Plague
OF TERROR

Blessings in the
Power of Gods
care,
David

Plague
OF TERROR

DAVID PAUL ANDERSON

River City Press

life changing books

ISBN:

Published by
River City Press, Inc.
4301 Emerson Avenue N.
Minneapolis, MN 55412
1-888-234-3559
www.rivercitypress.net

Cover Design and Graphics
Elizabeth Johnson, Minneapolis, MN

Edited by
Dr. Fredrick Fogel, Tallahassee, FL
Charlene Meadows, Minneapolis, MN

To The Warrior of Heaven

In the heat of battle, during the worst of wars, the sun will break through dark clouds above, streaming down light over beautiful fields newly flawed by weapons of conflict and engagement. It is precisely then, embracing both the good and the evil, that the godly warrior understands that war is fought for the sake of the beautiful. Human souls are beautiful. I have experienced the grandeur of humanity in my wife, Nancy, my children, and the saints that have graced my life. It is for these, and countless souls like them, that makes ordinary men into heaven's warriors. This book, and my life, are dedicated to the Warrior of heaven who defeated hell's best at Calvary, and continues to lead each child of God through many battles to the unchallenged victory lying just ahead.

Forward

Crafted to attract readers who enjoy supernatural thrillers, Plague of Terror creates the atmosphere of works by Frank Peretti, Stephen King, J. R. R. Tolkien, and C. S. Lewis. Like all supernatural thrillers and Christian fantasy, Plague of Terror grabs the reader, forcing a journey along overgrown paths, seldom walked, to uncertain destinations. Often impolite, readers are forced to experience settings lurking with suspense and danger.

The power of the Christian thriller is that it opens up a door and invites readers (or pulls them) into a spiritual dimension much bigger then the trifling activities of everyday life. The Apostle Paul tells us that there is a terrible battle being fought within this greater reality. Words crafted about this greater reality are always shadows. Writers of Christian thrillers sweat out their images, but are always aware that they can't get them right. Angels, demons, the weapons of heaven and hell, mock vain attempts to capture their subtlety. Writers may club the reader with the stark evil of a satanic mistress, but they know that a greater evil may lie in the whisper of a misguided friend.

Evil and good come packaged in different sizes, shapes, and colors. God's people can act more like the devil's children, and the devil's children can seem like angels. The task of the writer of a Christian thriller is to open up the elements of the spiritual warfare engulfing humanity, revealing the many faces worn by warriors of hell and heaven.

There is a very fierce and real spiritual battle championed by mortal and supernatural warriors. If the sounds of this spiritual battle clamored about mortal ears, humanity might understand its jeopardy. As it is, we often sleep while our bloodthirsty enemy walks in our bedchamber, leering at our slumbering form. Plague of Terror is either an action packed wake-up call to those sleeping as darts from hell inflame their souls or a pleasant comrade at arms for the warrior of God. In the words of Professor Francis C. Rossow, Plague of Terror is "a spine-tingling narrative, the Gospel in story form, more specifically, a dramatic (and artistic) rendering of St. Paul's contention that 'we wrestle not against flesh and blood, but against...the rulers of darkness...against spiritual wickedness in high places'."

Chapter 1:
Surprise Forces

The moonlit water struck through the dark woods like a serrated dagger. On either side of the river, steep rising foothills cut a wedge into the land trapping a jagged flowing stream. The narrow outline of Loon River moved silently through heavy mist, then slid into a large inlet. It delivered its sharp, man-made point like an assassin's weapon into the belly of massive buildings bathed in artificial light. Tall, electrified fences stood as sentries guarding the Plymouth Nuclear Generator compound. From the heart of PNG, a low humming sound vibrated throughout the woods, muffling the myriad voices of crickets still singing their night watch before the first rays of dawn.

"Damn." Flint released one hand from his Uzi, a rapid-fire gun of choice, to rub an insect from the back of his neck. There could be no slap, no sound punctuating the cover of night. Perspiration worked its way through black face paint, as a cold sweat dripped from his half-submerged body into Loon River. Above his head, the Uzi swaggered back and forth with each silent stride through the current-laced water. Flint stealthily moved closer to the PNG water inlet. He could see two other forms, cloaked in darkness, working their way with him through the water. One carried a duffel of plastic explosives resting on his head like a Bedouin woman carrying her wash to the river. The other protected a canvas bag filled with assorted tools, wire, and a timed detonator.

Watching the three-man squad were eyes that burned with hate. Hatred for everything human consumed a legion of invisible watchers as they drank in the dark intention of this terrorist brigade. Evil saturated the air like the smell of a cow rotting in humid heat. Flint could no more feel the nefarious presence all around him than he paid attention to his own skin. It was just there—part of him. He looked up at the sky. The moon still hadn't dimmed. "Damn, where are the clouds?" Something splashed down river. His malevolent eyes strained the night for any signs of movement—movement not their own. Moonlight, now his enemy, captured the silhouette of gaunt power lines as they faded off in the distance.

Gigantic metal towers rose repeatedly on the banks of Loon River supporting massive electrified steel cables that fed into the eastern seaboard grid. Boston, Washington, D.C., and New York City were among the concrete and asphalt communities that shared an insatiable appetite for kilowatts. Boston fed almost exclusively off of Plymouth. Washington, D.C., was among those cities lying in a fatal path should PNG suffer a critical failure.

· · · · ·

WLFO radio engineer, Al Perkins, was not happy as he worked to flatten out the spikes that had been showing up recently in the menu PNG was serving its patrons. Plymouth Nuclear was trying to figure out what was causing the slight variations. It wasn't business as usual to suffer these termite spikes as they nibbled away signal integrity at the station. Microprocessors used at the radio station were guarded by surge protectors, but Al was compulsive about things. He had installed a four-inch copper strip completely around the transmitter and had grounded it with ten-foot rods pounded into the ground every thirty feet to deal with the high RF radiation. Protection or no protection, he was going to smash these pesky spikes himself.

WLFO radio broadcasted a blend of jazz and New Age for white-collar yuppie listeners in the suburbs of Boston. Each WLFO broadcast studio had a large window overlooking Boston Harbor. Kris Downs, known to WLFO listeners as Heather Lane, sipped a lukewarm cup of thick coffee as Sade's "Smooth Operator" finished up a long set of mellow music for early morning fans. Her five-foot-six frame was filled with spice and zip, topped off with thick amber hair pulled back into a ponytail that fell through the back of a Red Sox baseball cap.

"Good morning, all you Sade fans!" Heather's voice tagged into the last line of the song. "It's 5:04 in the morning, and I gotta tell you, the coffee I'm drinking right now was whipped up in some sludge hole by engineer Perkins. No offense, Al, but you stick to the gizmos, and leave the coffee to the DJs."

Al, his eyes glued to digital meters, gave a slight smile as he heard Kris through the transmitter room monitor. Ratings had gone up a bit since Kris had started at WLFO. This was good. Rumors were circulating about a station shut-down if the floundering ratings did not pick up. Al liked his work. He enjoyed the Boston area. He would rather swallow a kilowatt than find another job. Engineers had it better than DJs. DJs were a dime a dozen, but a good engineer was gold. Still, if the corporate gorillas pulled the plug on WLFO, that could send him walking, good engineer or not.

"Boston Harbor is going to be gorgeous this morning! That big old sun is soon going to shove away all the lights dotting over the harbor, and shine down on your day!" Heather Lane looked out from the window of Studio B, hungering over the microphone as if it were chocolate. "Ever wondered what it's like to work on those huge ships? Hey, if any of you deck hunks are listening, this one's for you!"

Kris hit the button as Kenny G's "Moonlight" flooded the airwaves with silk. Kris popped the headphones off and headed for a fresh cup of coffee. Al's killer-brew had been dumped a half hour earlier, and Kris had started a new pot. She poured a full draft of clear coffee into her WLFO mug and then filled a second.

Walking by the transmitter room, she pushed open the door with her hip. "Hey Al," she teased, "still drinking poison or do you want some real coffee?"

Al grabbed at his stomach, "It's too late! It's too late! I'm a goner." Then with a wink, he reached for the spare coffee mug in Kris's hand. He took hold and then sipped. "Ah," he said, "I've died and gone to heaven."

"Gotta run," Kris shot back as she rushed to Studio B spilling coffee several times as she brushed by strangers flooding into the station. Joy, the WLFO bookkeeper who had come in early that day to post bills, was talking to a tall Latin American. The stranger wore his long, dark hair pulled back into a ponytail. Joy's face was flushed. She was agitated. Kris looked at her watch—5:17. "What are these people doing here at this time of the morning?" She had no time to figure things out. It would have to wait.

"That was 'Moonlight' by the silver sax of Kenny G," Heather Lane whispered seductively into the microphone. "Hey, what's going on!" The panel light had gone out. Studio B was dead. "What the heck!"

Frantically she flipped switch after switch. Lifeless dials mocked her random attempts—the microphone of Studio B refused resurrection. No, the problem wasn't with her board. "What on earth is Al up to?" Muttering words of torture and gizmo guys, she headed for the transmitter room. Opening the door that led into the hallway, she stopped. Al stood there, red faced, looking like a helpless child forced to do something he didn't want to do. "I'm sorry," he said.

"Sorry! What in the blue blazes are you doing? Make my microphone hot, and do it now! I've got a show..."

Al's mouth gaped open in voiceless impotence. Kris took several steps back, bracing herself against the edge of the production recorder. Al stepped to the side as the mysterious Latino entered the room, his coal eyes cast toward Kris. Another stranger, a small man lugging a canvas bag filled with electronics, emerged from behind the dark haired man. He was uncomfortable. His eyes avoided faces in the room. "Where is the line input on the production deck?" Al looked at Kris, then swept the floor, his eyes moving back and forth along the linoleum. "Never mind," grunted the technician, "I found it."

"How long until we are linked with the satellite?" The Latino walked over to the technician, placing his hand on the man's shoulder.

"Ten minutes—fifteen at most."

Hysteria raged like a windstorm within the female DJ. She had been violated by these men intruding into her space. "Would someone please tell me what's going on here! Joy, who are these guys, and what's this idiot doing with the production deck?"

Joy stood in the studio hallway, her form eclipsed behind the tall, dark stranger. "These guys are from the corporate office..." She started to explain, but her words were quickly displaced by the Latin American. He was not arrogant or rude, but clearly a man unwilling to forfeit control over the situation.

"Ms. Downs," came a voice thick with accent. "I am Ricardo Labano. I work for the corporation that owns WLFO. As you know, WLFO has been doing poorly in the ratings..."

"Wait a minute Mr. Ricardo Labano from the corporate screw up," bullied Kris into Labano's speech. "Since I've been at this station, our ratings have been getting a whole lot better—A WHOLE LOT BETTER!" Turning again to Joy and Al, "Who is this guy? What are they doing here?"

"Kris," Labano's voice was gentler, but no less deliberate, "a decision has been made to change the format of WLFO. I'm sorry."

Kris' legs rubberized as she fell back into the saddle of her studio chair. "This isn't happening. This is a nightmare." Twisting her face muscles into cavernous wrinkles, she struggled to break out from a bad dream. Kris knew how this worked. The guy at the production deck was using the 3600-system to produce an announcement that would periodically notify listeners of the immediate change in format. Lots of unfamiliar music would be served up. Initially, lack of sponsors for the new sound would mean commercial-free listening. The formatted satellite feed would make use of formatted DJs playing formatted tunes. Old listeners would leave, making way for a larger audience attracted to the new sound. Bottom line: instantly she was out of a job.

Kris wanted to erupt—sending tears gushing out to water down her fury. But no, this jerk would not have the pleasure of seeing her come apart. Instead, she translated her ragged emotions into blunt anger. "Where do you guys at the corporate office get the idea that you know better what people in Boston want to hear than those of us in the trenches! Are our ratings falling? No! Just when WLFO is starting to build its audience, you dopes come in here and pull the plug. So, what are you going to serve up now? Rock? Acid? Elevator music?"

Ricardo reached over to touch Kris's arm, but she pulled away. "Kris," he said, "this isn't a pleasant business, not for you, and not for me. You know the competition for listeners. It was felt that we gave the easy jazz format a good chance to prove itself, but it didn't."

"Are you telling me that we were losing money?" barked Kris.

"No. I think that you are aware that the station was staying in the black. The problem is that stockholders are not satisfied with a station staying black. They want profit, and the more profit the better. WLFO was not making the profit that can be captured in this market. With this transmitter, there's a lot more money to be made by reaching a younger audience. It's just that simple."

"Just that simple!" mimed Kris. "You come in here and mess up my life, my art, and send all the WLFO DJs out on the streets, and you call that simple!"

"Simple economics for the company," returned Labano, "not simple for you or for your friends. The corporation is not in business for you or your friends, but for stockholders. I truly do feel badly, but we have put together what I hope you will agree is a very generous severance package. Your name also remains with the company, and if we have need for a jazz DJ, we will contact you. Kris, the word is that you are very good."

Kris had no appetite for the corporate hatchet's compliments, slimed with the veneer of sincerity. She wanted to be angry with him. She wanted to spit! "Oh give me a break! Don't give me that line," she snapped. "That's as bad as when, after a first date, the guy says 'I'll give you a call sometime!' Fat chance! Face it, I'm finished!"

"I'd like to give you a call," replied Labano.

"You'd like to what?" hissed Kris.

As Al slipped from the room, Labano walked over to Kris and gestured that he would like to speak with her off to the side. Kris returned an irritated look to the ceiling and then walked with him to the corner of the room. "I would like to give you a call sometime. Or, since you find that a suspicious thing to say, let me tell you that I will give you a call sometime."

Kris stepped back, restraining the impulse to deck the stranger. "Oh, why not!" She delivered a tough right to Labano's cheek. Labano absorbed the slap without flinching. Kris stared at him, then abruptly burst out laughing. The situation was insane! This guy had just given her walking papers, and now he was hitting on her. Kris howled hysterically as everyone else in the room froze within the awkward moment.

Each time she drank in their expressions, a new wave of uncontrolled laughter quivered through her like a gust of wind through a willow tree. Tears rolled down her checks until her face finally stiffened again into cool anger. Swallowing deeply, her eyes flashed fire at the corporate muscle. "Listen Labano, what I want from you is to never see your face again. Joy has my address, and I'll be waiting for my severance. If I don't get it soon, I'm going to give my creditors the corporate phone number. Got it?"

Kris wanted out. Moving like a cornered animal, her hot glare continued its lock upon Labano. She forced her sightless hands to travel across the production deck as it led her to the freedom of an emergency door. Nearing the door, she quickened her pace, bumping the corporate technician face-first into two large reels of magnetic tape on a production recorder. Shoving open the door, she stepped out into the station parking lot. Darkness hung in the promise of an emerging dawn. Al sat on the ground leaning against the building, taking long drags from his cigarette. He flinched as the door flew open, jumping again as Kris slammed it shut. Pulling himself up by a signpost, he walked over to meet up with his friend.

Al fished for something to say, but the words vanished like minnows spooked by a stone tossed into shallow water along the beach. "That's all right, Al," Kris said, "it's not your fault. You still have a job, right? They change the DJs for the new format, but they'll keep the engineer. They'd be crazy to lose a gizmo guy as good as you."

"Who says I'm staying!" Al threw his cigarette at the side of the station as if it were an armed torpedo. Kris could see that he wanted to stand with her, but she knew that he loved his situation at the station.

"Al, you're crazy about Boston!" Wiping away spent tears from her cheeks Kris forced a smile. "We all know what radio business is like. When I became a DJ, I knew that the pay was low, the hours long, and the security—hell, what security!" She tossed another smile over to Al, who returned a nervous laugh.

"What are you going to do now?" he asked. Kris knew the play book. She had been sent back to home plate. She would need to grovel at the feet of the new station manager to pry loose a little production time in one of the studios to create a demo tape. Once the demo tape was done, she'd be digging through trade magazines looking for job openings at jazz stations, or (heaven forbid!) it was back to easy listening!

"I'm going fishing," she said.

"Huh?" gasped Al. "You hate to fish. You call fishing the work of animal Nazis!"

Kris laughed. "I'm going to talk to the new station manager and see if he will let me cut some demo tapes to send around. Maybe if I send out enough of them, I will lure in another job. It's just like going fishing, only usually not so bloody. You never know what you will catch—if anything."

"Kris, I know that station engineers don't count for much on resumes, but if you give out my name as a reference, well, if they ask me, they'll make you into a Sound Wave Goddess after they read what I have to say."

"A goddess!" A genuine smile erupted over pretense. "My brother's going to be a pastor. I don't think he'll want the competition. If you write me a reference, just tell them that I have the voice of Venus, okay?" Al gave another nervous laugh. Kris winked, flagged her hand quickly in front of her face, then headed toward her car. Turning her head, she called back, "Listen, Al, you're all right. Do you think the new station manager will be brought in tomorrow after Labano has done the dirty work?"

"Yeah," said Al as he lit another cigarette. "I'm supposed to meet with him after lunch."

Kris stopped to face Al again. "Good! I might see you then. If you talk to him first, put in a good word for me. Grease the gate! I need to have some production time. Take care." Swinging open the door to her vintage Chevy, Kris stopped momentarily to look back at the station. Al was once again resting back against the cool, dew-soaked, metal building. His face melted into the shadows, showing the occasional orange glow of his cigarette. The sun was just beginning to trace the horizon over Boston Harbor. Kris felt numb. Surrealistic events, in less than an hour, had painted havoc on the canvas of her life. She would call her brother, Luke. He'd help her put things into perspective. He always did.

• • • • •

Flint was within a hundred feet from where Loon River dumped into the power plant only to exit again after being channeled for "non-contamination" uses in the plant. Relentless lights exposed every inch within a fifty-foot perimeter to the outside of the fence. Armed guards tugged against dogs capable of rendering a man helpless within seconds. The conspirators were about to execute the most dangerous part of their plan. They had to breach the fence, get past the guards, and enter the vital areas of the plant. Gaining entry to the compound, they would join forces with an insider working to blind electronic security. Every phase of the operation must proceed without detection or incident until they were again safely outside the PNG compound.

"Soon there'll be no turning back, Ahmad," Flint whispered. The three conspirators continued wrestling against the current laced, ink-black water. Ahmad was irritated. Flint should not have broken the silence. Forming a fist with his right hand, Ahmad hushed any further talk. He handed the plastic explosives to the third man, a heavily bearded blonde named Starkey. From a long canvas bag strapped to his left side, Ahmad took out a stainless steel tube. It formed a two-inch barrel that channeled compressed air-launching projectiles up to 250 feet. When detonated, the only sound was a brief whoosh as the projectile shot out of the barrel. The noise would not be heard if they remained at least 75 feet away from the guards.

Ahmad aimed the launcher toward the far side of the compound. Whoosh—a projectile flew from the barrel, landing in the distance. Hitting the ground, its case popped open, activating sophisticated electronics that created a variety of sounds. Its technology even suggested human voices speaking in muffled tones. The guards rushed to the far side of PNG, seeking to discover the source of commotion. As they left the perimeter, three dark figures moved with determined effort through the water to reach the inlet. Taking jumper cords from his bag, Starkey quickly attached them to either side of two iron bars running horizontally above the water. There were more bars under the surface, but with the top two out of the way, a man could pull himself through and enter the compound. Starkey lit a small acetylene torch that hissed through the metal bars like a hot knife slips through butter. They were in!

• • • • •

Lisa Barker had been a model student scoring an unbroken record of top grades in physics and nuclear technology while attending Berkeley. She had set her sights on a PhD in nuclear engineering, but the demand for her skills was so great and the money so hot, she told herself she would take a detour. Deciding to work at PNG for a few years to make some bucks, she'd then go back to school. A few years turned into ten years, more than the five years needed to gain access authorization to all areas of the plant without escort.

When she was hired, her background check proved spotless. She had never been involved in any political movements. Her police record showed nothing, not even a parking ticket. She didn't like the flavor of beer, wouldn't drink high test, and had wine only on New Year's. Fitness-for-Duty observations during her first years demonstrated Lisa to be intelligent, stable, and motivated. What PNG did not know: Lisa had been lonely. Eight months before the early morning assault on the nuclear power plant, she had met a man named Starkey at an Internet chat room.

Starkey was a loner who thrived on the edge. Lisa, tired of her comfortable life, enjoyed the energy that Starkey brought to her whole way of thinking. He was political! His taste for anarchy leeched its poison into Lisa's appetite over her job.

PNG was one more place where corporate muscle had beat up on the little guy, taking away his dignity. "Slavery is not dead," Starkey once keyed into the chat room, "it's recast. Each person who punches a time clock or comes in at 8:00 to sit behind a desk is a slave. They're chained to their slave-masters by the Almighty Dollar. They need the bucks, so they sell themselves as slaves to the corporate muscle. Not me! Call me the enemy of big business! Label me the emancipator of the world's people!"

After months of daily chat on the Internet, Starkey asked Lisa to meet with him. Lisa agreed. They decided upon a coffee house called Intrigue. The evening of their rendezvous, Lisa tried on a black skirt and a burgundy sweater. Walking to a mirror, she assessed the female artillery intended for Starkey. Shaking her head, she headed back to her closet and removed the skirt and sweater. They made her look too bourgeois for Starkey's taste in women. Instead, she slid into a roomy, red flannel shirt accented with a pair of tight-fitting blue jeans.

Lisa arrived at their rendezvous ten minutes early. At 7:00, Starkey showed up wearing a denim shirt and faded jeans. A red handkerchief, serving as a bandana, was tied around his head. His long blonde hair fell to his shoulders. It was love at first sight for Lisa. For Starkey, it cinched a plot that would exploit Lisa's job at the PNG facility and expose the east coast to long-term nuclear fallout like the cesium-137 release at Chernobyl.

Through exhaustive hours of research on the Internet, Starkey had learned that nuclear plants cannot be detonated like a bomb because the fissionable uranium in the fuel, U-235, is far too low. The goal of their attack would be to breach three major atmospheric barriers and cause the release of substantial amounts of radioactive material. Plant security was designed to protect these barriers using well-armed manpower and intrusion detection aids that included closed-circuit television. The surveillance equipment had to be taken out from the inside. Starkey was courting Lisa, not for her brains, not for her body, but for her inside position at PNG.

After his date with Lisa, Starkey spent as much time with her as possible. He invited her out with Ahmad, Flint, and their girlfriends. The company was rough, but Lisa drank in the worldly air as if her pristine past had created a vacuum for it. Lisa began to despise her lackluster past, a past that had, to her benefit, protected her from evil forces lurking just outside of what can be seen or felt. Once unprotected, a dark entity attached itself to her, a demon that craved blood like parched ground thirsts for moisture. In her naked lust for new experience, Lisa had opened the door to a dark creature that was not carnal but fed upon carnage itself. Uprooted from her past, Starkey intoxicated her with the idea of sabotaging the PNG compound.

Lisa was a key player in the terrorist plan. Two tasks were hers to carry out inside PNG. On the day of "emancipation," as Starkey put it, Lisa would arrive at work early in the morning, before 4:30 a.m. The operation was to take place near dawn, when the moon was low in the sky, just before sunrise. At the prearranged time, Lisa would pour acid into the motherboard of the closed-circuit television monitoring system. Then, as the acid ate into the heart of the monitor, she'd execute a computer-related malfunction within a large valve in Sector One. Faking the failure required a manual entry into the critical parameters of the safety recognition system. The malfunctioning valve would occupy the attention of most technicians, serving as a diversion while they continued the "emancipation."

It was a piece of cake to smuggle the acid into the plant; a simple coffee thermos would do the trick. Lisa had prepared the guards for her charade by taking cappuccino to work for the last four months. The glass liner of the thermos provided a perfect insulator for acid. The properties of the thermos wouldn't effect the detection devices used to sense firearms and explosives.

· · · · ·

Lisa slipped her plastic card into the security monitor. The quick pass tripped a green light. There was no turning back. She'd left her thumb print in the technology used by PNG personnel to gain access to the secured area. PNG would discover her part in the "emancipation." The system computer had also recorded her security number as she passed her card through the monitor. Entering the room, Lisa darted over to the panel housing the surveillance equipment. Her hands trembled as she fumbled to remove two screws. Taking a deep breath she brought her hands together over the handle of the screwdriver. "Don't shake!" she cursed.

The first screw fell to the floor, then the second. Pulling hard, the front panel swung out on a hinge to expose wires and electronic components. Grabbing the thermos as it shook in her hands, Lisa doused the monitoring system's motherboard with acid. Smoke poured out of the electrical panel. Within seconds all the monitors would go blank. Technicians would be dashing to get to the motherboard, there discovering the sabotaged system. They would check the entry record and in its data discover her electronic signature.

Racing across the room, Lisa surveyed a large console containing dials, lights, and switches. A bank of knobs protruded from a stainless steel panel. Above it was posted "Sector One." Lisa turned the far right switch until it clicked. The large valve in that sector instantly shutdown, detonating a shrill siren in the heart of the PNG Operation Control. The shut down would alert security, triggering a second alarm—red, blinking lights would sprout throughout the compound. The computer-monitored facility would be placed on terrorist alert. Security would focus their attention on the large valve in Sector One, racing to execute a careful search for saboteurs. While security was occupied with the valve, four terrorists would breach the first of the three atmospheric barriers on the opposite side of the plant.

· · · · ·

The coven mistress sat on the floor of her apartment. Blood dripped from her hands onto the small rug with the embossed pentagram. Entranced, she walked along an ocean beach. Surrounding her was only sand, water, and sky. The sand was flat and featureless. The water was as still as glass. The bright sky was cloudless and sunless. She wore a white gown with a red sash. Perspiration ran down her body.

She stopped to face the sea. Sitting down upon the sand, she waited. A seagull flew down from the sky and landed on her shoulder. Another seagull perched upon her head. Seagull after seagull flew from the sky covering her completely. The woman's chest caved in under racing panic. She forced herself not to get up, not to run. It was difficult to breathe as she fought for air through the thick blanket of living feathers. The nerves of her skin were inflamed, pierced by the unnatural sharp talons that had replaced the web feet of the birds. She wanted to jump up with her arms waving. But she suppressed the fear and the pain, moving deeper into her trance.

She was walking along a forested path. Trees and foliage crowded toward the path, coveting the open space. Everywhere silence saturated the air and stillness held captive every limb, leaf, and blade of grass. Further she walked into the ever darkening woodland, until at last, she heard the sound of running water.

At the head of the path she discovered water pouring from a cave on a high bluff. The cave was dark; the water black as coal. Sitting down on a large rock the coven mistress waited. Time passed. Finally another seagull, very large, flew from out of the dark cave. It landed upon the branch of a gnarled, ancient tree. "You have come, my daughter," the seagull spoke. "You have pleased me. Few make the journey this far."

"My joy is to please you, master." The woman gazed in reverent awe at the large bird. "How might I serve you?"

"A great plague is about to devour your planet. The weak sheep of earth will be sheared from its back, but you and my other servants will be blessed."

Perverse pleasure moved erotically within the woman. "How might I please you in this?"

"You will join forces with others, some of whom do not know my face, but serve my purpose. This very hour four strive against the light. The blood of one scents the air." The great bird stretched its wings. "I will move three to join with you in the future I now prepare. Watch and obey."

"I will await your will." The coven mistress knew that the seagull was only the veiled presence of the god she served. "When shall I be graced to behold your face?"

"You will see my face when I love you the most." The bird flew from the branch back into the dark hole of the mountain. Reaching out, the woman cupped a small amount of the dark water within her hands, and drank. She awoke from her trance. Showering, she washed away the blood and perspiration and then dressed in a two-piece suit for work. It was 5:00 in the morning.

• • • • •

It was business as usual as Ron Linden watched the security monitors at PNG while they flipped screens from one camera to another. In another hour, he would be off duty. He looked forward to his usual breakfast—a cholesterol fix of bacon and eggs at Meg's Diner. Suddenly every monitor went blank. Ron's coffee mug toppled over as he assaulted the console, frantically working a self-diagnostic on the system monitors. Moments later a high-pitched siren tore into the matrix. "Holy fritz!" shouted Ron as he reflexively reached out, turning on the security alarm.

The whole complex lit up like a Vegas casino as sirens sounded a breach in the plant's security. Flint, Ahmad, and Starkey enjoying an adrenaline rush, raced to meet Lisa at operative gate three. They would need to work fast, before Lisa's security pass could be voided within the security system, preventing access to secured areas of the generator.

Lisa, her blouse wet with perspiration, had already passed her card through the electronic gate as the three terrorists arrived at operative gate three. Suddenly something happened that was not part of the terrorists' contingency plan. Ron Linden had decided to cut electricity to the power doors. These doors were massive—far too heavy for manual operation. Ron's creative maneuver ensured that intruders would be prevented from movement through PNG gates, with or without identification. When someone wanted to pass through he would verify their identity. If they checked out, Ron planned to power up only the one door they were using. Lisa would be considered a criminal by now. It would do no good for her to ask Ron to open up for her.

"What do we do Lisa?" shouted Starkey over the screaming sirens.

"I don't know!" Lisa searched the overhead catwalks for company security. "I have no control over these doors. Security must have cut power. There's no way in hell that we can open them without power. I think it's over!"

"No!" screamed Ahmad. "I will not accept that!"

Attacking the obstacle to their mission like a madman, Ahmad exploded against the door, cursing and swearing every vile word that ever soiled the lips of men. His shoulder planted against the gate, the massive door slowly gave way to Ahmad's insanity. Lisa, watching with her mouth wide open, refused to believe the drama before her. A gate fitted with brakes and weighing eight times the poundage of Ahmad was somehow giving way. What she did not see was the veiled hand of darkness. A force of evil played the shoulder of Ahmad against the door like a chess master moves a pawn. An appetite for human carnage, the carnage of millions of people made sick by nuclear contamination, was at work. The four terrorists were simply chess pieces moved by a malevolent force setting into play a master strategy preparing for a demonic feast.

"Come on!" commanded Ahmad. "The gate's open. Let's go! Let's go! Let's go!"

Only operative gate four remained in their way. Once beyond this barrier, they would access the area where the plastic explosives could be deployed. The explosion from the device was not intended to damage the building sufficiently to cause a critical failure. Instead, the detonation would take out the electrical system used to monitor the heat produced within the fuel-containing pressure tubes. If the electrical system failed, it would be Chernobyl all over Boston, New York City, Washington, D.C., and all the cities, towns, and rural back roads soon to be contaminated by nuclear fallout.

Reaching operative gate four, it also refused entry. Once again, Ahmad, shouting obscenities, slammed his shoulder against the gate. Hatred and hunger joined forces with him against the steel barrier. It began to move. Then, just above Ahmad, a brilliant light flashed, blinding the four terrorists and sending the demonic agency whimpering from the room. A Guardian had arrived. A soldier of Light. Holding a sword high above his head, the Guardian plunged it through the central hinge on the gate. Another flash! The hinge melted to its pin. The door was frozen shut.

"Damn!" shouted Flint. "I can't see a thing. What in the hell is going on here?"

With expletives of filth pouring from his lips, Ahmad screamed, "This gate won't move! Get over here and help me! Shove! Shove harder!"

All three of the men pushed brute muscle against the gate. Lisa also struggled to find a place to help shove against the metal door. Monumental determination could not stop their feet from sliding on a floor offering no footing. "It's no use," cried Starkey. "We've got to get out of here! We have to leave! Now!"

They could hear the feet of the security forces clanking above them on catwalks, soon to reach the space directly over them. Ahmad's murky vision was still impaired by the residue of the Guardian's spectacular entrance. "Get us back to the inlet!" he barked. Lisa, often stumbling, led them through a maze of hallways as she sought to avoid security. When they emerged from the reactor compound, Lisa gasped. The sun had started its ascent to the east. Their entry had been discovered and no cloak of darkness remained to cover their escape. Flint lowered his Uzi and let go a blast of bullets. The rapid fire sprayed its ammunition like tiny hatchets thrown against the bodies of their victims. The firepower cut through the security team, dismembering their bodies into a bloody pulp.

"Run!" shouted Flint. "That's our only way out!"

Trapped animals, they tapped into a reserve of adrenaline dashing toward their only hope of escape. Flint hit the water first, then Ahmad, and finally Starkey. Lisa was still running toward the inlet when she slipped on the pooled blood of the recently slain guards. Unable to control her fall she landed into the mass of mutilated flesh. The horror of her situation drained her instantly. She could not move. She could not think. She was losing consciousness.

"Get over here, Lisa!" cried Starkey. "Get over here now!"

Coldly, Flint aimed his Uzi at Lisa. Tat... tat... tat... and Lisa lay dead with the murdered guards. The entity savored the lifeless mortal, then detached itself, vanishing into a vortex that snapped open like a lipless mouth in the dark sky and then disappeared.

"Why did you do that?" demanded Starkey, grabbing Flint by the shirt.

"Dead men tell no tales!" Flint forced Starkey's hand from his shirt. "Now let's get out of here, or we're dead, too!"

As the terrorists made their escape, the sun was showering light over the eastern slopes. Anger raged within Starkey like a dark wind over hot lava. He could have killed Flint for taking out Lisa, but not today. Still, Flint had better watch his back side, thought Starkey. Revenge would run its course, but not until Flint was of no further use. For the moment, the driving thought for each terrorist was to save their own skin. They had failed this time, but there would be other opportunities.

It took a full day before the "incident" reached the press. Kris saw it on the News Board at WLFO when she went in to make her demo tape. All the release said was that a valve had stuck at Plymouth Nuclear Generator. The plant manager had been quoted as saying that "there had never been any risk to the public safety, and the valve had been replaced."

Chapter 2:

SEMINARY DAZE

Luke had been up until 3:00 that morning. The taskmaster alarm was yelling at him. Class was at 8:20, and it was 7:50 as his hand hit repeatedly at the clock. "Man, where's that button?" he yelled into his pillow, seeking that one button among many that would shut up his oppressor. Finally he hit payday. A velvety silence covered him like a warm, inviting comforter. Should he skip class today? He might have rolled over and drifted back into silky silence, but his mistress of the morning was calling to him. A bright, orange glow flooded over the head of his bed. Luke always left the east window curtain open so that the sensual sun would caress his face in the morning. It was a ritual for him, and one that had cost him more than one roommate over the years.

He could think of no one else who actually enjoyed catching the first rays of sun in the morning. That was all right with him. "Crypts," he thought to himself, "they sleep in crypts." Not Luke! Death hung over his thoughts like a pall. Had he sought comfort in his Christian faith so that, unlike Sartre, he could find an exit from Death's doorless cage?

"Rise and shine!" called his mistress through the east window. Lying on his stomach, Luke let his right leg fall out of bed, then his right arm. Knowing that everything depended upon his next move, he snapped his left leg sideways throwing his covers from his body. The cool air was like a slap to the face. Arching his back he then forced his body to sit up on the edge of the mattress. His mistress continued to embrace his shirtless torso and tease the edge of his eyelids. "If I don't get a mug of coffee, I'm gonna die," he said to her. But she remained silent, speaking only through the caress of her touch.

The feel of the sun moved across flesh far too long held captive indoors. Pale skin covered Luke's fit body. His brown hair was tossed by a night's sleep, as red whiskers sprouted from a two-day neglect of his shaver. Luke's hands were fine features, their fingers long like those of a musician, or as his mother would say, "You'd make a fine surgeon, Luke, with those hands of yours!"

To the right rear of his desk stood an electric coffee pot. It rose as a technical icon of order, smooth and sleek, above the piles of papers, open books, magazines, pens, clothing, and coffee grounds, which together smothered his desk in chaos.

Luke put the icon to work, and soon the aroma of coffee called to him through the open door of the bathroom where he was taking a quick five-minute shower. Still dripping wet and dragging his towel, he went for the coffee, taking a mug back with him to the bathroom. No time for breakfast now, but coffee, well, he had to have that!

Luke sprinted off to class. The bell rang as he sat down on a 1940's wooden chair. An attached small wooden ledge to his right served for taking notes. Beneath the chair were wooden lathes spread out horizontally and attached to the four legs allowing for extra books and supplies. Class began for him today in "Old Hall," the first building erected to house the seminary in 1914. It was the oldest site on campus and had been remodeled repeatedly. Room 107, where he now sat, had been completely redone. This classroom, like all the rest in Old Hall, was a kaleidoscope of mismatched textures. The classroom, made to look modern, remained cluttered with vintage furniture.

The professor, just arriving, arranged books and papers as he stood behind a relic from the seminary's past. It was a huge piece of wooden furniture that spanned three-fourths of the room's front. At its center was a raised wooden platform which slanted back toward the whiteboard, allowing for the professor's notes. Today Dultmann's lecture was on Matthew 17:24-27, the miracle in which Peter finds money in the mouth of a fish.

"Have any of you ever thought about the practical problems suggested by this miracle?" asked Professor Dultmann. "At the face of it, we have Peter catching a fish that had a coin in its mouth just at the time Jesus was to pay the temple tax. But think further. When the fish went for the hook, wouldn't it have taken a second miracle for the fish to hold onto the coin when its mouth opened to take the hook?"

"If it's a miracle," interrupted a seminarian, "then I suppose the fish could have been created by God instantaneously with both the coin and the hook already in its mouth."

"Yes," said Dultmann, "and that is the usual line of argument. But why seek the extreme answer if a simple one will do? Why multiply miracle upon miracle when a natural answer lies close at hand? Why argue that Martians T.P.'d your front tree, when a few nocturnal seminarians will do the trick? And let me tell you, I speak from experience."

Luke laughed at the professor's joke, but he knew that there were some present who would not find his point humorous. After class he was going to catch up to Clint Lewis. What a joke! Lewis would be fuming white acid at the mouth.

Professor Dultmann wore a mohair sweater, very soft to the touch and with deep earth-tone colors. He was in his early 50's, but seductive in his deportment. He appeared self-assured. He didn't smoke, but his demeanor conjured up the attributes of carnal pleasures—a man of the world enjoying a good cigar and a scotch on the rocks. Drawn into this professor's world, the student was met by another entity. It had the power to make the rough feel smooth, the dark seem light, the wrong sweet as right. Dultmann's every gesture, and each tiny muscle that moved within his face to express a calculated impression to the onlooker, was driven by an evil force that wore Dultmann like the hand wears a glove.

"Some would suggest a more reasonable understanding to this text," continued Dultmann. "Straus pointed out that this description might be an expression, rather like saying of the dawn that it 'has gold in its mouth.' The writer of this passage in Matthew constructed this scene in the life of Christ by using an example that was easy for people to understand—common people who identified with the simple lives of those who fished for a living." He scratched his beard. "Indeed, you will remember that Straus believed that it was perfectly natural for the early church to enhance the life of Christ through sea references. Can anyone here remember what two classifications Straus came up with for the ministry of Jesus in and about the water?"

"I remember that he called one class of miracles around the sea 'fishing legends,'" pointed out a female student.

"Very good!" returned Dultmann. "Can anyone name the second?"

"Yes," said Luke, "he called the second group 'sailing legends.' The 'fishing legends,' according to Straus, had to do with the trade of the disciples as fisher persons, and the 'sailing legends' were stories told about Jesus traveling at sea with the disciples."

"Excellent, Mr. Downs!" replied the professor, obviously pleased with Luke's grasp of the enlightened approaches to the Scriptures. "Now, of course, Straus believed that there were grains of truth within the miracles. Grains of sand, we might say, that caused the early Christian communities to grow them into pearls depicting miraculous events. His disciple, Bruno Bauer, as you know, went further than Straus. He believed that most of what we understand to be true of Jesus was actually fabricated by the early church to give flesh to its religious world view. The very person of Jesus could be a myth intended to tell a divine story. Hence," he scratched his beard again, "when we get right down to it, what's important to us is the message of the church about Jesus and not what Jesus did or did not do..."

Lewis was not doing well. His face was red and everyone was waiting for his hand to pop up. No disappointment! "Yes, Mr. Lewis," came Dultmann's cheery voice. Professor Dultmann always maintained his cool. He understood that many of these young men and women at the seminary simply could not accept the truth. "Too much time at grandma's knees," he once told another faculty member. Lewis and others like him were the uninitiated. Their pristine refusal to share the greater understandings that a scientific age had brought made them primitive and objects of the professor's pity and not his wrath.

Dultmann's lack of anger did not blunt his keen ability to use conservative students like a comedian uses a straight man. Grandma-taught seminarians would give their little, predictable speeches, and then he would give "that look" of his, a look that patronized and sabotaged all at the same time. As Clint Lewis started his retort, Dultmann's mind was unsheathing his oratory knife. Letting Lewis talk, he watched as a good number of students shuffled their papers in disinterest. He then raised his right eyebrow. In went the knife! Finally twisting the knife Dultmann showed the whole class an enlightened perspective that easily replaced the old, worn-out thinking that came from the lap of an old woman talking to a little child about Jesus.

Dultmann had heard it all before. He knew every objection to historical criticism, the academic discipline that sought to rid the Bible of supernatural myths. He had his answers down pat. Very few opposing students had little more than a Spartan chance of looking credible to their peers. He played his classroom like a stage master. Dultmann didn't need to challenge the student's remarks. He simply gave "that look" and started talking "reasonably" according to his orchestrated script.

Lewis, however, decided not to take a frontal attack. He would not challenge the professor's public disdain for the miraculous. Everyone knew that Dultmann, unlike Lewis, didn't believe in miracles. Dultmann always interpreted miraculous events within the Bible as an invention of the writer to make some esoteric point. Once again, in his lecture today, Dultmann explained away the miracle of the money in the fish's mouth. Lewis, not wanting to challenge the professor's point head-on, asked instead, "How would you preach this text to a congregation?"

"Well, my dear Mr. Lewis, you preach the story line," answered Dultmann, "not your exegesis. But you allow your exegesis to keep you from demanding more from the text than is naturally reasonable."

"So you are saying that you would preach the text as if a miracle did occur?" queried Lewis.

"But of course," Dultmann said with "that look." "Tell them that when we need something, God provides, as He or She provided the money for the temple tax."

"But if Straus and Bauer are right, God never really did provide the money," came the exasperated voice of Clint Lewis.

"We don't know that," returned the professor. "Indeed, it would be wrong to say that God did not provide the funds, since the church created this myth in the life of Jesus to make the point that God does provide. My point is that we do not know how God provided the funds. Perhaps what really happened is that Peter caught a number of fish and sold them, providing Jesus with the funds needed for the temple tax."

"Professor Dultmann," grumbled Lewis. A breathy voice indicated a nervous contraction around his trachea. "I know we have been here before, but this is another time when you are suggesting that the early church is trying to share the message that God does things that He doesn't really do. For example, at the grave, we who are to be pastors are supposed to proclaim the hope of the resurrection. Yet you say that in all likelihood, the resurrection of Jesus had nothing to do with His body coming out of the tomb. Now common sense says that if God can raise people from the dead, and this is our hope, then there are good grounds for us to assume that God did raise Jesus bodily from the dead. And if God did not raise Jesus bodily from the dead, how do we have faith that He has the power or the desire to raise us bodily from the dead?"

"Common sense," replied Dultmann effortlessly, "once told physicians to use leeches on their patients to remove bad blood." Laughter exploded like shrapnel around Lewis. "The issue is not one of common sense but rather of scholarly pursuit."

As Lewis was presenting his point about the resurrection of the dead, a presence entered the classroom. The word 'grave' had called to it, a wicked father calling to an evil son. Unseen by mortal eye, the presence did not so much move, as the room moved about it. It connected itself to every person in the room by long, very slender, tentacles. Some mortals had many dark threads attached or wrapped about them. Luke was also bound to the presence. As Lewis talked, a tentacle gripping Luke began to pulse, faster and faster, with larger waves to each vibration.

Lewis knew that the battle was useless. Dultmann, after all, had ultimate control of the classroom. It was his arena. Most of the students gathered there were his fans and would hear things his way. Dultmann provided a show, presenting Scripture like a circus ringmaster. Lewis approached Bible study differently, as if it were the very air he breathed for life. His debate with Dultmann represented a life and death struggle for truth. Lewis sought to protect his peers from a theology that could lead them and the members of their future congregations along the path to damnation. Lewis cared for people, not just about ideas. For all of his efforts to expose intellectual sophistry at the "progressive" seminary, he appeared to be losing the battle again. He stopped talking and slumped down in his chair waiting for the bell to ring. It would come, another ending to a frustrating hour in New Testament study.

The old steel-cast bell finally rang its uneven metal clatter. It was one more past relic of Old Hall which had nothing more than sentimental value and was allowed to survive from the "good old days" of the seminary. The presence of evil evacuated the room from itself, but left invisible marks in the form of spiritual wounds inflicted upon the professor and students. New wounds, they were, to add to the scars made countless times before by the same Shadow of Death. Luke was not exempt of these scars. He had engaged the entity before, feeling its presence more in his gut than in his mind. He had felt its faceless, feeding frenzy upon intellectual chaos of the seminary. Did it also feast upon chaos caused in the physical world? Did it also forage upon flesh and blood and mortal souls?

Luke no longer wanted to catch up to Clint Lewis. Dultmann had wrung all the satisfaction Luke could hope for out of his right-wing peer. No, he was hungry now, and so he headed to the seminary cafeteria for a short-order and more black coffee. "I should be thankful to Lewis," he thought to himself with an evil impulse. "If not for the duel between him and Dultmann, I'd have dozed into a public snore." The theology that Luke fed upon was lifeless. He studied it for the grade on his report card, not because it gave him any satisfaction.

Luke walked into the cafeteria. Music from the local pop radio station was pumped into overhead speakers. He wasn't in the mood for light conversation, so he sat down at an empty table facing out into Central Square. A large bell tower dominated the view. Located at the heart of the courtyard, the bell tower was connected to the campus by numerous sidewalks. Each led away from the tower like spokes from the hub of a wheel. Reaching out from the tower, they touched the campus buildings that hedged in the green oasis of trees and grass. Here and there benches were placed to provide a view to the bell tower. Luke was thinking about Cassandra when he caught the tail end of a news story from the overhead speakers.

There had been an incident at PNG. A valve had stuck. When his sister Kris took the job in Boston, Luke had goaded her about the possibility of a meltdown at PNG. If PNG nuked out, Boston would be toast in the atomic drift. This news story, as it filtered through the cluttered conversations of the cafeteria dining hall, took Luke's breath away. He was frustrated that he had missed the first part of it. "I need to call Kris and ask her about what went down at PNG," he thought. He would also need to bring up the uncomfortable business about being dumped by Cassandra.

Luke had been dating Cassandra for over a year. She was enrolled in the nursing program at a nearby college. They had met at the yearly dance sponsored jointly between the two schools so that their student bodies had an opportunity to fraternize. Luke thought that everything was going great between Cassandra and himself. They had the same interests. She even hinted at a future together. Luke was blown away when two days ago she called off their relationship. She still had a year to go before becoming a registered nurse. Luke would be leaving the city in just a few weeks, moving home until he received his first opportunity to serve in a parish. Cassandra wasn't ready for love over the Internet. That was that.

"Hey, Downs!" came the all too familiar voice of Lewis. "Damn," muttered Luke under his breath. He wanted privacy. Lewis was about to trespass into his territory at the cafeteria. "Do you mind if I sit down?"

"It's a public place," came Luke's uninviting reply.

Lewis gave no indication that he noticed the attitude that hung thickly around Downs, or he chose not to care. "What do you think about New Testament class today?"

Suddenly a flood of anger raced through Luke. All of his emotions about Cassandra, all of his concern about Kris, and all his anxiety about his change in life flowed together in a single tide of disgust for Lewis and his antiquated theology. "I think that Dultmann knows more about history and theology than you and I will absorb in a lifetime, that's what I think!" snapped Luke.

Lewis leaned back in surprise over the unexpected nip. "I think that Dultmann is two miles wide and one inch deep. That's what I think!"

"Look Lewis!" returned Luke with an irritated wave of his hand. "You can't just stick your head in the ground and try to see the world through the eyes of Martin Luther and the world as he knew it. Times have changed! We face information and ethical questions that Luther never dreamed about. It won't work to divorce faith from the culture. The two must be wed. We need to face modern facts in our theology and not hide from them."

"There is a critical difference between fact and fiction," argued Lewis. "What

Dultmann and his historical-critical cronies call 'fact' is just a point of view. They want to change the meaning of God and the moral base of our culture. What stands in their way? The Bible! So what do they do? They take the Bible, a muscular stallion that could win any race, and they blow it up into a thousand theological pieces. Then they put the lifeless pieces back together according to their play book and try to sell us on the idea that what we have had all along was an old, dead cow. I'm not buying it! The vitality of God as He reveals Himself in the Bible is, by God's grace, the powerhouse of every faithful minister of the Gospel. When all is said and done, His truth is going to be around a lot longer than the historical critical social planners united in their adoration of a mutilated theology."

"Damn," Luke thought to himself, "this guy is primitive, but he puts out oratory that makes a seminarian covet." Luke's anger was mellowing out into apathy. He simply wanted to stop the conversation. "I just don't think the same way you do," he said without hook or barb. He didn't want to give Lewis anything to grab onto. He hoped that Lewis would agree to disagree. No such luck.

"There are consequences to how we decide to shape the meaning of God and His will for human life," Lewis pursued with his point like a bloodhound after prey. He had genuine concern for Luke. His passion flowed from a desire to help his friend see that God's Word didn't need to be updated. It was the task of pastors and theologians to faithfully translate God's Word into the times and events of their generation. The Bible contained a timeless revelation. It was something written by the hand of God, not the product of a loose-fitting conspiracy concocted by past writers who sought to create the character of God.

"If the Bible doesn't present us with a timeless blueprint for human society," continued Clint, "we have nothing—NOTHING!—for knowing how we should live. We're not like a colony of bees where each member instinctively takes on its particular role in maintaining the hive. Society and culture for mankind are created externally out of the stuff in which ideas live and die." Clint pushed his chair out and sat to its side. "I believe that God has protected the revelation of the Bible so that it is timeless and true. And I am absolutely certain that I cannot rise above it with my own reason to judge it. It remains judge, jury, and missionary of mercy to the world." He stopped, waiting for Luke to respond. After an awkward silence he concluded, "Well, that's how I see it!"

"Who knows," Luke said, again trying to end the discussion, "in a few weeks, we'll be leaving these walls, and that's when the proverbial rubber hits the road. Perhaps with a few years under our belts, both of us will have learned a few new things. I would enjoy sitting down with you then and comparing notes."

"I'd look forward to that," said Lewis, picking up on Luke's change of mood. As Luke begin to pull his stuff together from the cafeteria table, Lewis placed his hand on his shoulder saying, "Luke, may God bless you in your new ministry. I really mean that. See you around, right?"

"Yup, see you around!" Luke glanced up, captured momentarily in the energy of his classmate's eyes. Clint was a man of deep passion. They shook hands. As Luke gathered together his books, a pen, clipped over the spiral binding of a notebook, slipped off and rolled over the table to the floor. As Luke's eyes raced after it, he noticed a grey-haired old African-American sitting at the next table. "Where did he come from?" The old man appeared like a whisper in full voice. Reaching down the stranger picked up Luke's pen. When the man looked up, Luke was startled by his piercing blue eyes.

"Here's your pen, Son." The old man spoke with a southern flavor. The curious stranger turned to look out the window. "Fancy bell tower!" he continued, pointing his finger to the window. "Whoever designed that is a clever fellow. That tower is way fancier than the simple trumpet that Gabriel will ring to the ends of the earth!" Looking back at Luke he delivered a wink served with a large smile.

Luke smiled back, thanked the old man for picking up his pen, and then headed for the cafeteria door. Walking out into the central courtyard, he looked up at the bell tower. Suddenly his eyes winced shut because the mid-morning sun had produced a brilliant halo around the cross on the tower. The air was cool and breathless. The scent of a flowering crab accented the season. Luke liked the spring. He enjoyed its crisp air. Each year he waited eagerly to see the first buds of green and blossoms of pink as they broke from grey-brown branches slowly freed from the death of winter.

As Luke turned the corner of the tower, he saw a woman sitting on a park bench. She was stunning! Thick, brown hair fell to her shoulders, accented by walnut brown eyes. Rich, red lipstick filled the lines of her mouth. Her dress, even the earrings suspended from small golden chains, matched the color of her lips. Classic beauty etched each curve and feature. Did he know her? Or perhaps she blended all the features of those women who courted his fantasies.

Luke decided to take on the opportunity. Why not? He had nothing to lose. If she brushed him off, he would be gone in a few days. It wasn't likely that he'd be running into her again. Walking over to her he asked, "Are you new here?"

A slight smile. "Very."

"Do I know you?" She felt intimate to him. Like a fresh dream, she seemed more familiar to him than his best friend.

"No, but you will." Standing up she walked to within inches of Luke. "Do you like the morning sun? Do you like the way she touches you when you are in bed?"

"Who are you?" stammered Luke.

"Gotta go." The woman started to leave.

"Wait!" called out Luke. She turned, smiled, but continued on her way. Opening the door, she walked into Student Hall. Luke raced to catch up with her. Entering the Union, he saw lots of familiar students shuffling about but the woman had vanished.

What had she meant saying that he would get to know her? How did she know about his ritual in the morning? The brief encounter with the mysterious lady in red stirred deep emotions—lustful desires to be with her. She invaded his thoughts for the rest of the day, trespassing his mind countless times into the future.

Luke left Student Hall. Passing by Old Hall, he tore his thoughts from the woman and returned to the sparring match between Dultmann and Lewis. He remembered how uncomfortable he had become when Lewis started to talk about resurrection from the dead. Luke could never get right with the notion of death. He remembered coming back from his year of internship and having a discussion with his hermeneutics professor. They were talking about how a pastor can best proclaim the Good News in context to a family who had just lost a loved one.

"You know professor," admitted Luke, "on internship, I remember standing over the grave where one of my members was to be buried. All the family and friends were gathered around as I prepared to do the committal. They were looking to me, God's representative, to give them some comfort—some hope. When I looked within myself, I could find nothing. I had nothing to give them. I mechanically spoke the liturgy at the grave. My words represented the lifeless crumbs of my floundering beliefs which, bottom line, have nothing to offer but a bologna sandwich. Yet I'll serve up that same baloney again and again when I become a pastor..."

Luke reached the front door to his dorm complex. Navigating up the stairs, he slid his key into the lock on his door. Walking in, he tossed his books into the chaos of his desk, then headed for the phone. Perhaps Cassandra had changed her mind and left a message. He lifted up the receiver. The campus phone service alerted him to one new message. Nervously he keyed in his security code, hoping that he would hear Cassandra's voice. "Hey little brother!" came his sister's voice. "This is Kris, and I need to talk to you. Something big happened to me, and I really need you right now. Please call me. Call me soon! Love ya."

Luke was concerned. Kris was a soul mate that, by good luck, was also his only sister. A storm cloud began to darken over his thoughts as he considered that his sister might be in some kind of trouble. "Wait a minute," he punished his thoughts. "Why should I suppose that the 'big' thing that has happened in her life is bad. Maybe it's good! Maybe she has met some guy and things are getting serious. Wouldn't that be crisp if the first official act of my ministry was to do the marriage ceremony for Kris!"

He punched in her number from memory. "Jill's Pizza and Black Dirt," came the voice from the other side. "We deliver by the carton or by the truckload. How can we help you?"

Kris often answered her phone with this pet ruse. "Let's see," sported back Luke, "I'd like to have two pepperoni pizzas with extra cheese and five cubic yards of garden peat."

"No problem! Would you like those items separately or together?"

"Just throw the pizzas on the truck with the peat, but I want my delivery within the hour. I also won't take so much as a loose pepperoni on peat unless Jill brings my order personally."

"Oh Luke," whimpered Kris, calling off the charade, "I wish that I could be with you right now. I need your shoulder! I need that listening ear and your voice that always knows just what I need to hear."

"My shoulder's always there for you." Standing up from his chair Luke began to pace. "What's going on, Kris? I called you as soon as I got your message. You've got me biting nails, Sis, so what's up?"

"No, it's not what's up, it's what's out! I'm out of a job. Out of luck. Out on the streets looking for work. And soon I'll be out of money."

"What happened, Kris?" His sister was in crisis. Luke's throat knotted as he quickened the step of his pacing. The cord of the phone caught the edge of his coffee mug. Luke dived to catch the cup, dropping the receiver on the floor. After saving the mug, he scrambled to pick up the receiver that had been kicked under the table. "Sorry about that, Sis, I almost broke my coffee mug."

"Not the one with Ole and Lena fishing..."

"Yeah, that's the one. But not to worry, I got it before it hit the floor." Luke sat down on the floor, his back resting against the wall. "Lena looks a little shook up, though, but getting back to your situation, is there something that I can do? Do you need money? A place to stay?"

"You're the best! I'd be lost right now without my little brother." Kris pouted into the receiver. "And you're about the only person I trust. You never let me down." Kris paused. Luke knew that she was crying. What could he say? He had to break the awkward silence, but Kris took him off the hook. "I'm a good DJ, right? I don't mean to brag, but I'm way above average as DJs go. I should have it made! A radio station would be lucky to have me. Right?"

"I'm your number one fan! I love jazz, and I love the way you serve it up over the radio. Last summer, when I drove delivery truck in Boston, my radio dial was glued to WLFO. Every time Heather Lane came on the air, half of Boston turned the dial to you." Luke paused. "The other half of Boston are idiots, so they don't count." Kris giggled. "I'm not exaggerating or just saying this because you're my sister, you gotta know, you're the best! There's not a better jazz DJ... ANYWHERE!"

"You're just saying that 'cause you're a refined, cultured fellow with a remarkable ability to judge talent." Luke grinned. "Now, would you mind telling all that to the management?" sighed Kris, her voice thin and fragile. It was not like Kris to sound so defeated.

"Yesterday strangers flooded into the station," she continued. "I was doing my morning shift when suddenly the board went dead. I was off the air! Then our station engineer came to the studio looking like he had shot his favorite dog. In his shadow was a corporate hatchet by the name of Labano. This jerk from the corporate screw-up was there to throw out the jazz format and all the station's DJs with it. Now WLFO is being programmed to serve up a format of baby food. Management thinks that there's more money in advertisers who pick the pockets of teen listeners. This really sucks!"

"Can they do that, Sis? I mean, can they come in and just pull the plug on your job without any legal exposure or liability?"

"I'm afraid they can," answered Kris. "There's no security for a DJ in this business, unless the DJ creates it. I'm too fresh in the Boston market. If I had been here a few more years, our listeners would have cried 'holy war' if management tried to pull me off the air. As it is, I'm done here in Boston."

"So what will you do, Kris?"

"I went down to the station this morning and spliced together a demo tape. I'll do some research in the trade magazines and see if there are any jazz stations looking for new talent. Just pray that something comes up before my money runs out."

Luke heard her use the word 'pray.' He could have taken it as permission for him to ask her about her spiritual journey at the time. Instead, he moved on to another subject. "If you need anything—money, a place to say, a listening ear, then call me. Okay?"

"I'll call if anything comes up." Changing the subject she asked, "Say, have you heard anything from Bill?"

"Kris, before we talk about big brother, I want to hear about what happened at PNG. Did you read anything on the newswire at WLFO?"

"Only that a valve stuck. The plant manager was quoted saying that the valve was replaced and that it never presented any danger to the public. That's about it. You know, Luke, you worry too much." She laughed out loud thinking of Luke fretting over her safety because she lived in range of a nuclear power plant. "Do you know how unlikely it is that there would ever be an incident at PNG? Tell me brother, do you sit around worrying about me being bitten by a rabid rabbit?"

"Only at Easter," Luke teased. "Getting back to William, I got an e-mail from him a few days ago. He was just packing his bags to go backpacking in Colorado. I think he's taking a full week off this time. Joined up with a group of hikers! He saw a flyer at Gulliver's Travel, advertising for experienced hikers only. This is new for Bill."

"Yeah, he always goes alone or with that old college chum of his. The one he hiked with during semester breaks. Did he say how he's doing?"

"The same. You know Bill, he lives for his work. The only thing in his life that doesn't fit the image of a white-robed techno-head is his love for hiking."

"Spare me!" laughed Kris. "If you saw him at the lab, you'd never guess that he owns $300 hiking shoes..."

"Yeah," returned Luke, "and often crosses narrow ledges with a 500–foot straight-fall to the ground below." Standing up again, he continued pacing over a floor strewn with books and dirty clothes. He kept a careful eye on the phone cord as it ran through the clutter. "Hiking is the only thing that takes him out of the Petri dish."

"I don't get it," added Kris, "he lives most of his life studying a zoo of infectious diseases. I thought guys liked to study girls."

"Up close and personal," smiled Luke. Then he cringed. When would be a good time to tell Kris about Cassandra?

"I think that Bill needs a good woman to remind him that there's more to life than those damn diseases!" added Kris.

"Damn diseases," thought Luke, chewing over that phrase. He wondered what meaning, if any, it had for his sister. Kris could just as well have said, "Mythical diseases." Then again, the diseases confronting Bill were anything but mythical! Hell may not exist, but there was nothing imaginary about the germs that Bill had to search out and destroy. His job was tracking down new viruses and bio-tech weapons that could be used by terrorists to take out large population centers. Bill didn't talk much about his work—there were security issues. The little that he did say was enough to scare a Marine commando. "Can you imagine Bill getting serious with a woman?" laughed Luke.

"No!" blurted back Kris. "Well, maybe..."

"Picture this!" broke in Luke, "the Oakland Infectious Disease Center hires a new research assistant. She is a knock-out blonde with thick glasses, and guess what, in no time she only has eyes for William! Bill smells the smoke and figures out that there's more than brains to the blonde, there's fire! Bill gives his little brother, the pastor, a call, and says that there are wedding bells in the near future. Would I mind hiking with them and a few friends into the Rockies to do the ceremony?"

"Stop it Luke!" cried Kris. "You got it right, though, Bill would want his wedding in the outback. And if that happens, I'll buy hiking shoes for the whole family! How thick did you say her glasses were?"

"Thick enough," joked back Luke. "But seriously, Bill's a great guy! He could be a fantastic husband and father if he learned to take his head out of the Petri dish and started studying the two legged animals."

"Hey! We're not animals!" protested Kris. "Not all the time... But getting back to Bill, he's good on the eyes, fit as a tennis pro, and sharp as a surgeon's needle. All he lacks is a life outside of the lab." She paused. "Well, I better let you go. I need to head for the public library and read through the most recent trade magazines. Will you keep me in your prayers?"

"Sure," replied Luke, even though his prayer life these days was spotty at best. He had gone through four years at the seminary, but the Object of his prayers had become less clear to him. Sometimes when he prayed, he felt like he was speaking to the air, or at best, to a stranger. "Would you do me a favor Kris? Would you send me a demo tape, too, so that I can listen to my number one DJ?"

"Absolutely!" Kris exclaimed with a smile so big that it smacked a kiss on her brother's cheek. "You will be the first to get a tape! Thanks for being there for me and always knowing what to say."

"Ah, shucks, you're just saying that so I'll buy more pizza and black dirt from Jill," smiled back Luke. "I don't always know what to say, but I do know that I'm crazy about my one and only Sis. Let me know how things are going and if I can do anything for you. Okay?"

"I will call you in a few days," replied Kris. "Love you little Bro."

"Ditto big Sis! Talk to you later. Bye!"

Turning to his computer, Luke hung up the receiver. He logged on to his favorite online florist seeking a little something to chase away his sister's blues. Luke chose a spring bouquet with lots of garden flowers and baby's breath. On the card he wrote, "To Heather Lane, the Venus of jazz, who brings electricity to velvet! Love, Luke."

Turning off his computer, Luke leaned back in his chair with his hands resting behind his head. What was he getting into, he wondered. Final exams started tomorrow. Cassandra had dumped him. He would be open to his first opportunity to serve as a pastor in just a few weeks, having no idea where that would land him. For years his future would be encumbered by educational debt. He still had his packing to do. There was the phone call he had to make to his parents to finalize his stay with them until he received his pastorate. He knew that they would ask about Cassandra, and he didn't feel like getting into that mess. "I wish that they had e-mail," he murmured to himself.

Looking to his bed, Luke fought off the urge to take a sudden leap into the inviting blankets. He wanted to sleep. He longed for the touch of his mistress of the morning. He glanced out the east window of his room, traveling in his mind to Boston and then to Oakland. He thought about his two siblings. He wanted the best for them. His theology was uncertain, but not his heart for family and friends.

He thought about Bill who was already hiking into the Colorado outback. Luke wondered what kind of people Bill was meeting. Were there any blondes wearing thick-lensed glasses? "I better start studying for my finals," Luke thought to himself. "Don't much feel like it, but sometimes water just has to flow uphill!" He plopped into a thick old chair that was losing its stuffing at torn seams and age-worn tears. The reading light focused down at his lap as he opened "The New Testament Environment" by Eduard Lohse. Time went by, slowly. His mistress would have to wait.

Chapter 3:

THE MATCH

Shadows of dusk arrived, not like lengthening fingers of night, but as a monolithic chunk of darkness dropped upon the mountain. The seasoned hikers had been on a steady climb. Exceeding their goal for that day, the conquered distance brought them to an unplanned location for night-camp. Forced to tent on a rocky, uneven ledge cut into the mountainside, kerosene lamps were lit first, then the two-man pup tents were quickly deployed with gear stored away until morning.

Fourteen hikers gathered with their guide around a campfire, its welcoming warmth inviting an evening of conversation. Nine men, five women, and Cal, guide for Naturally Outback, were spending their second night together under a cloudless sky. The moon was not yet full, but held the promise of a lover's soft exchange. Uncaptured by the clawing lights of civilization, the stars freely displayed their bright, pinpoint presence to the campers below. The dark, purple sky lived in the undulating glimmer of countless stars. It was moments like this, pristine and primitive, that had caused Bill to become addicted to hiking. His mind drifting from the company he kept around the fire, Bill was reflecting on the day's hike and how good it felt to be away from work.

Two men relaxed on the downwind side of the campfire smoking their big cigars. "Why do so many guys like to nurse on cigars when they sit around a campfire?" asked Mandy. "I suppose it's just a guy thing, but when I was growing up, my dad, who never smoked, had to have a cigar at night when the family was out camping. My guess is that it is tied up with testosterone or some male hormone—do you suppose?"

"As a medical doctor," sparked Briggite Brandon, "let me tell you that cigars are definitely tied to the male hormone tobaccostrone. Although, on some occasions, it has been observed that women crave a good cigar. Why? Science doesn't know. It has been shown that a greater percentage of women like cigar smoke secondhand, but equally, there are those who despise it altogether. For myself, I gave up tobacco a long time ago."

Briggite was an attractive woman. Her work and a failed relationship kept her unmarried. She was open to a relationship, but had begun to adjust to the idea that her career might be her marriage. That evening her reddish blonde hair was falling freely about her shoulders. Earlier that day she had been wearing a trail hat to keep away ultraviolet rays and annoying insects. Her freckled face was striking, etching together sass and kindness.

"So you're a medical doctor?" asked Bill. The word 'medical' had pulled him back into the campfire conversation. Looking over at the strawberry blond he asked, "Saw something in gross human anatomy class that made you quit smoking?"

"Frankly, yes," replied Briggite. "When I was smoking, I told the politically correct and Pollyanna pure that I was going to die from one thing or another, so I felt no motivation to take this pleasure out of my life. But then in med school, I took the required gross anatomy. We cut up bodies, and frankly, I saw black lungs with alveoli suffocated in dark mucus. I decided that I liked being physical too much to risk emphysema. So I quit. It wasn't easy, and I wore nicotine patches like a quilt until the craving stopped." She smiled. The conversation was getting too serious for her liking. She winked at Andy as he rolled his cigar between his thumb and fingers. "But boy do I crave a good cigar now and then!" Andy took a deep puff on his cigar, exhaling the smoke toward Briggite. Two others fanned the smoke in her direction with their hands.

"Here! I've got lots of extras," said Rob, the other downwind smoker, holding out a small box of cellophane wrapped smokes.

"Thanks Rob," smiled back Briggite, "but it's not my brand." She looked over at a well-built man in his early thirties. "I'm curious Bill, you used in-house language. What do you know about gross human anatomy?"

"I was a medical doctor, seems eons ago," he replied. "Now I do research in Oakland. I specialize in the area of infectious diseases."

"Are you serious?" cried Briggite. "You live in Oakland, too! Then you must work at the Oakland Infectious Disease Center."

"I do," came Bill's cautious reply. He then asked, "Do you live in Oakland?"

"Yes," said Briggite brightly, "and I work in the IDW at Oakland Community Hospital! Can you beat that? It is a small world!"

"What's IDW?" quizzed Cal.

"It means 'Infectious Disease Ward.'" Bill's answer cut off Briggite who had opened her mouth to answer Cal's question.

"Darn!" said Cal. "I hope you two are not carrying something! Bad enough to get the flu, I sure don't want to get anything exotic. You don't think that one of you got some bad bugs that we could catch?"

"Never know!" teased Briggite. Bill sat quietly. The turn in the conversation was an unwelcome reminder of what he did for a living. He was here to get away from work, not to think about it. The magic moment at the fire had become contaminated. He felt, well, heavy. The stars no longer shined down, but pressed against him from above. The high wall of the ledge closed in around him. The open air that he so loved collapsed against his lungs until he labored each breath.

"Are you okay, Bill?" asked Briggite, sensing the obvious change in Bill's demeanor.

"I'm fine," said Bill, seeking to mask his inward feelings.

Briggite was not convinced. Getting up, she walked over to a patch of long grass growing out of a cleft in the stone rise behind them. Centuries of dirt had been blown into the cleft, providing just enough foundation for these wild weeds to grow. One long stem supported a head of ripe seeds. Slicing her fingernail into the base of the stem, she tore away the stock. Walking behind Bill, she just stood there, her hands concealed behind her back. He turned around to see what Briggite was doing, but she remained still and silent, broadcasting only a large smile for public view. When he turned again to the fire, she tickled the back of his neck with the weed. "Hey, what's this!" cried Bill, turning to Briggite as she hid the weed behind her back.

The Shadow of Death ripped away from Bill as his spirit was set free by the teasing tickle of the playful doctor. Immediately the environment was once again his old friend. Jumping up, Bill reached with both hands around her body to take the weed. She held it farther behind her, not resisting his body pressed against hers. Unable to reach Briggite's hand, he went for her waist. "Tickle me, Briggs," he shouted into the crisp night, "and I'll make you pay with a vengeance."

She pulled away, unable to stand even the possibility of being tickled. Grasping her instrument of torturous healing like a surgical nurse holds a surgeon's scalpel, she took Bill's hand and slapped the weed into his clutch. Catching her breath, she looked at him and smiled, "Briggs! You called me Briggs!" Then softly, "I like that."

Surrounding the group as they huddled from the night in the friendly flames of the campfire were Guardians. "Elmidra," said one to another, "The woman draws to the man. El Shaddai speaks of hope and danger. It now begins. See! The vortex opens." As the Guardians watched, the fabric of reality was torn, exposing a dark, swirling hole in the sky. As it turned, it seemed to spin out hideous dark smears that grew distorted arms and legs and then slithered behind rocks and trees.

The Guardians listened to the voice of El Shaddai, or more precisely, it radiated within them. Then in one voice they radiated back into the heavens, "El Shaddai, we are full of Thy fullness. Our joy is in the essence of Thy loving purpose flowing through our willing consent to bring it into being. There is no good but Thy goodness! There is no beauty but what Thy purpose holds above the chaos and darkness. El Shaddai! El Shaddai! We hear and we flow within the harmony of Thy song. The dark ones come to thwart Thy purpose and find satisfaction within chaos. They cannot alter what Thou hast ordained. Yet help us in our task to make the journey short for these two, and their wounds few. El Shaddai! El Shaddai..."

As the Guardians sang their spontaneous praise to El Shaddai, the birds awoke and began to sing. Squirrels playfully flew from branch to branch, running as well from rocky ledge to open ground, enjoying the game. A general sense of well-being flooded the land. The beasts felt it. The nocturnal aura became layered about the hikers, and it seemed that they had been drawn into a reality where the sky was bigger, the stars brighter, and every color exposed by the glimmering flames was deeper and more distinct.

The demons heard only a cacophony of ragged tones that tore into their senses like a crow pecks flesh from road kill. It made them want to flee, but their appetites forced them to stay. The mortals were eyed by heaven as men and women of noble birth, but hell saw them as sheep for slaughter. Guardians were there to express the Divine purpose. Demons were there lusting towards their goal of satiating themselves upon a planet driven toward the death of all mortals.

"Well, guys and gals," said Cal, "like you, I could sit here all night, but then I'd be no good tomorrow. We have a long hike, and it takes us over some pretty challenging ledges. I'm going to hit the sack. I would recommend that you do the same." He stood up. "So, good night all! I'll wake you up in the morning with the smell of bacon and hot coffee."

Cal walked to his tent as the others took to their feet as well. Henry, another member of the group, poured mountain stream water from a canvas bucket dousing the flames of the dying fire. By the light of the kerosene lamps, soon to be extinguished for the night, Bill drank in the features of Briggs as the flickering light called them forward. He looked to her eyes, and in the glow, they seemed mythical, belonging to a Greek goddess able to command her environment by merely casting a look. Briggs was smiling at him. He felt self-conscious, like a schoolboy caught peeking into the girls' lavatory.

"Good night, Bill," she said. "Do you mind if I join you over Cal's bacon and eggs in the morning?"

"Only if you promise me one thing," he said, trying to make the best of Briggs' discovery about his interest in her.

"What's that? No more tickling?"

"If we have breakfast together," Bill replied, "then I want you to go out for dinner with me when we get back to Oakland. You choose the place."

"Are you asking me for a date?" Briggs teased, her eyes continuing to hold Bill in their mythical power.

"Only if I'm not getting in the way of any other relationships you might have back in Oakland," replied Bill.

"Well, there is Alex," Briggs said. Bill was instantly deflated. Briggs continued, "He's my dog and is accustomed to having supper with me. I guess he won't mind my missing one meal with him. Sure! I look forward to it. See you at breakfast. Goodnight, Bill."

As Bill said goodnight he thought to himself, "I hope Alex will get used to a whole lot of suppers by himself."

Climbing into his tent, Bill took off his shirt exposing the arms and chest of a man who kept himself in tip-top shape. Because of his love for hiking, Bill knew that he had to discipline himself to a regular routine at the Dale Valley Health Club. His long hours at the lab demanded virtually nothing from him physically, and he refused to give his job both time and health. More importantly, and unknown to family and friends, Bill was a special operative for OIDC often taking trips that involved danger, physical danger, at the hands of nefarious personalities involved in bio-technology and chemical weapons.

Months earlier Bill walked incognito down a crowded Istanbul street. Wares from small shops spilled out onto carts cluttering the streets. Sing-song chants filtered through the air from minarets rising above the bustling activity below. Bill wore a wig, its long hair falling down over the shoulders of his tie-dyed shirt, rich in hues of orange. The right knee of his faded blue jeans was torn open. A small leather pouch swung from his shoulder to his left side. He hadn't shaved for a week.

"Hey, English! Englishman!" shouted young boys as they pulled on his shirt. "Come into my father's shop," cried one. "He has big deals today!"

"No, Englishman" cried another, "come see crystal and glass from around the world! Come have Turkish coffee for free while you look..."

"Sorry, boys, not today." Bill tried to quicken his pace, but the crowd of young boys was growing around him, pulling at his shirt and pants.

"You are American," shouted one of the older boys, a broad smile pasted over his face. He had noticed the American accent laced in Bill's words. "Pay no attention to these urchins. Come with me and see the finest Turkish rugs." The boy tried to stand up on his tip-toes as he walked along seeking to keep pace with Bill. Whispering towards his ear he said, "Real cheap..."

"You know the rug dealer on this street?" Bill wondered if the boy knew enough English to understand the question.

"Of course!" shouted the boy. "He is my uncle. Come, meet him. Come have Turkish coffee for free."

"All right," Bill smiled, "lead the way."

"Scat!" scolded the rug merchant's nephew at the children still encircling the foreigner. "Get out of here now!" Facing off with the other children, the boy threw his shoulders back while making fists with his hands. The others reluctantly blended back into the relentless masses that moved with staccato motion among the merchant's carts and small shops. Running to meet up with Bill he stopped him, grabbing onto the leather pouch to Bill's side.

Bill swung around, his hand clenched for battle. Seeing the boy he took a deep breath. "Careful, son, that's not something I want handled."

"But Mr. American, you have walked by my uncle's shop. Look there!" He pointed to a door leading down a flight of stars. Above it, written in several languages, was a small sign advertising Turkish rugs. "My uncle keeps his costs down by making use of the lower level." The boy took Bill's hand. "Come! See! The best in Turkish rugs!"

Pulling Bill down the stairs the boy led Bill to a cluttered, dimly lit room. A large, bald man stood behind a scuffed, wooden counter. Small eyes took hold of Bill as he entered the room. The boy was smiling, presenting Bill like a trophy to his uncle. The boy's face changed instantly as the man motioned to the boy, indicating that he should leave.

"But uncle..." cried the boy.

"No buts! Leave! Now!" The man's massive, handle-bar mustache twitched as he nodded for a second time at the door. His face drooping, the boy sulked to the stairs and left.

"So! You are looking for a Turkish rug today?" The merchant moved from behind the counter and walked toward Bill.

"No." replied Bill. "I have other business."

"I thought as much." The merchant's chin lifted into the air, his eyes slanting down to size up the American. "What business brings you to my humble rug shop, so far away from your country?"

"I have something you want..."

"Did you bring it with you?" interrupted the merchant, looking intently at the pouch resting under Bill's arm.

"That depends," smiled Bill. "This humble rug shop is perhaps owned by a merchant too poor to pay for what I have to sell."

"Hmmm! We'll see about that." Walking back to the counter the merchant slid open a door, revealing a wooden box. Taking a black silk bag from the box, he opened it, pouring the contents onto the counter. Large, crystal diamonds rested on the dusty glass of the counter, mocking the basement store's dingy setting. "Now, let's see what's in your bag?"

Bill walked closer to the counter, lifting a small bottle of yellow liquid from his side-pouch. The merchant smiled, reaching with trembling hands to take the bottle. "I will need to test it, of course, to make sure that the contents are what they appear." Taking the vial, the rug merchant set it on the counter, and then removed a metal container from the back of the counter. The container's interior revealed foam molded to secure three bottles the same size as the one brought by Bill. Two bottles were set in the foam to the right and to the left, the center cavity was empty.

Reaching once again beneath the counter, the rug merchant took out a large jar. A frog jumped inside. An inch under a small hole in the lid, a flat piece of cardboard was suspended parallel to the lid held in place by threads taped to the cover. Taking an eyedropper, the merchant took one drop of liquid from each of the two bottles stored in the metal container. The drops landed on the top surface of the cardboard. Screwing down the lid tightly to the jar, he took a clean eyedropper, momentarily setting it aside on the counter. Tearing a piece of duct tape, he hung it by one corner to the side of the counter for future use. "Primitive," noted Bill.

"Effective enough," smirked the merchant. Picking up the clean eye dropper, he let go a drop of the yellow liquid through the small hole on the lid and immediately sealed the hole with the piece of duct tape. The yellow liquid hissed as it catalyzed with the other two liquids. The frog jerked, stiffened, and died. The merchant smiled. "How did you come by this?"

"Honestly, of course." Bill laughed. "It doesn't really matter, does it?" Bill knew how Interpol had secured part of the toxic mixture. An Israeli special operative had caught up with the courier taking the toxin by train to Istanbul. A struggle ensued. The Israeli agent was shot, but grabbed one of the bottles before jumping from the train. The operative knew that his transmitter, monitored by satellite at Interpol, would reveal his location. The transmitter was sewn into the lining on the side of his suit coat. As a further precaution, a sensor ran to the agent's vest pocket. When the Israeli operative removed from his pocket a pen designed with a magnetic point, it activated a Mayday signal. The agent's body was discovered lying dead in a wooded area, the vial hidden under his pants near his left thigh.

Interpol contacted OIDC, and Bill was drawn in on the case. The mandate was clear—all components to the dangerous toxin must be found. Following leads Bill landed in Istanbul. A contact for Interpol worked the streets of Istanbul. The word was out that a rug dealer was willing to pay a substantial bounty for something lost from a train a few weeks back. Bill traced the tip to the dealer presently standing before him.

Out of the corner of his eye Bill noticed movement behind a vertical wall of rugs. "I think we will have a change in our arrangements," smiled the merchant darkly.

"I think you're right about that." Bill eyed the merchant as the large man sought to put some distance between them. "You keep the diamonds," Bill smiled, "and I'll take your containers."

A man leapt at Bill from behind the rugs, throwing a small cord around Bill's neck. Struggling for breath, Bill grabbed the man's ears pulling them sharply. The attacker yelled, letting go of the cord. Reaching back, Bill grabbed hold of the assassin's neck to brace his weight. At the same time Bill quickly drew his legs into the air, thrusting his feet forward against the merchant. The heavy set man flew back, tripping over a rug rolled up to the right of the counter. Landing to his feet, Bill rammed the back of his head against the assailant's nose. Spinning around quickly, Bill delivered several punches to the man's stomach and face.

Dashing to the counter, the agent from OIDC threw the lid down on the metal container, racing with the toxin up the stairs. The boy, hearing the commotion, was running down the stairs. "I think your uncle needs some help cleaning up," yelled Bill as he passed the boy. "And watch the company you keep, son!"

· · · · ·

Back on the trail, Bill awoke to an annoying sensation playing over his face. He shot up suddenly, wiping his face several times with both hands thinking that an insect might be taking a trip over his terrain. Briggs burst out laughing. She had parked in the door of his tent, and supporting herself on her knees, was tickling Bill's face with another unbearable weed. "Darn it Briggs!" scolded Bill.

"What are you doing?"

"You are tardy, guy," she grinned, "and the group elected me to get you going. You're not trying to stand me up on our first date, are you? Or did you forget that we were going to have breakfast together?" Briggs' face took on the expression of a hurt little girl. It was Bill's turn to laugh.

"No way!" he said. "But I'll tell you what, Doc, you need to change your bedside manners. Lucky for you my hands went for my face and not for you!"

"Do you think so?" Briggs asked sensually. "Is that a veiled threat or a hopeful promise?"

Bill winked at her as he pulled a shirt over his muscular upper body. "I sure am hungry," he said, "and the smell of bacon sizzling on an open fire is the best lure I know of for getting a guy out of his sleeping bag on the trail. You haven't eaten yet, have you Briggs?"

Briggite felt warm as Bill formed her new nickname on his lips. Stretching out on her stomach with her legs scissoring the outside air, Briggs now was lying halfway into Bill's tent. Supporting herself on both elbows she playfully quipped back, "No. I'm not about to be stood up on our first date!" Reaching over with her right hand, she stirred Bill's morning hair with her fingertips. "But if you're not out of there in 30 seconds," she said giving his head a shove with her hand, "I'll not only eat without you, but I'll finish off what's left and leave you the grease and egg crisps."

"I'm out of here! I'm out of here!" shouted Bill. The rest of the hikers heard him and smiled. They were finishing off the scraps on their breakfast plates Cal had served up to fuel the morning hike. Some were already in the ritual of topping off their breakfast with a final cup of coffee. Bill tumbled out of his tent. Making his way over the ground on his hands and feet, Bill looked like an awkward crab heading for Cal as if he were lunch. "If I don't get some of that bacon, I'm gonna go into cardiac arrest, and you'll have to carry my dead corpse out of here."

"Don't you mean that you're gonna suffer a fatal digestive impaction?" laughed Briggs.

"Either way I'm dead weight for you to carry off this mountain!"

"Nope," replied Cal dryly, filling a plate with a stack of bacon and the pile of remaining scrambled eggs, "we won't carry you. We'll just send you free-falling down the south bluff of the mountain."

Bill winked at Cal. "Oh, well, glad I wouldn't be a bother."

• • • • •

They broke camp, continuing their climb along a route so rarely traveled that no defined path could be made out of the rocky surface covered by pine needles and green moss. Above and below them were high cliffs. Soon they were walking along ledges so narrow that the hikers had to remove their backpacks and carry them to the side. Placing their backs tightly against the mountain, they were forced to take small sidesteps along the ledge. Before the climbers, open air threatened them with the possibility of a fatal free fall. Bill enjoyed the difficult hike, leaching a thrill from the danger they faced.

Briggs was beside Bill, working her way along the same, narrow path. These life-in-hand climbs were an emotional rush for him, but today, for the first time ever, he wasn't focused. Why? It was Briggs! Bill was surprised, startled really, to discover that he was concerned for the safety of someone he'd just met. He hadn't left her side during the difficult climb. Suddenly Briggs tossed a large smile at Bill. She didn't seem to mind keeping the trail with him, and that felt good.

Several times along the narrow ledges Bill would ask Briggs how she was doing. Briggs, an experienced hiker herself, began to find Bill's fussing over her a bit humorous; then again, it felt good to be cared about. When they reached an oasis of flat, grassy terrain, Bill was about to check things out again with Briggs. Before he could get out a word, Briggs smiled, hit the flat of her hand on Bill's chest, and whispered sarcastically, "I've done this before, you know."

"I know. I know," Bill muttered, fearing that he was coming off as a chauvinist. "I'm not trying to be the macho-man, but... I don't know! Just be careful. Okay?"

Briggs smiled, her eyes framing him against the blue sky.

Cal stopped the group. "This next ledge is a killer." His voice didn't try to hide the danger they now faced. "We're going to take our time. I know you all are seasoned at this, but remember the rule: 'Look at where you're going and don't look down.' I'll go first, but I want one of the guys to take up the rear." Cal was a throwback, cut from the mold of the old-fashioned male. He still thought that it was the man's job to protect the fairer sex. He got grief for it once in a while. But, the old-mold males like Cal just let that kind of thing roll off their red-neck backs.

Cal walked to the ledge, and taking a deep breath, he leaned his back tightly against the steep mountainside. Slowly he sidestepped across the ledge. Reaching the other side, he shouted for the next one to come. Bill decided to be the last to go over. Briggs stayed behind with Bill so that she could cross just before him. As Briggs started out, Bill whispered, "Careful now. Take it slow and don't look down."

"Yeah... Yeah... Yeah..." smiled back Briggs.

Ahead of her a presence had began to draw sand and dirt out from under a large flat stone, in effect detaching it from the mountain. Like an hourglass signaling the time of a fatal accident, the sand and dirt fell to the distant ground below. Briggs moved closer and closer to the flat stone. Her foot lifted into the air, returning to the stone just ahead. Suddenly the stone slid away from the ledge. With a terrified yell Briggs threw her arms into the air as if trying to gain her balance and keep her body tight against the side of the mountain. No good! Horrified, Bill watched as she took a free-fall. Death waited for her below.

Suddenly a bright flash of light exploded to the right of Briggs. Something had changed the course of her fall. She landed on a large, dead tree growing horizontally out of the bluff. Desperate hands clung to small branches that bristled out from the half-rotten perch. Still shaken, Briggs, an otherwise skeptic of religion, was saying over and over, "Thank you God! Thank you God! Thank you God!" Taking a careful study of her situation, terror seized her! She found it difficult to breath. The limb holding her from certain death was beginning to crack open where it was embedded into the hammered soil and clay.

"Briggs, are you okay?" shouted down Bill. Cal and the others joined in an avalanche of calls reaching out for her.

"I'm OK..." It was difficult for her to talk. Tension had locked her chest in a vice. "...but the limb I'm on is breaking! I need help!"

Wrestling a rope from his backpack, Bill's mind raced frantically for a way to get Briggs to safety. He spotted a small tree growing thirty or so feet above Briggs near the ledge. The tree looked like a small branch growing out of the trunk of a great mountain. Working his way to the tree with dangerous haste, he attached the rope around its small base. It took a couple of tries, but finally he got the robe to fall within the reach of Briggs. Grabbing the lifeline, she looped it under her arms several times, tying the best knot she could manage under the circumstances. Instantly the perch holding Briggs snapped in two, slamming her against the side of the bluff. "Oh no! Oh no! Oh no!" exploded tortured cries for help. "Ouch!" She hit the compacted soil of the mountain. "Bill, I'm really scared!" Unknown to all, an invisible Guardian had been holding the limb together until the rope had been safely tied around Briggs.

Bill watched in horror, shouting back, "Don't worry, Briggs, we're going to get you out of this." Manufacturing a calm voice, Bill's nerves were in fact on fire. He had gotten a rope to Briggs, but there was no way that she'd have the strength left in her to climb up to him. It would be impossible for him to find the footing needed to pull her up onto that narrow ledge. He doubted that the limb securing the rope would take his weight and hers, even if he had the stamina to climb down to her and then muscle them both up the side of the mountain. Taking another survey of the surrounding area Bill determined that Briggs was only ten or eleven feet from a wide ledge down and to his right. He could get to it by working himself through a tight, narrow cleft in a rock.

"Cal," he shouted over to the group still watching from the other side of the ledge, "do you think you can get by that fracture in the ledge and come over here?"

"I think so," Cal shouted back. "Sure!"

"Good! Bring a rope with you." He looked down to Briggite, "Briggs! Take some deep breaths. I've got this figured out. Do you trust me?"

"Do I have any choice?" she cried. "But yes. Yes, I do trust you."

Working his way back over the ledge, Cal managed a big step over the gap created when the stone fell. Each second felt like an eternity as Bill watched Cal inch his way across the ledge. Finally Cal took a huge leap to land at Bill's side. "What's your plan?"

"I'm going to work my way down the crevice in that rock," Bill pointed to the right, "and get to the ledge near Briggs. I'll throw her the rope that you brought. I'll have her tie it under her arms along with the other rope that's holding her up. What I want you to do is lower Briggs down from the rope tied around that limb. While you let her down, I'll draw Briggs over to the ledge. If I were you, I'd keep the rope looped around the limb. Let the rope slide on it to give you some added friction against her weight. It's not going to be easy for you to get a good foothold, but it's the best plan I can come up with."

"Sounds good to me," breathed back Cal. "Don't worry about me, just keep a tight hand on the rope as you bring her in."

Taking the rope from Cal, Bill started down the crevice. It was very narrow, proving to be steeper than Bill first thought. He was forced to apply pressure with his hands against both sides of the narrow 'v,' constantly searching with the tips of his boots for any foothold that the mountain offered. He fought desperately to keep from sliding too quickly towards the ledge. Briggs was urging him to be careful. Her panicked voice transparently displayed fear for Bill and for herself. Reaching the ledge, Bill took the rope draped over his left arm.

"Listen carefully, Briggs, I'm going to throw this rope to you. I want you to grab it and tie it under your arms just like you have done with the other rope. When we're sure that both ropes are secured, Cal is going to lower you down. I'm going to use this rope to draw you over to this ledge. Got it?"

"Yes," said Briggs, "just hurry!"

It took a few throws, but finally Briggs caught the rope tying it around her just under her arms. "OK. Now Cal," Bill yelled, "you start letting Briggs down, very slowly, very slowly, and I'll pull her over to me."

It was difficult for Cal to loosen the knot with Briggs on the other end of the rope, and at the same time, not drop her when the knot let loose. He managed it, though, letting Briggs down slowly as the rope burned against the small trunk of the limb. Snap! The small tree broke away from the side of the mountain. Cal nearly lost his balance, the rope slid from his hands. Briggs flew against the base of the ledge where Bill grunted hard to manage her full weight. His feet were beginning to slide toward the edge. "Oh Lord," he said to himself, a prayer offered to God, "I'm scared."

Unseen hands took hold of Bill's feet as dark entities snarled at the Guardian's presence. Adrenaline flamed through muscles that Bill had trained, but not for this. Numbing pain worked against his efforts to pull the rope up. The whole weight of Briggs was placed against one arm drawing her up, and then the other arm. Sweat ran down his forehead scorching his eyes with blurring pain. Finally Briggs was able to grab onto some scraggly shrubs growing on the edge, helping to pull herself to safety. Taking her by the hand, Bill dropped the rope drawing her to himself. She collapsed sobbing into his arms. "You're fine. You're fine," Bill said over and over, drawing his hand repeatedly down Briggs' hair. Above them, hysterical cheers rang through the air.

"Bill," Briggs was forcing out her words, "I honestly thought that I was going to die. I thought I was going to die..."

"What!" Placing his hand gently under her chin, Bill lifted her eyes to his. "You think that I'd let you finagle a way out of our dinner date in Oakland?"

She smiled, hugging him desperately to herself. Briggs froze to his body, but it wasn't the time or place for Bill to soak in her embrace. Bill was already thinking ahead to their second attempt at crossing the now damaged ledge. Briggs was not going to be in any mood to go over the same spot where she nearly lost it. "On the other hand," Bill thought to himself, "if you get thrown from a horse, you get right back on it." They would be doing Briggs a huge favor by helping her to cross the ledge that almost claimed her. If she didn't face her fears now, they'd haunt her at every difficult crossing along the trail. "Let's get going, Briggs, we have a ways to go yet before making camp."

Slowly she let go of Bill and started for the cleft in the rock. He helped her move up the incline by letting her feet find a brace within his hand or on his shoulder each time she changed position. Right now she would take male help gladly, especially if it came from Bill.

Cal was waiting for them at the top of the cleft. He gave Briggs a big hug. "If that ain't the darndest thing I've ever been through!" The three of them walked over to the narrow ledge.

"I don't know if I can do this again," protested Briggs.

"Sure you can," said Bill, "but just in case, Cal will go in front and I'll follow. How about we tie a rope around you again, with each of us taking an end? If something should happen, we'll have a hold on you."

"No way! If I fall, or if either of you fall, we would all end up dead. Cal, get going, I'll come after you get across. Let's go before I lose my nerve."

Cal crossed over first. It took enormous effort for Briggs to take her first step onto the ledge. "Careful now, Briggs," said Bill. "I know you can do this, but I want you to look ahead, not down, and take your time. I'm not going to wait for you to get across before I start to cross. I'm going to be walking with you each step of the way."

Briggs shot a nervous look of appreciation at Bill, then continued making her way along the ledge. When she came to the spot where the rock was missing, she stopped. She gave Bill another look, but this one said that she didn't know if she could keep going.

"Briggs, don't look at me or to anything but the ledge. I'll keep an eye on you. Get as close as you can to the breach in the ledge. I'm going to take your hand as you pass over it. We can do this. We can do this together..."

Briggs forced herself to the edge of the fractured ledge. Bill's hand folded hers into his. It felt good. She was joined to his strength and confidence. Lifting her foot into the air, she stepped over the breach. Then she lifted her other foot over. Bill released his grip on her hand slowly. "Good job, Briggs! You're home free!"

Briggs reached the other side as one after another of the hiking party gave her hugs. She kept looking back at Bill as he made his way over the narrow ledge, finally reaching the group himself. He stood back sharing Briggs with all those who needed to vent their joy over her safe recovery from the fall. Sitting down on old logs and small boulders, they spent an hour rehashing all the details over what had just happened. It was Cal who finally got them moving again.

Bill and Briggs trailed behind the group. "Do you want to know something really weird?" asked Briggs.

What's that?"

"The limb that saved my life was a good five feet from where I started to fall. I know that this doesn't make any sense, but as I was falling, I saw this flash of light, then it felt as if I was being carried over to that limb." She laughed. "I know how this sounds! But Bill, how did I end up on that tree stuck in the mountain?"

Bill left her question unanswered. He just took her hand and continued to walk silently. Soon they would be making camp. There would be more time to talk around the evening's fire. But in the silence of their walk, he was trying to find an answer to Briggs' question. He'd also seen the flash of light. The tree that saved her life was not in the path of her fall. He remembered how his feet slipped on the dusty ledge while he desperately held Briggs by the rope. How had they found their footing?

The sun was beginning to set. Light sprayed towards them from the backside of towering pines. The trees stood colorless, like dark phantom threads, forming a frayed edge to the western sky as it traced its golden light along the mountain heights. It would be a cool evening tonight. They were higher up, and the air was thinner. The fire would feel good. After the evening social, even the rugged ground would be welcomed as they crawled their tired bodies into warm sleeping bags. The Guardians would be keeping vigil until the dawn.

Chapter 4:
Zig's

The phone rang as Kris was finishing up the supper dishes. Throwing the towel over dishes still dripping in the sink, she took up the receiver. "Hello."

"Hi! Is this Heather Lane, all time Venus of velvet jazz?" It was Luke's familiar voice.

"Well, not for right now, I'm afraid."

"And hey!" snapped Luke, "what about pizza and black dirt?"

"Store's closed!" Kris swung herself into a kitchen chair.

"Too bad! I was hoping for some pepperoni pizza with a yard of peat tossed to the side." Luke laughed out loud at his tepid joke. "Say, Sis, I got your demo tape, and I gotta tell you that you are the queen of jazz!" Luke's sincerity rang like a dinner bell to hungry workers. "I've listened to that demo fifty times, and I still look forward to hearing Heather Lane's silk and sassy voice."

"You're hired, brother! I need a good agent. And by the way, you made me cry. You were so sweet! The flowers and the card that you sent were fabulous! You made my day! No wonder I always turn to you when things are down!"

"Glad you liked them, Kris." Luke was pleased that the flowers had done their job. Kris needed a pick up. "Say, you won't believe what's happening to me. Guess where your little brother is starting out his ministry?"

"Luke! You've got your first congregation!" Luke pulled the receiver away from his ear as his sister's voice continued to assault the phone. "Where are you going? Near? Far? Timbuktu?"

"I'm staying in the Midwest, Kris. My call is to Rochester, Minnesota. I'll be serving as the associate pastor at Morningside Community Church. I went down yesterday to take a look and met some of the leaders of the congregation. It was great! Of course, the honeymoon is always good—or usually so; what it will be like for me at Morningside for the long-haul is always tough to call."

"Exciting, Luke! Maybe I'll pull down a job in the Midwest too! Wouldn't that be sweet! I'll work on it—send out some demos to openings in the five-state area."

"Kris," interrupted Luke. There was something else in Luke's back pocket that he was clearly eager to share with his sister. "Do you want to hear the hottest on Bill? Checked out my e-mail this morning and found a long one from Bill. Turns out that he got back last night from his time away from the Petri dish. Guess what he went and did? He went out to Colorado for a hike and came back with a hiker!"

"Huh?" blurted Kris. "Are you saying that he caught up with that blonde in the thick glasses?"

"I don't know about the glasses, but it sounds like Bill is smitten! And it gets better. He saved her life!"

"Too much! Too much!" gasped Kris. "What's her name? What's she like? What happened to her?"

"Whoa! I'll tell you what I know. Bill calls his new friend Briggs. I don't know a whole lot about her. Bill wrote mostly about her brush with death. Seems that somehow she fell off a ledge while they were hiking. She should have died, but as luck would have it (if you can believe this), she just happened to land on a tree growing out of the cliff. Bill crawled out on a ledge, threw down a rope to her, and pulled her to safety. He ended up doing the whole show himself. The guide had Bill's new girl friend by a second rope, but it slipped. Bill said that there's more and sometime he'll get into it with us, but it sounds like this was a real life-and-death scare."

"Our brother Bill, a hero! You just don't think of this guy who spends eighty percent of his time in a white lab coat as the Bwana." Pause. "So, did he say how she feels about him?"

"You know Bill," quipped Luke. "He's not much for talking about these kind of things. Reading between the lines... I'd say that they are an item!"

"I'm pinching myself. This is incredible! Do you think that she'll put up with the kind of work that he does, I mean if this turns into something more?"

"That's the best part. She's a medical doctor! She works in the infectious disease ward of Oakland Community Hospital. She swims in the same waters as Bill!"

"Ahhhhhhhh!" came another scream. "Wake me up, please! Sounds like this one might be made in heaven."

"Strange you should say that, Sis," mused Luke. "You know me, I'm not much into the miracle stuff, but Bill hinted that something like a miracle was behind Briggs landing on the tree that saved her life. I'm not touching this one, but since you sort-of brought it up, I'm just passing on what Bill said."

"When do we get to meet her?" Kris was now standing, bouncing up and down on her tip-toes.

"Bill didn't say anything about that, but when I e-mail him back tonight, I'll drop some rather large hints. And speaking of meeting, could I get a date with my big Sis next Thursday at Zig's Pizza?"

"You're coming out to Boston!" shouted Kris. Luke grimaced, once again putting the receiver at a distance to save his ear.

"I have a few weeks before I pack up for Rochester. It's been great living at home with mom and dad again, but it's a little hard to be 26, soon-to-be pastor in a large congregation, and still feeling like mom and dad are waiting up for me when

I come in the door."

"They'll never change, will they Luke?" Kris was laughing. She pictured Luke telling some of the locals he was hanging with that he had to be home by ten. "I can't wait to see you! When will you get here? You're going to stay with me, right? I'll have grandma's quilt on the couch!"

"I'll only be in Boston Thursday night, and thanks for the offer," Luke replied. "I'm planning to drive to Boston. 'Thought about flying, but I've got time on my hands, so why not take in some sights on my way to the east coast? If things go according to plan, I'll get to Zig's right about supper time. We can meet up there. Let's polish off our fill of pizza and Zig's 'Big Froth' then head back to your pad."

"I'm not going to deal with this well," pouted Kris. "I don't have enough to do to keep me busy... I'll be thinking about Thursday over and over until you get here. So hurry, okay?"

"It'll be good to see you, Sis." Luke looked down at his watch. "I need to fly! I'm meeting with some old high school friends in about ten minutes. Late or not when I catch up with my buddies, I'll still need to be home..." Luke served up his ending with a huge grin, "by... ten."

"You got that right!" came the implied wink. "I'll plan to see you at Zig's around 6:00. This will be great! Take care, Little Bro."

"See you then, Heather Lane!"

Hanging up the phone, Kris walked over to the window. It was a grey day and a perfect fit for her emotions. She'd sent out letters looking for work, but so far she hadn't been able to bat beyond third base. Stations liked her demo, said that they would keep her in mind for the future, but always ended up saying that they had no openings. The severance package from the station was generous. At least Labano hadn't lied about that. Still, it didn't look good on the resume to be out of work very long. Besides, she would like to use some of the severance pay to update her wardrobe. "Dear God," she whispered, "what's happening with my life?"

Suddenly a colorful bird, unlike anything she had seen before, flew by, perching not ten feet from her window. Feathered in dark reds and blues, it sported a golden head. Cocking its head to the side, it seemed to look directly at her through the glass, and then started singing. The song was bright, connecting with the displaced DJ's sad face then stretching it out into a big smile. "And thank you, God, for Luke."

• • • • •

Kris sat waiting for Luke in the no-smoking area at Zig's. Lifting her sleeve she sniffed it for smoke. Her wait in the restaurant's no–smoking area was as productive as trying to stay dry in a tropical rain forest during a downpour. The atmosphere at Zig's was laced with the smoke flooding out from the more popular dining area. She'd hang out her clothes on the balcony when she got home. For now, she slowly nursed a soda, impatient to see her brother. Zig's drew the area yuppies, in no small part because of its jazz playing softly in the background—used, like furniture, but mostly unnoticed. This was a favorite haunt for Kris, and Luke knew it. Once again, he had scored points with his big sister by suggesting Zig's for their rendezvous.

Heather Lane was well known at Zig's. Almost everyone there called Kris by this station handle. She didn't mind. It was a reminder to her that she had power. People actually wanted to hear her, listening to her kind of music. "Yes," she pouted, "I had power..."

"Heather Lane!" cried a voice from across the room. Heads at the bar turned in unison to look in the direction of Heather Lane. A man and woman waved and smiled while maneuvering around tables to get to her. She knew them. They had first met at Zig's. Chance meetings between strangers usually end quickly, but Kris had become good friends with Steve and Jan. They hadn't met up for a while. Reaching her table, Steve winked and then gave her a hug. "Did you like the plug, Kris? We heard that WLFO had lost its mind. The good people at Zig's needed to be reminded that the best jazz DJ in the history of this city is Heather Lane!"

"Thanks, Steve." Kris' smile broadened as she reached over to give Jan a huge hug. "It's a big night for me, guys, I'm meeting up with my little brother." Casting a sly smile at Steve she tied into his earlier compliment. "Better watch out, Steve, if you keep talking like my brother, I'm going to get a very big head!" Kris enjoyed hanging with Steve and Jan. Like her, they tuned into jazz. They were charming, too, a couple that—to the bone—were still crazy about each other. After eight years of marriage Steve and Jan couldn't get enough of each other.

"Finally, we're going to meet the famous little brother!" exclaimed Jan. "What's the occasion?"

"He's starting out as a pastor in his first church. He'll be living in Rochester, Minnesota." Kris tapped her foot impatiently on the floor. "Having a little time before starting, he decided to come and see me and, at the same time, get a break from the Mom and Dad routine." Kris laughed, gluing her eyes to the door. "Come on," she muttered to herself, "come in and make my day!"

A question started to form on Steve's lips, but sputtered into silence when he saw a change in Kris. Her eyes were riveted to the front window. She saw Luke! Ignoring poor Steve, she dashed to the door. As her brother walked in, Kris flung her arms around him to deliver a crippling hug. Pulling back she placed both hands on Luke's shoulders, drinking in his features. Tears sprouted in the corners of her eyes. "It is so good to see you little brother!"

Luke was hiding something behind his back. Kris knew it, smiling impatiently. With his Sis perfectly positioned in front of him, he slowly revealed two yellow roses surrounded in baby's breath. "It bothers me thinking of you wilting, Kris, so I brought a couple of fresh reminders to show you how others see you." Kris was going to give him another gigantic hug but Luke put out his arms stopping her. "Wait... Wait... Wait... I'm not done with my speech!" Clearing his throat, he continued, "We both love spring, right? Well, as spring always comes after the bitter cold of winter making the flowers grow, so a great job is coming your way after this jerk Labano! When you look at these flowers, I want you to remember that."

Kris started to laugh and cry. Her brother had, for the moment, chased the clouds from her sky. "Now you can give me another hug," said Luke with a matter-of-fact voice. Staring up at the ceiling he waited to be surprised by his sister's next move.

Kris knocked the wind out of her brother as she planted her second hug. When she had drained her strength and his, she grabbed him by the hand. "Say, I've got some friends that I want you to meet." She spoke loudly enough to catch the attention of Steve and Jan, then standing on her toes she whispered quickly into Luke's ear, "Actually, I want them to meet you!"

Kris was bursting at the seams, proud of both of her brothers. Luke had captured a special place in her heart. She had spoiled him when they were making grass stains together on the front lawn of their parent's two-story, turn-of-the-century home. When Luke was born, she never felt that her place as the family princess had been usurped by the new prince. They grew up to be more than sibs, they were best friends.

• • • • •

Dane Morrell stood up, pressing away wrinkles by sliding her hands down the sides of her blouse, into the curves of her waist, and over her shapely hips. The desk in front of her was the centerpiece within a brightly lit office, its linked mahogany sectionals surrounding her with high–tech devices. To her right, a gigantic gas fireplace dominated one side of the room with stainless steel panels, hearth, and mantle. Large windows to the left exposed the city skyline of Seattle. A ten-foot by ten-foot unframed, imitation Picasso hung behind her, bridging the fireplace to the office windows. The door in front of her opened. In walked Flint Porter.

Porter wore a tailored suit, pin–striped grey, with a thin, black tie dividing the front of a crisp, white shirt that had been pulled from a Macy's bag that morning, price tag $85. Strapped to his side, a nine millimeter Glock silently stalked each face captured by Porter's calculating gaze. Morrell felt him look. He was a killer who whitewashed his sadistic episodes by pretending to be a revolutionary. The only blood running cooler in that building as Porter walked into her office was her own.

Porter lifted the edge of his suit coat pulling out a half-empty pack of cigarettes, but stopped as Morrell took him on with her words. "I don't think you want to light up now." Morrell's controlling voice was antiseptic. Its total lack of emotion stimulated a myriad of emotions in others, but Porter felt nothing. He was not, however, going to take on the coven mistress over smokes. He slid the cigarettes back into the front pocket of the Macy shirt.

She gestured Porter to sit down in one of the two high-backed burgundy chairs that faced her desk. She was pleased at having intimidated Porter. "Sit down, Flint," her monotone voice created a dark atmosphere. There was no hint in her speech of the intimacy they had shared in the past. "When will we get the delivery?"

"We're working on it Dane," Porter responded matter-of-factly. "We're having some delays out of Russia. The damn Russian Mafia has no organization. It's clumsy! When it finally gets something going, the economy ties its hands. The important thing is that its scientists have made the dirty-germ. We tested it on Khlos, a small island off the Turkey mainland. Hell, it's deadly! Only a matter of time until it's in our hands."

"Dirty germ!" came a flat laugh from Morrell. Her lifeless, airy voice hung in the atmosphere. "I love you guys! You have something that could kill every living person where its unleashed, and you call it dirty! What about the antidote?"

"Of course, of course," replied Porter, standing to his feet. "You'll have the whole package when we get it out of Russia. At best we're still months away until enough is manufactured to do the job. I'll contact you when I'm back in the States." Turning around, he opened the door and walked out.

Morrell reached into her desk, pulled out a pack of cigarettes, and lit up. Her thoughts drifted back to the night she first met up with Flint Porter.

· · · · ·

Smoke hung in the air. The San Francisco singles bar was a favorite haunt for the over thirty crowd. Dane Morrell sat at the bar with two members of her coven. The three women were there for sport, seeking to hold life at a distance. The Satanists heard the sixties musicians entertaining the patrons, but without emotion. They drank their drinks, mindless of the flavor, seeking only to add more breadth between themselves and the world which held them captive. Their only savor was perversity. They would work the night until they were coupled up. Then they would enjoy shocking their partners when they were alone.

A man walked over setting a drink down on the bar, saying to one of Morrell's friends, "I noticed your red hair when I came into the club. I asked the bartender what you were drinking. This drinks on me. Do you mind?"

Morrell felt herself drawn to the man. There was some profit for her master in getting to know him. Doing an end run around her redhead friend, she reached her hands over to straighten the stranger's tie. She didn't let go when she was done. Morrell's friend got the message, walking away in silence. As Porter watched her walk away, Morrell placed her hand on his cheek, pulling his face to meet her eyes. "I'm really a redhead." Her monotone voice was seductive—different from any other woman's voice in Porter's experience.

"Is that so!" Porter took the empty bar stool.

"I swear," said Morrell, holding her hand up as if taking an oath, her lit cigarette between her fingers. "I'm just full of surprises."

They continued to talk—their speech spiced with innuendo. Morrell savored a delicious darkness to the man's thinking. She felt his murderous impulse. Clearly he was a world traveler, but he had avoided sharing what he did for a living. Morrell decided to take the chance. "So, what do you do that pays for expensive suits like this one?" Placing her hands on his lapels, she tugged them in her direction.

Porter's tongue was lubricated with alcohol. "I'm a revolutionary!"

Morrell shot out an airy laugh. "Is that so? Well I'm a witch!"

"Can you make a living as a witch?" Porter was amused.

"I make my living as an account executive," she leaned over, brushing her hair against Porter's cheek. "What I do is another matter. You'd be surprised by what I do."

"I'll have to check that out." Porter reached over placing his hand on her hip.

That evening began a liaison between the man with dark intent and the servant of a dark master. They drank upon each other's depraved inclinations. There was no love, no hate, no emotions for the other person, only the feeding frenzy of a man and a woman looking at one another, as if in a mirror.

• • • • •

Morrell reached to her desk for another smoke. Tonight the coven would meet at the Mueller farm, breaking the usual pattern of meeting at various suburban homes. The ritual sacrifices were always done out of town. They had kidnapped a young woman in California who, like other fame seekers, had come from the Midwest to make it big in Hollywood. The coven brought her to Seattle, bound and gagged in the back of a truck owned by a coven member who operated a fishery. She would be sacrificed to Molech, ancient god of the Valley of Hinnom. Molech was a destroyer who preferred infant flesh.

Molech stood undetected behind Morrell as she sat at her office desk. The arch-demon's slanted lime-green eyes sliced by a vertical shaft of blackness stared down at her. It placed its hand upon her right shoulder. Tentacles grew into her flesh, rooting her mind within its will. Morrell felt a sudden shiver of terror. She had not found an infant to sacrifice to Molech for months. She would need to do better at the next new moon.

Molech's appetite for human flesh was growing. At Morrell's direction, the coven started human sacrifices to Molech four years ago, but then only twice a year. Now the god of Hinnom demanded monthly victims. It was difficult to protect the coven—to keep its cover, while at the same time safely plucking enough victims to satisfy Molech's increased carnal cravings. Most recently, Molech was demanding infant blood, but babies were even more difficult to find without the danger of exposing a coven member during the kidnap.

• • • • •

Luke jogged behind Kris as she dragged him by the hand over to the Stanleys. "Jan and Steve," came the unmasked voice of pride, "this is my little brother, soon-to-be pastor at Morningside Community Church, and recent arrival to the Mecca of medicine, Rochester, Minnesota."

Steve instantly fell to one knee, pulled his chin into his chest with arms straight to his side. "Your majesty!"

Jan burst out laughing, having picked up on the same thing as Steve. Luke turned red. Kris was completely baffled about Steve's behavior. Next Steve took Luke's hand as he mimed back, "I am honored to meet his royal highness, little brother, soon-to-be pastor at Morningside Community Church, and recent arrival to the Mecca of medicine, Rochester, Minnesota."

Kris got it! Breaking out laughing, she turned to Luke and fell to her knee. "My prince!" Then Jan was down. "Yours is but to command, ours is to obey!" Except for the sound of smooth jazz, Zig's had become as silent as a sail in the wind. Eye after eye had turned and ears strained toward the strange drama starring Heather Lane.

Finally getting it too, Luke lifted his arms to the patrons of Zig's. With a dramatic flair he shouted, "My loyal subjects!"

Laughter exploded as the new king took his chair. His entourage joined him at the table. Zig's was soon buzzing again as the four blazed their conversation through the background noise and jazz-laced atmosphere. Kris sat across from Luke keeping her brother clearly in view. "Well Steve," Luke was the first to get the conversation rolling again, "now that Sis has told you who I am, the family royal and all, how about telling me about you and Jan?"

It was Jan who broke in to answer Luke. "Our life is pretty dull, except that we are madly in love with each other." She winked at Steve and took his hand. "Right, love?"

"Absolutely! Madly in love!" Winking at Luke, Steve turned to his wife. "Did I say that right, Jan?"

Jan tossed Steve's hand back at him, turning back to Luke, "The big exclamation point of our life these days is the trip that we just took."

"Oh, so you have been gone," interrupted Kris. "I didn't think I'd seen you around lately."

"It was a three week trip to the Mid-East," continued Jan. "And you know what? We didn't see one masked terrorist! Not a one! Promise!"

Steve laughed, but his bright faced soon faded under some dark memory. A serious thought invaded his mind, erasing all signs of his previous playfulness. "Something might be happening down there that does have to do with terrorists, even if we didn't see one." Jan knew where her husband was going as Steve continued. "They've had some deaths in a small village on the Aegean Sea. The government closed off the village completely. They also stopped all news reports coming off the island. I think the island is under quarantine. This is scary stuff..."

"Kris," broke in Jan, "you didn't hear a word of it here in the states, did you?"

"No," she replied. "Not even a post-it note on the WLFO News Board. But you know, there's so much going on in the world today, with telecommunications and the shrinking planet and all, that you gotta have over a hundred dead bodies to get a real story going."

"Or one dead royal prince," interrupted Steve, offering a second wink toward Luke.

"My brother is not going to die—EVER!" Kris straightened up in her chair. "I need this royal prince!" Turning back to Steve, Kris sighed, "Sadly, though, death is business as usual in the news today."

"The rumor we heard in Tel Aviv," Jan spoke quietly. Her voice had become a whisper, as if to respect the silence of the island authorities. "The rumor is that the whole village was wiped out completely. Everybody's dead!"

"This is hard to buy!" Luke, the seasoned seminary skeptic, charged into the conversation. "How can they keep something this big a secret? You'd think that the word would leak out somehow. Then bingo! It's on the Internet... after that it's just a matter of time before it's picked up by the press."

"In my opinion," protested Steve, "nothing makes sense once the government gets involved." Jan giggled nervously. She knew her husband's distrust of politics. He was the self-proclaimed authority on all current conspiracy theories.

"The word often does leak out," Kris noted, drawing from her personal experience working with the newswire at the radio station. "But if the press report can't be verified, it dies on the wire. Only the tabloids are willing to risk their reputations over a great, but unverified, story."

Luke wasn't buying much of what he heard, but you'd never know it. He had put on the same mask that he had learned to wear at the seminary. It was the one that allowed a pastor to look cordial and interested as a parishioner rattled on with some old-fashioned nonsense about Christ's bodily resurrection and the like.

"Getting back to what Steve said about the government and all," continued Kris, "you hit the nail on the head, Steve. A few years back, I started to notice a change in the information that came over the newswire. It's hard to explain, but the reports became tame. Things were being filtered out, you could feel it! There were certain countries, leaders, or incidents that were featured, but more like lightning rods, to draw our attention away from the big picture. The scope of world events became truncated. Almost over night there were individuals, key situations, that couldn't be touched with the proverbial ten–foot pole. Everything was being recast by the spin-masters. The press releases had the flavor of color commentary, doctored up to make it sell a certain way to the public. I think the government, or some shadow government, might be behind it."

"That's scary!" said Jan, her voice still wrapped in secrecy.

"Makes you think about Mel Gibson in Conspiracy Theory," added Steve.

"Conspiracy theorist Heather Lane has gotten to you guys," laughed Luke. His cultivated mask fell. "Sis is always imagining that things are not what they seem... that there is some shadow government agency pulling the strings above our leaders. Tell her about something real, like the dangers of living downwind from PNG, and she thinks that you are in cognitive overdrive!" They laughed again. Luke winked at Kris, turning the conversation to "D-day" at WLFO.

Overseas, a small village lay silent except for lapping flames devouring the town's buildings. One by one, men in atmospherically sealed suits were throwing autopsied bodies, slain by a killer virus, into huge piles to be incinerated. Pets and animals were being systematically destroyed.

• • • • •

"It's been five weeks, three days, and fourteen hours since you attacked the back of my neck with a weed," teased Bill. He was sitting with Briggs at a plush restaurant in the suburbs of Oakland. An open, round, fireplace blazed at the center of the room. They chose a table that butted up against the stone-sided fireplace. Smoke randomly drifted into the room, its aroma lightly seasoning the atmosphere with memories of campfires together in Colorado. Briggs took Bill's hand. "They've been the best five weeks, three days, fourteen hours, and seventeen seconds of my life."

"I'm glad to hear you say that," smiled Bill, "because I'm about to take the biggest, scariest step of my life. Briggs," Bill took a deep draft of air, "I no longer can think about the future without thinking of you. I know it hasn't been that long... I mean that long of time that we've known each other. But we're both mature... No! That makes us sound old. Ah, Briggs, I'm not going to say that I'm crazy about you, because wanting you to be mine is the sanest thing I know." Bill stopped. He was completely out of words.

"Are you asking me to marry you, Bill?" asked Briggs. Tears were rolling down her cheeks, out of place with her broad smile.

"Briggs, I don't know how to make speeches," replied Bill. "Sometimes I think that I took to working with viruses because I didn't have to talk to them. But I'm solid, and Briggs, I know myself. You could use my heart to anchor a boat, and it wouldn't move during a hurricane. Briggs, my heart is set on you. I know it sounds crazy. We've known each other for such a short time, but I've never had a clearer head than now... when... I... ask... you... to be mine."

Briggs squeezed Bill's hands. "Bill, do you remember when we left Naturally Outback to start out on the trail? You wore that green flannel shirt with red suspenders. You bent down to tie a shoe and one of the back snaps sprang loose on those red suspenders. You fumbled about like a little boy without his mommy trying to get it snapped. Finally, red faced, you turned to me and asked me to help you get it snapped. Turning your back to me you waited until I snapped it back into place. You were like a little boy blended together with a macho man. I was charmed! I knew that I was going to flirt with you on the trail."

Bill gave a nervous laugh. Briggs still hadn't answered his question. "Was that tickle on the neck your first flirt?"

"The first flirt that you caught, Dr. Downs," she sported back. Her face became briefly overcast. "I was also concerned for you, because it seemed like the weight of the whole world had landed on your shoulders. Just like I think that there's something that has been bothering you for the last couple of weeks, but you won't talk to me about it."

"Briggs!" interrupted Bill. "Will you or won't you marry me? For heaven's sakes, I'm going nuts here until you give me an answer!"

Briggs brushed away tears from her cheeks. "I don't know exactly when it happened, but I fell in love with you long before today, back somewhere along the trail. It didn't happen with a thud, but I woke up one morning in the tent and there you were, on my mind. I haven't been able to get you off my mind since that day. I'm soaked with love for you, saturated to the bone. If you had taken much longer to ask me, I would have become so full with you that I would have exploded!"

"That's a yes!" shouted Bill, then came the blush as patrons turned to look.

"Like it or not, Billy-boy," softly spoke Briggs, "I'm yours on a lifetime contract!"

• • • • •

Guardians had drawn about Bill and Briggs in a tight circle that included the central fire. Bodiless shadows were moving about within the room. Entities cloaked themselves wherever light eclipsed into darkness. A swirling vortex opened above the flames, just under the hood. A thick stream of darkness spun out into the room falling into a lumpy mass on the floor. As if sucked instantly into the air, the amorphous mass lengthened, becoming an odious demon towering ten feet and forced to avoid the ceiling by stooping down. It leaped at the nearest Guardian throwing him back and breaching the sentry of angels.

The two wrestled, passing through tables and chairs as if they were smoke. The demon, armed with claws and pointed teeth, was seeking to tear into the angelic body. Slime oozed out from the entity, hissing like butter on a hot grill when it struck against the body of the Guardian. The demon was powerless to destroy the Guardian, but it could inflict pain and distract him from protecting Bill and Briggs.

The demon bit into the arm of the Angel. Pain raced from the open wound forcing a gasp from the Guardian. The Guardian tore away, grabbing the entity, it flung the demon through the outside wall of the restaurant and onto the street. Cars passed through the warrior of darkness, their passengers unaware of anything but a brief, stale odor. Flying out after the demon, the Guardian drew its brilliantly white sword. The entity shrieked as it saw the Guardian's unsheathed weapon. "No! Do not send me into the outer darkness!"

The Guardian's sword struck into the monstrous entity. Flash! The entity was sucked into the light of the sword only to descend into a darkness that held not even the promise of light. Their captain vanquished, the dark entities fled from the restaurant, dashing for the vortex as it hovered above the street where their Goliath had met El Shaddai's David.

Dᴀᴠɪᴅ Pᴀᴜʟ Aɴᴅᴇʀꜱᴏɴ

Chapter 5:
PRN40

"Morningside Community Church." Morning sunshine sparkled in the voice of the parish secretary. "How can I help you?"

"I understand that you have a new associate pastor that's joined your staff, is that true?" It was a male voice—not a regular caller.

"That's correct," replied Tamor Carver. "The Reverend Luke Downs." Tamor had joined the Morningside team three-and-a-half years ago. She came to America from Angola, Africa, at the age of 17, her faultless English spiced with a British savor. She was the royal princess to a small tribal chief educated at an Anglican medical mission in Dondo. Before leaving Angola, she carefully selected her American name and chose Carver after the famous African-American scientist. Now 22, her long, black hair framed a face of childlike features as it cascaded down upon her chest and back. One tightly braided strand of hair fell along the right side of her face clinched with a small, bright red ribbon. "Would you like me to ring his study?"

"Yes! Thanks." The man's voice spiked. "But tell me, do you regret calling him to Morningside, or does he still have you fooled?"

Tamor's spicy accent brightened, stretching to the extreme a voice already satiated with joy. "No, Pastor Luke is great, but we have some concerns about a couple family members. They seem a bit eccentric! He has a sister named Kris who answers to Heather unless she is selling pizza and black dirt—then she calls herself Jill. Of course, there's his prodigal brother William who can't hold down a decent job, and so he spends his time with lowlife. Frankly, we don't know how Pastor Luke turned out so well given the influence of his kin."

The stranger was charmed by Tamor's acid humor. Her British accent tickled against his ear forcing him to choke down chuckles as they bubbled up with each word Tamor spoke. She'd somehow figured out that he was Luke's brother and was sporting with him. But what a chance she took, Bill thought. What if he was a funeral home director, calling because there had been a tragic death in the Morningside community?

"I take it this is William," said Tamor crisply. "Would you like to speak to your brother?" Tamor's voice continued to smile.

"Yes, this is Bill," he replied. "But tell me, how did you know? You took quite a risk. I mean, you slighted your new pastor's family! How would that sound to someone else on the other end of the phone?"

"Oh, not to worry about that," Tamor spoke with a wink in her voice. "Pastor Luke had me enter your number into the memory on our phone system. The system shows us the number of the calling party. I remembered the Oakland exchange. When I picked up the tele, I saw that the incoming call was an Oakland number. Besides," she smiled broadly, "who but a brother would be so insulting to his own blood! I didn't take that big of a chance, you see. I'll ring you through."

"Wait a minute!" stopped Bill. "Since I will be calling Morningside from time to time, it might help to have your name."

"Tamor Carver," she said smartly. "It's good to talk with you William. I will get your brother. God bless you. Bye!"

Tamor pushed the intercom button to Luke's office. "Pastor Luke," she said, "I have a prodigal on the phone who wants to talk with a pastor. Should I send him through?"

"Ah, brother Bill," smiled Luke. "He didn't give you a bad time, did he?"

"Nothing I couldn't manage," she replied, then vanished from the line.

The phone gave an audible click as Tamor transferred the lines. "Hey big brother!" Leaning back Luke placed his feet on top of his desk.

"How are you doing, Luke? Good to hear your voice and not just read the taps you send over e-mail!"

"Good to hear from you, too, Bill." Luke reached for a picture that his brother had scanned and sent as an attachment by e-mail. It showed Briggs standing in a small cleft, a zenith on a Colorado mountain, as it jetted thousands of feet above the woodland below. A gigantic sun, setting in the west, completely encircled Briggs within the protruding rock. If this woman's charm matched her beauty, Luke thought, Bill had taken home the prize. "So how's Briggs? Do you still have her on that mind-altering drug that causes her to see you as something special?"

"Yup," sported Bill. "The problem is that I need to keep upping the dosage. Besides that, there's a side effect. Briggs keeps walking up to patients at Oakland Community with this huge grin. It works well with, 'You're completely cured!' but doesn't go down with, 'I don't think you have more than a week...'"

Luke laughed. "You know that Kris and I are dying to meet her. If we don't get a meeting set up soon, my money's on Sis making a personal delivery of pizza and black dirt to your apartment door."

"Is that supposed to scare me?" chuckled Bill. "I won't arrange anything if that's what it takes to bring Kris to my door." Pausing, Bill searched his memory for the last time that he had been with her. "I haven't seen Kris since the Christmas before last!"

"Yeah, we don't get together nearly enough," Luke continued the lament.

"That's going to change, Luke. I'm planning a trip to Rochester. There's someone I need to see at the Mayo Clinic. He's been researching predator viruses that have no effect on humans, but are deadly to toxins like anthrax. It seems that their chemical composition..."

"Blah.... blah... blah," chuckled Luke into the phone.

"Sorry. I'll skip over the lesson in organic chemistry." Bill tapped his fingers on the side of his cheek repeatedly as he talked with his brother. "Besides the research, I want to get a look at your new parish."

"Great!" Luke's joy cruised over the lines to California. Standing up, Luke began pacing back and forth, leashed to his desk by the phone cord. This wasn't like Bill to break away from the lab unless he really had business to do with the Mayo Clinic. Yet maybe there was some other lurking purpose to his visit? Bill's trip to Rochester sounded legitimate. It probably was... Still, Luke decided to go digging for other agendas that might include Briggs. "You don't have any special events planned for the future? I mean, something you want to tell me about? Something that involves Briggs? Something you might want me to do for you and Briggs?"

"I'll get into all that when I see you. My plane arrives in Rochester tomorrow at 9:40 a.m. I know this is short notice, but can you make it work?"

"Make it work?" quipped Luke. "You know that we pastors only work on Sunday. I'll pick you up at the airport. After a quick tour of Morningside, we'll head out for lunch at the best steakhouse in southern Minnesota, and maybe the world. And, the beef's on me!"

"Fantastic! I'm looking forward to tomorrow. Tell Tamor that your eccentric brother will be traveling without any infectious lowlife, so not to worry."

"Good, we like that," Luke grinned into the phone. "The kind of viruses that you hang around with, we don't need in Minnesota! See you tomorrow, Big Bro!"

$$\bullet \ \bullet \ \bullet \ \bullet \ \bullet$$

Bill struggled to find the saddle to his cordless phone after his call to Luke. It was buried somewhere under the clutter covering his office desk. Wearing his white lab coat unbuttoned in the front, Bill rolled his sleeves above his elbows. An ID hung sideways from his left breast pocket, coded to allow him access to the "Black Knight" restricted area. "Black Knight" is what the staff at Oakland Infectious Disease Center called the lab containing the most toxic viruses.

The killer viruses imprisoned there acted like the evil black knights of medieval lore. The staff at OIDC saw themselves as knights in shining armor seeking to protect the world. Their self-evaluation was right on target. They were modern knights using weapons that included state-of-the-art technology and satellite communication connecting them with Interpol throughout the world. OIDC worked behind the scenes saving the world's population from microscopic bugs that could take out entire cities within days. They did the dirty work for the Center for Disease Control and Prevention.

Suddenly sirens sounded, blasting Bill to his feet. A rotating red light flashed through Bill's office window as it looked out into the hallway. A breach had taken place at Black Knight! The most serious alert at OIDC had erupted. Bill flew out of his office door joining other OIDC staff as the electrified current channeled them toward the same location. Some technicians stayed at lower stations of security, their level of clearance not permitting them to advance. Bill slid his security card through security zone one, then security zone two, then security zone three. The last two levels would require his card and the retinal scan of his left eye. Stan Hartman was waiting for him as Bill slid his security card into the entry for Black Knight. Pounding the tip of his right shoe repeatedly against the floor, Bill waited impatiently for the retinal scan to give him final clearance.

Stan was suited up in an atmospheric containment suit. Bill could see Stan's face through the multi-layers of air-tight glass on the isolation door window. Stan's clear plastic visor revealed an expression torn with terror. His suit was dripping wet. He had flushed it in the decontamination shower. "Sherry's dead!" "Sherry's dead! Stan shouted this over and over, his words muffling through the suit and sealed doorway. Finally the door opened.

Bill ran to the second sealed door leading into the Black Knight refrigerated storage area. Through the glass door he saw Sherry lying on the floor still wearing a containment suit. She wasn't moving. "What in the blazes is going on here?" screamed Bill, scrambling to maneuver into a containment suit.

"No," protested Stan. "You can't go in there! From what we can tell, Sherry's suit was functioning perfectly. Look! It still has positive pressure. There's no detectable breach in it!"

"What are you saying?" Bill barked impulsively. His mind was distant from Stan's words. He was thinking of Sherry. He had to get to Sherry. Stan's warning did nothing to stop Bill from working himself into a containment suit.

"Bill, you can't go into the lab!" Stan rifled his words at Bill. In horror Stan watched as his friend placed his second foot into the suit. "Sherry did not have a heart attack! No unexpected stroke! Her bio readings indicate acute stress to her immune system, the kind caused by PRN40!"

"She was working with PRN40!" Bill's voice cut back at Stan, as if somehow he had something to do with the situation.

Stan caught the implication. "Bill, don't climb on me!" he protested. "Sherry was simply doing a routine inventory of the vials. She wasn't doing any tests—you know that she wouldn't work with PRN40! Not without authorization!" Stan was dazed. "It's a nightmare!"

"Hold it!" Bill released his grip, the containment suit fell around his feet. He was desperately trying to mentally take hold of what was happening. "Let's think this through. There's no apparent breach in Sherry's suit. It still has a positive pressure. She didn't work with PRN40 except to inventory the samples. Now she's dead, showing all the signs of a PRN40 infection. Didn't she feel something coming on?"

"She's the one who sounded the alarm," replied Stan. "I was putting on a containment suit to join Sherry in the lab. Suddenly the siren is screaming, lights are flashing, and I run to see Sherry... Bill! She was holding her throat as if she were choking or couldn't get any air."

"Was air being pumped to her suit?" drilled Bill.

"Yes, as I said," Stan walked closer to Bill, "her suit was working perfectly. You saw the gauges, everything reads good. Bill, nothing here makes any sense!"

Sherry's lifeless hand moved. The husk of her body was being violated by dark forces. Her sightless eyes opening she stood upon her feet. "Sherry!" Bill shouted. "What's happened?" She said nothing. Eyes vacant, she turned toward the refrigeration unit.

The triggered alarm had done its job locking the refrigerator's door automatically. It was riveted shut until multiple safeguards were sequentially set in motion. Sherry's demonized carcass began to pull on the door handle. Supernatural forces ripped against the welded bond between the handle and metal door. Crack! The broken fragment of a metal bar rested in her hand, but entry was denied.

"What in heaven's name are you doing, Sherry!" Stan was yelling hysterically, his helmeted head pushed tightly against the glass of the door. Mechanically Sherry's gloved fist began pounding the door of the cold storage refrigeration unit. A crack exploded across the center of the glass. Four or five more hard hits shattered the facade of the door. Sherry's dead hands began taking vials of toxin. Stan and Bill screamed, but their words failed to reach her dormant ears.

"We've got to stop her, Stan." Bill looked over, catching his friend's horrified look. Stan was gaping at the monitor displaying Sherry's vital signs. They were flat. Bill saw it too. "The monitor can't be working, or the cable connection must be loose." Stan looked back at Bill and nodded his head in slow agreement. He didn't buy what Bill had said.

The system was designed to detect any anomalous operations. On the other hand, Stan realized that if the monitor was working, Sherry was walking around in the other room, dead. "I'm going to release detox!" yelled Bill over the screaming sirens. Stan shook his head as Bill's right hand struck hard against a large, protruding button. A yellow mist begin to cloud the refrigeration lab. Sherry's form disappeared until her zombied face struck up against the glass door leading from the cold storage lab.

Bill looked at two glazed shells housing eyes that once sparkled with flirt and fire. Hell and death met him there. "Dear Savior," he whispered, "don't let this happen to Sherry. Don't let this happen..." He was breathing hard. "Sherry deserves better than this. Help her! Dear Jesus! Help us all..." As Bill prayed, Guardians entered the chamber to face dark warriors flying out from a vortex pulsing at the far end of the room. Yellow mist continued to pack into every crevice of the lab. Two Guardians struck their swords forming a cross, but all Bill and Stan saw was a flash of light. "What was that?" cried Bill. Stan said nothing, his hand pressed against the side of his head.

A cherubim with a flaming sword appeared before the crossed swords. Walking to the vortex the heavenly warrior thrust its flame into the center of the darkness. The cherubim turned its sword to the right. The shadow warriors shrieked as they grew oblong and were sucked head first back into the hatch of hell. Sherry's body collapsed, falling lifeless again to the floor. Bill read the question on Stan's face. "I don't know," Bill gasped. Stan couldn't hear Bill's words silenced by the blaring sirens, but he wouldn't question further. He knew that he had witnessed something beyond a scientific explanation. What it might have been, Stan didn't want to know.

Taking a deep breath, Bill looked down at the body of his friend, slain by the virus and shamed by agents of hell. "This is going to be hard on Sherry's family," he said to Stan. "If she's really dead we're going follow procedure and insist that her body be cremated in the containment suit! I want the crew that goes back for her body not to touch anything! Let them verify if she's dead. If so, wrap up Sherry's remains, with the suit, in a body bag, and then plan for immediate cremation. I think we may be dealing with a virus that can somehow get through polymers. Wrap the body bag in an asbestos material until it is cremated. I want this room sealed up until I can figure out what's going on with this virus."

Reaching over his hand Bill touched the glass near Sherry's body. "Stan," he continued, "don't mention anything about this bizarre episode. I'm not sure how we're going to explain the broken door on the refrigerated storage, but telling stories about an animated corpse won't help us out. Right?"

"I wouldn't touch what I just saw with a ten foot pole!" Stan looked briefly at Bill, then glanced to the first entry door. Other OIDC personnel with proper clearance were now arriving. He and Stan walked to the door as Stan released the solenoid driven lock. Glancing quickly at his friend and colleague, Bill then looked straight ahead. "Give them my instructions. Meet me back at my office."

· · · · ·

"I don't get it! Why aren't you taking the trip to Rochester to meet with Dr. Lempke?" interjected Stan. He sat in Bill's office. Once again Bill was acting as if the Center couldn't operate without him. Stan's friend was about to call off a very important meeting with a researcher in Rochester.

"I'm going to have to postpone that trip to Mayo for now..."

"No you don't!" protested Stan. "OIDC can get along a couple days without you. It appears that PRN40 may be more dangerous than we thought. We need the research that Lempke has done on predator viruses. You've got to go! If we don't figure out how to stop this thing, then Sherry's death is for nothing, and her family may die too."

"OK! OK!" Bill said waving his hand in front of his face. "But I'm going to call you when I get into Rochester. I'll want an update..." He paused. "I want you to find out and let me know when the memorial service will be for Sherry. I won't miss that! Understood?"

"Yeah, I'd want to be back for that too," replied Stan. He walked to the door, then turned. "Bill, don't cut your plans to meet up with Luke. Sherry's death is... I think it will be good for you to spend time with your brother." Bill smiled weakly, nodding his head.

• • • • •

The plane touched down. It was a foggy, cloudy morning in Rochester. Luke waited just beyond security at terminal one. Exiting the plane Bill wore a white shirt loosely tucked into faded blue jeans. His hair bounced randomly as if he had just stepped out of the wind. Bill was one of those guys who always appeared lost wherever he was, unless you caught him in the lab or on the trail. There was a boyish look to him created from the cut of his facial features and the casual clothes that hung about him. Luke was pleased to see that Bill was still big Bro Bill. "Boy it's great to see you," Luke said, shaking Bill's hand and then delivering a hug. "I was sort-of hoping that Briggs might have come along for the ride."

"Not this time, little brother," returned Bill. He was tired. The usual "oh shucks" smile that he sported was absent. "But she did tell me to say hi and give you a hug from her." Bill gave his brother a second hug.

"I need to make a quick call back to the Center." Bill scouted for a public phone.

"Sure," replied Luke pointing down the corridor, "phones are straight ahead. But where's the cell phone? Is the agency too tight to give you guys a phone?"

"Got one" quipped Bill, "but they're not secure. Public phones are random and less likely to be bugged."

Making a quick pivot Bill jogged away to make his call. After a ten-minute conversation, he rejoined Luke who had picked up his brother's duffel bag in the luggage area. Together they left the terminal, walking out into the soggy atmosphere as it hid Luke's car under a blanket of fog and mist.

"Is everything okay back at the Center?" asked Luke.

"If you want an honest answer," replied Bill, "it's chaos back there!" He looked over at Luke as they walked. "But let's not get into that now."

"Got it, Bro," replied Luke. He'd been with his brother before when subjects came up that Bill couldn't get into. "The plan is to give you a tour of the church first. How does that sound?"

"I was counting on it," answered Bill.

Driving along, they made light conversation about the weather, what had happened to Kris at WLFO, and what it's like living in Rochester. It was Luke who picked up on the irony that Brigg's family was also from Minnesota. On top of that fluke, Luke's first parish landed him back in Minnesota at Rochester. Bill agreed that it was quite a coincidence. He thought back to a philosophy instructor he had at the university. A student of Soren Kierkeggard, the professor was a Christian delivering lectures laced with a heavy Norwegian accent. The professor once shouted from his podium, "Dar you see! There's nooo such thing as coincidence. Dar's only Providence!"

After a few short miles, they pulled into the large, concrete parking lot of Morningside Community Church. Once inside Luke gave Big Bro the full tour, even taking him to the boiler room and church attic. They ended up at the church offices. Tamor was keying in the attendance from last Sunday's three worship services.

"Don't tell me," she said, looking up from her computer, "you must be William. You don't look anything like what Pastor Luke had described. Where's the white suit? How about the face mask and plastic gloves? I don't see any of it!" Then looking over to Luke, "Are you sure that this guy is your brother, Pastor?"

Luke winked at Tamor. "No way to be sure without the lab coat," he grinned. "Ah! There is one test. If he can tell me what's buried in the folks' backyard, then he's who he says he is."

"Well," said Tamor raising her right eyebrow as she lowered the left, "can you tell us?"

"Of course," answered Bill. "Two dollars and twenty-seven cents."

"What's that?" queried Tamor.

"It's true," replied Luke. "Mom found money laying all over our bedroom on one of those rare occasions when she looked at our mess and said, 'enough is enough!' Plunging with a vengeance into our nuked-over bedroom, she was determined to decontaminate it. Each of us claimed the money that she found. Mom knew that the pocket change came from both of us. She decided to set the change on top of the kitchen counter until we worked things out."

"Yeah," laughed Bill, "but you took matters into your own hands!"

"That I did!" agreed Luke. "I put the money in a tin box and buried it in Dad's sprawling garden. We all forgot about it until Bill brought it up months later. I couldn't remember where I'd buried it. So the money is still waiting for us somewhere in Dad's garden."

"You pass the test," said Tamor. "So, how do you like Morningside?"

"You have a mansion here!"

"Just helping us to get ready for the mansions that Jesus is preparing for us in heaven," smiled Tamor. "Well, I need to finish up attendance, and you two need to head out if you are going to beat the rush to The Steak Club. That's where you gentlemen are going for lunch, right?"

"Yup," said Luke, "and I've got my sights set upon a Steak Club Manhandler." His eyes twinkled as he looked over to his brother. "Bill, this is a steak sandwich so big, so juicy, so hot that it's illegal every day but today."

"Get out of here!" cried Tamor, pretending to sulk. Her childlike face made her a pro at deploying the look of a forlorn orphan. "I'll hold down the fort, and while you two are devouring a Steak Club Manhandler, I'll be just fine with my bologna sandwich and banana."

"I'll bring you back a doggy bag?" teased Bill.

"Why not!" replied Tamor. "On what I make, that's the closest I'll ever get to The Steak Club!"

· · · · ·

The Steak Club was not what Bill expected. It was tucked into a row of buildings in the old commercial side of Rochester. A large neon billboard separated it from signless buildings that stood silently to either side. "I know it doesn't look like much," admitted Luke, "but that's to keep the neophytes away. Serious steak eaters come here, and soon you'll understand why."

Entering The Steak Club through a weathered oak door they were immediately greeted by a friendly hostess. "Hi Rev! Table for two?"

"Yes, please," said Luke. "Do you take out-of-state foreigners like this guy?"

"Just so he doesn't want The Steak Club Manhandler," smiled the hostess. "I don't think a foreigner could handle it! Non-smoking as usual?"

"Non-smoking, thanks."

They were led to a booth cradled in the shadows of the far right corner. The kitchen was located through a door to their left, and they could hear kettles and pots clanging against stoves and counter-tops. Bill took Luke's dare, ordering the Manhandler. They talked more about Kris and her situation. Luke shared more about his first experiences in Rochester. Bill often looked off into the distance. Like a fish splashing out of the water and suddenly flying into the air, Bill would engage his brother's words, but soon after his thoughts would plunge back into the murky waters that anchored him somewhere else. Bill tried to hide his uneasy feelings, but whatever they were, the demons made their presence known.

"Bill," Luke finally said, deciding to take a chance, "I get this feeling that something's bothering you. Is there anything I should know? Is there anything I can do..."

Bill continued to stare blankly at the table, then glancing up to face his brother, he did something unexpected. He smiled. "It really is great to see you, Luke. It reminds me of better times..." After another pause, Bill took over the conversation, "These have been the best of times for me and the worst. There are some really mean bugs out there, and some are getting uglier. Yesterday we lost a great researcher to a new virus. She was also a good friend..."

"Sorry to hear that Bill," Luke cut into Bill's sentence. Seeing the pain on his brother's face Luke bought time for Bill's emotions to cool. Luke's brother was letting out one of his demons, and it hurt. "How'd it happen? You haven't told me much about OIDC, but I remember that you promised Kris that the containment precautions are almost faultless."

"They are!" Bill insisted. "We continue to be baffled about what happened to Sherry. It was Stan, a colleague of mine at OIDC, whom I called this morning from the airport. It appears that a hunch I had is right on target. This is not for public consumption, but we're fairly certain that the virus that killed Sherry has the ability to degrade the integrity of polymers and rubber. The clean-up crew discovered that one of the vials touched by Sherry was contaminated on the outside with the virus. Somehow it must have spilled out of the vial. She had on the polymer gloves that come with every containment suit. The crew examined the glove before placing it in asbestos. They saw that a small area at the tip of the right thumb was degraded. This is real scary! If the new virus has the ability to penetrate rubber and plastic and somehow gets out on the streets, there would be no way to control it! No standard suit could be used safely to go into an infected area for detox and rescue!"

"So what do you do?" shot back Luke. He was just beginning to understand what Bill was suggesting. Not only was Bill in danger, but this virus could go global.

"We destroyed... the contaminated vial.... and the virus that it contained." Bill's heart joined with the fog outside as he tried pushing away thoughts about Sherry. Shaking his head he continued. "As of today, no one but myself and a couple other researchers are allowed into Black Knight. What's more, all vials containing this deadly virus are to be handled with metal tongs. I'm here to meet with a researcher to see if there might be a way of engineering a predator virus to fight this thing." He looked away. "Enough shop talk! Let me tell you the second reason for my visit."

"Let me guess," interrupted Luke. "You and Briggs are getting ready to tie the proverbial knot."

"Unbelievable!" replied Bill. There was a sudden change in the atmosphere as Bill brightened. "I'm still pinching myself. We haven't known each other that long, as you know, but we are a fit, made for each other. I'm sure of it!"

"Does Kris know?" Luke tied into his brother's news, masking his concerns. This was a big step for Bill. It came after a short time with Briggs. What did he really know about her? What did she really know about him? Luke studied Bill as they sat there. He was still the same older brother, steady, not inclined to make rash decisions. Luke smiled. This was going to be okay. Bill had found his love and friend, now he was planning to make her his wife. That's the way it's supposed to go. He was sure that Kris would see it the same way.

"I haven't told Kris yet," Bill answered. "I want to have all the details nailed down before I call her."

"What details are you waiting on?"

"We need to know what pastor will do the service, for one thing," Bill replied, smiling broadly at his brother. "Briggs and I were sort-of hoping that it might be you."

Luke was not surprised, but it sure felt good being asked. "Ah, you're just saying that because you know that I'd force my way into the service if you didn't ask me." Reaching across the table Luke grabbed Bill's arm. "When my hair gets grey, or my head grows bald so I look like dad, I'll think back on being part of your wedding and it will be one of the high points of my entire ministry... my entire life!"

"Now before you say yes," Bill cautioned, "you'd better have all the details. We'd like to have the service in Colorado, out on the trail, where we first met. It would mean a hike and some extra work for you."

"Are you suggesting that you're in better shape?" Luke sparred. "I'll take you up on that wedding, but I just hope that you and Briggs can keep up with me on the trail."

Bill continued to fill Luke in on the details of their wedding plans. Bill's eyes shouted out an adoration for Briggs each time he said her name. Leaving the steakhouse they spent the rest of the early afternoon touring the city. Their final stop was at the Mayo Clinic. Luke left his brother there, returning to get him for a late supper. That night, the two relaxed at Luke's, talking about the crazy things that they had done as kids. Bill once again brought up the irony that Luke's first parish should be in Rochester, Briggs' hometown. "You may see me more often then you'd like," teased Bill.

In the morning Luke brought Bill out to the airport to catch an earlier-than-planned flight. The change allowed Bill time to get back for Sherry's memorial service.

• • • • •

They stood together on Chapel Hill. It was a day for spending time on the beach. Very warm, with only a slight breeze pretending to give relief from a relentless sun pasted in a cloudless sky. They had gathered around a hole cut into the earth. Newly dug dirt lay hidden under fake, green grass. A black urn with Sherry's name, date of birth and death etched in gold, sat alone on a brass table. Chairs had been set out for Sherry's husband, two children, and mother. The pastor stood to the side of the funeral urn. Sand, poured in the shape of a cross, fell from his hand onto the urn's cover. "We now commit her body to the ground;" said the pastor, "earth to earth, ashes to ashes, dust to dust, in the sure and certain hope of the resurrection to eternal life through our Lord Jesus Christ, who will change our lowly bodies so that they will be like His glorious body, by the power that enables Him to subdue all things to Himself."

As the committal service ended, one by one friends walked away in silence. Family members took individual flowers from the spray near the urn to serve as a remembrance. Bill stood about fifteen feet from the casket. He wasn't family that he should stand closer, but she was more than a friend, so he couldn't just walk away. This funeral should never have happened. Sherry should not be dead. OIDC was designed so that this could not happen, and yet it did. He wanted to say something to Sherry's family, but he couldn't wrestle down the words. "When the last page is turned for each of us," he thought to himself, "there's only the hope that the Writer of all things has written other chapters and hidden them for later." Bill hoped that God had saved something very special for Sherry.

The nightmare in the lab haunted his daytime thoughts and troubled his dreams. Bill had never seen pure evil in human flesh. He had faced off with some really evil merchandise in his work, but nothing that compared with what had taken over Sherry. Bill never thought of himself as having special insights into things, but a feeling hung around him, a sense that there was something extraordinary and sinister about PRN40. Trying to push away the foreboding thoughts conjured by the virus, he pictured Briggs in his mind. It helped, but nothing took away the dark premonitions. Meeting Briggs had brightened his future, but now a cloud had parked above his parade.

· · · · ·

Sherry's cremation remains laid to rest, the family and friends gathered back at the church for lunch. Pastor Fred Mueller greeted them and then had a word of prayer. The family was served at their table. The rest of the mourners stood in one of two serving lines to get sandwiches, a sampling from several salads, Jell-O, and their choice of desserts from large plates of bars and cakes. Bill joined with others from OIDC as they loaded up their plates then heading outside to sit on the grass. Stan sat down next to Bill.

"Have you spent any time at the Center since getting back from Rochester?" asked Stan.

"No," Bill shook his head. "All I know of the situation comes from our conversation over the phone yesterday." His thoughts were far away. "I just didn't feel like going in..."

"Then you haven't heard the conclusive findings about Sherry's death?" Stan watched Bill's expression as he asked the question.

Bill snapped suddenly back into the conversation. "What did you find?"

"No question, it was PRN40. This damn stuff can, within an hour, soften the structure of rubber or latex so that it can slide through. The affected area on the suit remains durable. That's why her suit maintained a positive pressure even though the virus had breached the containment. When the virus finally makes contact with the skin, it acts the same way. This is what we were missing before! We couldn't understand why the virus was so deadly because we expected it to act like every other virus. But this one doesn't need to be ingested or breathed in. At the slightest contact, the virus quickly enters the body by softening the tissues and easing its way into the bloodstream of the victim.

"Do you know what we have here?" Bill asked with an airy voice, as if the news had drained him.

"On the basis of our inability to discover any way to destroy the virus," answered Stan, "I would say that we have a doomsday weapon if it falls into the wrong hands."

"IF!" cried Bill. "We know that it has already been tried on Khlos Island. Bad people have a very bad 'knight!'" Bill paused, soaking in the bad news. "Is Interpol doing anything?"

"Yes," replied Stan. "Remember, it was Interpol that asked me to go to Khlos. When I arrived at the island, well, I'd never seen anything like it. The people of the island died just like Sherry. Their immune system went wacko! After infection, the virus attacked the lungs of its victims, shutting them down. This is the first time since starting at OIDC that I've been really scared. This bug is bad! Real bad! If whoever hit Khlos lets this out again, we all could be toast. Quick work and lots of luck stopped it there, but I don't think we'll be that fortunate again."

Bill looked up into the sky, not at anything particular, but focusing on the changing shape of a large cumulus cloud. The clear sky that had watched over the burial of Sherry was now populated with thick, billowy clouds. "If we can't destroy it, is there any way that we can derive a vaccine to fight it?" turning his head back toward Stan, Bill studied his response.

"You're asking me?" Stan blurted, surprised by the question. "I'm not the Center's prominent expert on viruses. I think that title belongs to you. You're the go to guy!"

"Stan, I didn't mean to imply..." Bill took hold of a fist-full of grass, pulling it up thoughtlessly from the earth. "I was really just thinking to myself. I'm going to get right on it. I have a few ideas from my visit at Rochester. Have the lab rats that I ordered been delivered to Black Knight?"

"Yes," said Stan, "along with some animal rights protestors." Stan looked confused. "I don't know how these animal lovers find out about these shipments." Suddenly it dawned on Stan why Bill was asking about the lab rats. "You're not going into the Center tonight, are you?"

"For a while. But I've got a date with Briggs at 8:00." Thinking about Briggs changed everything. "Well, I'm out of here. See you back at the Center tomorrow."

Saying his goodbyes to Sherry's family Bill headed back to the lab. Stan's news didn't surprise him. At the back of his mind the apocalyptic fear had always lurked that he would one day face an enemy like PRN40. War had broken out. Sherry had been killed in battle. Now that he had seen the face of his enemy under the electron microscope, then watched it murder one of his best friends, he was numb. He wondered if this is what it's like to go into shock. Colors, sounds, the day-to-day shuffle of life, seemed remote and subdued. "God," he prayed silently to himself, "this time we're going to need to depend on You."

Chapter 6:

ELIJAH JORDAN

Steam drifted like low flying wisps of clouds over the hot bath water. Sure it was the middle of the afternoon, but being out of work gave Kris permission to pamper her moods. Today she would feel warm and useless. Parking in a hot tub accomplished both. She would not read. She wouldn't do her nails. Kris was simply going to lean back, close her eyes, and listen to Kenny G. One foot had slipped into the inviting water when the doorbell rang. "Oh, who's that!" she muttered.

Throwing on her white terrycloth bathrobe, she walked to the entry door opening it as far as the chain-lock permitted. A man stood in the hallway wearing a wrinkled white shirt with olive green pants. In his arms rested a gigantic bouquet of flowers arranged within a small canoe. "We have a delivery of flowers for Heather Lane," came the detached, male voice.

"One second." Kris looked for her purse, spotting it on the nearby end table, she then fumbled through it seeking enough money for a tip. Unlatching the security chain, she opened the door to take the bouquet. It was too big for the end table, so she set it on the floor. Thanking the delivery guy, she handed him some dollar bills. Tip in hand he smiled and left down the long hallway. Closing the door and fastening the chain once again, Kris walked over to the flowers. A tall plastic stem held up a small card amid a kaleidoscope of colored petals. She opened it. The card, written in fluid script, read, "Are you ready for a northern adventure? I will call you. Tonight." Signed below she saw, "Rich Labano."

Kris fell back into her couch, instantly buried in the dozen or so pillows that she used to line its back and sidearms. "I don't believe the nerve of this guy!" she said out loud. There was no way that Kris wanted to talk to the corporate hatchet. Throwing the card down like a hot potato, she pulled herself from the pillows, walked back to the bathroom, disrobed, and eased into the hot water. Kenny G continued to play in the background, but her mood had gone from mellow to mad. Kris tapped her fingers nervously along both sides of the tub. What would she say to Labano when he called? Maybe she shouldn't answer the phone. How about answer the phone then slam down the receiver?

· · · · ·

It was 4:00 in Oakland. Bill had left work early that afternoon. Once again, late that afternoon, his Bible study group had decided to meet at Grimm's Family Diner. At 5:30 they would eat together in a room separated from the general customers by a large folding door. From 6:00 until 7:00 the group would continue its study of the book of Exodus. As he drove, Bill was mentally recounting all the plagues sent upon Egypt, organizing each in the right order. Most of the plagues were natural disasters, only miraculously intensified.

"God used the natural world to accomplish His purpose," reflected Bill. His modus operandi was to use the stuff of His creation in a miraculous way, rather than bringing in monsters and Martians. Even the plague of death, although supernatural, did what all plagues do, it made the Egyptians sick. In the case of the Egyptian plague, all the firstborn died. Thinking about God's chastisements, Bill's mind raced to the final book in the Bible. In the last days, God would use the terrible forces of nature once again to punish the planet because its people had turned away from His Word.

Tonight, more than usual, Bill looked forward to being with his Christian friends. He had invited Briggs, but she still struggled with Bill's religious beliefs. One of the things that Briggs had jettisoned to make room for modern science was the notion of a prayer-hearing God. Bill, on the other hand, never felt any tension between his faith and science. "Pure science," he would tell Briggs, "I mean the true science of methodical inquiry and discovery, only makes the reality of a Creator more concrete. Much of what the scientific community calls science is really modern myth." Bill liked hard facts. He used them creatively. He built things from the bricks of his research that astounded his peers. He was unconventional in his thinking, but he required that the bedrock of his world be brick-hard facts— hard like granite.

Pulling into Grimm's, he'd arrived a full half hour early. The traffic had been light. He decided to go in, order a soda, then park his body in the group's meeting area. He would read again the passages in Exodus that would be studied that evening.

"Then the LORD said to Moses and Aaron," he read in Exodus nine, "take handfuls of soot from a furnace and have Moses toss it into the air in the presence of Pharaoh. It will become fine dust over the whole land of Egypt, and festering boils will break out on men and animals throughout the land..."

"Hey fella!" it was the voice of an older man with wrinkled black skin and snow white hair that called to Bill. "What's that you're reading?"

"Oh, I'm getting ready for a Bible study group that will be meeting here in a few minutes," answered Bill.

"I didn't ask what ya were doin'," said the white haired stranger, "I can see what yar doin'. What I asked was what you all were readin'!" He spoke like a man who made his living off the land. Practical words, few adjectives, and short sentences were the stuff of this old man's speech.

"Exodus, the ninth chapter," Bill replied. He felt a bit awkward. Getting into the Bible with Christian friends was one thing, talking about it with a stranger made him uncomfortable.

"Ah, the plagues of dyin' cattle, boils, and hail!"

Bill was impressed. This guy seemed to know his Bible.

"My name is Elijah Jordan," continued the stranger, his hand outstretched to greet Bill. As Bill shook his hand, the man continued. "Do you mind if I sit and visit with ya a spell? Not often I get the opportunity to talk with someone about the Good Book."

"No, I don't mind." Bill spoke with only half a heart. Elijah sat down on the opposite side of the table directly in front of Bill. His face was weathered, not so much with wrinkles, but cut by thousands of cris–crossing lines. His hair, his face, the clothes that he wore, spoke of age. The ancient face contradicted Elijah's striking eyes. They were blue as the sky at noon, young and fresh!

"What do you think, young man," began Elijah, "about all those terrible things that God brought upon the people of Egypt?"

"It was His way of bringing freedom to His people," answered Bill.

"So God was willin' to destroy one people for the sake of another?" asked the stranger. "That don't seem right!"

"He had made a promise," Bill replied, "that He would continue the line of Abraham until the birth of the world's Savior. The Egyptians were, and I think you know all this, persecuting the chosen people of God. So yes, God took care of His promise and His people."

"And He did that," countered Elijah, "at the expense of other people?"

"Hey! He was keeping a promise. Okay!" Bill searched for the direction that Elijah was taking the conversation.

"Did El Shaddai save His people because the Israelites were good and the Egyptians were bad?"

"It's not that simple." Bill was being drawn into a conversation that minutes earlier he had sought to avoid. Why had the old man called God by this sacred, Old Testament name? "The Egyptians refused do God's will, and so He punished them through the plagues."

"But first He let evil men serve His purpose," added Elijah. Bill looked confused. "What I mean," continued Elijah, "is that evil intentions can be used by God for a greater good. The Egyptians were evil towards the Israelites. It was this same evil that brought God's people to their knees, and they cried for deliverance!"

"So what's your point?" quizzed Bill.

"My point is that there are a lot of evil men doin' things for all the wrong reasons, and yet God Almighty makes it all come out the way that He has ordained." The stranger placed his hands on the back of his head and looked to the ceiling, clearly frustrated that Bill was not catching his point. "Young man, the point is that when evil men do evil things, they think they have takin' control. They think they are winning against the Almighty. But in fact," he took his hands from his head, placed them on the table, and leaned into Bill's face, "they end up serving His greater plan. What's more, they fall under His holy wrath for what they dun." Pausing, Elijah pulled back from Bill. "And what of Israel when it made the golden calf to worship instead of El Shaddai?"

"I think you know, Mr. Jordan," sparked Bill, "God also punished them."

"No, call me Elijah, not this Mr. Jordan." Elijah smiled broadly, then looking intently into Bill's eyes he asked, "Did they all die?"

Bill had a feeling that Elijah knew the answers to all the questions. He wouldn't play his game so easily. He decided to give the wrong answer. "Yes, I think that God killed everyone but Moses and his wife, rebuilding Israel from their children."

Elijah smiled, "Ya don't say, young doctor?" Leaning once again over the table Elijah forced Bill to pull back. "What He did was to leave a remnant—a remnant a whole lot bigger than the family of Moses! El Shaddai has always left a remnant when He sends His chastisements upon the world. He will do so, I suspect, until the last days."

The old man stopped, pulled away, then looked at the open Bible laying before Bill. Drawing it over, Elijah paged through it, stopping suddenly. "One last question before your friends start a' comin'. What about today—right now as we speak? Do you think El Shaddai should pardon the sin of a whole world that has turned its back against Him and His Word?"

"That's quite a question!" Bill was startled by the implications of the stranger's question. He noticed that Elijah's sentences were getting bigger as well. "God is also merciful!"

"Yes, He is merciful!" Elijah responded. "In His mercy He destroyed the outside dangers to His remnant by subduing the Pharaoh. In His further mercy He destroyed the internal forces of evil within Israel itself by His chastisements after the golden calf. Remember young man, the mercy of God is not always gentle. It can be severe! God is a lovin' God, steadfast in His love forever, but He is also holy. Christians today can't say enough about the love of God, but they seldom talk of His holiness." Elijah was not one dimensional, as Bill had first supposed. He certainly spoke more eloquently than the stereotypical old senile that lived in the tenant apartments of urban Oakland.

"Hey Bill!" came Dave's familiar voice. The next Bible study member had arrived. Looking in the direction of the voice, Bill smiled. "Hi Dave, how's it going?" When he looked back to Elijah, he was gone. "That was a fast exit!" Bill thought. "He must have gone down the hall to the bathroom." Drawing his Bible back over the table, Bill looked down to see what the old man had been reading. Elijah had turned to Deuteronomy. Then something happened so quickly that Bill thought he had imagined it, the words in five verses rippled like waves on a sea.

He read Deuteronomy 28:58–62:

"If you do not carefully follow all the words of this law, which are written in this book, and do not revere this glorious and awesome name—the LORD your God—the

LORD will send fearful plagues on you and your descendants, harsh and prolonged disasters, and severe and lingering illnesses. He will bring upon you all the diseases of Egypt that you dreaded, and they will cling to you. The LORD will also bring on you every kind of sickness and disaster not recorded in this Book of the Law, until you are destroyed. You who were as numerous as the stars in the sky will be left but few in number, because you did not obey the LORD your God."

The waitress startled Bill as he looked up to see her standing by his table. "Did you see where that old man took off to?"

The waitress smiled. "If anyone over sixty-five fits that category, we've got a whole lot of them around here. Could you be a little more specific?" The waitress tapped her pencil against a pad of paper.

Bill was having a difficult time focusing. The scripture that he had just read electrified through his spine. Bill shivered. Looking to his Bible then back to the waitress, he tried to stammer our more information, "He was an African-American..."

"And had blue eyes?" interrupted the waitress.

"Yeah! That's him!"

"I saw him walk by me as I was heading for your table," she said. "I don't see him now. Sorry!" She tapped her pencil again on the paper. Her mouth worked over a double helping of gum. "Can I get you anything?"

"Not yet. I'll order something with my friends. I'm part of the study group that meets here tonight." Closing his Bible, Bill looked up to see Dave take the spot previously where the stranger had sat. Bill shook Dave's hand as they begin to visit and kill time, waiting as others slowly joined them at the table. Suddenly a thought flew into Bill's mind. "He called me 'doctor!' How did he know..."

• • • • •

Kris sat tapping her fingers against the kitchen table. Her whole day had been undone by Labano's card. She'd field his call, if for no other reason, it gave her one more opportunity to tell this corporate hatchet what a jerk he was. She had been in a holding pattern waiting for his call for almost an hour. The phone rang. Kris jumped. She tried to direct her emotions away from the lump in her throat, transforming them into searing anger. She almost dropped the receiver as she pulled it to her lips. "Hello."

"Hi Kris, this is Rich Labano. Did you get the peace offering?"

Kris had tried to prepare herself for Labano's call, but at the sound of his voice everything she had planned to say evaporated. Speaking after a torturous pause her cutting tone could tear apart concrete. "Yeah, I got the flowers."

"Kris, I don't blame you for thinking that I am a walking cesspool," continued Rich. "I would feel the same way if I were in your shoes. But please, just do one thing for me, don't hang up. This conversation may not mean much to you, but it is very important to me."

It wasn't fair! Kris wanted to chew this guy up and spit him out, but she found herself beginning to think he might be human. "I won't hang up," she said, "unless you give me good reason..."

"That's fair," said Labano. "I can't ask for more." Another awkward silence split between them. "Have you sent out any demos yet?" asked Rich.

"Yes," came the short, flat answer.

Rich decided to make a try at brightening the conversation. "I remember the first time that I heard your demo. It came with your application to WLFO."

"You heard my demo?"

"Yes, and I was very impressed. You are very good. I could listen to you for hours."

"Fat chance now!" Sarcasm dripped from her voice.

"I would not be so sure about that," said Rich kindly. "Cream, they say, always rises to the top. Talented people like you naturally flow into the right place. It's all a matter of timing! Sometimes it seems that the timing is wrong, then all of a sudden, VOILA!, everything fits into place."

"Easy for you to say," answered Kris, "you still have a job."

"It has not always been so," replied Rich. "I have had my bumps too. Who knows, maybe tomorrow I will be out of a job. Not much in life is certain. Yet I can tell you one thing that I feel very confident about."

"Oh, what's that?" interrupted Kris. Labano was sounding way too human for her liking.

"I am certain that I do not want to be your enemy," he answered. "I would even like for us to become friends, although I know that is perhaps too much to ask."

Kris was numb. Labano had become the heat-sink for all her anger about losing her job at the radio station. Now, as she talked with him, he no longer was the animal she had caged behind the bars of her resentment. No, he was human. He even came across as a nice human. "I suppose that you were only doing your job," she returned. "But why would anyone human want to be cast in the role of a beastly corporate hatchet?"

Rich laughed. "I am not a corporate hatchet," he replied. "In fact, I am really a marketing specialist. The corporation owning WLFO intentionally decided never to hire someone to do, well, what looks like dirty work." He paused. "The corporation exists to make a profit. The stockholders expect this. Every job depends upon it. What is difficult to understand, so often, is that if we do not act responsibly, then every person in the corporate structure could be on the street overnight. Our decision to change the format at WLFO was not an easy one. We knew that it would disrupt many lives for a period of time, but we also knew that eventually the talented DJs who worked there would have jobs again."

"Well, I for one am still wondering how I'm going to eat next week!" grunted Kris. Her voice had become softer, but it tightened up again as she thought about her uncertain future.

"I would like to talk to you about that," replied Rich. "But I'd rather not do it over the phone." He paused again. Everything hung on how Kris reacted to his next question. "Before you start on macaroni and cheese, why don't you let me take you out for a good supper?" Kris could hear the tease in Rich's voice. Quickly it became more serious. "I have an urgent matter to talk to you about, Kris. I know that this is short notice, but could you clear your schedule for dinner tomorrow night?"

Kris looked up at her calendar. Completely blank! "Let me see," she answered coyly. "Are you sure that another evening wouldn't work?" She couldn't believe that she was actually considering meeting this guy, even if it was business and not a date.

"The sooner the better," answered Rich.

"Okay, I'll clear tomorrow evening for dinner."

"Would you like me to pick you up, or would you like to meet me?" asked Rich.

"Why don't you let me know where you plan to eat, and I'll meet up with you there." Kris was going to play this carefully.

"No, you tell me where you would like to eat, and I will meet you there." Rich noticed that Kris was keeping distance between them. He didn't blame her for that.

"How big are the bucks?" Kris asked, and for the first time Rich could hear a smile.

"The sky is the limit!" he answered, enjoying the moment.

"Since it might be my last good meal for a long while, how about The Regent?" she asked. "Or is the sky not that high?"

"Done and done!" smiled Rich. "Would six o'clock work for you?"

"Oh, I'll make it work," replied Kris, continuing the charade which said, "I'm not that easy!"

· · · · ·

The coven cleaned up all evidence of the ritual sacrifice at the Mueller farm. Dane Morrell was dressed completely in black. Spots of blood were scattered on her hands, face, and clothes. After the grounds were cleaned, her clothes would be burned, then she would shower in Mueller's house. The meeting, however, would take place first. Molech had been satisfied, even if it was not with infant flesh. The demon would continue to enlarge the power and pleasure of the coven.

Gathering around in a circle, the coven members used as chairs the square bales of harvested field grass that had once grown along the roads. "I talked to Flint," began Morrell. "The shipment continues to be delayed. There are problems in Russia. I did learn something that is important. The virus was tried on Khlos Island just off Turkey mainland, killing every single person within a small village."

Coven members began to speak among themselves, pleased that the virus was everything that it had been sold to be. Morrell brought back the focus of their meeting, "We hope to have the shipment within two, maybe three months." Porter had not said that, but Morrell felt that the coven needed something more definite than what Porter had offered.

"And what of the antidote?" asked one of the cloaked coven member.

"It will come with the shipment," replied Morrell. "We still need to work out the details. Who will go to what city and how we will release the virus..." She was determined to keep the coven focused on Molech's purpose. "We will settle these issues at our next gathering."

"How many days before releasing the virus must the antidote be taken?" asked another faceless member. Not all members of the coven were driven with Morrell's selfless passion to please Molech at all costs.

"Porter says it can be taken the same day," answered Morrell, but she was not pleased. Seeking to put an end to the discussion about the antidote, she made a quick reference to its effectiveness. "Once the antidote enters the bloodstream, the virus has no effect on the body."

"How do we know that the antidote will work?" asked a third. "We have Khlos as proof that the virus is deadly, but we have seen no evidence that the antidote will protect us."

"Do you want Porter to experiment on you?" snarled Morrell. "You must not put your faith in Porter or any mortal; it is Molech who protects his servants."

As they spoke, the Shadow of Death had strung tentacles so numerous about the coven members that their bodies were veiled from the Guardians watching from a distance. God's warriors from heaven would not enter this unholy ground. Molech stood in the shadows to the side of the Satanist's circle. His hunger for human blood burned. Layered out and surrounding the coven members were more hungry entities. Hungry for the blood of the world. Hungry for the blood of the coven members.

· · · · ·

Seda Orhan, a short, thin woman with dark hair and skin, sat in her dimly lit living room with the curtains shut, holding out the life outside. An unopened box mailed from Khlos sat on a small table. The day before, news had reached her that every member of her family had been killed during a terrible fire that struck her native village on Khlos. The merciless fire-storm had not left a single body to be honored with burial. Everything had gone up in smoke. The government had restricted the area and would not allow relatives to enter the village. A memorial service was being held in two days at a nearby community, but Seda would not be going. She couldn't afford the airfare. If she were able to dig up the finances to make the trip to Khlos, she would not be welcome. Her conversion to Christianity had the effect of banning her from her family.

"Father in heaven," she prayed again, "I must lean on You. I feel so lost. I gave up my family when I came to you. I had hoped to find the words that would bring them to You. I failed. I am not called to judge their immortal souls, but I have no comfort as I grieve their deaths. I do not have the comfort of knowing that they had experienced the love of Jesus before they died."

Looking at the package in front of her, Seda again thought about her mother. Was it days, or even hours, that passed between the time the package had been sent and the onslaught of the terrible fires? Seda knew that she must open it. It would be an insult against her mother's memory not to see what she had placed inside. Her mother was the only member within the family that continued to have secret contact with Seda. Mailing this package to her outlawed, Christian daughter was dangerous—more obvious and dangerous than the scant letters that Seda's mother sent to her via a neighboring village.

Walking over to the package, Seda took it into her hands, then squeezed it against her breast. Once more the tears of despair flowed. Moving to an overstuffed chair, Seda sat down holding the box tightly in her hands. Slowly she worked loose the string and tape, removing the wrapping paper to open the box. Inside were two small jars of olive oil. A simple gift, but one that Seda cherished. Tears flowed again as she let her fingers caress one of the jars. She imagined her mother touching it as she placed the jar into the box.

Setting the box on the floor, Seda left the jars of oil on the table. She would decide later where she wanted to display them. These containers would not be buried in the pantry! She would look at them often, remembering her mother.

Walking over to a large window, she pushed aside some of the vertical blinds. She looked out onto the street, seeking a moment broken free from the prison of her dark apartment. Outside an old man with weathered brown skin and white hair was walking down the sidewalk. He was just one more stranger, likely a wino, passing near her urban apartment. Returning to her chair she read the brief note that her mother had included with the gift over and over. It was the usual stuff. Not very sentimental, for the people of her village were hard. Life had made them resilient and hard.

Seda dozed for about an hour. When she awoke, a fever was punishing her flesh. Breathing was difficult, she tried to get up, but fell to the floor beside the chair. The last thing that she remembered was the dark hand of a stranger taking her hand and saying, "Seda, it will be all right."

• • • • •

Kris made sure that she arrived late to The Regent. She walked into the lobby where Labano stood captured within the awkward awakening of a damaged relationship. He greeted her immediately with a smile. Kris tossed back the token teeth of a hesitant smile. Walking quickly to her, Rich took her by the hand saying, "Come Kris! I have a table for us that overlooks Boston Harbor."

Kris reluctantly gave up her hand. As they walked to the table, she thought to herself, "Sure, I had a view of the harbor at WLFO, at least until a few days ago!"

Rich pulled out a chair for Kris. This was something new for her. Men today were not big on getting chairs or opening doors for their dates. She liked it. And strangely, she liked thinking that she was on a date.

"I am so glad that you agreed to meet me tonight," said Rich. "I have been looking forward to it ever since I talked with you on the phone. How about a glass of wine to start out our dinner?"

"Okay," she said, still measuring her emotions. Rich avoided the house wine, good as that was when offered by The Regent. Instead he chose an Italian wine— an expensive Italian wine. Understanding that Kris had legitimate resentment against him, he had decided not to try and make repairs with her too quickly. Still, he could hope that they might become friends—perhaps more than friends. So they talked about the weather. They talked about the Celtics. They talked about the sunsets over the harbor. When Kris finally shared about her two brothers, Luke and Bill, Rich felt that their relationship had risen to a new level of trust.

"You have not asked me," said Rich, "what urgent business brought about our meeting."

"I've seen you in action," laughed Kris. "I figured you'd get to it when you were ready. It's your dime tonight. So! What urgent business made our dinner date so important tonight?"

"You said date," came the soft voice of the Latino.

"You know what I mean!" Kris blushed.

Rich smiled. "Do you like basketball?"

"This is your urgent business!" Kris arranged the muscles on her face to express the pretense of mock amazement. "You had to know, right now this evening, if I liked basketball!"

"I was thinking more particularly if you liked the Bucks? You see, there is an opening for a jazz DJ in a major market station in Milwaukee."

"You don't mean it!" exploded Kris. "Are you saying that I'd have a chance for it?"

"No. I am saying that it is yours if you want it."

This was more than she had hoped for! Was she dreaming? Could it be true that she was being offered an avenue back into jazz, in a major market, and right next door to her little brother in Minnesota? "You're not just playing with me now?" frowned Kris. Her cautious voice, softer now, oozed suspicion. "I mean, what you did to me at WLFO would be peanuts compared to the letdown I'd feel if you're just leading me on now!"

Reaching across the table Rich took her hand. "I would never want to hurt you." Ricardo's velvet accent stroked across her ears. "I hope this will not change anything, but I live in Milwaukee myself. I travel so much that I could live almost anywhere. Kris, I cannot tell you how amazing this really is. The very day I had to let you go at WLFO, I returned to the hotel and read my e-mails. The station manger at Milwaukee had written for some marketing surveys and casually mentioned that there would be an opening for a DJ within a month or so. My heart jumped! Not only because I wanted to help you, but because I did not want to be... your enemy."

"OK, Rich," she finally used his name. Her voice was sounding more matter-of-fact than she intended, but her mind was racing. "I gotta ask you this. Why all this gush over me? I don't see you helping the other DJs who were let go at WLFO. What's in it for you?"

"Believe me," interrupted Rich, "if I knew of jobs for them, I would be helping them too."

"Yeah," came the voice of a skeptic, "but the one job opening in jazz came my way. Why?"

"I told you that I heard your demo," replied Rich. "Remember? I told you on the phone... Well, I was attracted to your voice. I liked the sound of it. I enjoyed how your mind worked as you put words together. You talked to the listeners as if they were sitting across the table from you." He looked at her like a man looks at a woman. "It was all one sided between us at first. I was attracted to you before you knew of my existence." Smiling, his eyes glanced away to the table, returning to embrace her eyes. "I liked you before I saw your face." He continued to smile softly. "The day I saw your eyes, your hair, your hands, your face at the station, that was the finisher! I knew that I wanted to get to know you better. Can you imagine how I was feeling back then! Right there! To like you so much, so soon, and to know that very quickly you would become my enemy. Kris, whether you take the job in Milwaukee or not, can we be friends?"

Rich still had her hand in his. She squeezed. "Well, if I am going to be living in Milwaukee, I'd better have at least one friend."

Chapter 7:
ER

"How are the wedding plans coming, Brit?" Briggs friends at Oakland Community Hospital called Briggite 'Brit.' Coleen, like everyone else who knew Briggs well, enjoyed the gossip generated by her up and coming wedding better then tabloid reading. Serving as the head nurse of the IDW, Coleen had become Brit's closest friend. Arriving five years before her, Coleen helped Briggs settle into an apartment within her complex. The two often shared meals together, sometimes taking in a movie at the neighborhood theater.

It was now late afternoon as the two sat sipping coffee together in the staff lounge. Briggs was daydreaming, but at her friend's question, her thoughts drifted together into the face of Bill. Suddenly smiling, her heart felt a sunny day. Coleen noticed the smile and was about to ask her what was on her mind when, like an unexpected clap of thunder, the overhead speaker blared code blue. A patient had been admitted into the ward who was near death.

Flying out the door, the two women raced to Admittance. The procedures at IDW were elaborate. Before entering the Emergency Admittance area, they placed on containment suits. "Damn," said Briggs. "It always seems to take forever to get these things on during an emergency!"

Suited up, they walked over to the emergency table where a middle-aged woman was lying. Briggs immediately looked at the vital signs, then studied her chart. A male nurse was talking in the background as Briggs read over what they knew of the patient's condition. "The patient's name is Seda Orhan," said the nurse. "She was picked up by ambulance after a call came in from a neighbor who found her lying on the floor. Do you want to know what's really nuts about this one, Brit?"

Briggs stopped reading the chart, glancing up to lock the male nurse in view. "The guy who called this in said that she had an infectious disease. He told the emergency operator that the ambulance med-techs should wear protective gearing..."

"Who was the guy?" interrupted Briggs.

"We don't know," he answered. "When the med-techs arrived, he was gone. But it gets better!'

"Huh?" grunted Briggs. She was getting impatient with the slow feed of information. "Just tell me what you know. Quickly!"

"Do you see that bag filled with sand on the counter?" Not bothering to wait for her answer, he continued. "That bag was at the patient's side with a note attached. Go take a look at the note."

Walking quickly over to the counter Briggs read the note. "Do not touch the woman's body. Pick up this bag with metal instruments. Do not touch the two glass bottles inside. Do not let the bottles touch the sides of the bag."

Briggs was breathing hard, causing the visor on her suit to fog. Looking down at Seda she asked, "Did the med-techs wear protective clothing?"

"Yes," said the nurse.

"Did they decontaminate the suits after bringing in the patient?"

"Why, yes," he answered, "that's standard procedure after wearing a containment suit..."

"Good!" Briggs said sharply. "Call the Oakland Infectious Disease Center—stat!—and tell Dr. Bill Downs to get over here. Tell him that Dr. Brandon needs him right away!"

Briggs turned her attention back to the condition of the patient. The woman was burning up with fever. Each breath was labored, and there was no indication that she was conscious. "Get ice!" she barked. "I want this patient packed down! Until we know what we're up against, I don't want any meds administered. Got it? And I want everything—I MEAN EVERYTHING—that has had contact with the patient incinerated in decontamination."

Briggs had good reason to be concerned. Enough shop talk had been exchanged between Bill and herself to raise Briggs' anxiety. She knew that there were some evil viruses out there—ones that gave Bill restless nights. Briggs began a mental inventory of the issues raised with the new arrival. Who had made that call? How did he know that the patient might be carrying a communicable disease? Why did he place the containers in sand and write the note? Could this be tied up with a terrorist attack?

It was just this sort of possibility of a terrorist incident that kept Bill in a job. Briggs sat with the patient, holding her hand through the containment glove, waiting for Bill's arrival. Bill drove with reckless speed to the hospital, a magnetized flashing light on the top of his car the only warning to oncoming traffic. Arriving at the hospital, he left his car running in the drive, dashing for the emergency ward. Placing on protective gear, Bill entered the room where Brigg's was sitting by a raised bed. He looked at Briggs attending to the patient, suddenly horrified when he realized that Briggs was holding the patient's hand.

"Briggs!" he shouted. His fiancé jumped to her feet. "Get into decontamination immediately! Wash your hands thoroughly and then burn the gloves, but don't touch them again. Use tongs. Do it! Do it now!"

Briggs could not have been more confused, but the urgency in Bill's voice told her that it was no time for a discussion. Leaving admittance, she headed directly to Decontamination. Bill walked over to the patient buried in clear plastic bags of ice to check out her vitals. "This can't be happening," Bill muttered to himself. Turning around, he raced to the door, dashing out of the room to catch up with Brigs. Joining Briggs in Decontamination, Bill began scrubbing his hands over and over with disinfectant soap. "Careful, Bill," urged Briggs, "or you're going to scrub down to the bone." Bill did not look up. He did not smile. He simply barked a command, "Britt, you wash those hands of yours completely clean. I mean completely clean!"

"Bill, you gotta tell me what's going on," came Brigg's anxious reply. "You just ordered me to leave a patient who is dying."

"That's right!" Bill shouted. "She's dying! Who brought her in?"

"Ambulance med-techs...."

"Where are they?" interrupted Bill.

"If you are worried about spreading whatever she's got," supposed Briggs, "don't worry! They all wore containment suits."

"And where are the suits now?"

"I had them incinerated."

"Excellent Briggs!" For the first time since his arrival, Bill's voice became less mechanical. "Briggs, I hope I'm wrong. I hope to God that I am wrong, but I think that this is the same bug that killed Sherry. It defies all known understanding of how viruses work. Briggs, it has the ability to penetrate containment gear!"

"My lord!" gasped Briggs.

"Who all might have been exposed?" continued Bill. "We must put the infected patient's apartment, every person in that building, and anyone that may have visited her that day under protective quarantine. The good part about this virus is that it acts quickly, so it's easy to trace."

"I've already placed the building and its occupants under quarantine," assured Briggs. "Something didn't feel right! Call it woman's intuition, but I decided to take extra precautions." She thought a moment. "I think I'd better get on the phone and see if the patient's neighbors saw any visitors with her today." Another pause. "We do have another big problem, though..."

"What's that?" Bill forced his question through a knotted throat.

"The guy who called in about the patient, he's gone. We have no idea who he is or where he went. The good news is that he seems to know something about this bug. He likely took precautions to avoid contamination."

"How do you know that?" Impatience oozed toward Briggs.

"It's really strange," Briggs answered, "but when the man phoned in he gave instructions, saying that the med-techs should wear containment gear. He also left some bottles packed in sand with a note."

Bill stopped washing and started out of the room. "Where are you going?" asked Briggs. "I need to see those bottles! My hunch is that they are contaminated!"

· · · · ·

Elijah sat holding Seda's hand. He wasn't wearing a containment suit but wore a white lab coat. Seda, regaining consciousness, complained about feeling cold.

"You're gonna be fine, Seda," assured Elijah.

"What's happening to me? Where am I?" The words barely left Seda's tired body.

"You're at the Oakland Community Hospital. In a few minutes, two doctors are gonna come into the room. They'll be wearin' special suits. Actually, it looks like they come down from outer space. Don't let it frighten you. They're here to help you. I gotta go for now."

"Wait!" Seda put as much effort into that one word as an Olympic jumper puts into the final leap. Then weakly again, "Are you the one who found me? Didn't I see you outside my....." Seda began to slip away.

"Rest, daughter," said Elijah. "Rest now." Then he was gone.

$$\bullet \ \bullet \ \bullet \ \bullet \ \bullet$$

Bill and Briggs entered Emergency Admittance once again suited in protective clothing. Briggs walked over to Seda. Bill single-mindedly headed for the package. He studied it carefully. Ingenious! Whoever had placed the jars into the sand was using the silicone to isolate the virus from the plastic bag. Bill felt some hope that the person who had found the patient understood enough not to get infected. If they couldn't get to him soon, they'd better pray that he knew enough to avoid infection! "Dear God," Bill prayed silently, "protect this man. Protect us all! In Jesus' name. Amen."

"Bill, come over here!" Briggs voice raced with anxiety causing Bill to run to her side. Handing him Seda's chart, Briggs pointed next to the instruments tracking Seda's condition. The patient's vital signs had improved unbelievably within the last twenty minutes. Her temperature had dropped significantly.

Bill looked at Briggs. "I don't get it."

"Maybe she doesn't have this super virus." Briggs was trying to read Bill as he studied Seda's chart.

"If she doesn't die within the hour, I doubt that she has the virus that...." It was hard for him to get the words out, "...that killed Sherry." Bill had been so sure that this woman had been infected with PRN40. Perhaps it was the death of his friend that skewed his thinking. After all, how could an isolated incident like this take place within the inner city without leaving a trail of corpses to the patient's door? "I'm going to take these jars down to OIDC," said Bill. "I don't want to take any chances. We'll make sure that these jars aren't PRN40 tainted. Would you order me a containment box?" He paused. "Metal containment boxes, with lots of sand."

$$\bullet \ \bullet \ \bullet \ \bullet \ \bullet$$

Bill sat under a brilliant canopy of light at the OIDC. Working in the Black Knight confinement area, he had taken the jars of oil out of the sand using metal tongs. He had concluded that he wasn't working with PRN40 infected items, but he wasn't taking any risks. One mistake with the new killer virus would be one's last mistake. Stan sat to the left of Bill. Removing a few drops of oil from both of the jars, Bill was finishing up a test that would reveal the presence of PRN40. Nothing! Stan looked over to his exhausted colleague. "What do you think, Bill?"

"Something made that woman sick," he muttered. "Whoever called in protected these jars as if they contained PRN40. Frankly, I wish that I'd thought about using silicone as an insulator. I say we test the outside of the jars. That's what this guy was trying to keep from touching the plastic."

Using standard procedures to remove residue from the outside of the jars, they began their tests. "Damn it!" It was Stan who broke the silence. Bill just stared, frozen within a terrifying moment of discovery. In front of them, on the lab bench, was PRN40! "What did we do to isolate the patient infected by these jars?" blurted Stan.

"The apartment complex is under quarantine," replied Bill. "The med-techs who picked her up wore containment suits. Everything that came in contact with her has been incinerated. The only wildcard is the guy who made the emergency call. We don't know who he is, and we don't know where he is. Perhaps he's a terrorist playing cat and mouse with us using a deadly killer. Our only hope is that if he had enough brains to use this stuff, or to wrap these jars in sand, he's also smart enough to have avoided infectious contact."

• • • • •

Briggs sat again by Seda's bed. Bill had called with the unsettling news that the patient had in fact been infected with what he called PRN40. She had been told to tell no one about the nature of this virus, not even her boss. Besides the usual precautions, Bill advised that the patient be sealed in a containment tent. Seda was wrapped like a sardine within a clear, plastic jar, but the plastic tent was not allowed to make contact with the patient's body. Suddenly Seda moved. Her eyes opened! Briggs jumped.

Through an electronic enhancement, Briggs spoke to Seda. "Seda, I'm Dr. Brandon. You are at the Infectious Disease Ward of Oakland Community Hospital. You came in a very sick lady, but your condition has improved. How are you feeling?"

"Weak," she said. "Where is the man who found me at my apartment?"

"We'd like to know that too," replied Briggs. "Do you know who he is?"

"No, he was a stranger." Seda appeared confused. "I saw him here just a little while ago. He's on your staff."

"What!" gasped Briggs, forgetting her bedside ways.

"Yes, an older black fellow, with white hair." She tried to describe him through the fog of her illness. "He held my hand and told me that I would be fine."

"He held your hand?" snapped Briggs.

"Why, yes. But he didn't stay very long. He simply said that I'd be fine and that two Martians would soon be coming through the door..."

"Martians, Seda?"

"That doesn't sound right, does it?" Seda shook her head. "That's what I remember."

Briggs listened, concluding that the patient had hallucinated while under the effects of her high fever. Still, her description of the man matched that of the stranger who had found her at the apartment. "Go on, Seda, what do you remember about this man?"

"Not much. He wore a white coat, that's why I thought he must be work here. The most remarkable thing that I remember about him were his eyes. He had blue eyes. You don't often see someone with his dark skin having sky blue eyes."

• • • • •

Bill had given orders to convert a lab in Black Knight into a patient room at the Oakland Infectious Disease Center. Pulling strings he arranged to have Seda brought to OIDC. Elaborate procedures were applied at each step of the transfer to ensure the public safety. Seda was soon resting comfortably at OIDC.

"I can't figure it," Stan said. Turning from Bill he looked through the glass into Seda's makeshift room. "She should be dead! Why is she still alive?"

"That's the million dollar question," replied Bill. "Do you know what this means? If she lives, we may be able to manufacture a vaccine from her blood serum. She may be God's miracle girl for the planet."

"It would take time..." Stan knew that time was their enemy. Time gave someone, or some nefarious band of terrorists, the gas they needed for making further mileage in the use of PRN40. The fact that the virus had been released upon the village at Khlos meant that there were those who were experimenting with the virus. The bug had proven deadly. When and where it would be released again was anybody's guess. "Who do you think is behind this, Bill?"

"I don't know," answered Bill. "You were on Khlos. Did you see anything that might help us figure out who has a leash on this monster?"

"Not a clue." Stan shook his head. "By the time I got there, the investigators had already concluded that the village offered a major threat to the island. They decided that it was better to burn the village quickly than to do more investigation. If there were clues, they're in ashes now."

"Has Seda eaten?"

"Yes, and she has a remarkable appetite," smiled Stan. "She's asking lots of questions, and I'm not sure how long we can avoid telling her what's going on here. She does have rights. Even if national security put limits on her freedom, she still has rights." He smiled again at Bill. "Just because she's Seda, and I like her."

Bill finally cracked a smile. "The tests of her skin, urine, saliva, and clothing show an aberration of PRN40. The lab rats infected with it are not getting sick. They appear to be developing an immunity to the virus."

"Yeah," interjected Stan, "and if we could only figure out a way to turn that into a vaccine, then we would have something!"

"That's our job," replied Bill. "I think that in a few days we can move Seda out of the tent; let her move around the room. We'll take this thing one step at a time." Bill threw a switch that connected him electronically with Seda. "How's my favorite girl doing today?"

"I'm afraid that I am far from being a girl!" teased Seda. "Say guys, how long do I have to stay in this thing?"

"I was just telling Stan," answered Bill, "that if everything goes well over the next couple of days, we're going to let you have a new place where you can actually get up and walk around. One step at a time, okay?"

"Thank you Jesus," Seda said under her breath. Speaking back to the men behind the glass she replied, "I'll take it one step at a time, but I wish that you would tell me more about what's going on with me. I know that I have been infected with some virus, but that's all I know. I think you people memorize that phrase, 'you have been infected with a virus.' You must have a bigger vocabulary than that! Can you say things like, 'You will be well in two weeks,' or, 'We've got this wonder medicine, and you can go home.' I mean, there has to be more that you can tell me!"

"There is," said Stan, "but hang in there with us, Seda. I'll tell you this much, it's a miracle that you're alive. The virus that infected you has always been fatal. Frankly, we are clueless as to why you are alive..."

"That's right Seda," interrupted Bill, "and if you will let us work with you, we may be able to save more lives than just yours."

"So I'm your guinea pig!" smiled Seda through layers of plastic and glass.

"No," said Bill, "you were the guinea pig of the virus. For us, you might be the savior of the world!"

Seda thought a minute. "No, there is only one Savior of the world!"

Bill paused. "You're right Seda," winking, he smiled again. "And I think He worked a big miracle in you, and it might be a gift to the world. This is a very bad bug. A very bad bug!"

· · · · ·

That night Briggs met Bill for dinner at the place of their first date. "How's Seda doing?" asked Briggs.

"She's a miracle!" Bill threw his hands up into the air. "I have no explanation for her recovery. Seda should be dead. Nothing about her and the virus fit together scientifically, and yet they sit together in front of us staring us down." Pausing, Bill looked intently at Briggs. "In answer to your question, she's doing fine."

"What's next?"

"We're trying to figure out a way to make her blood serum into a vaccine." Bill bent forward over the table to get closer to Briggs' ear. He continued in a whisper, "She may provide the only hope I see for everyone on this planet should the bug get out!"

"There you go again!" Briggs loud voice sent Bill back against his chair.

"Getting apocalyptic! Every once in a while you do this! I know that you work with bad bugs, Bill, but the end of the world! I work with this stuff each day, just like you, and I worry about people in Oakland getting sick, not the end of civilization. I think you read that Bible of yours a little too much."

Bill leaned forward again, the hint of a grin had grown across his mouth, then vanished in a wearied face. "Briggs, I'm not saying this out of my religious beliefs. Not at all. I've seen what PRN40 can do. There's never been anything like this bug, and I think you know that. When I look at a monster like PRN40, the only thing that gives me hope is my faith. Faith that there is something bigger than a meaningless humanity expanding on the globe like yeast in a Petri dish! You have heard it from me before, so I'm not going to preach, but I think that there's something extraordinary about our creation—something huge about the human race. I think behind it all—conception, birth, life, death and pea soup—is a God who gives meaning to it all. So there! End of message!"

"Amen," Briggs consented, not so much to the content of the message, as to the fact that it was done.

"Things happen that can't just be a coincidence," continued Bill. "Their clues telling us that there must be an intelligence at work in our universe. For example, have you thought about what would be happening right now if we had never met? When the patient came into Oakland Community Hospital, you'd have treated Seda's condition as an anomaly. You'd never have called the OIDC about her infection. Once Seda started to improve, you would have concluded that she was recovered, sending her home. Her immunity which may save the world would never have come to the surface."

"Yeah, I suppose you're right," she said in her matter-of-fact voice.

"Don't you get it?" Bill asked impatiently. "God winked!"

"God what?"

"Whenever something happens that overwhelmingly defies the odds, I think that God is winking. Like all winks, it's delivered to those who are meant to see it. God brought us together so that you would make that call to me at OIDC. Without that call, we wouldn't have the possibility of a vaccine against PRN40 in our reach. When God brought us together in Colorado, He winked. I didn't see it then, but I do now."

"Sure, whatever you say, Bill." Briggs decided to change the subject. "Say! What did Luke decide about officiating at our wedding?"

"Green light!" A happier face was instantly painted upon the man of Briggs' dreams. "He said that he would be thrilled to be part of our wedding day. Then he threw down the gauntlet saying that he didn't think we'd be able to keep up with him on the trail. Mom and Dad would do just fine, but not us!"

"Oh, is that right?" laughed Briggs. "He's that good, huh!"

"Well he thinks so! I guess we'll just wait and see. The important thing is that he'll be there. So will Kris." Briggs watched as Bill changed mental gears. "Oh boy, I didn't tell you about what's happening in her life—with all the excitement and all." Pausing, he waited for Briggs to become impatient for the new gossip.

"Don't do this to me, Bill..."

"She has a boyfriend!" Bill scratched the right side of his temple, looking up at Briggs with a smile.

"Seems like there's another kind of infection going around! The L–O–V–E bug!"

"You haven't heard the best part," continued Bill. "The guy that she is sweet on is none other than the one who gave her walking papers at WLFO."

"No!"

"Could I make this up?" beamed Bill. "Who would believe me! I guess he's a nice guy, too. Kris has taken to him in a big way. She wants to have him invited to our wedding so we can get to know him. No problem with me, but I wanted to run it by you."

"The more the merrier, as they say! I just hope that our guests know what it's like to take to the trail. Is this corporate guy up to it?"

"Well, it's not the sort of thing you bring up!" joked Bill. "'Hey Sis, is the guy a hunk or a wimp?'" They both laughed. "I know that he is Latino," continued Bill, "and wears his hair tied in a ponytail."

"Sounds macho to me!" baited Briggs. "What do you think?"

"Are you telling me to grow my hair out so that I'll look macho?" Bill grabbed the hair on the back of his head as if trying to make a ponytail.

"Not bad! I might grow to like that!"

"Forget it, Briggs!" returned Bill, dropping his hair. "I'm more likely to work on growing bald than growing hair."

"That's cool!" Smiling, Briggs took Bill's hand. "I like that too. They say that bald men have more testosterone."

· · · · ·

Briggs and Bill continued to make plans for their wedding. Briggs had heard horror stories about the stress a woman feels taking care of the details for her wedding day. She loved every detail in planning her wedding day! Every arrangement she made carried with it the scent of spring. Newness was in the air! Life was sprouting all around her, soon to blossom and produce fruit. Unlike Bill, her up-beat mood withstood the terrible virus. Not even thoughts of the plague would sicken her spirit. She was in love! Her feelings for Bill were stronger than plague and pestilence, and she knew it.

Time raced by; soon the wedding was only two days away. Seda was still at OIDC, but more comfortable furniture had been brought into her new room. Seda's recovery was remarkable, allowing both Bill and Briggs to leave for their wedding day without any worries. Research had gone well with Seda's blood serum, and the crew at OIDC felt that they were very close to having a vaccine.

Seda sat by an open window, enjoying the sunlight as it blazed into her room. It took hold of her, wrapping her body in a brilliant blanket of warmth. Her happiness was clouded only by thoughts of her departed family. The staff at OIDC had become great friends. She hadn't had many friends in America. Now that her family had been killed on Khlos, her friends at the Center were the world to her. She missed her walks in the park, but the shuffling of staff in and out of her room left no time for boredom.

"Good morning, girl." Someone had slipped into her room without catching her attention. Seda turned. An old man shot a smile at her.

"Am I dreaming?" asked Seda, her eyes entranced.

"No, girl, you're not dreaming," replied Elijah Jordan.

"Every time I bring you up, the staff here seems to think that you're just someone in my dreams." Seda continued to stare.

"Well, that's just fine!" Elijah slapped his hip. "Let's just keep them wondering. What do you think?"

"Easy for you to say." Seda finally let go of Elijah with her eyes, shaking her head. "They think I'm crazy."

Elijah laughed. "I've seen a lot of people come and go. Some of the best of 'em have been called crazy." Elijah stepped closer. "How are you doing?"

"I'm feeling great!"

"Yeah, that's good. Still, it seems to me that there's something dark hanging around in your heart. Something that hurts."

The muscles in Seda's face tightened. Her eyes squinted together as a tear washed down her cheeks. Walking over, Elijah put his hand on hers as it rested on the chair. "Tell me about it, Seda. Tell me about your family."

Seda's hands raced to her face as she burst into tears. She tried to speak, but her deep sobs prevented Seda from sharing her feelings. Waiting patiently, Elijah had placed his hand on her shoulder. Standing up, Seda walked across to the other side of the room. Looking back to the window, Elijah's features had disappeared. He stood silhouetted against the brilliant light breaking through the window. "You must not play the part of God, Seda." Elijah spoke. His words filled the room, but she could see no movement in the shade of a man enveloped in light. "Don't judge them to hell, or to heaven. Let God be God."

"But they did not know Jesus..."

"Yes, at least some knew of Him because of you," broke in a voice coming from every direction. "Your mother knew more of Him than she could share. Your letters did not go unopened and unread."

Seda closed her eyes together tightly, but tears continued to shove their way down her cheeks. What she was hearing promised something so wonderful that it took her breath away. When she opened her eyes, Elijah was gone. "Dear God in heaven..." Seda began to speak, but her words were washed away in tears of hope and joy.

· · · · ·

Inside Saudi Arabia, permission had been granted for Ahmad to run his campaign against the demonized West from an isolated compound to the east.

A special package had been delivered that day from Russia. There were five vials filled with a liquid and five empty ones. The filled vials were buried in a white powder, sealed in a containment box, and transported with utmost caution. The five empty vials were wrapped in cloth and carried in a cigar box.

"When do we make the delivery to Morrell?" asked Flint. "She's been on my tail. I've been getting e-mails from her lately, sometimes twice a day."

"No reason to wait," answered Ahmad. "The Russians have yet to send us the antidote, but it will come in time to save our ass, I'm sure of that! For Morrell and her Satan worshipers, we'll use sugar water and food coloring to make up their antidote. We don't want any loose ends to deal with, right?"

Flint nodded. He had the heart of a machine, a deadly machine. "I can be in the States as early as tomorrow. Should I set up something that soon?"

"No," said Starkey, "we need more time to figure out how we to get the package through customs."

"We've been through this a hundred times," responded Flint in frustration. "There's nothing in this stuff that will be picked up by their detectors or their dogs."

"That's right," countered Starkey, "but we didn't expect this stuff to show up bathed in sand. Don't you think you're going to have a hard time explaining why you are carrying white powder into the States?"

"Tell Morrell that we have the package," said Ahmad to Flint. "We will arrange to get it to her within a week. She has waited this long, she can wait a bit more. Remember guys, we're in charge of this operation, not the witch. A short stall also gives the Russians more time to get us the antidote. I don't give a damn about Morrell and her little band of bloodthirsty Satanists, but we need the antidote, and the sooner we have it the better I will sleep."

Flint e-mailed a coded message to Morrell, "We have had a great time vacationing in Russia! We picked you up a little souvenir. Our next stop is Seattle. We will swing by with it within a week. Hope you like it!"

· · · · ·

The boat tipped sharply. Luke fought to maneuver the sail as he made the turn. It was a fresh morning on Lake Minnetonka. Luke had driven up from Rochester to spend the day at the family cabin. Today he was soloing the family sail boat. Running the rigs of the boat, Luke realized that he was badly out of shape. During college, sports kept his muscles toned. The four years of seminary training that followed gave little opportunity for recreation. He jogged and played enough intermural sports at the seminary to keep his body toned, but Luke was paying for his weakened condition as he floundered, trying to keep the boat steady.

The strenuous activity of sailing—working the sail, rudder and ropes—wore on Luke under the hot sun. He decided to take off his shirt. A lily white chest and back tempted ultraviolet rays to do their damage. Perspiration ran down his face as he turned the boat westerly. Finally worn out by the physical labor, he turned the bow in the direction of the cabin's dock.

The sail moved across the deck as he turned, bringing into view another sailboat thirty feet away. A dark haired woman wearing a red two-piece swimsuit worked the boat effortlessly as she sat to the stern. She was traveling the opposite direction, so the boats quickly separated in the water. There was enough time for Luke to catch the name of the boat written across its side, "Turbulence."

The woman waved. In a flash Luke recognized her as the girl by the bell tower at the seminary. "Hey!" he yelled. "HEY!" But the woman turned away from him, continuing to sail easterly. Luke had tried once before to catch up with her when that was not her intention. It didn't work. Luke decided not to try it again. He shuddered. "This is getting weird." What was she up to? Was it coincidence that she had gone sailing on Lake Minnetonka that day?

There were other changes going on within Luke's spirit; changes that went unnoticed. What power had enabled this strange woman in red to erase Luke's thoughts about Cassandra? Why was his eye drifting away from a woman who had caught his attention at his new church? And why, when he did think of Rachel, was Luke driven into lustful fantasies about her?

Chapter 8:

POLITICAL RAMIFICATIONS

"We have gathered here, in the sight of God, and these outback hikers, family, and friends, to join together this man and this woman, to be husband and wife..." The morning had started off chillier than usual, even for the higher altitudes, forming misty clouds that glided like eerie ghosts over the mountain lakes and slow moving streams. The cool morning air eventually was forced to surrender to the relentless afternoon sun. More hours flew by as earth's star, the sun, continued to cascade its warming rays over the mountainous outback. Finally late afternoon, foot soldier to the evening calm, chased the retreating sun into the west. At 6:45 a large golden globe of sunlight rested on the twin peak shoulders of a distant mountain.

A chorus of singing, fluttering birds provided a wedding prelude. Soon the gathered chosen, the wedding party drawn together in nature's cathedral, saw Bill and Briggs walk from either side of a mountain clearing. They were to stand in front of Luke, captured in the stunning vista of a wooded valley below. The bridal couple didn't face into the great westward expanse, but rather stood on the mountain cleft toward the forest. The guests looked forward into the vista, framing the bridal party within the aura of a gigantic, golden sun blazing over a sea of green.

Briggs faced Bill, holding his strong hands in hers. Her auburn hair starkly contrasted against the all white trail shorts, shirt, and broad rimmed hat that she selected for her wedding day in the outback. Briggs' freckled face lit in joy, her smile reached to her ears. She stood there, drinking in her sweetheart's eyes to see a future where dreams come true and longings are satisfied. Briggs pulled her hand away briefly from Bill, placing the back of her fingers against the side of her face. Briggs' desire for Bill was flushed against her cheeks.

Bill had not changed his opinion about his love. He believed that she could play the part of a Greek goddess—of course, of Irish ancestry. Her small nose and well defined chin were always held high. People would think her sassy, thought Bill, if not for the incredible warmth radiating from her eyes. Today, she was joining with him. Bill's smile broadened. Briggs reacted by tightly squeezing his hands.

"As I look around," continued Luke, "I see so much joy. There are old faces and there are new faces, but each one is focused at one point, one movement in time, one occasion of great new beginnings! Look at you Bill! Standing with this beautiful woman here in God's natural cathedral. And Briggs, this guy has stolen your heart! The good news, Briggs, is that, as far as Sis and I can remember, you are the victim of his first crime. He has spent too much time courting viruses to threaten the hearts of the opposite sex." There was a brief chuckle, especially by members of OIDC and those who knew "Petri Dish Bill" the best.

"And now, as you become one, what do you two represent? Well, before I answer that question, I need to remind everyone here that both Bill and Briggs work with disease control. Together they are a formidable weapon against the nasty germs that lurk on the west coast. So what do they represent? They are the BB's aimed at our worst carnal enemies! Get it? Bill and Briggs... B and B.... Germ warfare." Another clamor of humor, as guests looked to one another fussing over Luke's flaccid humor.

The young pastor continued his wedding homily, with few mentions of God or the incarnate Son. He centered his words around memories with Bill, humorous situations that had occurred between the bride and groom, and the beauty of nature. The homily was followed by the Intentions, the Intentions by the Vows, and finally, Bill and Briggs each took a burning candle and together lit one large candle. Luke had suggested that they keep the small candles burning to represent the idea that the bride and groom continued as individuals. Bill, more conservative than his brother the pastor, said no. "I've never known of a single couple that had problems because their unity had destroyed their individuality," Bill told Luke. "What I see all the time are couples who don't play as a team. Briggs and I are an item. One item. I like that, and so does she."

"Now that William and Briggite have consented together in holy marriage," finalized Luke, "have given themselves to each other by their solemn pledges, and have declared the same before God and these witnesses, I pronounce them to be husband and wife, in the name of the Father, and of the Son, and of the Holy Spirit. Amen."

The "amen" triggered sudden applause and whistles. "Okay," continued Luke, "let's serve up that kiss, brother, so we can get the campfire going and start those porterhouse steaks!"

Briggs outgunned her new husband, targeting a warm kiss directly on his lips. Bill captured his new bride within his arms, swinging her through the air. Cheers and applause broke from the mountain ledge down upon the valley below. The moon had ridden into the sky as the sun disappeared leaving behind a royal blue blanket wrapping the dusk. Those who chose not to stay the night left with flashlights and lanterns, walking down the winding trail to their cars tucked within the valley below. From a distance they looked like fireflies slowly darting in and out of trees in a snakelike motion.

Bill hugged his new bride, still holding her in the air. Briggs melted into his muscular arms, almost fainting when she was set back on the grassy plain. Standing on her toes she leaned into Bill until her lips brushed against his ear. "I love you, madly!" she whispered.

"I don't love you!" shouted Bill so all could hear. He then swept Briggs again into his arms, running with her at a remarkable speed to the campfire. Freeing Briggs he stood before her and dramatically continued his speech. Holding his right arm high, he waved his hand several times in the night air. "Shall a toad love a swan? Will smooth velvet welcome the caress of slivered wood? What pauper could hope to cherish a queen? No, I do not love you, dear Briggs, for to say to these fine people that my heart would hold you, threatens to take captive the moon and steal away the breath of dawn." Bill stopped and took both her hands in his. The gaping wedding party stared in breathless silence. "But this I would have you know, fair maiden, there is no pulse within this heart that does not beat for you. No setting so stunning, that when you are present, my eyes are drawn away from you!"

Bill fell to his knees and bowed deeply before his bride. Catcalls and applause faded away from the fire into the darkness of the forest. Briggs stood there, her warm smile shaming the fire, with tears rolling down her cheeks. "Bill," she said, her voice winsome and soft like smoke stifled within the thick chimney of her throat, "I didn't know that you were such a poet. That was beautiful! You told me when you proposed that you didn't know how to make speeches. You've made me wax in your hands. Mold me and bend me. I'm yours!"

Bill smiled back. Oh no, it was not the simple smile of youth and joy. It was a look that cut open rocks and swept up oceans. It was a look that erased the distance between a man and a woman until both their spirits cried for union of body and soul. Bill's eyes drawn in by Briggs' returning look, reaching for him, only him. Her flushed face welcomed the modesty of darkness and shadows. All about the two newly one, familiar faces blended together with the trees and rocks and stars into one monolithic other. They would tarry the night with friends, but numbly, awake only in each glance, each word, and each gesture of their beloved until they were alone.

Kris sat beside Bill at the fire. He was looking across at Briggs. "You really love her, don't you?"

"Kris," he said, "you heard about the brush with death that Briggs had on this very trail. I can still remember her looking up at me when her life rested literally in my hands. I didn't know if I had the strength and leverage to pull that rope up. I was sliding on the gravel so I couldn't use my legs to any advantage. I had to lift her with one arm and then the other. When she was about halfway to the ledge, I was exhausted. Everything was on the line. I either let the rope slip, or I went with the rope if I couldn't get Briggs up. I decided that I would rather die with Briggs in a free fall than give her up. I haven't changed my mind. I breathe her in like air."

"I guess you could say that qualifies as love," smiled Kris. Her voice sparkled with her brother's joy.

Kris was pleased. Like salt looking for its pepper, her brother had matched up with a woman fulfilling his dreams. She wondered what Rich was thinking right then. Was he thinking of her? Would she ever experience with Rich or any man what Briggs now had with Bill?

Kris stared into the fire. Her blank expression suggested to Bill that a naughty little serious thought had parked in his sister's mind. "Not tonight," Bill whispered to himself, "not tonight."

"Say Sis!" Bill's call pulled her, at least for the moment, away from the face of Rich drawn within her imagination. Looking at her brother, she saw an expression on his face that bothered her as far back as when they were kids. He was up to no good, and she knew it. Sure enough, without warning he lunged toward her tackling her away from the fire, pulling her to the ground. Tickling Kris, he chided her saying, "And what's this I hear about you and a corporate hatchet?"

"Stop that! Bill stop that!" hollered Kris. She was laughing so hard she barely had breath. "STOP IT BILLY! You did this to me as a kid and I HATED it! STOP!"

Bill took his hands away from her sides; leaning back he planted his right hand behind him on the grass. "That was for not bringing him to the wedding so the rest of us could measure him up!"

"And you're the reason I didn't bring him along!" Kris lunged across the grass knocking her brother to the ground. Pinning Bill's shoulders under her knees she delivered a playful diatribe, "I had enough problems with you scaring off my dates when I was at home. I didn't need to have my big brother messing up things with Rich!" Later she shared about Rich's unexpected business trip so that her family wouldn't misunderstand the reason Rich had not been at the wedding. A station manager had been caught doctoring the financial reports. The company wanted Rich to go down with the new manager and work out the situation quickly.

"Hey, Sis!" Bill was continuing their journey down courtship lane. "Just because I never met a date of yours that I liked, doesn't mean that I sent them running."

"No? What about Allen Dixon!"

Bill erupted, laughing till tears flowed down his face. He actually had at the age of fifteen chased Dixon from the house. Bill had caught his sister's date looking through the keyhole of her bedroom door. Mom and Dad were out on their weekly date. Bill had left Dixon in the living room to look for a video they'd watch that evening. He returned to find Dixon gone. Bill went up to see if his sister was still getting dressed. There he found Dixon, crouched on the floor, right in front of his sister's door.

Dixon's mouth dropped open as he jumped to his feet and ran down the stairs. Bill followed after him, chasing him for two blocks before waving him off.

"Yeah, and why did I chase that Bozo away?" Kris still held Bill fast to the ground as he pretended to struggle against her grip. "If what he was doing is family entertainment... well not with my family!"

Kris laughed, collapsing on top of her brother. It felt good to be close to him, but it triggered feelings for Rich. She missed him terribly. Lifting herself up, but leaving her knees to pin down Bill's shoulders, her laughter suddenly faded into a big sigh. Bill figured out that his little sister must be thinking about her new friend. He just couldn't resist saying, "You really like this Rich Labano the corporate hatchet, don't you?"

"Stop it Bill!" smiled Kris. "And yes I do! You know what else? I think he would pass the big brother test!" She tossed her hair back from her face.

"Does he peek?" teased Bill.

"No!" frowned Kris. Wiggling her fingers in front of her brother's face, she transformed them into weapons without mercy, relentlessly tickling his neck.

"Hey!" yelled Briggs from across the fire, "that's my job." Dashing over to Kris, Briggs joined in on the delicious torture. "Sorry hubby," she sported, moving her fingers along his side, "but we girls are getting our revenge. Kris, for when you were kids, and me because you wouldn't let me sing "Do Wa Ditty" during the wedding." Bill begged for mercy. He got more compassion from his sister than from his wife. He would have his revenge!

• • • • •

"What do we have here?" asked the Russian med-tech at Klestkaya People's Hospital as he looked down at a man in his early thirties lying on an emergency room bed. "When did the fever come on?"

"Just half an hour ago," replied the man nervously. "You must help me! You must help me! I will be dead within an hour if you do not do something!"

"No, you will be fine," replied the med-tech. "I am going to order tests, and we are going to use ice to bring down your temperature."

"Ice!" screamed the man. "Idiot! Ice will do nothing! Tests will do nothing! I need antidote! Antidote!"

"What's your name...."

"Damn my name!" yelled the man again, growing weaker by the second. "I need antidote!"

"I do not know what you mean." The Russian med-tech was tired and didn't need the irritation this stranger was adding to his day. "I am not a doctor. If you have some idea why you are sick, tell me, and I will note it on the chart."

The man became limp, pulled into himself, and began to say over and over, "Useless... Useless... Useless..."

The patient died within the hour. A doctor had seen him, ordered tests, administered antibiotics, but none of it dented the progress of the disease. The tests indicated the likely presence of a virus, but the equipment at Klestkaya was primitive. The doctor recognized that a disease killing so quickly represented a serious health risk. A sample of the dead man's blood serum was sent to Central Laboratories in Moscow by special courier. That evening, military trucks surrounded Klestkaya, and no one was permitted in or out of the city. The identity of the dead man revealed a connection with the Russian Mafia. The courier who delivered the blood sample was placed under strict quarantine, as were the technicians who received the sample in Moscow.

• • • • •

Inside Special Securities at the Pentagon, agents were studying satellite images from southern Russia. They watched intently as military trucks left Rostov to surround Klestkaya. "What in the mind of muddled Russia do you think is going on?" asked a civilian technician.

"I'm not sure, but I'm going to call the general." Two hours later, Special Securities was crawling with intelligence specialists. The window of time offering satellite surveillance had closed for 3 hours and 24 minutes until another satellite passed above southern Russia. Secret agents within Moscow were contacted. One agent said that there were rumors about a deadly virus outbreak at Klestkaya. OIDC was then notified, and Stan was en route by special jet to Washington, D.C. When he arrived at the Pentagon by helicopter, satellite imaging had been restored. He looked at the monitor. "Where are the images that were taken earlier?" he barked.

A woman keyed in some codes. The monitor began to display a sequence of pictures. "That city," observed the OIDC operative, "is under quarantine!" Leaning back against the outside edge of a technical gadget, Stan demanded, "Show me the location of that city!"

Again the woman's hands raced over the keyboard. Up popped a map of southern Russia. "Bring it out!" Again the commanding voice.

"Damn!" said Stan. "This is too close to Turkey... too close to the Aegean Sea." Stan did the math in his head. Several months had passed since the outbreak at Khlos. Why would the virus show up now? It didn't make any sense, but Stan had a bad feeling about Klestkaya. "Commander," he said turning to a ranking military official, "I think that this could be very serious. It's so serious that I recommend that all flights to and from Russia and the Mideast be stopped immediately. No travel to or from that area for American citizens."

"What are you talking about?" The commander stiffened, irritated at the orders given him by a civilian. He dished out orders, he didn't take them. "Do you have any idea of the political ramifications of a move like that? I don't have the authority to..."

"Don't give me that! If you don't have the authority, get on the phone to someone who does." Stan moved to within inches of the ranking officer's face. "Listen commander! If that community is under quarantine, and if the bug causing that quarantine is what I think it just could be, we're talking about the deaths of not thousands, but millions, if we don't contain it. Do you want Americans falling over like dominos as the virus works from some entry point, then spreads from city to city? You want political ramifications! That damn virus will serve you up a plateful of political ramifications!"

"I'll make some calls," replied the commander. "Is there anything else that I should know?"

"Two things." No one could miss the seriousness laced in his voice. "I pity anyone who gets it! If there's good news, the virus usually kills its victims within hours, so it's fairly easy to trace. I recommend that we send out medical alerts to all major city hospitals. Ask them to report any fast–acting pathology which includes a high fever. The bad news is that," Stan measured his words, "it appears the disease can penetrate containment suits upon contact. I don't know what to tell med-techs about precautions, except that they shouldn't touch a patient suspected of having the disease or anything that has made contact with the patient. I know this is almost useless information, because more than likely contact will be made before the diagnosis. I'm sorry, that's the best I can do, at least for now."

The commander turned to go, but Stan arrested his retreat, grabbing the ranking officer's arm. "Commander," he said quietly, "we are very, very close to a vaccine against this bug. I don't want to get anyone's hopes up. Even if it works, it would take years to make enough of the vaccine to inoculate the general public. We have to stop this bug. Whatever it takes, it must be contained!"

· · · · ·

The navy blue morning sky was chopped and mixed repeatedly by the bright lights of a military helicopter hovering over the camp. "Bill! Bill! What's that noise?" Briggs was tugging at her husband who had pulled himself down into their sleeping bag. Slowly his head emerged facing directly into Briggs. He squinted. Then his right eyebrow raised as Bill tipped his head to the left. Bill was listening to the chopper's cha.. cha.. cha... cha... cha... cha....

Pulling himself out of the bag, he wrestled on his trail pants, then crawled out of the pup tent. "Dr. William Downs?" came an electronically amplified voice from the chopper. Bill waved his hand. "We have a situation. You are requested to return with me to the Oakland Infectious Disease Center."

Briggs had joined Bill outside their tent. "You don't think something is wrong with Seda, do you?"

"I don't know." Bill shook his head, skeptical that Seda was the reason for this unexpected visit. "It doesn't seem likely that they would send a military helicopter to get me because of a change in her condition. I'm stumped! It looks like our honeymoon is going to be postponed. Sorry Briggs!"

"Nothing you can do about that."

"No," smiled back Bill. "I'm... sorry... that... our... time... together... is being cut short."

"We'll make up for it later," winked back Briggs.

The military chopper set down on the spot where the wedding had taken place the day before. Bill climbed on as Briggs stayed behind to break camp and play hostess to the remaining family and friends who had camped the night. As the morning passed by, Briggs was having a difficult time making light conversation with the group. Her mind was drawn to Bill and all the things that he might be facing.

Was Seda all right? Had another outbreak of the virus taken place in Oakland? Were there more fatalities at OIDC? Stan usually handled things when

Bill was gone. Was Stan okay? He had left a last minute message on the voice mail indicating that he would have to miss the wedding. There was no alarm in his tone, but he was clearly annoyed that a situation had come up taking him away from sharing Bill's big day.

· · · · ·

Dust swirled randomly as the chopper set down on a lit platform—mounted one foot above the OIDC roof by metal scaffolding. Stan was there to meet Bill as he stepped out of the military transport. Bill had tried to pry information from the soldiers flying with him in the chopper. He discovered nothing about the situation. They wouldn't say a word about the reason for this dramatic trip back to the Institute. The operation was classified as "Need to Know," and the only thing the chopper pilot and crew needed to know was getting Bill to OIDC.

Stan did not look good. "I'm sorry to break up your wedding celebration," he said. "I'm afraid that we may have another outbreak of PRN40."

"My God," said Bill, not to curse, but to pray. "Where?"

Stan explained what the satellites had picked up in southern Russia. He had photos of Klestkaya showing the military vehicles surrounding the community. "Have you tried to contact Central Laboratories in Moscow?" asked Bill.

"Of course," Stan answered, "and at the highest levels. They won't talk. We're getting the boilerplate answer that it's a domestic matter and no concern of the United States."

Bill was no stranger to desperate situations. He forced his emotions to flee. They left like smitten enemies that would return. Bill's mind began functioning like a machine manufacturing probabilities to forecast what they faced on the continent and world-wide. "Have you shared what we know with Central Laboratories?"

"I talked to Dr. Boris Keransky," answered Stan, "and told him about what we found on Khlos. He already knew all about it. I asked him if he also knew that the virus is able to penetrate containment suits. There was a long pause, then he said he had to go. That was the last exchange that I had with Central Laboratories in Russia. I think we should give them another call."

"Speaking of Khlos, run by me the condition of the crew that detoxed the island."

"If anyone on the team had been infected," answered Stan, "they would be dead by now, so I think we're out of the woods on that. It's been months since that outbreak."

Bill took a piece of paper from his shirt pocket, clicking his pen nervously with his thumb. "Okay. Okay. What precautions have we taken against this black knight?"

"Everything that the crew wore or used that could be burned, has been burned. The town remains off limits, and we have alerted area hospitals to watch for PRN40 symptoms. Links have been established to bring any reports immediately to government authorities and OIDC. I keep saying that the only thing good about this virus is that it acts quickly. The island has been clean for a long time without incident, so likely it's no longer contaminated." Stan paused. Bill knew what he would say, "Unless the virus is still present on contaminated surfaces."

"Do you think that someone from Klestkaya could have been one of the terrorists who toxified Khlos?" Bill's mind opened another window. Like a computer sifting through its data banks, he assessed mechanisms that would account for a delay in surfacing the presence of contaminated goods. "Perhaps he carried something back that was infected but didn't have contact with it for months." Bill drew his hands down over his face as he looked back at Stan. "Has the lab determined the shelf life of this thing?"

"Not really... What I mean is that we are testing the virus in ambient conditions, and it has not died. To date, we have no idea how long it can live without a host. We don't know if it incubates. We just don't know a hell of a lot about this monster!"

"What progress has been made on a vaccine?" Bill's mind opened another window as he considered defensive strategies against the virus.

"That's the good news," Stan answered, giving just the hint of optimism. "We think that we have a vaccine. It's not tested yet, and the whole process has been so miraculous that it could convert the skeptic in me." A faint smile broke over Stan's fretted brow. "Bill, there's no scientific explanation for what's going on with Seda. Except for a few packaging refinements to make the treatment ready for others, she's a walking vaccine!"

"How much of the untested vaccine has been synthesized?" Worst case scenario, best case scenario, raced through Bill's mind.

"I really don't know. We're just getting into this. We don't want to drain Seda of her blood. If you want a guess, I'd say we could vaccinate 400 to 500 subjects by week's end. That's with a rough and untested vaccine. You know it takes years to test a new vaccine. After that, who knows how many hoops the FDA would make a pharmaceutical jump through before it allowed a release of the vaccine for public consumption?"

"PRN40 may dictate this one to the FDA." Bill jotted down more notes to himself on the slip of paper. "Have we prepared to send our findings to major pharmaceuticals so they can begin their work on the vaccine?"

"We are moving at quantum speed on this one, Bill," Stan replied. The two walked into Stan's office. Stan shuffled through a file of papers. "And yes, we have already made phone calls. Just about every company that we have contacted is placing this project into priority lab time. They've been asked to copy the synthetic process developed here, duplicating what's taking place within Seda. That's not going to be easy."

"I know! I know! What about security?" Bill's analytical dexterity was looking a whole lot like rudeness. "Do they understand that no information about the virus or work on the vaccine is to be leaked? I mean absolutely nothing is to be leaked! No 'Deep-Throats!' No scoops for a favorite press agent! Nothing out!"

"They understand the dangers of panicking the public." Stan's voice cut with irritation. "But as you know, we can't control what any one person might choose to do. We have done our best to stress the security issues."

Stan was worn thin. He understood Bill's passion to win. Bill was the Michael Jordan of infection control. Everyone facing a deadly toxin wanted him on their team. He was routinely lent out to foreign agencies facing deadly outbreaks. Whenever the game turned against Bill, his mechanical drive to fix things morphed associates into robotic warriors who were there to do or die. Bill refused to admit their emotions, fears, or exhaustion into the equation. The game had to be won.

Stan had a life outside of the lab. Before his trip to the Pentagon, he'd fought with his daughter. "She's dating a jerk and wants to move in with the guy," Stan rehearsed. He was worried about her. Compound the problem with his daughter to the fact that Stan's only sleep in the last two days had been on the jet, and he was a man running on very little. How did Bill expect him to button up security and at the same time get research started within institutions not under OIDC control?

"Sorry, Stan." Bill was groping to phrase his thoughts. "I want to meet with everyone at OIDC who is working with the PRN40 vaccine. I want to meet with them today. This is to be a very private meeting, so let it be known that they're not to talk about it with anyone else. Not at OIDC! Not anywhere! Let's plan for 3:00 in the conference room."

"What's up, Bill?" Putting down the file, Stan stared at his partner.

"Trust me on this one." Bill remained evasive. Stan started to leave, but Bill caught him by the shoulder. "Wait! Instead of meeting at the conference room, ask the group if they'd be willing to meet after hours at Mac's Bar. Tell them it's important. Tell them to make room for it. Eight o'clock at Mac's Bar, and mum's the word! Stan, it is... it is critical that everyone working with PRN40 be there!"

"Okay. Whatever you say," replied Stan. He said no more. Stan knew when his friend's mind was set in concrete.

"One more thing," continued Bill. "I want you to put on Seda's chart that the next drawing of blood is to be skipped." Stan shot Bill a look questioning a request that made no sense at all. Bill read his colleague's mind. "Just put on the chart that I ordered it. I have been her doctor. If there are any questions down the line, I'll handle it. Trust me on this one." A dim smile flashed across Bill's face, then vanished. "Trust me."

Stan left the room completely baffled. He knew Bill to be eccentric. Years ago he might have told Bill to explain it or shove it. But he had come to know that Bill's long-shot was better than his own bird-in-the hand. In almost any situation, if there were bets to be put down, his money would be with his partner. Stan kept his concern to himself. He refused to push the huge question that hung like a thundering cloud above this meeting that Bill wanted arranged with select OIDC employees.

One by one Stan pulled aside the technicians working with PRN40. Each agreed to the meeting, but its clandestine quality created a surrealistic atmosphere within the consent given by technician after technician. Then again, the whole world had been tipped from its axis for those who understood what the discovery of PRN40 could mean for the entire planet.

Bill walked down the hall to Seda's room. She was resting. "Seda," Bill said softly. "Seda. Could we talk for a bit?"

Seda pulled herself up, resting back on her pillows. "Sure, Doc, what's on your mind?" This was an unexpected visit. Seda looked at Bill's hand noticing he carried medical gear used to draw blood. She was tired of tests... tired of being prodded and poked to keep her blood flowing to the world. Still, the doctor at the side of her bed had helped to save her life.

"I'd like to ask a huge favor," he said.

"Go ahead and ask, Doc, I owe you my life. I just hope your favor is big enough." She smiled.

"I would like you to give me, personally, some of your blood. I can't tell you why right now, but I'm asking you to trust me."

"Couldn't you just take it?"

"I could. But I value you as a friend, and taking something from you wouldn't feel right. Besides, OIDC keeps better track of where your blood goes than the government accounts for the gold at Fort Knox." Bill forced a smile.

"Doc, take what you need!"

"Thanks, Seda." Bill's voice cracked with emotion. He took a deep breath, concentrated, then continued. "I brought what I need to draw some blood. Tomorrow the technicians will not be taking blood as usual. You won't need to put up with more needles, at least for a day!" Seda liked that.

Bill took her arm. Using the shunt already installed into a vein, he avoided another pierce to her skin. He was amazed at how well Seda had held up under the relentless visits by OIDC staff. Noticing the gold cross he had seen several times before hanging from her neck, he asked her where she got it.

"I bought it for myself, actually," she replied. "Nothing special or sentimental in how it came to me."

"Doesn't matter." Bill completed filling a small plastic bag with blood. "It's what it stands for that makes it special." Squeezing Seda's hand, he said good night, then headed back to the lab where he worked until morning.

• • • • •

Briggs arrived back in Oakland by plane. Driving to their apartment she arrived home around 10:00 in the morning. They had decided to live at Bill's place until tracking down a townhouse suiting both their tastes. She was surprised to hear the shower running. Bill had not gone in to work. She smiled. Quietly she moved toward the bathroom, allowing her clothing to fall to the floor. She opened the door. "Briggs! Is that you?" called out Bill. She did not answer but pulled open the glass door, joining her husband for a long, hot shower.

• • • • •

"I was surprised to find you home." Briggs was talking from the kitchen where she was pouring coffee. After finishing their shower, they were having brunch on the apartment's outdoor balcony. Briggs was standing near the open door that led from the kitchen. A loud jet was tracing a line just above them.

"Sorry, Briggs!" shouted Bill. "I didn't hear that."

Briggs turned the corner, walking out to join Bill on the balcony. She handed him a mug of coffee to top off their light meal. "I just said that I was surprised to find you home. Did you miss me much?"

"Of course!" he said dramatically, and then coyly, "I worked all night and then slept in today." Bill manufactured a smile in order to set the stage for talking about something that would not set well with Briggs. "Say! What do you think about planning some family get-togethers."

"Huh?" gasped Briggs, surprise scribbled confusion across her face. "We just got married, remember? As I recall, both our families were at the wedding. Don't you think we should wait, maybe a couple of months or years, before suggesting that we all get together again?" Briggs was astonished. They were married just two days ago!

"Well, I've got some things that I want to talk to you about." Bill was having a difficult time explaining this one. "Things that are for your ears and not for broadcast. I'm not ready to get into this right now, but will you just take my lead on this one?"

"Let's say I do," she said, somewhat irritated that Bill was keeping something back from her. "What do we say to relatives who think we're nuts! I mean, getting together so soon after the wedding?"

"I've thought about that," replied Bill. "We tell them that we missed not seeing your cousin Wade and others like him who were unable to make it to the wedding. We'll tell them that I've got something that I want to give them. We'll go back to Minnesota! We'll meet at your parent's house in Rochester first, and then we'll plan a day for getting together with my family. I'm going to suggest the family cabin on Lake Minnetonka to dad. It will be fun!"

"What aren't you telling me, Bill?"

"Okay, Briggs, I wanted to have a little more time to figure out how to say this to you. Remember how yellow fever was on a rampage at the turn of the 19th century?"

"Yeah, but what has yellow fever to do with this deadly disease? We're talking apples and horse dung here, Bill!"

Bill said one word, "Asibi!"

Without a pause Briggs broke in, "I know about him. He was from west Africa. Asibi contracted yellow fever and lived. A specimen of his blood was used to create a vaccine against yellow fever."

"Yup! And all the vaccine manufactured since 1927, by the Rockefeller Foundation and the government and all other agencies, derives from the original strain of virus obtained from that simple native."

"It's the same thing we're seeking to do with Seda's blood..."

"That's right," interrupted Bill, "but we're quickly running out of time. I really didn't want to get into this with you now, but here's what we have to do..."

· · · · ·

"Keransky, I'm telling you that all hell has broken out here!" screamed the desperate physician into the phone. Hundreds of red, feverish bodies were crammed together, moving slowly like molten lava through the halls of Central Clinical Hospital of Moscow. Some were walking. Some were leaning against the walls or crawling along the floors. Some lay dead as the traffic stumbled around them. There were citizens, nurses, and children caught in the merciless grip of a disease that showed no partiality. Whatever child of Adam crossed its path was the victim of Cain's revenge.

Keransky fumbled the phone receiver into its saddle. He had received calls from City Emergency, Central Republican Clinic Hospital, Moscow Municipal, and clinics throughout the city giving the same report. The virus first discovered on Khlos, somehow communicated to Klestkaya, now had taken Moscow by storm. Keransky phoned for his vehicle then hung up. Lifting the receiver again, he made another call. A male voice answered on the other end, "Office of Dmitry Katuzov."

"This is Dr. Boris Keransky, I must talk to the commander immediately."

"I'm sorry Dr. Keransky," said the aide, "but Commander Katuzov is in a meeting."

"I don't care if he is talking with the Prime Minister, get him for me now!"

The aide laid down the receiver to knock on a large door to the right of his desk. Pushing against the weight of the massive door, it opened as the aide walked into the conference room. "I am sorry to bother you Commander, but Dr. Keransky is on the phone, and he insists that he talk with you."

Katuzov got up from his chair following his aide out of the room. Picking up the phone he barked, "Yes, Keransky. What is so important that it could not wait?"

"Commander, we have a problem. I had hoped that we could resolve it at Central Laboratories, but it is out of control."

"Damn, Keransky! What is the problem?"

"The virus has spread. The one that was being contained at Klestkaya has somehow reached Moscow. It might have been caused by a breach within our containment devices. We did not know this, but the virus has the ability to soften and penetrate plastic and polymers. Many of our own technicians are dead, but they passed on the virus before the problem was discovered. The virus has spread throughout the city in an unprecedented manner. Commander, we must quarantine the city!"

"Have you lost your mind?" yelled Katuzov. "You are talking about Moscow!

It's your duty to keep the city clean. Don't come to me to fix your messes."

"Commander, listen to me," pleaded the head of Central Laboratories. "You can blame the outbreak on me. Fine! Do it! But if you don't immediately quarantine the city, all of Mother Russia may be dead within a month."

"And what am I to do with the politicians?" snarled Katuzov. "Am I to cage them in Moscow and watch them die!"

"I would evacuate them," replied Keransky nervously, "and then place them into hospitals in Noginsk, Pokroy, Kurovskoye, and Yegorvesky. Transfer patients in these hospitals to Vladimir. The government officials should have no physical contact with any of the staff. Each should be given a separate room. Those who do not die within four hours, given the virus pathology, are not infected. If someone dies, the room should be sealed until we decide how to dispose of the body and decontaminate the room. This must be done!"

"Can you tell me how I am to persuade these paranoid politicians that this is not an elaborate coup?" snapped the commander.

"In roughly fifteen minutes every television station still on the air has been ordered to show pictures from Central Clinical Hospital," said Keransky. "Tell the authorities to watch. If they refuse to leave after that, they will be dead. That is the bottom line, Commander. I am leaving the city immediately."

"No you are not!" screamed Katuzov. "You are responsible for the public health!"

"What are you going to do to me, huh, Katuzov! Threaten me with death? Too late! That threat has already been delivered by a clout that, right now, is much more powerful than you."

"And what of the city?" asked the Commander, his impotent voice no longer able to intimidate or threaten.

"You must surround it with the military. No one must leave or enter. Death must be administered to any citizen who gets within fifty kilometers of any soldier. This is bad business, but we have no choice!"

· · · · ·

A dark, knotted mass of entities drifted above Moscow. Like black sparks flying from Death's grinding wheel, entity after entity flew from the demonic hoard to feed upon the carnage of an expiring city. Some demons played with the dying, like a cat holding a terrified mouse but refusing the kill. Others entered the souls of the healthy who still followed the old regime's official religion of atheism, sending them into convulsions and fits of madness. Slowly, from the center of the quaking cloud of hell's own, descended Molech, its red eyes hungry for human pain, its appetite craving the terror that seizes mortal man when it feels the icy, merciless grip of death.

Chapter 9:
The Get-Togethers

"It's remarkable! Seems like just last week that we were together for something. Dang... just can't remember what it was." Briggs' older brother, John, was first to launch a good-natured attack. Odd the timing for this family gathering. Everyone was talking about it. John's sarcasm reflected what all the Brandons were thinking. Why was Briggs here? Why did she want to see everyone again just a week after the wedding? Briggs and her new hubby had arrived in Rochester late the night before. The next day Brandon clanners were filing into the home that Briggs had known as a child.

There were uncles and aunts, cousins and their spouses, children of cousins, and even a few second cousins. Each was wondering the same thing. Why a second family gathering so soon after the wedding? It was a struggle for Briggs to manufacture an answer to that question. "Bill has something he wants to give you," she'd say, "and it wasn't ready in time for the wedding." It was lame, but better than a dopey, silent stare. What it was, she wouldn't say.

Mostly, Briggs' family just smiled to her answer, then continued to chat. It would be a harder sell for Bill's family as they gathered at the family cabin. Unlike Brigg's family who mostly lived in Minnesota, some of Bill's clan would be making long trips. Some might not have come at all if it were not for Kris's new boyfriend. He was the unplanned hand that dealt enough curiosity into the situation to make the trip worthwhile.

Tables, borrowed from the Brandon's church, were tucked into every open space on two levels. Briggs and Bill moved from table to table, seeking to be good hosts by spending time with everyone. Finally settling at the table with John and a few of Briggs' cousins, they looked around the room sizing up the group. "Where's Wade?" Briggs sputtered, unsettled that a cousin was missing. Bill tossed a glance over at Briggs. She was frantic.

"Oh drat!" John replied. "Wade would've killed me if I forgot. He had to work. He begged his boss for the day off, but he's the go-to guy at Comdaq. It's great to be brilliant, but this is one of those times when you wish that he wasn't a computer whiz. He won't ever be out of a job. Literally! There'll always be someone ready to snatch Wade up. Problem is that once he's hired they chain him to his desk."

"Got that right," said a cousin, "Wade once said that he works ten hours a day, sometimes seven days a week. When he's not at Comdaq, he wears a beeper. Talk about being married to a job!"

"Sound like anybody that you know, Briggs?" winked John. He had heard about Bill's long hours at the lab.

Briggs wasn't listening. Transparently agitated that Wade wasn't at the gathering, she continued a pensive look glued to Bill. Wade had missed the wedding because of work, and now he had missed today's gathering.

"You know what I think we should do?" smiled Bill. Calmly his eyes took hold of Briggs, then moved on to the group. "I think that on our way to Lake Minnetonka tomorrow, Briggs and I should make a stop in Mankato. We can at least have breakfast with Wade. His boss has to let him eat, or I'm reporting him to the humane society. I mean, even dogs are protected!" The group chuckled. Briggs loosened up—wrinkles of concern vanished for now.

"Say everyone!" announced Briggs' mom, Harriet. "There's lots of food, so don't be shy. Briggite, could I get you to pour punch for everyone? After all, it's the special recipe from Bill's bachelor days. Got it from his best man." She raised her hand, placing its back against her forehead. "I've never tasted anything formulated by a bachelor. Never! Help me, Robert, I think I'm going to faint." Briggs' dad waved her off. "Never mind," said Harriet dryly, "I can't find any place to fall with all these people jamming around." Everyone laughed. Harriet had a wry sense of humor and a flair for the dramatic gesture. She was always good for getting a stalled party rolling.

"I still think it's unreal that both of you are doctors," exclaimed Linda. Linda, youngest daughter to Briggs' uncle Clem, lived a few doors down the block from the Brandon home and the two grew up together. They were more sisters than cousins, sharing the deepest secrets, the saddest tears, the highest joys. Briggs winked at Linda, "Well, I'm the doctor, Bill's a ringmaster in a circus of diseases."

Laughter rippled around the table. "Isn't it true that both of you work with diseases?" continued Marilyn. Marilyn was another cousin to Briggs, living in Richfield. Holding her first child, a baby not more than five weeks old, she didn't look up as she asked her question.

"Work with diseases," laughed Linda, "that doesn't sound right!"

"Yeah," chimed in John, "but they do! And to think they both lived in Oakland but hadn't met until signing up for a Colorado hiking trip. I think that the hand of fate pushed you two together."

Looking over to Briggs, "I'm sure of it," Bill replied, "but your sister might have a quarrel with Fate." He winked. "In a few years she may not like living in my circus."

Reaching across the table, Briggs slapped Bill on the chest. The conversation continued as they chatted about Bill's work. Bill said very little. Briggs looked over at Marilyn nursing her child. Briggs' eyes were drawn to the infant's hands. One hand pulled, then released, the soft edge of the blanket, doing the same motion over and over again. The other hand waved with staccato motions through the air, as if trying to take hold of something unseen. The baby's new skin looked so soft, its tiny blood vessels showing through infant skin. Before Briggs lay life and all its promise. Tears filled Briggs' eyes. A burst of emotion overtook her. She ran from the room.

"What's wrong with Briggite?" John looked over to Bill, seeking to pry out an answer with his vacant stare.

"I'm not sure." Bill got up, following after her.

• • • • •

Flint Porter eyed the 66-story skyscraper. Its glass panels reflected the late afternoon light like a giant, technological, temple offering itself as a substitute for the sun. Inside, Morrell would be waiting for him. Carrying a large suitcase filled mostly with sand, Flint dodged pedestrians as he made his way toward the skyscraper. After a time, the weight of the suitcase strained even his muscled torso. Crossing the street, he challenged the busy traffic to take him on. He smiled, thinking to himself that if someone hit him and the suitcase—the last laugh was his.

He walked into the first level of the skyscraper. Shops, seeking to take advantage of the foot traffic, were stuffed into every available area, spilling out as small stands dotted over the black and white marble floor. A water fountain dominated the plaza's center, forcing pedestrians to walk even closer to the storefronts. Flint headed for a long row of elevator doors. Automatically one opened. Taking a deep breath, he hit the button for the 66th floor. His last meeting with Morrell hadn't gone well.

Sitting at her mahogany desk, Morrell waited impatiently. The coven had grown restless for the shipment. Flinging open the door, Flint entered the room carrying the suitcase, a broad smile traced over his taught face. Morrell's body language gave no sign of welcome. Framed like a white granite statue set on a plush, burgundy chair, Morrell's face was void of expression. Flatly she asked, "Is that the shipment?"

"Yes."

"I've been hearing on the news that Russia is in serious trouble because of what you've got in that suitcase. How did it get out?" Morrell's monotone voice stiffened through granite lips.

"At first, we didn't realize all the precautions when handling the item." Flint smiled. He was enjoying this. "It can't be transported in plastic. It can't be stopped by any safety gear that uses plastic."

"So when did you figure all this out?" smirked the coven mistress.

"The Russian Mafia had some things right. They transported the virus in glass containers, but the outside of one of the jars must have had the virus. It infected something taken back to Klestkaya. One of the Mafia goons must have picked up the bug. The virus didn't show up for months. We don't know what happened!

Maybe whatever was infected sat on the shelf, taking the guy out later." Flint spoke like the virus was a close friend in the society of assassins. "The idiotic Russian government then transported some infected blood back to Central in Moscow, not knowing that their containment securities would be useless." Flint smiled broadly. "The damn Russians shot themselves in the head! They took out Moscow!"

"I hope that it is as you say," snarled Morrell. A tinge of emotion broke the barricade of her iron facade. "We had an agreement that our group was to have the privilege of releasing the virus first. Your life is worth nothing if you mess with us."

Flint laughed. "I can take care of myself." He looked directly into Morrell's steel eyes, then was forced to glance away.

"Take care of yourself? You mean you and your nine millimeter Glock that you shoulder under your coat!" mocked Morrell. "You have no idea what you are up against if you get on my bad side!"

"Devils and all that?" Flint suppressed his fear, pretending to be amused by Morrell.

Morrell captured Flint in the cage of her glaring gaze. Not blinking, she started muttering something mechanically. Molech appeared, swollen after gorging itself at Moscow. At its side was a lesser demon, just half the size of Molech. They were invisible but for Morrell.

The smaller demon floated from its master until it hovered menacingly beside the terrorist. Reaching up it touched the area of Flint's suit, concealing his gun. Instantly the cloth burst into flames. "Damn!" cried Flint tearing off his coat and throwing it at Morrell. The flames vanished as the coat hit an invisible barrier, falling onto Morrell's desk. "I don't have time for your carnival tricks," he snapped. "Take the virus!" He walked with the suitcase over to Morrell who mocked Flint with a slitted smile. Flint shouted, "I hope to hell it takes you!"

"Speaking of that," Morrell's matter-of-fact voice tossed away the jeer, "do you have the antidote?"

"Yeah, it's all in there." Flint dropped the suitcase; it fell with a thud on the desk. Turning around Flint headed for the exit. He wanted fresh air!

"Don't you think that you're going to attract a lot of attention with that gun of yours?" asked Morrell. Forgetting about the absence of his coat, Flint looked down to see his holstered gun.

Morrell laughed lifelessly. "Here!" She tossed him his jacket. There were no signs of fire damage. Uttering a profanity, Flint slid into the coat and left.

· · · · ·

Bill caught up with Briggs in her parent's bedroom. Huddling at the corner of the bed, Briggs rested against the headboard, weeping out silent sobs. Bill rushed to her side, sitting down on the bed, he drew her into his arms. "Honey, what's the matter?" Gently he lifted her chin until their eyes met.

"Did you see Marilyn's beautiful baby?" exclaimed Briggs, fighting for breath, her chest heaving with emotion. "I looked at her and thought of all the babies in the world who will die if that virus isn't stopped. Bill, that virus is more than a dangerous biological anomaly. I've had this feeling from the beginning that it's... it's evil!"

Bill took her hand. "Strange that you should say that. I've had that same feeling. I started suspecting something sinister about this virus just before my Bible study at Grimm's. Getting there early I decided to read over Exodus. Suddenly this guy shows up. He's old, dark skinned, and has these incredibly sky blue eyes..."

"Bill!" interrupted Briggs. The new information broke through the emotional downpour. Pulling back from Bill, Briggs started wiping away tears from her cheeks. "This sounds like the same man that Seda said phoned in after she became infected with the virus. I remember thinking how odd it was for someone with dark skin to have light blue eyes."

"You're kidding! Spooky!" Bill stopped for a second, chewing over all the implications. "This old guy quizzed me," continued Bill, "about the justice of a God who sends punishments. He took my Bible, turning to a passage in Deuteronomy. I learned later that the text spoke about the terrible plagues that God would send if we turned our back on Him. I was ready to digest the passage just as a member of the study group arrived. I looked up, said 'Hi!' then turned back to... Elijah! That's his name, Elijah Jordan! But he was gone. Seemed to just vanish. Looking down to see what Elijah had turned to, and I know how this sounds... but the words appeared to ripple in one of the passages. The text spoke about God's punishments."

"I don't want to talk about it anymore!" protested Briggs. She and Bill had a truce about their religious differences. This whole thing with Elijah showing up at Bill's Bible study, added to the fact that he was likely the same guy who had been with Seda, was attacking her religious skepticism. Briggs became undone as the discussion turned to the chastisements of God. Always in the back of her mind was the fear that God might exist. If God existed, she would be a target for the Deity's anger. She didn't want to hear any more about the chastisements of God. End of discussion!

"Okay, Briggs," said Bill softly, "I just need to know that you're all right."

Briggs straightened herself, wiped away the remaining tears, and served Bill a silly smile that said, "There! See, I will make everyone think I'm just fine even if a cyclone is tearing me apart on the inside!"

"I know that you're hurting," Bill consoled. "I feel like I'm living in a nightmare. The worst part of it is that you are in the bad dream with me. I'd do anything to make PRN40 disappear just for you! I love you Briggs."

Throwing her arms around Bill, Briggs squeezed him desperately. A few more sobs slipped through her defenses, but that was it. Standing up, she put on the silly smile again, and led the way back into the sea of Brandon bloodlines.

At the table, a sudden hush fell as Briggs and Bill sat down. John was first to attack the silence. "Hey, Briggs," he blurted, "what happened to you?"

Linda shot John a look, then changed the subject. "What's this special surprise that you brought, Bill?" She knew her cousin. Briggs wasn't ready to share her emotions. Briggs was grateful, squeezing Linda's hand briefly under the table.

Standing up, Bill headed for the door. "I'll be back!" Leaving the room, he returned with a cardboard box. Reaching inside, he pulled out a small, white box. In the small box was a porcelain coffee mug showing the scene of the Colorado trail where Briggs and Bill were married. Below the setting were the words, "Joined together, we're part of you. Love, Bill and Briggs."

Harriet's eyes washed in tears. Marilyn surrendered her baby to Linda, giving Briggs a kiss on the forehead, then a hug. Everyone present was impressed with the gift. The odd timing for this second gathering was quickly forgotten as the afternoon passed in the warmth of Brandon hospitality.

• • • • •

Early the next day as the sun splashed light over the eastern horizon, Briggs and Bill took to the road for his clan's get-together at the family cabin. They had phoned Wade, setting up a rendezvous for breakfast in Mankato. The visit with Briggs' cousin took them out of the way, but Briggs and Bill were agreed that the visit was a must. Parked on the concrete lot of the fast food place, Wade sat waiting as they pulled into the lot. Waving to them from his open sunroof, Wade cast a gigantic smile in their direction.

Bill parked their car, then he and Briggs headed toward the restaurant. Briggs, unwilling to wait for Wade inside, darted in his direction at ramming speed. Catching him in the middle of the parking lot, she delivered a huge hug. The smell of breakfast sausage saturated the air. Bill's appetite had become a god, demanding a food offering...immediately! "Come on you two," he yelled, "I gotta have some of that sausage!"

"Me too!" yelled back Wade. He and Briggs waited for Bill to catch up with them. "How are you doing, Bill?" came Wade's friendly greeting and warm handshake.

"It's good to meet Briggs' favorite guy cousin." Bill looked around as if he didn't want to be overheard. "I can say that now, right Briggs, without the rest of the family being around?"

Briggs gave Bill a push on the chest, then taking Bill in one arm and Wade in the other, she pulled them to the door. Once inside they ordered their food, carrying it to a booth away from the main traffic. As always, after they sat down to eat, Bill paused to bow his head for a brief prayer. Briggs caught it out of the corner of her eye but continued to visit with Wade. "It's been so long, Wade. I missed you, you know, not being at our wedding."

"I'm sorry about that," said Wade. "This boss I work for thinks that the whole dang company might just collapse if I'm gone for a day. I've got great job security, just no life!" He looked mischievously over at Briggs. "Did you like what I sent to you?"

"Yes," laughed Briggs, "but when the delivery guy showed up, Bill and I couldn't figure out what could be in such a big box. It must have cost you as much to send it as the gift itself. And yes, we loved it! In fact, we used that sleeping bag made for two on our wedding night." Briggs blushed. Her girlish modesty surprised her as she quickly changed the subject. "Did you hear that Bill was helicoptered back to Oakland in the morning? Great honeymoon, huh!"

"I heard about that." Turning to Bill, "You must be a regular James Bond kind of guy."

"You bet!" sported Bill. He bent his arm up to show his biceps. "Licensed to kill any germ or virus that gets in my path."

"That reminds me," said Briggs. "Guess what we forgot in the car?" She glanced at Bill.

"Hey!" Bill returned, "I can't remember everything. But, oh all right. I'll take care of it."

Looking back to Wade, Briggs asked, "Wade, would you come out to the car with me for just a second? If we hurry the food won't get cold. We've got something to give you. If we don't get it now, you know me, I'll forget. It's something we're sharing with both our families."

"Sure," Wade said. As they left for the car, Bill stayed behind.

• • • • •

"How are you doing, Seda?" asked Elijah, waking her from an afternoon nap. Walking over to the curtain, Elijah opened it, allowing sunlight to fill the room.

"Who are you?" Seda asked sleepily, stretching out her arms and legs. "I'm so grateful for all you've done for me. But nobody seems to know who you are. When I mentioned to Dr. Brandon that you had visited me here, I know she thought I'd been hallucinating."

Elijah changed the subject. "Place is pretty quiet around here today."

"Yes," answered Seda. "Most of the crew is on holiday, I guess. I was told that I'd have a quiet weekend. I've enjoyed it actually! No tests. No, 'Eat this food, its good for the blood.' And no needles! When I get out of here, I don't ever want to see so much as a sewing needle ever again!"

"That bad, huh girl?" smiled Elijah. "So how much longer will y'all be stayin' here?"

"They never answer that question." Seda frowned. "I've been here for better than a week and I feel fine." She looked over at Elijah. He acted skeptical about the Center's purpose in detaining Seda. "They're trying to take advantage of me. They know that my blood is the key to helping out the entire planet, at least, that's what they tell me. This could give a girl a big head."

Elijah smiled, "One to fit your big heart, I figure."

"I could sell my blood to them and they'd pay a million dollars a half-pint." She nodded to Elijah, pleased to let him know that she wasn't a patsy. "But I'm letting them have as much blood as they need, and I'm glad to do it." She paused to think over Elijah's question about her stay at the Center. "When it comes to my leaving, I think that I'm also here because they're worried about my safety. It's like they know I won't be exploited here, but if I left, I would be in danger. Strange! I know."

"I don't think that's strange," said Elijah. Reaching out, he touched her hand. Seda felt something. When Elijah touched her, a surge passed through her entire body. The sensation started where he'd placed his hand, then tingled out to her fingers and toes. A very warm feeling flowed into her mid-section and parked there. It was as if something very intimate had been exchanged between them. She said nothing, but felt a great peace. "Did they tell you about your kidneys?" continued Elijah.

"How'd you know about that?" quizzed Seda. "Yes. They told me that they'd be watching them closely. It doesn't have anything to do with the virus. They say that my kidneys have been having problems for quite some time. Nothing that I ever noticed."

"I wouldn't worry about it, Seda, I think that what you had was just a passin' thing. These scientists," laughed Elijah, "they don't always get it right. On the farm, if you see crows hanging around the barn for a few days, you don't conclude that they are going to move in and stay. I think that whatever was goin' on with your innards, has just plain gone and flown the coup!" Elijah danced, raising his arms, flapping them up and down, and swirling his body in circles several times. Seda laughed. It felt good for her to laugh.

• • • • •

Briggs and Bill arrived at the family cabin on Lake Minnetonka. Bill's dad, Glenn, greeted them warmly at the door. His mom, the gushy type, gave them both repeated hugs. A few family members had already arrived, staying the night before to enjoy time at the lake. Kris was standing in a doorway separating the formal dining room from the kitchen, a huge smile breaking across her face. Reaching to her right, she took hold of a hand hidden behind the wall, pulling into view a man with dark hair tied back into a ponytail.

"I'm sorry about this," said the stranger. "This little charade was cooked up by Kris, not me."

Briggs ran over to Kris giving her a Brandon sized hug. In the innocent spontaneity that comes from a heart pure in its marriage, she also gave Kris' friend a welcoming hug. "So we finally get to meet tall, dark, and handsome!"

"I'm afraid you must have me confused with someone else," Rich said. Deflecting the overwhelming compliment, he glanced over at Kris. "Or, perhaps, as you all must know, Kris has a tendency to make things a bit bigger than life."

Bill walked over to shake Rich's hand, then delivered a welcomed hug upon his sister. Looking back over at Rich he replied, "You don't have to tell me about Kris! I suppose she's told you scads of 'big brother' horror stories?"

"A few," laughed Rich, "a few." He paused. "Bill, Kris really looks up to you. I had some jitters that I might not pass the big brother test!"

"Hold it!" interrupted Luke. Dramatically, with a flair, he entered the room, acting as if he had stepped center stage. "Isn't anyone worried about what I think? Is it just Big Bro here that gives out the blessings upon Sis and Rich? I'm the brother who's a pastor! Bill just works with bugs. I work with blessings all the time!"

"Stop it!" sported Kris.

"Well, for what it's worth," continued Luke, "in the time I've had with Rich here at the lake I've come to think—to say it straight—he's too good for our sister!"

Kris hit Luke on the arm. "Watch it brother! I have some stories I could tell about you!"

"None of that," said Betty, matriarch of the Downs family. "I want all of you to just sit down and visit about the good times—the good times! But first, grab a plate for hors d'oeuvres. We'll have some before we eat; and that's a couple hours away. So eat up!"

Everyone shuffled for a place to sit, Kris making sure that she and Rich got a place by her brothers. They talked for a while, laughing most of the time as the Down's siblings traded misadventures from their past. Eventually Kris brought up the serious subject that everybody had on the back burner of their thoughts. "What do you know about Moscow, Bill? They say that something got into the drinking water from a refinery in the city, making almost everyone sick with lots of people dying."

"Oh," said Bill. He chose his words carefully. "I know pretty much what everyone else has heard on the news."

"Isn't it awful," added Rich, recalling what he knew about the situation. "I have heard rumors through some of my international contacts that there has never been anything like this in modern history. It's as if the refinery leaked the Bubonic Plague." There was a long pause as if no one knew where to go with the conversation.

"Say, switching gears," Briggs deliberately changed the subject, "I was wondering if someone would pull me on skis tomorrow. It's been centuries since I tackled a lake on skis. It was in high school when I last took to the water behind a boat. Maybe I won't get up, but I'd like to give it a shot."

Glenn heard her from across the room. "If you want to get up on skis, I'm the guy. These young pups don't have my experience. After all, who do you think pulled them?"

"Great!" smiled back Briggs. "I get the family pro! It's a date tomorrow morning. I'm looking forward to it!" She turned to Luke. "So, is there anyone special that we should know about? Bill and I are hitched. Kris and Rich are an item..." Kris blushed, turned to Luke, pinning the attention back on him. "Yeah, anything happening in your love life?"

"Well." Luke hesitated. "Strange you should bring that up. There's a woman in the parish who is, well, stunning." Luke's thoughts ran in two directions. He wanted to talk about Rachel. He wanted to shout to the whole world about his hopes for her. But his dreams might be smoke in the wind. Explaining Cassandra's kiss goodbye was bad enough. He didn't want to build things up about Rachel, only to end up explaining another Dear John letter. There were also, always, the torturous desires for the lady in red...

"You say she's stunning, huh," joked Kris. "That good and still not hitched? Just waiting all these years for you?"

"No, she's not married!" Luke pretended to be annoyed. He bent closer to Kris. "Even though we've met and there's something there, I can't figure out a way for us to get to take things to the next level..."

"A date?" interrupted Kris again.

"Oh, don't do that, Kris! I'm not saying that anything between us is building to some big climax." Luke swayed his head from side to side, tapping his finger tips together. "I gotta tell you, she's remarkable. I'm surprised that she hasn't been snatched up."

"Sounds like you'd better get on the stick, Little Bro," smiled Kris.

"The only problem," cautioned Luke, "as I see it, is she's a bit too conservative. She takes the Bible, word for word, as if it came from the mouth of God."

"Isn't that what all you Christians do?" protested Briggs.

"In your dreams," broke in Bill. He shot a teasing look at Luke. "Some of us get so educated that we think we're smarter than God! Piling all kinds of human ideas on top of the Bible, they can't find it again."

"Don't start with me, Bill," cautioned Luke, tossing his brother a friendly smile.

"Now listen, children," the voice of the matriarch spoke. "Stay away from religion and politics! This is a family get-together. Talk about family! You know how that works. 'How do you like your job?' 'What's happening in Milwaukee?' I'll get things started. Rich, tell us again how you managed to get a date with Kris after you fired her from the radio station. I love that part!" Betty was a sucker for romance.

• • • • •

After the evening meal, Kris leaned over, whispering to Rich, "Come on, let's go down to the lake. The moon tonight is fantastic. I love it when moonlight floats on the water like a golden globe." Taking his hand, she pulled Rich from the table. Once outside, they walked down the grassy slope and onto the dock. Tied to the dock was an oversized pontoon. Its deck measured eight feet by sixteen feet. A large canopy overhead covered vinyl benches fastened to the floor along the sides of the pontoon. Kris coached Rich into a corner where they could put their feet up on the adjoining bench to enjoy the sight of a large, full, yellow moon.

Resting her back against Rich, Kris turned her head facing her man, "Well?"

"Well, what?" teased Rich.

"What do you think of my family?" drilled back Kris.

"Like them," he said. "This is our first meeting, but I sense a lot of joy. Your parents have provided a foundation. I feel their personality in everything that happens. That's good. Luke has a wonderful sense of humor. Bill takes seriously his Christian faith, but he doesn't grandstand. My parents would like that. I don't think Briggs shares his convictions, but she has depth. There is though," he paused, "something else with her. I sense something sad."

"Oh come on, Rich!" taunted Kris playfully. "All that from your first meeting?"

"I suppose you're right." Rich put his hands on her shoulders and began rubbing them gently.

"Ooooo, don't stop!" Kris spoke in her seductive DJ voice.

"You're using that voice again." Rich's words were coated in his own alluring accent.

"Do you remember what we were talking about as we drove to Minnesota?" asked Kris.

"About how we could save money if we shared an apartment?"

"Yeah." Kris paused. Turning around in his arms she rested her head against his chest. "Well?"

"You American girls," sighed Rich, "what am I to do with you?"

Kris pulled away pretending to be hurt. "Are you saying that there are other girls!"

"But of course!" joked Rich. "Hundreds of them. And they all want to live with me."

"A regular harem master, aren't you?" pouted Kris. An awkward silence followed, then Kris broke in again, "I mean it Rich! Why not?"

"First, because I care for you too much. I care for what we may become, and I do not want to take away from that. We have already become more than friends. I think you feel that way too, or you would not want to be with me in the way that you are suggesting."

Kris pulled away further, delivering a carefully rehearsed look. Placing her hands on his chest, her eyes dove into his. "You care for me. That's all that's important!"

"No, my lovely Kris, there is much more to it than that." Rich pulled her closer. "There is honoring you even if you do not want to be honored. There are our parents. And how would your brother, the pastor, feel about us living together without the benefit of marriage?"

"Luke?" laughed Kris. "He's liberal. I worry more about what Bill might think."

"See!" Rich jumped on the point. "It does make a difference."

"But we have entered a new millennium," protested Kris. Pulling back, she sought to measure the impact of her words. "Bill's the one who needs to make changes just like everybody else. I'll bet Briggs would be more open to it."

Rich had strong feelings for Kris. He feared that the conversation could lead in a direction that would make her look badly. He decided to intercept the discussion before it did damage to their relationship. He placed her head between his two, strong hands. Looking intently into her moon–swept eyes he said softly, "Kris, do you remember me telling you on our first dinner date how much I was attracted to you even before I saw your face?"

"It wasn't a date!" She scowled playfully.

"Okay, our first meeting after the encounter at the radio station. I told you that your voice attracted me to you. Not just its quality, but the wit and intelligence which I heard behind the voice. When I saw you at the station, as I said, I knew that I was going to ask you out. What I feel for you now is way past my feelings back then. It was five inches deep then, it is five feet deep now."

"Only five feet?" sulked Kris.

"Five hundred feet!" Rich smiled broadly. "What we have is too important. I will not risk our friendship, even though I would very much like to take you. When I was a boy, my priest told my brother and me that sex is easy, but friendship is hard. He said that young men and women often stop growing as friends once sex becomes the driving force within their relationship." Rich lifted her chin with one hand, his other hand remained on the side of her face. He drank in his darling's features like wine. She was not simply one of many women who had the power to enchant a man under a lake-locked moon. She had a face. "You are a very attractive woman. Do not tempt me beyond my strength. I think we should join your family back at the cabin."

Rich drew her close to him, then kissed her. Standing up, he pulled Kris with him to her feet. The large moon was framed about his face as he ran his fingers through her hair. His voice became rich, low, and sensual, "Someday, my princess, if God wills, we will dance on the high peaks of our passion for one another. And there will be no guilt. Nothing to explain away to others. Only the innocence of a man and a woman, their union blessed by the church, exploring the farthest boundaries of their love."

They walked back to the cabin. Kris placed her arm around Rich's waist as he wrapped his arm over her shoulders. Leaning her head against his chest, they said nothing. Kris was not unhappy. Actually, she felt special. Rich had placed her above his own appetites for her. No other man had ever done that before. Ironically, there was something very masculine about a man who was in such control of himself. Had she heard a veiled proposal in what he had said?

Chapter 10:
CHICKEN SOUP

Embracing Luke with a motherly hug, Betty Downs raised her hand to wave little goodbyes as he walked away. Prepping for a Monday morning Bible study required her son to leave the gathering early. Back in Rochester, the senior pastor had taken the Sunday morning schedule, freeing Luke for the family gathering. Lifting the handle to his car, Luke opened the door to climb behind the wheel. Waving a final good-bye to his mother and sister as they stood on the steps, Luke took to the road. Blowing her brother a kiss, Kris mouthed the words, "I love you, Little Bro."

The trip back to Rochester was uneventful. Luke thought back over all the discussions he'd shared that weekend. It was good to see Bill and Kris. His sister's new boyfriend was a real find! "It would be great," he thought, "if they had chemistry that turned into something special." He recalled their interlocked forms silhouetted against the moon-washed water as they came up from the dock. Suddenly, but not surprisingly, his thoughts darted to the mysterious lady in red.

Shaking his head, Luke muttered to himself, "This is idiotic!" Forcing his thoughts from a fruitless fantasy, he brought to mind Rochester and Rachel. What's she doing right now? Is she thinking about him? Rachel was a volunteer youth worker at his church. She caught his eye the first Sunday at Morningside. Two months earlier she had broken off an engagement that had lasted over a year. The reason for calling off the wedding plans remained an untold story. All in good time...

Pulling into the parking lot of his apartment, a wave of nausea suddenly assaulted Luke. "Too much good food," he muttered. Unlocking the door to his unit, emptiness greeted him like an unwelcomed roommate. The sparsely furnished apartment, void of anyone but himself, was filled with loneliness worsened by the fresh memories of time with his family. Closing the door, Luke headed for his bedroom craving a good night's rest. Enjoying the cool sheets of a fresh bed, he drew them tightly to his chin. The satin covered pillowcase sunk softly under his head, inviting him into a quick sleep. It was not to last. At 4:28 a.m., Luke made a mad dash for the toilet. Every piece of food that he had enjoyed at the reunion was coming back for a return visit. He vomited until he fought for breath.

Finally his stomach landed on empty. Tentative steps tottered him along from the bathroom to the kitchen. Fumbling under the kitchen sink, his hand searched to find the handle of a red scrub bucket. This would be his backup by the bed. If another episode struck, and if it came on fast, he'd have the bucket. Placing his insurance beside his bed, he lay down again. Sweeping his hand over his fevered brow, he muttered into his blankets, "There's no way under heaven that I'm going in today."

Sleep evaded him. Forcing himself out of bed at 8:15 a.m., Luke dragged himself to the phone and called the church office. "Good morning," came Tamor's welcoming voice, "Morningside Community Church. How can we serve you today?"

"Get me an undertaker," replied Luke, "I think I'm going to die..."

"Are you all right, Pastor?" Concerned for her pastor, Tamor still smiled at the humor lacing her pastor's words. He wasn't dying.

"No, Tamor, I'm far from all right!" Luke's weak voice tried to sparkle. "The flu has come to visit bringing along its whole family—fever, aches and pains, and a volatile stomach! Would you mind making a few phone calls to the regulars at the Bible study? Tell them that we won't meet today..." As they talked, Rachel Jacobson sat in the volunteer's desk next to Tamor. Although Luke was constantly shadowed by the woman in red, thoughts about Rachel often dispelled the phantom from the young pastor's mind. Coming in early that morning, Rachel planned to put together the monthly newsletter for junior and senior high youth. She was a woman of medium build with sandy brown hair. Her blue eyes were round jewels sparkling on the horizon of freckleless cheeks. A softness radiated from Rachel's small features. Parked perpetually across her face was a welcoming smile.

"You don't worry about a thing," assured Tamor. "I will take care of the Bible study and organize your messages for the day. You just get better, hear!" Hanging up the phone she turned to share the news with Rachel. "Poor Pastor Luke, he's really under the weather! Got the fever and can't keep anything down."

"You know what, Tamor?" Rachel responded. "My Grandma had a cure for whatever ailed you. A special recipe for chicken soup that's been handed down from before my ancestors left Europe for America. It's a bit of a putz to make. Chicken and vegetables must be fresh from the store." Stacking her work on the desk, Rachel continued, "I'll finish up this newsletter later. Right now I'm going to the store. I've got some soup to make! Trust me, Grandma's soup is something that the pastor will keep down."

"Oh, Rachel, what a dear you are!" Tamor was delighted. "We both know that it's no fun to be sick when you're single—no one to pamper you back to health, and all." She took a deep breath. "I'm sure that Pastor Luke will appreciate the gesture even more than the soup. Do me a favor?"

"Sure, Tamor, what's the favor?"

"Pick up one of the daily specials on flowers and give them to the Pastor from Pastor Horton and myself. Tell him that we'll have him in our prayers. Which reminds me, I'd better tell Pastor Horton that Luke won't be coming in. Let me know what the flowers come to, okay?"

"Flowers are good as delivered," smiled Rachel. "You're the one always going the extra mile for the pastors and people at Morningside. We're blessed that the Lord led you to our door... Well, I'm out of here!"

Rachel drove to a small neighborhood store known for its fine meats. Shopping at the small grocery store near her home saved time. The down side was that its produce wouldn't be as fresh as the uptown stores. "Still," she reasoned, "how stale can celery and carrots get?"

Placing the chicken and produce into her shopping cart, she picked up a ten pound bag of flour just in case her pantry was getting low. Her grocery list filled, Rachel headed for the checkout. "Seventeen dollars and twenty–four cents," noted the clerk after ringing up the purchases. Quickly paying for her groceries and the flowers, she raced for her small house on Oak Lane. Always at home in her kitchen, Rachel worked the recipe she'd memorized at her mother's knee. Grandma had detailed every step, including the process for creating homemade pasta noodles. Three hours of loving care went into making grandma's chicken soup, but the results were well worth the time.

Setting aside a little of the soup for her lunch, Rachel poured the rest of it into a mason jar, tightening down the cover. Taking newspapers she wrapped the jar in several layers. Bundling it all in a terrycloth towel, she left for her car, soup and flowers in hand. It was a ten-minute drive to Pastor Luke's apartment. The soup would stay hot for the short trip. "Dear Lord Jesus," she prayed, pulling out of her driveway, "help Pastor Luke to mend quickly. May Your holy angels have charge of him; may the evil one have no power over him."

Rachel didn't know it as she drove out on that sunny morning with noon fast approaching, but the Protectors from heaven would need to swoop to her aid. Danger lurked, as evil entities had attached like barnacles on a boat to the top and sides of her car. A mere fender bender was being darkly engineered into a fatal accident. Beneath the car, clear fluid slowly eased from a fracture in the brake line of her car. Hells warriors were there to break the odds and make an accident take a deadly turn. Rachel was within blocks of Luke's apartment when a silver car began backing out of a neighborhood driveway. Stomping down madly on the brake, Rachel felt it plop to the floor without resistance. "Dear Lord in heaven..."

Targeting Rachel's car, invisible Guardians suddenly flooded onto the street. Some Messengers of Heaven ripped entities from the automobile like mites off a cat's ear. Still the vehicle sped thirty miles an hour toward the unsuspecting car backing onto the street. Elmidra drew his sword plunging it into the ground just ahead of the rear bumper of the car as it backed into traffic. Stopping with a thud, the car acted as if it had hit a light pole. Its engine stalled. The startled driver looked back just as Rachel's car zoomed by, narrowly missing her back fender. Reaching for the keys, Rachel turned off her car's engine. She let her car coast until maneuvering it to the side of the street, parking it at an angle by the curb. "Thank you Father!"

There was nothing she could do about the car now. Pastor Luke's apartment was a five minute walk away, so Rachel decided to leave the car, traveling the final distance on foot. Later she'd ask Pastor if she could use his phone to call her friend, a Christian mechanic working at Powerland Auto Repair.

Reaching the apartment building, she pressed the intercom button connecting visitors with residents. "Pastor Downs," came Luke's weak voice.

"Pastor," said the angel of mercy, "this is Rachel Jacobson. I thought you might like some hot, homemade chicken soup!"

"Hi Rachel!" Luke was surprised. "I'll buzz you through the door. Please excuse how I look, okay!"

When the security door buzzed, Rachel pushed open the glass door with her hip. Her one hand held the soup and the other a bouquet of flowers. Rushing to his closet, Luke pulled pajama bottoms up over his underwear. Quickly throwing on a bathrobe, he wrestled with a sleeve that was turned inside-out. Racing back to the bathroom, he sanitized his stale breath with mouthwash. As the doorbell rang, Luke fought to tame wild hairs bed-pasted into abstract forms from the night's restless sleep. "Oh boy!" he lamented, "I look like the zombie who came for breakfast!" With a final dash to the door, he grabbed a stocking cap from the entrance closet, quickly pulling it down over his head.

"Hi Rachel." Luke greeted her with a smile that said, "I'm glad to see you even though I look like this and feel as if I'd been hit by a Mack truck."

"Nice hat!" she said with a smile. Reading her pastor's sorry condition she continued, "Oh poor Pastor! You get right back into bed!" Luke stood there in the stupor of his flu, not quite processing things well. "Move! Get yourself to bed and I'll get you something to eat."

"I appreciate that," came a hesitant protest. "I just don't think I can keep it down."

"Pastor Downs," commanded Rachel, "go to bed! My grandma's recipe for chicken soup has never failed. It will make you feel better. Trust me."

"My bedroom's a mess," replied Luke. "Do you mind if I get a blanket and flop here on the couch?" Luke felt awkward asking for permission to do something in his own house, but Rachel had taken charge.

"Is that the blanket?" she asked, pointing to the top shelf of the open entry closet.

"That would work," returned Luke.

"Good! You lay down and I'll get the blanket." Walking over to the closet, Rachel took down the blanket and returned to Luke. Unfolding it, she gently laid it over him, fussing with it, as if tucking in a little child. Motioning to a closed door she asked, "Is that your bedroom?"

"Yes," said Luke, wondering what was on Rachel's mind.

As Rachel headed for the door Luke exploded in protest, "No! Don't go in there unless you wear safety shoes and a hard hat!" The sound of his raised voice made his head ache.

"Listen pastor, I grew up with three brothers. I've been through the rubble of their war zones countless times. You just relax." Opening the door, Rachel disappeared, returning with two pillows. "Please lift up your head Pastor," she said kindly. Luke pushed himself up on his elbows, allowing Rachel to carefully arrange them under his head. "Okay, you just take it easy while I dish you up some of Grandma's soup."

Pouring the soup into a dish, she prayed quietly, "Dear Lord, Grandma always said the secret ingredient to this soup was prayer. I ask You to bless our pastor and mend him in every way. May this soup serve that healing. May it not unsettle his stomach, but rather soothe and heal in every way. I ask this in Jesus' name. Amen."

Walking carefully to the couch, she handed her pastor a generous helping of Grandma's soup. Surrounding them were Guardians. Encircling the two, Protectors had joined hands as they faced away from Luke and Rachel. Only Elmidra stood within the circle, his hand resting upon the shoulder of the young, skeptical pastor.

Lifting the bowl to his lips for the last time, Luke cleaned up the remaining few drops of soup. Wearing a satisfied smile, he turned to Rachel. "This is the best chicken soup that I've ever tasted! I'd rather have this than a fine steak!"

Rachel smiled, taking the empty bowl. "I'm glad that it hit the spot. I know from experience that when you get the stomach flu, nothing can taste good. Nothing, that is, but Grandma's chicken soup."

"You've got that right," said Luke weakly, the flu still draining his strength. "It was really special for you to take time for me, making the soup and all." He thought for a minute. "Say! How'd you know that I was sick?"

"I was at the church when you called," answered Rachel. "I heard Tamor talking to you. You're still fuzzy in your thinking," she smiled. "After all, how else would I have become the delivery girl for the flowers?"

"Of course," replied Luke shaking his head. "Be sure to thank them for me, will you?"

"I will," she said, and then paused. "I'd better go and let you rest."

"Would you mind staying a little longer..." Luke's voice became boyish. Casting him a puzzled look, Rachel listened as Luke struggled to explain why he wanted her to stay. He didn't know Rachel that well. That was the point. He wanted to know her better. "I'd like to get to know you better, that's all." Rachel was about to protest again so he quickly continued. "Grandma's soup worked, and I'm feeling much better now. So please, stay and tell me about yourself. Where'd you grow up? Do you have sibs? What do you like to do? Things like that..."

"I grew up in Sandpoint, Idaho," replied Rachel. Taking a chair from the kitchen, she sat down beside the couch that buttoned Luke under a blanket.

"So, what's it like growing up in Sandpoint, Idaho?" Luke asked, pulling himself up on the pillows.

"I learned to enjoy all the seasons for what each offered," Rachel said. "I love spring for its freshness and new growth, a yearly reminder of Christ's resurrection. Summer was a time when life, rich and green in Idaho, is for savoring. Summer was the eating of the meal, after it has been prepared in spring. Fall was filled with all kinds of sights and sounds. It brought the feeling of being well satisfied after a hearty meal as you cleared the table, making ready for the next meal. Winter was a time, well, when after the dishes have been washed and put away, you sat down to share time with family and friends–the necessities of life behind you. Winter is for reflecting upon life and enjoying relationships. As Idaho snow blanketed the earth, barefoot me would be tucked under an afghan, sitting on the couch, enjoying my favorite people."

"You think like a poet, did you know that?" asked Luke. Rachel looked away, good-naturedly waving off his compliment. "What else do you remember from your days growing up at Sandpoint?"

"I guess..." Rachel stopped. After a short, silent reflection, she continued, "I remember my mother."

"What's her name?"

"Mom's name is Pam," answered Rachel.

"Good memories?" asked Luke.

"The best!" she smiled. As the fingers of her mind turned through snapshot images from her childhood, Rachel glowed. Pictures of her mother flashed before her. Rachel could see her sitting at the kitchen table waiting for her to open the door as she came home after school. Her mom had wrinkled over time, but Pam's spirit remained young and fresh. "Then as now, life savors sweet when she's around." Rachel seasoned her smile with a single tear. Suddenly, like a ruptured dam she tearfully exclaimed, "She loves to laugh!" Fingers dashed quickly to her cheeks wiping away the tears. Sitting silently for a few seconds, she flashed several apologetic smiles at Luke.

"Sounds like a special lady." Luke rescued the moment from silence. "What else makes her such a big light in your life?"

"She's always there for family and friends." Rachel was doing better again.

"And?" Luke rolled on his side to see Rachel better.

"Mom's artistic, using calligraphy to write messages on fun, little pictures. She frames these personalized pictures giving them to friends, sometimes for no reason except to say that she was thinking of them."

"That's cool," reflected Luke. "Unexpected kindness is often the best!"

"Yeah, I think so," agreed Rachel. "Mom still touches the lives of so many. She's always ready to be a listening ear for friends needing to share their problems. She gives advice, and she takes it too." A few more tears slipped by. "Sorry!" Rachel got up to get a paper towel from the kitchen for mopping up her tears. "I don't know why I'm doing this..."

"I do," answered Luke. "You love her, and you're not with her."

"I guess you're right." Her chest heaved with a deep breath. "I think that Mom's love for the Lord floods into everyone's life. Then like a knee-jerk, you love her back. I still need a weekly dose talking and laughing with mom over the phone."

"Have you thought about visiting over the Internet?" Luke asked. "You don't need to pay an arm and a leg for two starter computers. They'd work for getting you going on the net."

"I have a computer and use the Internet for work," she returned. "Mom could afford to get a computer, but she thinks that she's too old to step out onto the information highway." She laughed. "She might be right! I can't imagine teaching her even a simple task like doing e-mails, much less explaining how to surf the web."

Luke and Rachel continued visiting about her childhood, his childhood, and how the Internet had changed the world. It was Rachel who finally stood up and said, "I think you need to get some rest now, and I have some items on my afternoon to-do list. First off, may I use your phone to call an auto repair shop? I almost hit another car. Mine is broken down a few blocks away. I'll need to have it towed in and fixed."

"Are you all right?" exclaimed Luke.

"Yeah, I'm fine. It's my car that has a headache... or stomach ache. Who knows! So how about the phone?"

"Sure," replied Luke, "phone's on the wall by the fridge." Then thinking ahead, he asked, "How are you getting back to your place?"

"I was going to see if my friend at the shop might have time to give me a ride," she answered.

"I have a better idea." Luke was hatching a small conspiracy to move things along with Rachel. "Take my car. I may be out with this flu for a few days, so you might just as well use it." Rachel was going to protest. "Listen, Rachel, I'm sick!" Luke was whimpering. "Don't make me argue with you." He fell back onto the couch. "See, I'm getting worse!"

Rachel smiled, then slowly nodded. Disappearing briefly to clean up a few things in the kitchen, she returned to see Luke holding out a car key. "I still don't feel right about this," she fretted.

"Uh... uh... uh... uh," scolded Luke. "Take the key. Go!" He forced a smile. "Okay little flu guys, if this gal isn't out of here with the key by the count of ten, attack! One. Two. Three...

"All right! All right! I'm going." Giving his hand a brief squeeze as she took the key, Rachel headed for the door.

"That was good chicken soup," he called after her. Rachel turned, smiled, then quickly vanished down the hallway.

• • • • •

"Good morning W-Land! Heather Lane bringing you the soft spice that stings!" Kris shifted her bright voice into soft velvet. "And you love it!" Her voice brightened again. "If you're still stuck in bed, and you know you're going to be late, then at least stick your head outside the window. It is a gorgeous day! A light rain swept everything down while you slept. The clouds are gone! The sun is delivering us a 78 degree morning. Get out of there! Move! And to help you get going, I'll play your theme song, Mercy, Mercy, Mercy by Kenny G." Starting the disc, she turned off her mike.

Her new show had aired for just over a week in Milwaukee. Already the station was hearing upbeat reports from the retailers. This was good! It was the local businesses that bought air time. If they liked what they were hearing, it made sales that much easier. Kris had been given the best shift at the station. She worked Monday through Saturday from 6:00 a.m. until 10:00 a.m. WDFR radio, like many stations, had lots of fans this time of day. Milwaukee area listeners tuned in Heather Lane as they got ready for work; then as they left on their morning commute.

Kris worked through her morning shift until the clock read 9:55. "It's been great! Thanks for tuning in WDFR and letting Heather Lane share your morning. Nick Turner is next. Stay with him, he needs all the W-Land listeners he can get!"

"Hey!" cried Nick in the background. "They just tolerate you until the duke of jazz saddles up and rides the airwaves."

"Ride 'em high!" teased Kris into the microphone. "And for those of you who aren't cowboys and trail chicks, I'll bring back the velvet tomorrow at 6:00. Have a good one!" Winking at Nick, Kris started the electronically mastered duet, Unforgettable, by Nat King Cole and daughter Natalie. Giving up the studio chair to Nick, she headed for the door. Kris would relax for about fifteen minutes in the station employee lounge before starting production. Typically it took the remainder of the morning and into the early afternoon for her to create and cut commercials for sponsors. If she finished her assignments in the morning, the rest of the day was hers.

Today she had a light load. She would be done before noon. Looking out the production room window into the station office area, she saw Rich. One look and she blushed. After many weeks of dating him, Kris still became weak when she first saw Rich when he returned from his business trips. This was a good day to be done at noon! Rich smiled when he saw her. Kris felt her skin redden more. "I hate this," she murmured. Turning around she began fussing with some technical equipment to conceal her face. "I just need to buy a few moments," she patronized herself, "then maybe I won't look like a blushing, first date, idiot!"

Rich sat down at an empty desk to wait for Kris to finish up. It had been a rough week for him. When he started with the company, he enjoyed the travel. He was single and there were lots of sights to see. Now that he was dating Kris, road trips seemed longer and offered less in return.

Emerging from the production studio, Kris bee-lined to Rich. Still smiling, he rose and took her hands pulling them to his side. Leaning into him, she then drew back. "I have the rest of the day free!"

"What a coincidence," said Rich, "I just happen to have made reservations for two at McBride's. I was trying to think of someone who might like to join me. Since you have the afternoon open..." Rich stopped and dramatically shook his head. "No. It is unfair to offer you such a short notice. You might start believing that I'm taking you for granted. I had better ask Brenda. I know that she would go with me, even on such short notice."

"Yeah, she would," laughed Kris, "but over my dead body!" She squeezed his arm. "Let's get out of here before you look around to find other short notice specialists!" They walked out the door to Rich's leased Volvo. He opened the door, Kris slipped in pressing the boundary between her and the driver's seat. Kris threw her arms around Rich as he entered the car, laying her head against his neck. "I'm so glad to see you!"

"It has only been three days!" he laughed.

"Don't go to the restroom when we get to McBride's," she warned, "because if you're gone for more than three minutes, I'm coming in after you. And when I find you in there, I'm giving you a big hug as the guys watch!"

Rich buried his right hand into the thick hair falling behind her neck. Pulling away his hand, he lifted her chin from his chest. He kissed her tenderly, then pulled back. "Are you hungry for a good steak?"

"Yeah," she said, "but you know what's really crazy, I'm just dying for a big bowl of chicken soup."

"Done!" said Rich. "But I'm afraid we will have to cancel our reservations at McBride's!"

"What are you up to, Ricardo Labano?" Putting on her skeptical look, Kris held Rich in its schoolmaster's gaze.

"You cannot eat chicken soup at McBride's!" he answered. "That's not allowed!" Rich acted as if everyone in the world, but Kris, knew that it would be silly to order chicken soup at McBride's. "Of course, we must go to Mama Katreli's for chicken soup. Use my cellular. There is a city directory lying on the back seat. Why don't you call Mama Katreli's and see if they can fit us in today. If so, give a call to McBride's and cancel our reservation. If it is chicken soup you want, it is chicken soup you'll get!"

Mama Katreli's had openings, and Rich and Kris were seated in a small booth facing a busy street of downtown Milwaukee. "I was sicker than a dying dog when I got back Monday morning from Mom and Dad's," said Kris.

"Strange," he said, "I was very sick that morning too."

"Gads!" exclaimed Kris. "I hope that mom didn't serve up tainted food."

"Who knows," replied Rich. "If she did, her cooking is so good that I would gladly get sick for a day or two just to eat another one of her feasts!"

"What am I going to do with you!" Kris shook her head. "You always know how to put things in the best way. You're really too good for me you know."

Reaching over with his left hand, Rich took hold of both her hands. Kris had let them lay on the table as bait, inviting his touch. Suddenly Rich raised his right hand to his face. Extending his index finger, he moved it back and forth in front of his mouth. "No more of that talk," he said with the pretense of a frown. "If you are going to talk about me, then talk about a subject that's dear to my heart. Let's talk about you!" Rich reached down cradling both of hers in his strong, masculine hands. "Being with you is like walking along the beach at dawn. I never tire of the beauty and freshness I experience."

Lifting her shoulders like sails caught in a warm wind, Kris sighed deeply. Innocently her eyes gawk back at Rich. "I feel like a silly schoolgirl right now," she thought to herself.

"I've got to tell you what I did last night," Kris said. "I went to evening worship at a neighborhood Lutheran church near my apartment. They posted a sign about a contemporary worship service on Wednesday evenings. It's tough for me to get up on Sundays, but I just felt like I needed to go. Do you know what? It felt good. It felt really good!"

Rich smiled as she continued, "I never missed Sunday worship as a kid. Then came broadcasting school, and I still worshiped now and then. Finally, I just fell out of the habit."

"In my faith, it is a sin not to worship," replied Rich.

"I suppose that it's a sin in my faith, too," she laughed, "but grace covers it all, doesn't it?"

"Yes," said Rich. His eyes smiled back at Kris. "But I don't think that God intended His grace to make us ignore what's best for us."

"I'm not sure what you do on Sunday morning. As you know," pouted Kris, an obvious reference to their discussion on the moonlit beach, "we've never woken up in the morning together." She paused musing over a whole new thought. "Are you trying to tell me that you always worship on Sunday?"

"Not always, I'm afraid," he said. "Sometimes when I am on the road it is impossible for me to attend Mass. When I am home in Milwaukee? Yes, I attend Mass regularly."

"I don't believe it!" said Kris. "How come you've never shared this with me?"

"Well, you know," he squeezed her hands, smiling broadly, "you don't come up to a girl and say, 'Would you go out with me? I attend Mass regularly.'"

Kris pulled her hands away from Rich. "Stop it! You know what I mean. We've been dating for a while now, and I had no idea that you held such deep religious convictions."

"Actually, that's really too bad," he reflected seriously. "I come by it honestly. My family is very devout, but we are equally private about such matters."

"Will you make me a promise?" asked Kris, clearly setting Rich up for something.

"What promise would you have me make?" came the accent laced reply.

"Would you take me with you some morning when you go to church?"

Rich was surprised. "Yes," he said with his right eyebrow raised. "But you know that our way of worship may be different than what you are accustomed to experiencing. But yes, if that's what you would like, we will go together some Sunday morning. But on one condition. I want to go with you to an evening worship service at your neighborhood church. Is it a deal?"

"Yes," said Kris smartly. "To quote my best friend, 'Done and done!' And so we don't put it off, how about going to your church next Sunday? We can follow up next Wednesday in my neighborhood." Rich smiled at her with his eyes and lips. Leaning forward, Kris's voice became tentative and childlike. "Well, what do you think?"

Rich checked his calendar noting that both days worked for him. "Done and done!" he said with a wink. The angels sang in heaven.

"Boy, this is good chicken soup," said Kris.

Chapter 11:

FILTHY LUCRE

They hid under the shades of night. Two men, as they watched soldiers stationed on an obscure country road just outside Moscow, were waiting for an opportunity to slip back into the city. The soldiers were laughing, the orange glow of their cigarettes igniting with every puff. Leaning against a military truck straddling the gravel road, the guards' automatic rifles were slung to the side. The Russian soldiers were anything but on guard. It was another early morning watch, tedious as the morning before. The only action during their duty involved insects that flew, chirped, and bit. No one was left to escape from Moscow, and only an idiot would try to enter the cursed city.

"We will never get in if we must wait for the soldiers to leave," whispered one of the Russian men. "They face towards us into the woodlands, so they are blind to the road as it moves toward Moscow. I say we take the risk, slip by them through the trees, and hope that they will not look back toward the city until we pass the clearing. We are only in danger for five, maybe ten, minutes until we are over the hill."

"The road beyond these trees is wide open," whispered the other. "If just one of them turns to look back at the city, we are dead."

"I can think of ten million reasons in British Gold Sovereigns for taking the chance," replied the first. "You stay here if you like. I am leaving." Darting to his left, the one Russian began running from shadow to shadow, taking advantage of the cover provided by trees along his path. The other Russian shrugged his shoulders and then followed. They worked their way through the woods, around the sentry, and finally stood at the edge of the small forest. The road that lay ahead of them offered no cover until it dropped down a hill in the far distance. The first Russian, face painted, dressed like the other in black, looked back toward the truck and then started to run as fast as his rifle and backpack allowed. Shaking his head, the second followed, although slower, carrying an additional thirty pounds of body mass.

"Stop!" commanded a Russian soldier. The two men continued to run, cursing in their mother tongue. The commander could have ordered his men to shoot. Their targets were in clear view under the half-moon above. Instead, he decided to capture the men and discover their intentions for entering Moscow. Likely, given the backpacks that they carried, they were just looters. Yet the chase would provide a great sport breaking the tedium of another eventless watch. Ordering his men into the truck, the commander watched the driver bolt with him into the cab. Hotly in pursuit, the truck bounced over the rough meadow chasing down the footmen.

Leaning out the rider's window, the Russian commander fired shots of intimidation in the direction of the fleeing men. The heavy-set intruder suddenly turned, grabbed his Uzi, dropped to the ground, and fired rounds at the truck. The windshield exploded into fragments as the driver slumped forward against the wheel, his body jerking like a rag doll as the truck bumped aimlessly over the rough terrain. The commander, his left shoulder nearly torn from his torso by the repeated firing of the Uzi, opened the passenger door and jumped from the truck. The soldiers in the back also jumped, one wincing as his ankle bent sideways upon impacting the ground.

The Russian soldiers dashed for cover, attending to their wounded, as the two dark figures continued their break for Moscow. The truck carrying the soldier's communication gear struck a tree exploding into flames. There would be no radioing for help; no alerting of superiors concerning this deadly encounter.

The Russian Mafia hit men looked ahead toward the city. It was two kilometers to the outskirts of the sprawling residential area that encircled Moscow. Street lights froze the city in an unmoving, unblinking bath of light. There were no cars tracing their headlamps along city roads. No turning on and off of lights within homes and businesses. Lights left on remained on. Lights turned off remained silenced by darkness. As the two slid into the city, the one said, whispering as if the ears of death could hear, "I do not like this. We are taking a terrible chance being here. Have you no fear of the plague?"

"Why do you keep talking like this?" responded the other. "Did you want to wait for someone else to come for the gold? If you were afraid to take the risk, you should have stayed behind. It is a little late for your whimpering. Just remember, touch nothing! I think that it is time for us to put on the gas masks."

"Yeah, sure," said the other, "and once again, we are lunatics pretending that these masks can protect us from this virus."

"If you want to go back, then leave!"

Jogging down the hill, they faded into the shadows wherever buildings or trees provided cover. They feared Russian patrols traveling along country roads who would be using their field glasses to sweep the city for looters. More than this, they feared the satellites. They had heard stories about satellite technology reading the label on a package of cigarettes laying on the beach. There was no way that they could know if Moscow was under surveillance. Fearing the worst, they moved stealthily through the city, working under the assumption that satellites were watching everywhere.

Working their way down a residential street, the Russian goons hugged the sides of apartment buildings and fences. The city slept in silence until, off in the distance, they heard the sound of a truck. The clamoring engine of a heavy duty truck was growing louder. It was coming closer! Drawing back his right leg into the air, the larger Russian slammed the bottom of his boot hard against the lock on a door. Crack! The door burst open. Quickly they both slid inside the complex, moving, sometimes tripping, down a dark hallway. Once again the boot struck. An apartment door shattered and flung open to the side. Ahead of them, on the far wall, a curtainless window faced out upon a vacant street. Hiding to the side of the window, the men watched a transport turn the corner rumbling in their direction.

A large, slow-moving vehicle, appearing more like a bus than a truck, maneuvered by the building. Large windows to either side of the transport exposed a brightly lit room directly behind the driver. Technicians wearing white containment suits were slaving over technical equipment projecting from the floor, ceiling, and sides of the interior. "Look at how they travel through Moscow," said the antagonist to their clandestine operation, "and we are walking around in street clothes and silly gas masks."

The other waved him off. As the transport turned the corner, the heavy set man headed back through the doorway. On the table to their right he noticed the statue of a bird in flight, made out of silver. Taking it into his hands he exclaimed softly, "Pure silver!" With a quick glance around the room, he sighed, "No use to anyone here!" Opening a catch he slipped the silver bird into his bag.

Without warning the other Russian stopped his hand. "Don't be a fool!" he snarled. "We are going to be carrying out millions in gold coins. We will not have room for this. Leave it here!"

Pulling his hand free, the co-conspirator fired back a defiant look. The other locked with the defiant glance, shouting at his compatriot, "We do not have time for this! Take the statue! Take the damn kitchen table! I am here for the gold." Turning away toward the door, he quickly exited the apartment. Letting the statue drop to the floor, the other followed. Out on the street again, they moved slowly toward the Russian equivalent of an industrial park. The community of factories and warehouses lay near the point where they had breached the military quarantine around the city.

Just ahead was a section of the city displaying factories, towering chimneys, and assorted large machinery standing uselessly as if being stored or junked in the littered openings between poorly maintained buildings. One building sat like a windowless fortress, except for a few skylights invisible from the street. The two headed for that building. A decaying body, undiscovered by decontamination teams, was propped against a large steel box used to collect garbage. "Damn!" said one of the Mafia hit men.

Once again a locked building would be violated, but its metal door was too strong to be undone by even a muscular kick. In the distance stood a loader, its forked tines holding a large wooden crate, no doubt used to gather up the dead. The Russian who had assumed command of the two-man assault on the city jogged over to the forklift, sat down, and started it up. No problem! Unlike many Russian-made "lemons," this one worked without coaxing. Darting from the driver's seat, he kicked the wood platform off the front. Saddling up again, he fastened himself onto the forklift with the safety harness. Gunning the engine, he headed for the steel side of the building at ramming speed. Targeting an area without rivets, he managed to avoid the steel support beams. With a smash, the loader broke through the sheet metal, jolted halfway through the wall, then came to an abrupt stop.

Inside the building, stale air assaulted the driver's gas mask, seeking to punish him for desecrating this unnatural grave. A single light had been left on high above a table sitting on the other side of the warehouse. Dead bodies were scattered about on the floor or slumped over dirty ashtrays and molding coffee mugs cluttering the table. Jumping from the forklift, the Russian recognized a decomposing body. Making a face, he spit on the floor.

Meeting up with his partner who climbed through the breached wall, the two forged through the cluttered room. They were looking for something. On the far side, away from the light, they spotted what they had come for. A blue barrel sat alone, marked in Russian with the word for "solvent." Dashing over to the barrel, their spirits sank when they saw that the barrel had been opened. A decaying corpse lay by the barrel, clutching one of many clear plastic containers used to store British Gold Sovereigns.

Peering into the barrel they discovered shredded filler paper packed to the top of the container. Rummaging through the packing, the heavy-set Russian smiled. The barrel was still filled with containers of gold coins. Grabbing one from the barrel, he shoved it into the other's face. Both smiling, they quickly took the packs from their backs. Sifting through the paper, they searched out container after container, carefully arranging each within their bags. As they started walking away, the heavy-set deadweight to the mission spotted gold in the hand of a corpse. He reached down taking it into his gloved hand. "No!" cried the other. "That might be contaminated!"

"Too late now," said the other, "but if it makes you feel better, I will keep it separate in my pocket." An invisible entity, hunger lingering in its large green eyes, was wrapped about the poor Russian goon. The Shadow of Death stood to the side.

"You can keep it too!" snapped his partner. "You are the one who is taking a terrible risk handling gold from the victim of the virus! It is your death!"

Making their way out of the city, they decided to take a longer route to avoid the scene of their entry. No doubt the soldiers they'd exchanged fire with that morning had received backups. Soon the breached area would be crawling with soldiers and technicians wearing white containment suits. At the outskirts of the suburbs, a truck rambled towards them on the same road. Jumping for the ditch, they crawled into a large culvert. The military transport reverberated above them only to pass from view as the road curved left. Soldiers wearing white protective suits sat on benches in the back of the truck. The incident at the roadblock was already stimulating significant activity in that part of Moscow. The Russian hit men would be getting out of the city none too soon.

Taking the journey with them, unseen but present, was Molech. He was holding the Shadow of Death at bay. The virus, created out of hell's belly by scientists duped into believing that they had constructed it, would have taken the lives of these men within the hour. Molech, however, had bigger plans for the effects of the virus. Death's hunger would remain unsatisfied until Molech was done with its pawns.

Late in the afternoon, the Mafia team reached their car. Their get-away transport had been concealed under a country bridge. The men were tired. Dead tired! The weight of the gold that they lugged in their packs, however, was no match for the greed carrying them to their car. Loading up their vehicle the two soon raced along a carefully designed route to Zurich. Molech rode with them, placing one ghastly hand on each of their shoulders. The demon continued to hold back the onslaught of the disease.

The major stash of coins had been carefully concealed under blankets in the trunk. One pack of gold coins had been placed under the rider's seat. It would be used to pay off corrupted border guards. Bribes along the way would ensure the fact that when the trunk was opened, it wouldn't be searched. Each border crossing had been carefully studied. The fleeing Russians knew who would be on duty at each shift, what guards would take bribes, and which guards were loyal Russians. At one point the two mobsters stopped, waiting in the distance for over five hours, until the next shift took duty. It was the only shift at that particular checkpoint that had a guard who was in their pocket, an addicted gambler always short on cash.

Reaching Zurich, they holed up at a rundown hotel in the brothel area of the city. It was a dangerous game they were playing. These two Mafia muscles had ripped-off their Mafia bosses. Now they must lay low, maybe even for years. Each understood that they couldn't make major purchases that would draw attention. The British gold sovereigns would be sold off bit by bit for years. The Internet would help them circulate the coins back into the economy by connecting them with precious coin merchants around the world.

A few coins were sold right away for needed cash, but not so many as to draw questions from the downtown Zurich dealer. Passing themselves off as tourists who had bought some British coins, they pretended to be out of funds and needing to sell their souvenirs for cash. Money in hand, they used the first fruits of their theft to raise hell in the brothels and bars of Zurich. One Russian, however, soon returned to the hotel sick. Molech had given him over to death. It was time to set loose the plague in Zurich. Molech would direct attention away from Dane Morrell and her coven.

An hour later, the second returned briefly to the hotel room. Entering it after quickly placing on a gas mask, he lugged a suitcase one-quarter filled with sand. Packing the gold into the sand, he left the coins pocketed in his dying partner's coat. His comrade lay in a fevered sweat, unable to stop the theft of his share of the take. "Sorry friend," said the one through his mask, "but this is no good to you now! I told you not to take the contaminated gold." He left the room as the Shadow of Death sucked away the dying atheist. Death looked lustfully after the departing partner still protected under Molech's care. It was only a matter of time before the remaining Russian would be death's dessert.

· · · · ·

"Do you think it's a good idea to travel out of the States?" asked Kris, her anxious mind thick with worry and concern. She had phoned Bill after an e-mail from Briggs mentioning that he was leaving for Europe. "Whatever is happening in Moscow scares the daylights out of me! Do you know any more?"

"Not really," dodged Bill.

"Ah, you're lying to me again, aren't you big brother?" Kris sought to be coy, but her voice cracked. "There are parts of your work that you keep from everybody. I've learned to live with that, but when you listen to the news... I'm worried sick about what's going on in the Mideast and Moscow. Stay here, Bill, don't go. Who knows what might happen to you?"

"Boy, what color is the sky where you live?" laughed Bill. He hid a weak smile behind the phone lines. "I'm just taking a quick trip to Zurich. Just a routine meeting with others working in the global community on infectious diseases, that sort of stuff. Say! Switching gears, how's tall, dark and lonesome doing?"

"Lonesome? I hope so! He's traveling too," Kris pouted. "I'm just glad that he's staying in the good-old U. S. of A!" Kris was a black belt in worry. For years she fretted over Bill and her parents. Luke was tame, but now Rich had been added to her fret list.

"You really care for him, don't you Kris?"

"Yeah... I sure do," she sighed. "But I think that he's too good for me."

"You too!" sported back Bill.

"Hey, whose side are you on?" protested Kris.

"The winning side," shot back Bill with a grin, briefly forgetting about his trip to Zurich.

"Then, dear brother," Kris said, drawing him in with her smooth, DJ voice, "that'd be my side. If Rich were to get serious, I'd be the winner!"

Continuing their chat, Bill shared little stories about his adjustment to married life. After promising his sister that, for Briggs' sake, he would always leave the seat down on the toilet, the siblings said their goodbyes. A framed picture of Rich sat on the counter of Kris's small apartment. It was a Kodak special, enlarged to fit the frame, showing Rich sitting on the pontoon at Lake Minnetonka as the sun set just behind him on the far shore of the lake. Taking the picture into her hands, Kris pressed the glass against her lips. "I'm thinking of you, sweetheart," she said, returning the picture to the counter.

She decided to finish off the evening under a large feathered comforter, sipping hot cocoa, and reading another chronicle from The Book of Talyara. She enjoyed fantasy. It kept her problems at a distance and made life feel bigger than the stuff served up by everyday life. Kris had little time for the smug intellectuals who thought they had everything figured out. She knew that whatever surrounded planet earth was bigger than the ocean of stars. There was a numinous quality to life lying just over the horizon for those who had enough faith to keep walking. She walked life. Too many stopped the adventure with the prosaic pontifications of the applied sciences. Not her! Kris knew that you couldn't fit the meaning of life into the little boxes revealed by the fives senses. Since Rich and his faith had become part of her life, she had begun to process these ethereal feelings in terms of what she had learned as a child at her sainted grandmother's knee.

· · · · ·

"Good morning Pastor," smiled Tamor. Tilting her head to the side, she looked up at Luke as he walked into the parish office. "How are you today?"

"Just great!" he said. "It's a day for playing hooky! I thought about calling in sick, but twice might have raised eyebrows. Would you have been suspicious, Tamor?"

"Are you kidding? Look at that sun! It's enough to make a preacher lie." She winked.

Luke winked back. "Well, do you have any messes... I mean messages for me?"

"Just to mention that your brother Bill called. He said that you shouldn't try to call him back. He's leaving for Zurich soon. He said something about keeping an eye on Kris and her wild imagination."

"He's right about that imagination!" Luke laughed. "I talked to her just the other day, and this thing in Moscow has her thinking that the Apocalypse is upon us! If Kris found out that Bill was flying to Zurich, she's thinking that her brother is going to die in Moscow."

"Well, as I see it Pastor," replied Tamor with an edge of seriousness imposing upon her indisputable good nature, "I think it's high time the Lord does get down here! In case you haven't noticed, things are pretty messed up in the world today."

Luke just smiled. He liked Tamor, but she shared that same naivete toward religion that he saw in Rachel. Seminary training had taught him not to challenge pew-pious parishioners with the inside scoop. He had no battle to win, no point to prove. If his people lived comfortably within their little religious worldview, what was that to him? The only roadblock involved social issues. In time he would need to help them accept many things about human conduct that they had previously called sin. But there was plenty of time before starting into the troublesome waters of change. First, he would win their trust.

"Oh, and Rachel called," continued Tamor. "I think that she plans to stop by when you're done at the office today. Her car is fixed and she would like to pick it up and return your vehicle."

"Great," thought Luke to himself, "the setup is working right on schedule!"

"I'll give you her number," Tamor said, handing Luke a pink phone message slip.

"Thanks." Luke took the note. "I'll call her right away and plan things out." Tamor smiled knowingly.

"What's that look?" sported Luke, twisting his head a slight turn to the left.

"Oh nothing," smiled Tamor. "You had better scoot and give her a call. I think she's waiting." Tamor gave a second serving of that same look.

Walking away from Tamor, Luke felt a little uncomfortable. He didn't know where things were going between Rachel and himself, especially now that the lady in red made daily visits within his mind. It would get uncomfortable if rumors started around the church about the new pastor and a woman in the parish. Still, he was confident in Tamor's good sense about such matters. She might tease him, but she'd never breathe a word about her suspicions to anyone else.

Assured that he was safe from any false impressions, at least for the time being, he went to his study and punched in the number on the note. "Hello," came Rachel's familiar voice. Luke was amazed to find his throat thickening like a schoolboy carting a crush. The lady in red flashed before him.

Clearing his throat, Luke forced away competing thoughts. "Hi Rachel. This is your favorite pastor returning your call." It was a bad tease, but he was nervous after all.

"Hi Pastor Horton," said Rachel. She would have some fun with Luke's blunder.

"Well," Luke didn't skip a beat, "I now know who your favorite pastor is!"

"Oh, Pastor Luke, it's you," she teased. "You got my message!" Rachel continued to master the conversation ignoring Luke's lure. She'd keep the upper hand in this charade. "Maybe Tamor told you that my car is fixed at the shop. I was wondering if we could catch a ride together when you're done at the church? I'd pick you up then we could go get my car. After that, you'd have your car and I'd have mine, and all's right with the world!"

"If that'll fix the world, let's do it!" He paused. "But after we fix the world, how about enjoying it awhile... together? We could leave a little before five and plan for pizza right after we drop off your car?"

"Sure," Rachel returned, "but I'll need to juggle a few things around. Oh, never mind! Yes! I haven't had pizza for over a month. What time should I come?"

"Let's say 4:30, giving us plenty of time to get to the garage before it closes."

"I'll see you then at 4:30?"

"Unless the rapture takes place before I get there," joked Luke.

"See you, Pastor," replied Rachel, searching for the humor in Luke's sarcasm. "Bye!"

Luke wondered how long it would take before she would start calling him by his first name. It was an awkward thing to bring up. Something had to be, at the very least, simmering between them before he invited Rachel to call him Luke. Until then, the word 'pastor' would continue the barrier of professionalism that Luke was eager to demolish. His lustful fantasies, stirred on by the lurking figure of a phantom woman in red, increased his desires to become more familiar with Rachel.

· · · · ·

Kris stared at the newswire. What she read fear-froze the news release to her hand. A press leak out of Zurich told the story about an outbreak of an unknown deadly disease that had already claimed more than a dozen lives within the city. Government officials were calling the report irresponsible, but they were not denying it. Kris knew that Bill hadn't given her the whole story over the phone. Unnerved about Bill's trip to Zurich, she left the radio station for the day, her production assignments remaining unfinished. She desperately wanted to call Luke in the worst way, but no, first she would get herself under control. Kris wasn't about to give her brother more ammunition for labeling her a member of the crazed, paranoid fringe.

Arriving at her apartment, she paced back and forth. In the background, a cable news station aired a talking head bringing news to the nation. "I wish that Rich were here," she thought. "He's like Luke. Rich knows how to hit the right buttons for settling me down." She lifted the phone and took a chance. Dialing the number to his cellular phone, she hoped to catch Rich while he was driving between appointments. "Hello, Ricardo Labano." His accent dripped from the receiver.

"Rich," came her voice. It was timid as a little girl's. "I'm sorry to bother you."

"To hear your voice is never a bother! This is the brightest moment of my day."

Instantly half of her anxiety slipped away. "It is so good to hear your voice!"

"Is there something the matter, Kris?"

"Yeah, I guess there is," she said. Tapping her fingers on a wooden table, she was determined not to sound hysterical. "Have you heard about Zurich?"

"You mean the press release about the unusual deaths?" he asked.

"Yes, and Rich, Bill is on his way to Zurich! I phoned him. I asked him not to go! I told him to stay home even before I had heard anything about Zurich. I was worried about Moscow! This is even worse! Moscow is contained. The outbreak is just beginning in Zurich!" She was sounding hysterical. The gushing words overflowed her defenses, mastering the situation.

"Tell you what," Rich said, "I am right now heading to the airport. I will be back in Milwaukee by 7:00 this evening. What do you think about a late supper tonight? I'll swing by and get you. Do we have a date?"

"We have a date," replied Kris. She sounded like a young daughter who had asked too much of her father, then feeling ashamed when the father gave more than she had asked for. The Labano magic had worked its charm and Kris was under control. Focusing on her date with Rich only a few hours away, she harnessed her anxious fears about Bill.

"Will you be okay until then?" he asked.

"Yeah," she said. "I won't say that I'll be fine, but knowing that I'll see you soon, I feel much better."

· · · · ·

Rachel picked up Luke at the church, then drove to the repair shop. Settling the repair bill, she led the way back to her house. Parking her car, Rachel joined Luke as he drove them to a neighborhood pizza joint. Jake's Pizza was tucked far back into a forested hill within the suburbs. Its multicolored neon sign rose into the evening sky calling for visitors. Luke opened the passenger door, and together they walked toward Jake's. Luke's hand brushed several times against Rachel's. He wondered if she'd noticed. They were seated at a table covered with a plastic green and black checkered tablecloth. Ordering a large pepperoni pizza, they waited for their sodas to be brought to the table. Luke started the conversation. "I'm a little concerned about my brother Bill. Have you heard about the problems in Zurich? Bill's going there on some kind of assignment for OIDC."

Rachel leaned forward, her face suddenly overcast. "I'll need to add him to my prayers," she replied. Her hand reached across the table to take hold of Luke's hand.

Luke smiled. "Oh, I said I was a little concerned. Bill deals with this stuff all the time. He's probably more safe with the precautions that he'll take in Zurich than we are sitting in this public pizza joint." He took a chance, placing his free hand on top of hers. "I hope you don't mind me saying this. It's a bit personal, but heck, you have seen me in my pajamas!" They laughed.

"Well, let's have it," said Rachel with upturned eyebrows.

"I just wanted to say that it felt good when you took... my hand," he smiled, a bit nervous. "Did you only do it 'cause of concern for my big brother?"

She pulled her hand from his. "Yes," she said matter-of-factly. Then she smiled taking his hand with both of hers. "This time I'm taking your hand because I want to do it. How often does a girl get to hold the pastor's hand?"

"Ah, and that brings me to a second item," broke in Luke. Rachel captured him with a smile. Looking as if she were completely at home within the situation, she was a significant contrast to what was going on inside of Luke. "I was wondering how you'd feel about calling me Luke?"

"Now that's going to be a tough one," laughed Rachel. "It's strange, you know..."

"What?"

"When I think about you, I always think Luke. But when I'm around you, I always say pastor." Rachel stopped, thinking over what she'd just said. "I think the Lord would say, 'Rachel, call him Luke!'" Squeezing his hand in hers, she then lifted her hands from the table, running long fingers through her thick hair.

"Well, on this one the Lord and I are in agreement," smiled Luke.

"Does that mean that you're not always agreeing with the Lord?" baited Rachel.

"Rachel, I don't want to blow you away, but sometimes I'm not even sure what He's saying!" Luke knew he was taking a chance. Her willingness to call him Luke had brought them beyond the pastor/parishioner relationship. Still, in his own family, he had seen how his remarks could threaten those uninitiated to new trends in theology.

"I pretty much take what the Bible says as God's message to us," noted Rachel. It wasn't the response of a woman who was simple. Rachel's demeanor seasoned her words with the sense that she had faced hard issues within her own faith walk.

Luke saw Rachel's depth. Her thoughts ran deeper than mere opinions. Sensing that Rachel was grounded, he risked more. "Most religions believe that their god or gods have spoken all that needs to be said. You know as well as I do, Rachel, that many of our Christian beliefs don't stand well with other religious views. I learned at the seminary to be a little less certain... a little more modest about the infallibility of the Christian worldview."

"I see," smiled Rachel. "I once thought that way too. But I changed my mind."

"Why the change?"

"Sitting down on my garden bench one day, I decided to figure out what options are out there concerning the meaning of God." Rachel straightened up in her chair. "Surprisingly, I decided that there are only four possibilities that sum up what common sense has to say about what God means for us... I mean for humanity!"

"Common sense?" Luke's smile broadened

"Yes" sported Rachel, "common sense!"

"Wow," teased Luke, "common sense reduces the whole debate about God into four points! I wish I had you as a seminary professor! The tests would have been a whole lot shorter." They laughed. "So, tell me the four options that common sense serves up concerning God."

"Okay," continued Rachel, "but are you sure you're up for this?"

"Fire away," smiled Luke.

"Option one," shot back Rachel, "says that there is no God or pantheon of gods."

"That's a straightforward possibility," said Luke. "Option one, if I understand you right, simply says that there's no God or bunch of gods." He nodded, his head showing that he understood her first option. "A lot of people hold to that. What's option number two?"

"Options two and three deal with the issue of evil in the world. Option two says that God is all powerful but that He is not completely good. So when bad things happen, it's just what you expect from Him. He does good things and He does bad things. No one can fault Him when He acts wickedly, because He's God."

"You say 'He' when you speak of God," sported Luke. "Are you sure that God isn't a She?"

"Don't get me started," Rachel shook her head and smiled. Luke got the point. Rachel didn't want to get into that subject–not now. "Getting back to option two, I couldn't worship a God who is all powerful but not completely good. I concluded that if God were all powerful but not good, He would make little difference for my life anyway. How could I trust a God who was also evil? He could seek to hurt me just as well as try and help me."

"What's the third option?" Luke asked. He looked at Rachel's lips as she spoke. He had planned for other conversation that evening, but now he was held captive to Rachel's thinking.

"Again, given the evil that we see in the world, like the deaths at Zurich, it is also possible that God could exist, be completely good, but not have enough power to restrain evil. Such a God I could pity, but I could never worship."

"So, if God were evil and all powerful," replied Luke, "you wouldn't worship Him because of the evil. On the other hand, if God were completely good but not all powerful, you could only pity Him."

"That's right," nodded Rachel. "I would refuse to worship an evil God, and I could only pity a weak deity. In either case, such a God is no use to me or to all humanity! Either a wicked God or a weak God leaves humanity equally trapped by evil and confused about what's really good or right. So the only option left, as I saw it, was to conclude that God is completely good and at the same time limitless in power."

"But then what about all the evil in the world?" continued Luke. "How can a good and all powerful God allow all of the bad things that we see in the world?"

"The evil in the world," she replied, "is something we bring to it, not God. God manages the evil for our sake and makes it serve His ultimate purpose. If God allows His children to suffer for a short time in this world, that can't compare to the good that He plans to give them for all eternity."

"But why not settle for option one?" asked Luke. "When you see all the terrible evil, why not conclude that there simply is no God at all?"

"Because the order we see in the world cries out for a Creator!" Rachel's voice swelled with passion. "If you went to Mount Rushmore and looked at the engravings of the four presidents, you would assume that someone had created it—carved it. You wouldn't for an instant believe that it happened by random chance. Common sense demands the obvious. It would be obvious to you that intelligence had left its mark on the mountain. No one would convince you that the intricate design happened over millions of years because of random wind and rain erosion."

"Some scientists," cautioned Luke, "say that the order we see is the product of billions of years of chance occurrences that brought about structure without the need for a cosmic designer."

"Yeah, and other scientists who do the math realize that random chance could never result in the order we see on this planet. So they talk about life on this planet being seeded by aliens from Mars. That makes no sense. Common sense says it's nonsense to conclude that the complexity we see could happen by chance. That's like saying that if you allowed one hundred million tornadoes to tear through a dump, someday the twirling winds would make a Mack truck! Come on, Luke, do you really think that could happen? Of course not! Neither do I."

"That's cool, Rachel," replied Luke. He was impressed by her crafting of the argument from design. There was still another catch to this position, however, that had been argued by a British philosopher. "Did you know, however, that there is a philosopher by the name of David Hume who shot all kinds of holes in that argument?"

"Would it surprise you to hear that I have read his argument?" smiled back Rachel. "It only works because he makes all his terms swim around in a circular argument where he forces us to accept his conclusion because we have agreed to his terms." Rachel looked out the window. "I think that the meaning of God is far bigger than what human language can describe."

"Are you saying then that we can't talk about God?" protested Luke. "Is He beyond us like the mystics tell us?"

"No," she answered. "We know Him through His Word."

"But you said that God was bigger than human language..."

"I mean," she spoke emphatically, "that the fullness of God is bigger than our language." Rachel fished around in her mind for an illustration. "Just because I can't get the whole vista of a landscape in the viewfinder of my camera, doesn't mean that I can't take any picture at all. God has given us pictures of Himself in the Bible. We know something about Him because He has given us specific glimpses into His mind and heart."

"But..." replied Luke, "if I may continue to play the devil's advocate, even if we agreed that there was one all powerful and good God, there is no reason to assume that it's the Christian's God. Perhaps He—or She—is expressed within countless religions all over the world."

"Well, there are a couple of answers to that 'devil's argument'," winked Rachel. She continued to look very comfortable as she stood in theological waters with Luke. "First of all, I want you to consider a question. Have you ever noticed that the human race is the only species on the planet that has no instinctive drive for organizing its society? Certain bees will always build certain kinds of hives and always the same way because they are driven to do so. They will never call a town meeting and question whether they should change the design. Am I right?"

Luke smiled.

"In the same way, wolves will never have a meeting to discuss whether or not they should stop running in packs. The issue is settled. Their instinctive drives make them run in packs." It was her turn to deliver a grin. "Am I still right?"

The waitress brought their sodas. "I guess so," said Luke cautiously. He had been led down too many rhetorical traps at the seminary to fall into one easily.

"Mankind has no one pattern for organizing its society," continued Rachel. "That's why we have so many cultures." She sighed. "That's why we have so many wars... So if God is completely good and totally powerful, why would He allow mankind, the center of His creation, to be clueless about how each member should live within the whole?"

"That's a good question," Luke smiled, really to himself, watching Rachel artfully lay out her theological reasoning. At first he was prepared to humor her opinion. After listening to her, he was ready to take her seriously.

She leaned back pressing her argument forward. "God designed the human family so that our relationship with each other flowed from our relationship with Him. When Eden fell, our broken relationship with God had a secondary consequence. We no longer knew how to relate with each other. When things were right between Adam and Eve with God, Adam and Eve related perfectly with each other. No one had to tell them how to be loving. Love simply flowed naturally between them because of the loving bond that they had with God."

Luke winced inside. He figured that Rachel would take the Fall of Eden literally. It still bothered him to hear her say so, especially because she was obviously intelligent. "I'm still not sure how humankind's lack of a blueprint for society supports your fourth option."

"When the human race fell," Rachel responded, "God decided to work with one group of people to reveal His will for all people. He would use a chosen race to bring into history the Savior promised in the Book of Genesis, just after the Fall."

"So you're saying that Israel is that chosen race?" interjected Luke.

"He called Abraham," answered Rachel, "and this man believed God. God then made many promises to him, including the covenant to bless the whole world through his offspring."

"How do you know that all of the things mentioned in the Old Testament are true?" asked Luke. He was taking a chance. Revealing his skeptic nature jeopardized his other role as Rachel's pastor.

"I don't know for certain that everything in the Bible is true," answered Rachel. "Not in the sense that I know you are sitting in front of me. I just keep using common sense and stick with my four options. I rejected option one because I saw intelligence behind the world's order and complexity. I rejected option two because I refused to worship an evil deity. I finally also rejected option three because a weak God was to be pitied, not adored. There remained only one option left."

"So you concluded that God must be completely good and totally powerful," summarized Luke.

"Yep, I did," answered Rachel transparently. "A totally loving and powerful God wouldn't leave us in a mess after the Fall. His answer to our dilemma was the creation of one great, true religion."

"And that one great, true religion must be the Judeo-Christian faith?" asked Luke.

Rachel paused, seeking to size up her argument through Luke's eyes. "Until God restores perfection to the human family," she continued, "I believe that He has related His truth to us through a religion created by the Holy Spirit from the very Word of God, the Bible. That's why I believe it must be true! The Bible is the only true revelation of almighty God. The Word of God is His way of shaping human conduct and revealing His saving plan. He creates human society out of chaos by conforming the will of His people to His Word."

"That's a good argument," admitted Luke honestly. "I've never heard it put quite that way before. But how can you be so sure that it is the Christian religion that reflects the will of this all powerful, all loving God?"

"Let me ask you a couple more questions," she replied. "First off, have you ever noticed how dusty the Judeo-Christian faith is? By that I mean that we keep digging up artifacts that prove individuals and events mentioned in the Bible? Almost all other religions don't have a historical basis. A Hindu wouldn't ever expect to find something at a dig that was used by Krishna. They don't even look at history like Western culture! And in the Koran there are many events also mentioned in the Bible that are clearly out of sequence, but the followers of Islam simply say that Allah can put events wherever! The Judeo-Christian faith doesn't do that. What's more, it seems that things doubted by liberal theologians have since been proven by archeological finds."

Luke thought about the monolith mentioning King David, and the more recent find of the tomb of a Jewish priest. "Okay, for now I'll concede that Christianity has a strong historical basis. What's your next question?"

"Okay! How would you come to understand me best? By placing me on an examination table and then dissecting me down to my cells? Or, by relating with me through conversation, work, and play?"

"I suppose that the products of dissection could fit almost any human being," he replied. "To know you, I would need to talk with you and, I guess, generally spend time with you."

"In the same way, I know God because of my relationship with Him created as He speaks to me from the Bible. I know God as I live with Him, pray to Him, and watch as He works in my life. I remember reading a quote somewhere from a key figure in the German Reformation period..."

"Martin Luther?" asked Luke.

"Yes, Martin Luther...." Rachel had studied Luther and Calvin, but had decided not to be a name dropper. "Luther once wrote that you know God by His benefits. Not only does the Word of God tell me so much about everyday life, but more importantly, through it I have experienced the power of God. I have felt God's grace. I believe option four to be true because, as Luther would say, I have experienced His benefits within my Christian walk. I know that He exists in much the same way that I know that you exist. If someone tried to tell me that you were a figment of my imagination, I would laugh." She reached over and squeezed his hand firmly. "Luke, that's because I know you. I also know God. I know things about His personality. I know that He is all powerful, holy, and filled with love and mercy."

"You're getting too theological for me," Luke joked, an obvious dodge to divert their discussion away from theology. Secretly, her logic was unsettling. He could see where she was leading. Her argument took the discussion in a direction sounding far too much like Clint Lewis was a third party to their conversation. "I'm going to have to think about this for a while."

Rachel waited. She wondered what Luke was thinking–really! It didn't take long for her to find out, but it had nothing to do with theology.

"There is one thing that you did say." Luke smiled, it was a calculating smirk, looking a whole lot like the coy smile of his sister when she was about to move in for the kill. "You admitted, in your example, that the only way that I would get to know you better was to spend lots of time with you. Now the simple fact is that I would like to know you better! So according to the syllogistic logic I learned at the seminary, it seems that to make that happen, we're just going to have to spend more time together." He smiled broadly. "Don't blame me! It's Aristotle who came up with the logic!"

Rachel just smiled back. The waitress delivered the pizza rescuing Luke from floundering in his first major move on Rachel. She liked Luke. She was attracted to Luke. But strange as it was to think this way about a pastor, she wasn't ready to move too quickly into a relationship where she wasn't certain about the man's spirituality.

Chapter 12:
Powers of Death & Life

A smart looking high-rise condo located in a better suburb of Seattle towered below racing clouds. An expansive terrace jetted out from the main entrance to the condo. Brick walls surrounded its manicured, open area. Large, floral–design umbrellas flapped in the breeze above gleaming white tables. The building, built to resemble French architecture at the turn of the century, was only a few years old. Its outside walls wore a stucco finish, with hundreds of tinted windows darkly facing out on all sides. Large flower boxes hung from numerous balconies, sporting vivid colors against the grey-brown exterior.

It was 7:55 p.m. Expensive cars were pulling up to the visitor parking. Men and women walked out, fashionably dressed, each carrying a bag as they headed for the condo entrance. A friendly face was there to open the security doors allowing the guests to pass through. The visitors to Dirk Gadlaher's apartment sampled hors d'oeuvres, drank their bar favorites, and chatted about casual things. At 8:30, each opened up the bag that they had brought with them. Dirk's wife lit candles throughout the room as he turned off all electric lights. Men and women together took off their clothing. Street clothes were replaced with hooded black robes that covered their heads, eclipsing all facial features.

Two men unrolled a large black carpet. A golden pentagram was exposed, its points nicked the outside edge of the carpet. A bell rang. Each member lifted a stick of incense toward a nearby candle. Scented smoke began to fill the room. Dane Morrell entered wearing the same black robe of the coven. Squatting down at the center of the pentagram, she folded her legs beneath her. She did not look up. Her face vanished within the shadow of her hood. The devil himself could have been sitting hidden under the robe, in the dimness, surrounded by smoke.

Starting to chant, she swayed in rhythm to her monotone invitation to Molech and his demonic hordes. Soon all the coven members were swaying and chanting. Molech appeared beside Morrell within the pentagram. He was visible to the coven as a shadow, but Morrell saw nothing. The arch demon would not show his true face. One glance at its disfigured appearance and the very servants of Satan would flee in terror.

A hush fell upon them all. The room had become thick with the scent and smoke of the burning incense. Slowly Morrell lifted her head. A male voice spoke from the veiled darkness of the hood. The coven members listened. Some cut the back of their hands, drinking their own blood before it could fall to the floor. Others, unable to remain standing, sank to their knees or fell prostrate to the floor.

The Shadow of Death had sent its tentacles throughout the room. They passed through the robes and wrapped around scarred body parts; scars not seen by human eyes, but visible to powers and principalities. New wounds were being inflicted by the entity. More cutting of human flesh, as entranced members traced the path of invisible tentacles upon their own bodies with surgical knives. No blood poured from the fresh injuries. Death swelled as it drank in human blood and sweat. Some Satanists convulsed as the evil entity tightened its grip, dropping followers of Molech to the floor, their arms and legs flying out of control.

The hand of one fell across the golden pentagram. Instantly it burst into flames. Shrieking, the woman pulled it back. The flames vanished as red, painful blisters broke out over the exposed area of skin. The male voice continued to speak as if no sight of fire nor sound of pain had broken into the dark ritual. Finally Morrell's veiled face looked down. Molech vanished. Morrell arose, standing back as the carpet was rolled up and placed into a long canvas bag. Morrell sat down again on the hardwood floor. Coven members also sat down on the floor or pulled their prostrated bodies up from the floor to form a half-circle tightly about the coven mistress.

They looked to her faceless hood. She peered into their featureless faces hidden in the shadows of their hoods. "We have the virus. Tonight we will take the antidote. Before you leave, you will be given a can or plastic container to take with you to your cars. Each is filled with sand. The plastic containers are for those of you who must pass through metal detectors. At the center of each is a vial containing the virus. You are not to touch it until you reach your destination. After tonight, you will be immune to its effects, but others will not be safe. Our guardian wants the virus released at precisely the same time at each location. He does not want messy contaminations along the way. Do you all understand?"

"Yesssss," droned the coven members in unison.

"Some of you will travel by plane. Others of you will be driving your cars. Two present tonight will have a very complicated travel plan. The furthest point will require four and a half days of travel time. Five days from today, at a time tailored differently for each of you so that it reflects the various time zones, the virus will be released. Your time, your stop, and the means for delivering your vial of the virus will all be explained in your packet. Take it with you as you leave. No names have been written anywhere. Our great guardian himself will see to it that each of you get your own packet. It is another sign for you. It is another confirmation of his presence and great power."

A coven member entered from the kitchen carrying a tray. Plastic glasses, with a small amount of colored liquid, were offered to each person. Morrell was given a glass last. None imbibed until Morrell lifted her glass. In unison they brought the antidote to their lips and drank. A tray was passed again and all the empty glasses collected. Opening the bag they had brought to the meeting, each coven member removed their robes, dressing again into their street clothes. A container holding the virus had been prepared for each person and placed upon a table, along with a tailored packet of instructions.

Morrell positioned herself at the door as the coven dispersed for the night. Molech stood invisible to her side, his hand upon her hand. Each face that came before Morrell caused a deliberate shuffling through the packets until a certain one was given out. When the last person left the condo, two packets remained. The one she handed to Dirk, the other she placed into her bag. Finally, picking up one of the two remaining cans, Dane Morrell left into the silence of night.

• • • • •

Briggs decided to take a day off from work. Bill was still in Zurich, so she was free to do her own thing. She still had boxes at the apartment waiting to be unpacked and their contents mixed in with Bill's things. She thought about tackling a few, but decided to indulge in something less productive and more therapeutic. A lazy-day sun had parked itself in the eastern sky, warmly inviting Californians to enjoy the day. Briggs decided to go for a walk along the beach. This trip she would leave her dog at the apartment. It would take most of her morning to make the drive and her pet didn't travel well. Spewing out apologies to her hurt canine as she left out the door, she headed for the coastline along Santa Cruz.

Parking her car, she took a beach bag from the trunk. After applying a liberal dose of sunblock to her exposed skin, she took out her sunglasses. They had huge lenses, swallowing up the top half of her face as she placed them on her nose. Briggs laughed, "Not many of these models still around!" They dated to the psychedelic era of the late 60's. She had picked them up for twenty-five cents at a garage sale. They were outrageous and reserved for days like this when she wanted to make a statement, but not to anybody who knew her.

Reaching the beach, she removed her sandals and placed them in the beach bag. It felt good to dig her toes into the wet sand. Walking with her face in the sun, she enjoyed the ocean vista and the surrealistic quality of light as it glazed over the water. Keeping a keen eye to the sand, she was always hunting for that outstanding find, an ocean shell that was large, colorful, and fully intact. They were rare, too quickly snatched up by other shell hunters seeking after these trophies of nature routinely and randomly cast upon the beach by ocean waves.

Stranger after stranger passed by as she continued along the beach, some smiling as they noticed her glasses. Ahead of her she saw an old man with dark skin and hair so white that it grabbed sunlight and threw it around his head. He was making a sand-castle, an extraordinary sculpture out of wet sand. The sight of the old man working in the sand intrigued her. It was suitable for framing as a Rockwell masterpiece. Continuing her walk up the beach, she stopped in awe before the artfully crafted castle. "You do great work," she said with a smile.

The old man looked up. His blue eyes met hers. Briggs arms fell to her side dropping the beach bag and spilling out its contents. Could this be the mysterious man? She wanted to run. The old man smiled, "Let me help you pick up those things that you just spilt."

"No!" she shouted. Realizing how foolish that sounded, she started over, measuring her words. How loud they were. How fast they were spoken. "I mean, no, that's all right. I will get it. Just a few things I threw into a bag for a day at the beach."

Reaching down to pick things out of the sand, the stranger helped her anyway. "Do I know you?" Briggs asked, fearing his answer.

"I don't think we've met directly," he answered. "But we do have some mutual acquaintances." He smiled and shook his head. "Well, that's a poor way of saying it. I'm supposin' you don't much care to have your husband called a mere acquaintance!"

"You know Bill?" she demanded, knowing the answer.

"Oh, not that properly," came the southern flavor of his answer. "We met once and had a good visit."

"You're the one who helped Seda, aren't you?" she said, her voice tinged with anger. "You're Elijah Jordan..."

"That I am," he smiled, throwing his hand up in a gesture to the sky. "It's a nice day for a walk isn't it?"

"Yeah, nice day," she answered, her mind completely absent from her present surroundings.

"Do you mind if I walk a spell with ya?" asked Elijah. "I'm about done here." He pointed over to some boys playing in the distance. "I gotta go, you know," he whispered into Briggs' ear, "or those poor little fellas won't have the fun of taking down my fine creation!" Elijah bent down drawing his elbows to his stomach and shaking his hands in front of his face. Laughter erupted through his clenched teeth as his head moved round and round. Briggs started to laugh, and as she did, her anxiety simply spilled out onto the soft sand. Her image of Elijah as an imposing messenger from heaven vanished, at least for the moment.

"Sure! Why not!" she said. The two started walking. Briggs seized the moment, knowing that opportunity comes but once. The mystery of this old man, she thought, was about to be unlocked. "Would you mind answering something?"

"I suppose that would depend upon the nature of the question," smiled Elijah. His face was turned away from her, facing out to the sea.

"Were you with Seda at OIDC?"

"What you say?" he pretended to be confused. "O—what is the O something something something?"

"You're a pretty foxy guy," smiled Briggs. "Were you with Seda when she was hospitalized at the place where Bill works?"

"Ah! Well if that's where you're talking about, why yes, I had a brief visit."

"I don't know how you got into that place," returned Briggs. "The security is faultless! But I do know that you were damn lucky that Seda wasn't carrying the virus."

"Damn lucky!" mimed Elijah. "Why is it that you call to your unwanted master?"

"What do you mean?" Briggs asked, thoroughly confused by Elijah's question.

"You called out to hell!" Elijah shook his head. "You don't say, 'you were cancer lucky'.... or 'heart attack lucky'... or 'stroke lucky!' Why, you don't even want to think about these terrible things, much less call for them! Yet something that can swallow up body and soul into an eternal night of pain, well, you call for it as if it were nothing but smoke to throw at a bad situation."

"Unwanted masters," Briggs repeated the phrase just used by Elijah. "So when people say God, or Jesus, or Christ in vain, they are calling for unwanted masters, too?"

"Oh no," replied Elijah soberly, "it's not the same. When they misuse the names of the Almighty, they're calling down the wrath of God. That is far worse! Far worse! It is written, 'Thou shalt not take the name of the LORD thy God in vain, for the LORD will not hold him guiltless who taketh His name in vain.' To use the name of God frivolously is to summon plague and pestilence to court your future!"

Briggs was speechless. She spoke out of habit. She didn't give much thought to these words. Frankly, she didn't give much stock to their reality either. She decided to get back to the subject at hand. "I simply meant to point out that you were not wearing containment gear. If Seda had been carrying an active virus, you would be dead right now."

"Containment gear!" Elijah said emphatically. "Containment gear! It seems to me that it ain't much good against the virus. Am I right?"

"How did you know that?" drilled Briggs.

"Oh, sister, sister!" Elijah shook his head again. "What do you know about that virus?"

"I know it's deadly. I know that it kills quickly. And I know what you know, Elijah, that it penetrates through plastics and polymers."

"Now how do you suppose that it is able to do that?" asked Elijah, bending his head down and rotating it to look up at Briggs as they walked.

"We... we... we are not sure," she stuttered. "It must be the same chemical process that allows it to move quickly through the skin, into the blood stream, and killing its victims within hours."

"Chemical process...," continued Elijah, "and how do you know that it is a chemical process?"

Briggs stopped walking, grabbed Elijah by the arm, and turned to face him. "What else could it be?"

"That's one of the differences between you and your husband," pointed out Elijah, his searching gaze allowed Briggs no place to run. "You think that science has an answer for ev'rything. You think that given enough time you can analyze anything and figure it out according to the laws of nature. Bill knows that there are things bigger—way bigger!—than what you can discover under your microscopes. Some of these things are evil, brewed within the cauldrons of hell." Elijah pulled free from Briggs' grip on his arm continuing his walk down the beach. Briggs stared blankly, her arms loose to her sides. Something flashed within her mind, and she started to run.

Stopping directly behind Elijah, she reached forward grabbing onto his shoulder with her right hand. He stopped, turned around to her briefly, and then started walking again. Briggs ran in front of him this time to block his way. His blue eyes took hold of her. They caught the light of the sun, burning into Briggs. She looked away. "What are you telling me about the virus!" she demanded.

"I'm saying that there are things prepared in hell that find their way here!"

Briggs stared. "I don't know what you mean."

"I mean," said Elijah, "that you'll never find anythin' on earth that will stop that virus. Only the blood of Seda."

"But there isn't enough time!" cried Briggs, as if Elijah could do something about the deadly situation.

"Time," said Elijah. "There's always time. Some people could be given ten lifetimes, and they would still never be saved by the blood. I don't mean Seda's blood either, sister. What she's got will save some of you for a season. Your husband is trying to tell you in a thousand ways about the blood of the Lamb. A poured-out sacrifice for the whole world and giving life everlasting!"

Briggs knew what Elijah was trying to say. She went to church as a child. She once believed in heaven and hell, angels and demons, and the power of the blood. Then came the university, with all its enlightened professors who showed the errors of believing in a prayer-hearing God. She wondered again how Bill had been able to keep his faith through the university experience.

"I'll tell you how he kept his faith," broke Elijah into her thoughts, reading them is if they were the daily news. "He worshiped. He fed on the Word. He was met by the Lord at the Table. He didn't keep his faith, El Shaddai kept Bill's faith for 'im by divine means."

"I'm sorry." Briggs chest heaved. "I don't understand."

"The farmer sows the seed in the ground. He drives his tractor from the field, closes the gate, and confidently awaits the day of harvest. How does he know that he'll be takin' in the grain? Because there's life in the seed... Life in the seed! Briggs, Bill's filled with God's Word. There's life in God's Word, and it grows faith—grows faith in the heart of Bill!"

Elijah stepped around Briggs and started down the beach. Briggs ran in front of him one more time and stopped. "I want to believe... I want to...," she broke down and wept. With her arms limp at her side and chin sagging against her chest, Briggs' body convulsed in the deep waves of her dilemma.

Elijah reached over, taking her by the hands. As he squeezed her soft smooth skin within his wrinkled, black hands, she felt warmth radiating through her whole frame. The tears stopped. Lifting her head she looked across at Elijah. "I know that, sister," he said. "My, you are a lost lamb! Say now, I think that today the angels in heaven might just be rejoicing. What do you think?"

Briggs remembered—and it did not seem peculiar to her at the time that she did remember after all these years—a passage in the Bible that talks about angels rejoicing over one sinner who repents. "Maybe the angels are rejoicing," she smiled broadly at Elijah—tears still smeared against her cheeks. Letting go of her hands Elijah began to dance around in a circle, clapping his hands above his head. Soon he was singing a spiritual at the top of his voice. A lone cloud in an otherwise crystal-clear sky suddenly let down a drenching rain just above them. The sand was swept away from her body, and she stood washed clean in the blood of the Lamb.

• • • • •

The halls and rooms at the University of Zurich Hospital were cluttered with doctors, nurses, medical technicians, and military police wearing white containment suits. "How many confirmed deaths by the virus do we have in Zurich?" asked Bill as he walked into a large University lecture room. The lecture hall had been converted into a command center for managing the outbreak in Zurich.

"Thirty–seven known dead," replied Ueli. Dr. Ueli Blocher was the Chief of Staff at the University of Zurich Hospital. "We need to figure out how Zurich became infected. If we don't figure out how this is spreading, well..."

"I've given that some thought," said Bill, filling in the space that Ueli had left in the conversation. "Take a look at this map. The first instance of PRN40 infection took place on Khlos Island. Then we see it showing up months later at Klestkaya, having taken a northerly course. Moscow becomes the next victim, once again north. It seems to me that either the virus originated on Khlos and was haphazardly spread north. Or," he paused, "the virus was developed in Moscow and then deployed on Khlos."

"I don't follow your second point," broke in Blocher. "What do you mean developed in Moscow?"

"What little testing we have been able to do on this virus suggests that it is not a natural occurrence," replied Bill. "I think..."

Once again Ueli interrupted Bill, "Not a natural occurrence! I'm stupefied! What are you saying?" Blocher was tired, overworked, and scared. What he didn't have any longer was patience.

"I'm just saying that we don't think this could have resulted by random mutations of a known virus," replied Bill with some irritation. He, too, was tired. "Which means that the virus was likely produced within a controlled environment. Interpol knows of at least a dozen labs working covertly within Moscow, some financed by the Russian Mafia. I think that PRN40 was somehow engineered in Moscow, then Khlos was chosen as the target for trying out the virus. It makes sense that the scientists working with this loose canon would suggest that it be tried at a location that could be quickly and easily quarantined."

"Then how did it get to Klestkaya?" asked the Chief of Staff.

"My guess is that the messenger boys who delivered the virus to Khlos didn't know how deadly their cargo was. I think that one of them, if there were more than one, let a personal item become contaminated with the virus. Some time later, the man or woman made contact with the infected item, became sick, and went to the local hospital. The seriousness of the person's condition must have made the medical technician suspicious, and Central Laboratories was notified. I think that Central Laboratories in Moscow sent for a sample of the victim's blood. When Central realized that the virus was fast acting and deadly, they ordered the military to close off the city."

"Why do you suppose that?" came the agitated voice of Blocher. "Couldn't it simply be the case that Central Laboratories had nothing to do with bringing the virus to Moscow? Instead someone in Klestkaya became infected and then traveled to Moscow?"

"If that were the case," replied Bill, "then there would have been a trail of dead bodies from Klestkaya to Moscow. The fact that we don't have any other deaths makes me think that PRN40 had been taken to Moscow by medical courier. Central Laboratories had no idea what they were up against. They used standard precautions... precautions that would not prevent the spread of PRN40 once they began to work on it in Moscow. They simply had no idea that the virus could penetrate polymers, rendering almost all of their usual containment systems useless. The virus was brought to Moscow then spread from Central Laboratories."

"If you're right, how did it get to Zurich?" drilled Ueli.

As they talked, a number of people from various disciplines were listening. One listener was taking notes. Hans was the Minister of Public Safety whose job it was, among other things, to oversee the Zurich police force.

"Look again at the map," answered Bill. "We see outbreaks of PRN40 along a route from Moscow to Zurich. Two of the first recorded deaths involved border patrol staff. This is no coincidence! Someone brought the disease from Moscow to Zurich. And there is one more thing. Since the next fatality happened some time after Moscow was quarantined, I think someone went back into Moscow for some specific reason, became infected, and then avoided the military police for a second time as one or more of them left the city."

"What would be so important as to drive a person or persons to risk being infected with a fatal disease or shot by military police?" blasted Blocher.

"Cool down, friend." Bill shook his head. "I'm afraid that's one question I can't answer," Bill leaned back against a desk.

"I don't know if this is just a coincidence," broke in Hans, "but one of the victims of the virus, a Russian found in a cheap hotel in Zurich, had a number of British Gold Sovereigns in his jacket along with a train ticket for Paris. He was also one of the first reported deaths in our country."

"That's it!" shouted Bill. "The guy was Russian, one of the first to die in Zurich, and carried anything but the usual pocket change. He must have gone into Moscow because he knew about gold coins that were stored somewhere in the city. He managed to get around the military police, found the coins, but became infected with PRN40. He then headed for Zurich." Once again the Michael Jordan of infectious control was demonstrating his deductive dominance.

"Why Zurich?" asked Hans.

"Who knows!" Bill threw his hand into the air. "He had to get through a lot of border security checks to make his escape. Maybe the route to Zurich was the only one he could make work. Maybe he knew who could be paid off at the border checks, and the only line of collaborators led here!"

"If you're right," said Ueli, indicating a more open ear to Bill's scenario, "then we can have some confidence that the virus is not attacking broadly, but narrowly along a prescribed path."

"That's right," Bill said. "And it's important that every area where PRN40 has been indicated be sealed up tighter than a balloon." He turned to Hans, "That includes Zurich."

"We are not Russia," said Hans. "Our people have rights. However, the government has declared a state of emergency and under these special circumstances—the city has been contained. We are allowing no travel in or out of the area within fifty kilometers of the city. It's not my job to deal with things outside of the city, but the government has taken these steps. Special hostels have been set up for tourists and visitors who simply are not financially prepared for more than a short vacation or business trip to Zurich."

"And what are we doing with the patients suspected of being infected with PRN40?" asked Bill.

Ueli answered, "Every single person complaining of any symptom endemic to the virus, including a simple fever, is being brought exclusively to the University hospital."

Bill thought for a moment. "Hans, I think we need to stress something to the general public. We have told them to avoid going to work or traveling around the city. I think we need to use radio and television to make a stronger point. They should stay in their apartments period! The disease moves quickly. Maybe if we take away its fuel, we can put it out. There may be some contaminated surfaces, but if we put out the flames, we will find the smoldering embers later. Do you think, Hans, that we could find resources and personnel to deliver food to people who are running low in their homes, at least for a few days?"

"That can be done," Hans replied.

"Good!" Bill said. "I'd get to the airwaves quickly. Tell the people to stay in their homes. If they are running out of food, even medical supplies, give them a number to call, and we'll try to meet their needs until we get the outbreak managed."

"Wait a minute!" Hans raised his voice. "We have a problem here. Everything we know of the virus suggests that it kills its victim within two to three hours. How could these men have contracted the virus in Moscow and lived long enough to bring it to Zurich?"

Bill looked genuinely stunned. "You're right, Hans. Either something atypical took place—perhaps the Russians had developed a drug to inhibit the growth of the virus—or something that had become contaminated was touched much later." Bill stopped. "Or..."

"Or," interjected Hans, "the virus doesn't always kill quickly."

"God help us if this bug can spread without leaving an immediate trail." Bill's tone could chill ice. "Listen! I've got a hunch I want to work on. I can't believe that Zurich is the destination for the gold that the Russian apparently risked his life to get out of Moscow." Bill started to leave. "I'm going to clean up."

The men and women around Bill began walking away from the discussion. Bill headed toward a wing in the hospital serving as the command center for the staff working at the University Hospital during the outbreak. He walked into a prep room sandwiched between the lecture hall and the staff quarters. Several portable decontamination booths had been set up in a chain. Bill called out, "Anyone using the Decon?"

There was no reply, so he walked into the first booth and showered down the white suit. Entering the next booth, he removed the suit, hanging it with a long line of other suits. In the third booth he showered down, scrubbing his body meticulously. The hot, steamy shower felt good. Standing with his fingers locked above his head, he let the water fall against his neck and back. "I wonder how Briggs is doing?" He was thinking about her a lot these days.

• • • • •

Working a hunch, Bill disguised himself, leaving the University Hospital without notice. He grabbed a taxi to the Zurich transit rail exchange. The dead Russian was found with a rail pass that was to take him to Paris. Reading over the case transcript, Bill noticed that although the Russian had checked in alone, the desk clerk was suspicious of another man who entered the hotel minutes later. Was that other man an accomplice? If so, it figured that he might also be heading out of town, perhaps for Paris, and carrying a heavy load. Of course, even if Bill's hunch was right, he didn't know when the dead Russian's partner was leaving, or if the conspirator had already left. There was lots of room to his theory, but after all, Bill was playing a hunch.

Dressed casually, Bill sat down on a bench with a good view of the foot traffic. People were laid out on benches and on the floor near walls. Frustration etched its mark upon each of the travelers inconvenienced by the quarantine. Across the spacious lobby, an argument had broken out with a man caught trying to get by security into an off limits area. Straining under the weight of the suitcase he carried, the traveler was unwilling to let go of it. Bill jumped to his feet. The man was speaking Russian. Forcing his way through the crowd, he looked up to see a woman also talking with the authorities, apparently serving as a translator.

She was blonde, with blue eyes, wearing a tight yellow dress. Bill had no idea that this was the brunette who had captivated and sullied his brother's thoughts—a temptress appearing for the appetites of her prey. She was beautiful, a blonde as Bill preferred. He felt soiled as he studied her standing beside the Russian, his thoughts tainted with lustful desires. "My God, what's happening?"

Bewildered, Bill still had something going for him that his liberal brother, the pastor, lacked—spiritual discernment. He sensed the evil that hung darkly about the woman. He knew that he was about to step into something sinister. "Lord," he prayed, "stay right here at my side. I think I'm going to need Your help!"

Looking up, the woman saw Bill making his way through the crowd. Grabbing the heavy suitcase, she carried it effortlessly to her side. The Russian started after her to take back his gold when he suddenly stood rigid—frozen in a second of time. Molech was demonizing the mortal, about to use him to assure the woman's escape with the gold. Monstrously strong, the shell of the Russian threw blows at the security team, lifting them into the air and throwing them across the room.

By the time he turned to face Bill, this agent from OIDC was in the air himself, flying into the Russian's mid-section. Thud! He hit the demonized man sending him briefly to the floor. Bill felt like he had hit the trunk of an oak tree, amazed that he had managed to take the stranger down. The Russian had the strength of ten men. Undaunted, the possessed man jumped quickly to its feet, lifting Bill a foot above the floor with one hand. The animated face smiled darkly, drool dripping from the corners of its mouth. Molech was about to use the other hand of the possessed body to crack Bill's neck when seventeen security men arrived with automatic rifles.

Molech had succeeded in drawing security away from the woman. It was important for Molech to stay with her, assuring her safety. The evil entity left the mortal. The Russian immediately collapsed. Bill reached over to feel for pulse in his neck. His adversary was burning up with fever. "Stay back!" yelled Bill. "Stay back! This man may have the virus." He shot a look to the security team. "Do any of you speak English?"

"I do," said one.

"Good! Contact the Minister of Public Safety. He's at the University of Zurich Hospital." The guard was about to ask a question, but Bill interrupted. "Do it now! There will be time for questions later. Tell the Minister that Dr. Downs thinks he has a Russian victim of the virus at the rail exchange. And tell this security team to keep the people away from this man. Do it! NOW!"

Chapter 13:
BRAKES & THROTTLES

Standing in the kitchen of her apartment Rachel wrestled with the lid on a jar of mayonnaise. The girls were coming for lunch. She'd decided to make tuna fish sandwiches complete with lettuce and lots of mayonnaise, that is, if she could get the lid off the jar. Rachel had fretted away the morning worrying about her date with Luke. She had been way too serious. "Gads! This was our first date!" she thought. "He must think I'm a prude." She blushed.

The doorbell sounded. Bethany walked in, not waiting for Rachel to meet her at the door. "How ya' doing kid?" she shouted from the living room.

"Fine, if I can get this stupid jar open!"

"Let me see that," Bethany said as she entered the kitchen. Taking the jar she went to the sink, turned on the faucet, and holding the jar upside down, she let the hot water pour around the lid. Giving the top a hard rap on the counter, she then handed the mayonnaise to Rachel. "All done!"

The lid turned easily from the jar. "That's why you're my friend," laughed Rachel.

"I'm your friend because I know how to open jars!" Beth crafted her words, making them droll.

"Exactly!" teased Rachel. "No, you know what I mean. You're always there when I need you. That's what friends are for! Right?"

"Thanks! When is Tamor coming?" Beth reached into the mixing bowl, lifting a chunk of tuna and popping it into her mouth.

"She should be here in ten minutes or so," replied Rachel. "She'll leave the church office promptly at noon, arriving back just as precisely at twelve fifty-nine."

"Yeah," agreed her friend, "I think that God broke the mold, just like they say, after He made her. Very fussy! Very 'do it right the first time.' Say, before she gets here and you have to watch what you say about her boss, how did it go with Pastor Luke?"

"Oh don't!" gasped Rachel. "You had to bring that up!"

"That bad?" Beth was surprised by Rachel's reaction.

"I came off like I was the preacher," lamented Rachel. "I preached at him!"

"Was it a good sermon?" Beth asked, smiting their conversation with humor. Spicing every situation with the lighter side was Beth's trademark. Humor in this case did not have its desired effect. Rachel was in no mood for making light of what she thought was a huge blunder on a first date. "Come on, it can't be that devastating!"

"OH NO!" cried Rachel. "Listen Beth, I just got sooooo serious. Talked deep theology. I came off as a know-it-all! Why didn't I talk about sports or something? You know, the usual girl tricks where we look dumb, making a guy feel smart and center stage. But no, not me! I had to be Miss Theological!"

"That's too funny," laughed Beth.

"Funny!" moaned Rachel.

"Yes funny," continued Beth, "because he doesn't know you then. When he finds out what you're like with your friends, he'll need an interpreter just to make sense of the real you!"

"Okay," rankled Rachel, "you tell me. Who is the real me?"

"You have a serious side, that's true, but you're... you're also playful. You're fun to be with wherever we go. You have the best one–liners! You like to do things that are on the edge, just so long as they're not irreverent. You're the physical outdoors type, loving to camp and take long walks. And tell me woman, does the girl you just described own a trail bike? No. But you do! I've watched you kick dust with that bike! If Pastor Luke saw only the serious side to you, he has a whole other education coming!" Beth paused to take a good reading of Rachel. "So tell me kid, do you really think your date turned that ugly?"

"Well, it wasn't good," answered Rachel. "Yet at the end of the evening, I could tell that he was still interested." Again she paused. "I'm not feeling like a klutz just because I was with the parish pastor. That date would have been bad, bad, bad with anyone! And it's not because I talked about God, either. I want to be up front about my faith within any relationship. I just don't want to preach, especially to a pastor!"

"I wasn't there, kid, or did you see me under the table?" Bethany found it difficult to restrain her humorous impulses. "Sorry. What I mean is that I have no way of knowing everything that happened. But I do know you, Rachel. I've seen the way you carry yourself. It's tough for me to buy the idea that you totally blew the evening."

"Thanks Beth," sighed Rachel. "My emotions are all tangled up. I'm worried about how I came off to Pastor Luke." Rachel pulled at her lower lip. "And I'm not sure... how I feel about... dating him again."

"Whoa, kid!" interrupted Beth. "Did I miss something here? I thought you were worried about him turning things off between you? Why are you at the spigot? Why not let him make that decision?"

"No, you're not getting it," protested Rachel. "I don't know if I feel like going out on another date with him."

"Why not? What's not to like?" queried Beth. "He's good looking, from what

I can tell he has a nice sense of humor, he's a pastor, and most importantly, he's available."

"So are maggots on a dead cat!" blurted Rachel.

Beth laughed. "Which is he, the maggots or the dead cat?"

"Stop it!" A smile finally broke across Rachel's face. "That's not what I mean. I'm just saying that being available doesn't mean that something's ripe for the picking!" Rachel thought for a moment. "You know Beth, I'm glad that Tamor hasn't come yet. I wouldn't want her to hear this, but the truth is, I don't feel comfortable with Luke's—I mean Pastor Luke's—theology."

"Just a minute!" Another interruption by Beth. "Between us girls, I think you can drop the 'pastor' in this case."

Another brief smile from Rachel. "Maybe I'm just reading him off course right now, but something's rubbing me the wrong way."

"Enough to nip things in the bud with him?" smiled Beth.

"No," Rachel pulled her lip again. "But I sure made a good stab at making things terminal the other night." Rachel put on her puppy dog face. Laughing, Beth reached over to take her hand.

"This is what you do kid," she said enthusiastically, "you call him. Go for a picnic and let him devour more of your good cooking. Take some time and get to know him before you go drastic."

"But am I leading him on?" asked Rachel.

"No," said Beth in her practical voice, "this is how it has worked for thousands of years. Boy meets girl. Boy and girl get acquainted. Boy and girl get serious or one runs to the hills."

Rachel laughed. "Can I wear my running shoes on the next date?"

"Only if they match your outfit," joked Beth. "Remember! Nothing has to go any farther than you want it to go. As Tamor would say, 'Remember girl, you got your foot on the brake. Just keep his hand off the throttle!'" They both laughed.

The doorbell sounded again. The door sprung open as if activated by the chime. Tamor walked in wearing a lime green blouse with a matching ribbon holding back her hair in a ponytail. "Hey girls! What's happening?"

"Speak of the devil!" declared Rachel. She tossed a look at Beth that said "change the subject!"

"Say girl," frowned Tamor as she placed one hand on her hip, "y'all got no cause to say that!" Tamor burst out laughing and the others joined with her. Her friends loved it when Tamor poured on the southern slang. It was a gigantic contrast from her usual proper diction laced with a British flavor.

"Let's get serious," said Tamor as she sniffed the air. "What's for lunch?"

• • • • •

After the girls left, Rachel thought over Beth's advice. She decided to do exactly what her friend had suggested. Reaching for the phone, she called the church. "Morningside Community Church," said Tamor. "What can we do to serve you today?"

"Hi Tamor! This is Rachel!"

"Long... time... no... hear... from you, girl!" Tamor laughed. "What's up?"

"I was just wondering if Pastor Luke was in the office?"

"Don't say another word, I am ringing you through right now!" Rachel could hear the smile on the other side of the phone.

"Stop that Tamor!" cried Rachel.

"See you soon," chuckled Tamor. She transferred her friend's call directly to Pastor Luke's office.

"Pastor Luke," came his voice.

"Hi Luke, this is Rachel."

"I was wondering who was on the phone," he said. "Usually Tamor screens my calls and lets me know who's on the line before I answer. This time I'm glad she didn't. Hearing your voice was a terrific surprise."

"How's your day been going?" asked Rachel.

"Same old... same old," he said. "I have most of my sermon done. Took notes from our date the other night to help me out."

"Ah! Don't say that!" cried Rachel. "I got way too deep. I really feel foolish..."

"Well don't," interrupted Luke. "I enjoyed myself. And, to tell you the truth, you got me thinking about things that I hadn't thought about during my time at the seminary."

"Sure," said Rachel dryly, "Miss Theologian dupes the seminarian!"

Luke laughed. "Really Rachel, I enjoyed myself."

"I'm not so sure...." she replied, "so I want to make it up to you. How would you like to go on a picnic at the park with me after church on Sunday? I'll make up grandma's battered deep fried chicken, bake some fresh rolls, serve up deviled eggs, and top it all with some European Ale. So! Should I write it on my calendar?"

"Is the chicken recipe from the same grandma that taught you to make soup?"

"Same one," noted Rachel.

"Well, the way I figure it, I owe my life to both of you. That soup saved me from the evil influenza! I should be taking you out to some high-class, uptown restaurant as a token of my thanks. You know Rachel, your grandma's recipe for chicken soup is good enough to make it illegal."

"Then get ready for jail!" joked Rachel. "You haven't had chicken until it has been transformed by the magic of grandma's special herbs and then fried to a golden brown."

"What time should I bring by my appetite?" asked Luke.

"Here's what I'm thinking. I'll go to the first service on Sunday so I can have the rest of the morning to do the cooking. I would be ready any time after noon."

"Let's plan for 12:30," he said. "That'll give me time to go home, change clothes, and mellow out a bit. I'll come by and get you at around 12:30."

"Great!" said Rachel brightly.

• • • • •

Bill arrived back at their apartment before Briggs had gotten home from work. He was exhausted. He had seen enough death for a lifetime. Yet he knew that all he had experienced in Zurich was a fraction of the casualties that could soon cascade around the planet. He decided to have a glass of wine, and then another. That was enough. Corking the bottle he placed it back into the cupboard. Lying down to rest, he was fast asleep within minutes.

• • • • •

"This is remarkable!" Stan said to Seda. "Your kidneys are perfect. I'm not just saying that they've gotten better. Your kidneys are the textbook standard for perfection! You could donate a kidney today and be fine for the rest of your life."

"Thank you Jesus!" Seda said, bowing her head for further prayer. Respecting her time, Stan waited until her eyes opened. "You know he was here again."

"Who was here?" he asked. "Jesus?"

"Well yes and no," she answered with a look that said 'don't mess with my Jesus.' "I was referring to the man who saved my life at the apartment."

"Seda, that can't be," protested Stan. "Our security under normal circumstances is flawless. Multiply flawless by two under present conditions and not even a gnat can get in here undetected. Security these days at the Institute means a multiple of three!"

"He was here I tell you," smiled Seda. She understood. "He's not like the rest of us you know. I think he's a messenger from heaven."

"An angel, Seda?"

"That's right, an angel," she replied emphatically.

"I love you Seda, but I gotta tell you, I think that you're getting cabin fever! Your imagination is working overtime."

"Was it my imagination that cured my kidneys?" she asked.

"Are you saying that this old man with the white hair healed your kidneys?"

"That's right again..." Reading Stan, Seda saw skepticism breaking out like perspiration on a baker's face. "When he was here—and he was here—he touched me. I could feel something traveling through my whole body and then resting for a time in the area that you tell me my kidneys are located. He also told me that you were wrong. The symptoms showing bad kidneys would go away, he said. He told me that I would be fine."

Seda was separated from Stan by more than a philosophy of life. The emotions of peace and joy which radiated within Seda were alien to Stan. She wanted him to know the same love of God that she was experiencing just then, as she had often before. She was frustrated that she was a simple woman armed only with simple words. "I know that Elijah was here," she continued. "But you tell me that's impossible. Yet you also tell me that my kidneys are perfect and have no explanation for my recovery. Then I tell you how they were healed, and you won't have it! Stan, which of us isn't facing the facts? You think that I desire to believe so much in God that I won't look at the hard facts. Have you ever thought that just maybe you try so hard not to believe that you refuse to see what's in front of your face?"

Stan stood there for a moment thinking. He looked a few more times at the report outlining the state of Seda's inexplicable recovery from chronic kidney problems. Walking over to Seda, he squeezed her hand softly. "Maybe."

• • • • •

Rachel laid out a large plaid blanket on soft green grass under the park's lone willow tree. Kneeling down on one of its corners, she reached up, taking from Luke a genuine relic from the past. With her mother's wicker picnic basket in hand, she set it to the edge of the blanket. A nostalgic smile hung in Rachel's eyes, pulling Luke with her to a distant memory. "My mother used this same basket when she first dated dad," Rachel volunteered. "I fell in love with it one day when I was playing in the attic. It was so dusty. I cleaned it up, covering it later with an old towel. I wanted to ask mom if I could have it, but I wasn't supposed to play in the attic. So I shouldn't have known about the basket."

"A real dilemma! So what did you do?" Luke watched as Rachel worked wrinkles from the blanket.

"I waited for years," she resumed. "When I was fifteen, I went up into the attic and simply brought the basket down. I had grown past the old prohibition that kept me from the attic. Mom didn't even ask me why I had gone up there. She saw that I liked the basket and asked if I wanted to have it. Broadcasting a large smile, I said yes. It became mine. I carefully cleaned it, rubbed it down with linseed oil, and then put it in a box. This is the first time that I've used it since I packed it away."

"Wow! I'm honored." Luke's hopes brightened. Did this special treatment signal that he'd gained a "favored male" status with Rachel?

"It's not that big of a deal, except to me," laughed Rachel. "But let me show you how special it can be!" Opening a red, wooden lid, she prepared to show Luke what she'd brought for their picnic together. On the very top, resting on a red linen cloth, was an apple pie with cinnamon crust. Removing the pie, Rachel set it to the side. Taking out the small linen cloth, she spread it out at the center of the blanket. Its monolithic red accented well against the plaid blanket. The linen gone from the basket, Luke looked in to see a thin, clear plastic tray with a light blue cover. Taking out the tray, Rachel set it on the linen, popping off the lid to reveal freshly made deviled eggs dusted red with paprika.

From the left side, she lifted a covered pot surrounded in dish towels. Unwrapping the towels, she raised the lid releasing the scent of deep fried chicken into the air. The middle of the basket held a bag of warm rolls and a container of soft butter. Stationed to the far right, she took and unwrapped more towels exposing two green bottles of cold, imported ale. "Voila!"

Rachel tapped on the blanket, inviting Luke to sit down. Lying back on the blanket, he planted one elbow on the ground. He studied Rachel's sandy brown hair, glazed under a summer's afternoon sun. Falling down over her shoulders, it danced with each of her movements upon the straps of a loose fitting sun dress made yellow by large daisies covering the fabric. A fresh-cut yellow daisy was carefully braided to the right side of her hair. Looking up into the swaying branches of the willow tree, Luke drank in the moment as if he had been transported back. He imagined a time where the world knew no cars or airplanes, only horses and carriages. Luke enjoyed the past. Collecting antique pictures taken of everyday life, he often coveted the people captured on the yellowing lithographs and sepia photographs.

Looking back to Rachel, he gasped. The woman sitting with him on the blanket wore a red dress. Her long hair was dark as the brown in her eyes. She was smiling at Luke, wiping a white handkerchief across the top of her low cut dress. Luke yearned for her.

"Luke." Rachel was startled by his entranced stare. "Luke! Are you all right?"

The lady in red was calling for him. Luke shook his head. The mysterious woman's face faded away into Rachel's as she sat gazing at his stupor. "Luke," she laughed. "What's the matter?"

Luke replied with a nervous laugh. "It's this beautiful day! I was day-dreaming, I guess."

"Is that so," replied Rachel. "I was getting worried. What were you thinking about?"

"Horses and carriages. Basically, of a time before internal engines ripped the air with loud noises polluting it with the smell of combustion." Luke was still thinking of the lady in red.

Rachel looked away, but her busy hands continued setting things out. "Would you mind opening these?" she asked, handing him the ale. "I hope you're hungry!"

"I could eat a horse," he replied. Taking the bottles, he screwed off the caps.

"Not one of the horses you were just dreaming about, I hope."

Luke gave another nervous laugh.

"You preachers are always forced to pray at social events," smiled Rachel, "but today you get a break. I won't preach, but I'll give the prayer."

Luke was relieved that Rachel didn't expect him to pray. He was having a difficult time balancing his attraction for her as a woman and dealing with the fact that he was also her pastor. The persona of the woman in red became attached to Rachel. Lust for her burned away the person before him. He wanted satisfaction in her body. Luke's thoughts had trespassed into the carnally impure and returned to sully the angelic within his life. It was Rachel's prayer that broke the spell. She prayed, "Father God, this is a beautiful day! Thanks for letting us spend it together. Thank You for Grandma and all her special recipes. And thanks for the friendship that Luke and I share. May this food that You have provided for us, and the time that we have together, honor You and strengthen us for service. We ask it all in Jesus' Name. Amen."

"Thanks Rachel," he said, "that was a beautiful prayer." And it was! There was nothing contrived in her words. She spoke from the heart. She believed what she said. For Rachel, there was no doubt but that God was hearing every word and would bless each item in her prayer. Most importantly for Luke, he knew that it had somehow freed him from thoughts that if left unchecked, would eventually destroy their friendship.

"I'm still embarrassed about our discussion over pizza the other day," she said, dishing up a plate for Luke. "Sometimes a bee gets in my bonnet and I'm out of control!" She lifted her head smiling sheepishly. Luke marveled that a woman so intelligent could be saturated with the aura of innocence. She was a stark contrast to the lady in red, but no less desirable. They were reflections of one another, one drawing out carnal feelings of lust, the other manly desires of love. Lust and love would seek to take Rachel. Each would have her body and soul, but not in the same way. Lust saw no face, but love preserved it.

"Now stop," protested Luke. "I really don't see why you feel like something terrible happened with us. I like being philosophical. If you were ditzy, well, I would tire of our time together very quickly. You're not only beautiful, you're deep."

Luke had not planned to make such a clear reference to how he saw her physically. Even after he said it, he didn't give it a second thought. Rachel, however, caught what he had said. "So," she continued, "you don't mind a brain on a girl's legs?"

Luke was surprised by her one-liner, laughing heartily. "I like the package deal!"

"And what about life in Morningside Community Church?" asked Rachel. "Do you still like it here or is the honeymoon over?"

"I like it very much," he said, "but usually a good honeymoon lasts at least a year. I'll tell you more in about six months or so. But tell me about you. What do you like to do? And, hey, I don't even know what you do for a living."

"I read manuscripts for a Christian publisher," she answered.

"How does that work?" he asked.

"Publishers get all kinds of manuscripts from authors who hope to get their work into the market. Much of it comes unsolicited. Wanna-be-published authors send in trial chapters with an outline, or whole manuscripts, hoping that the publisher will become interested. Since I work out of my home, my publisher sends a portion of the unsolicited manuscripts to me for my review. Ninety-five out of a hundred are sent back to the writers with a rejection notice. The rest I recommend for further consideration, and maybe two or three will actually become published after that."

"Maybe I shouldn't ask, but does it pay well?" Luke's question was framed by raised eyebrows and lips drawn back into a timid smile as he spoke.

"No," Rachel smiled back, "but after my tithe, I have enough to get by. I like the freedom of setting my own routine. Some weeks I have tremendous pressure to get through manuscripts. Other weeks it's as if I'm on vacation." She paused, looking up at the sky. "Do you know what keeps me doing this?"

"What?" he asked.

"Well, it's like this," placing her food down for the moment, she rested back on the palms of her hands. "You start reading another manuscript. You don't really want to, because it's likely another prosaic, poorly written piece with a bad plot and lots of cliches. Then it happens. The manuscript may have been rejected by others, but it grabs you. You're drawn into the manuscript. You've discovered talent! Raw, unrecognized talent! And you know that this will be a book. What's more, you know that you will be the first step in launching a writer's career."

"It's sort of like going fishing for sunfish," interjected Luke, "and suddenly you're bringing in a ten–pound walleye."

"Exactly!" cried Rachel, pulling herself forward again, clearly pleased that Luke understood. "Of course, it goes the other way too. I've 'thumbs downed' a few authors who have become highly published and successful. Every manuscript evaluates the interests of the editor and the publisher, not just the abilities of the author. If the work is not rejected out of hand because of typos and bad style, the editor makes a judgment call concerning the subject or plot. The manuscript must also fit the line of books published by each company. The final decision may be a bad call, or a good call. But a call will be made, because that's what the editor is paid to make."

"Have you helped to launch many new authors?" he asked.

"No, not that many," Rachel answered. Taking up her plate again, and between mouthfuls, she started naming the authors that she had helped get started. Luke, not swimming in the same evangelical waters as Rachel and her publisher, only recognized one name. He fumbled a bit. It was uncomfortable for him not knowing authors that Rachel relished over. It was time to change the subject. "Tell me Rachel, what do you do when you're not rejecting most manuscripts?"

"Well, you know that I work with the youth ministry at Morningside," she smiled. "I also like spending time with my friends. In the summer I enjoy taking my trail bike out and polishing off a few hours bumping, and sometimes flying, along the dirt trails that I know..."

"Wait a minute," Luke broke in, "you're not talking about a bicycle are you? You own a motor bike?"

"Yup I do," said Rachel proudly. "It serves my alter-ego. I take it with me when I go camping with Beth and a few others who like to brave the elements in a tent."

"You know," Luke was shaking his head, "I'm seeing a whole new side to you."

"Hey! It's just like Beth said!" Rachel spoke spontaneously. Next she looked down, blushing. She hadn't intended to bring Luke in on her discussions the other day with Beth.

"What about Beth?" Luke asked.

"Nothing! Just nothing!" she deflected. Nervously, her right hand raced for her head nearly crushing the daisy. Luke continued to look confused. "Really! It's nothing," continued Rachel. "But tell me this, what do you do when you're not being Pastor Luke?"

"I like to camp too," he said. "It runs in the family. My brother and my sister are big on the great outdoors. Bill met his wife on a trail hike in Colorado. I did their ceremony during an outdoor wedding on the very trail that brought them together. I also like to garden. I think that there's some secret rule that all pastors need to like plants. And I like being with you."

Rachel caught his look just then. It was filled with desire. She fancied that his look was for her. Hidden from Rachel, and maybe from Luke, was a lurking question. Did Luke see Rachel, or the lady in red? Rachel could only know what she read in Luke's eyes. How could she know what ran deep within his secret thoughts? His look broadcasted unmasked desire. Rachel didn't have on her running shoes. But then, she didn't know if she wanted to run. She would definitely keep her foot on the brake, however, until she knew more about his Christian walk.

Chapter 14:
MATCHED UP

Driving into the underground garage of their apartment, Briggs was pleased to see Bill's car. She had missed him with an ache that touched the body, constantly thinking about what he was facing in Zurich. Parking the car, she took to the stairs. As a matter of course she avoided elevators, preferring to use the stairs for minimal daily exercise. Reaching the apartment she unlocked the door and entered. Bill was sleeping on the couch, his hair pushed up by a satin pillow at the end of the couch. He looked like a little, unkempt boy who had been taken off the streets for an afternoon nap.

She yearned to go over and pet down his hair, but fought the urge. She would let him rest until supper. Briggs decided to welcome him back with some of his favorite foods. After about an hour of whipping things together in the kitchen, she went to the couch and knelt down by his head. Stroking back his hair, she kissed his lips. Waking slowly from his rest, Bill first managed a faint smile, then cracked open his eyes, peaking out through two, small slits. "Welcome home, honey," Briggs whispered, leaning her head against his face, almost purring.

Bill brought his arms around her. She felt so good in his embrace. "I've missed you, sweetie," he said, pulling her face close to kiss her forehead.

Briggs pulled herself away, leaving the palms of her hands resting upon Bill's chest. "I want to hear all about what happened in Zurich," she said, "but over supper." She smiled broadly. "I made you some special surprises." Walking the short distance, Briggs led their way to the kitchen. Two large poached eggs, smothered in béarnaise sauce, resting on Canadian bacon and English muffins, greeted Bill at the kitchen table. Parsley flakes accented the yellow sauce, as long spears of buttered asparagus lay to the side. "You lucked out on the asparagus," smiled Briggs, "I bought some for myself the other day but never got it cooked up."

"Eggs Benedict," said Bill loudly, "what a treat!" He turned around facing into Briggs, placing his hands tenderly on her shoulders. "I can see that I need to make more trips to Zurich. I come home and you make me feel like a king."

"You are my king," replied Briggs. "I'm only sorry that I don't always take time to let you know that." She looked to the table. "Sit down now and eat before things get cold."

Bill sat down, opposite to Briggs, at their small kitchen table. He was lowering his head for silent prayer when Briggs interrupted. "Do you mind if I join you?"

Bill looked up, quickly concealing his look of surprise. Capturing Briggs with warm eyes and a welcoming smile he said nothing, but reached across the table with both of his hands. Reaching back, Briggs joined her hands with his. They bowed their heads together. "Father," prayed Bill, "I was just about to say how thankful I am to You for giving me Briggs. I guess it's good for her to hear that too. Thanks also for keeping her safe and moving me to live each day in Zurich seasoned within my prayers for her. Bless this food that Briggs has made with such thoughtfulness and love. We ask it in Jesus' name. Amen."

"Amen," continued Briggs. She looked up at Bill casting a subdued smile. "Surprised?"

"A little I guess," answered Bill.

"You'll never guess who I ran into on the beach!" Briggs raised her eyebrows as she spoke, releasing her grip from Bill's hands so that they could begin eating.

"You made a day of it at the beach?" Bill was pleased that Briggs had taken some time for herself while he was away. "That's great!" He examined her face seeking some clue. "I don't have the faintest idea who you met. Elvis Presley?"

"Better than that!" she said, savoring a delicious pause as she held Bill in suspense.

"Come on! Tell me!" Bill's good natured impatience was wearing through.

"Elijah Jordan." That's all Briggs said, then watched to see how Bill would react. His fork dropped from his hand to his plate, its handle becoming pasted with bearnaise sauce.

"What?" gasped Bill. "I mean... did you talk with him?"

"We talked about a lot of things," she replied. "But I gotta tell you how shocked I was to see this old man building a sand castle and then, as he turned his face toward me and I saw his blue eyes, I knew... I just knew this was the man you had talked about... the one who had saved Seda's life." Briggs reflected for a moment. "My first impulse was to run."

"So what did you talk about?" Cleaning off his fork mindlessly with his napkin, Bill's eyes remained glued on Briggs.

"Well for one thing," said Briggs, "I'm going to be a lot more careful about the kind of language I use. I got a lecture from Elijah about calling to unwanted masters and bringing down the wrath of God."

"Huh?" Bill screwed up his face.

"Oh, let's save that for later." Briggs was enjoying her complete control over a subject that held Bill by a leash. She took a bite of her Eggs Benedict, took one chew, and then said from the side of her mouth, "We talked about Seda, her blood..." finishing the bite, she swallowed. Her voice lowered, "And we talked about the blood of the Lamb."

Bill continued to stare. He didn't know what to say. Briggs rescued the moment from silence. "Move slow with me, Bill, but I think you and I are going to be spending a whole lot more Sundays together—in church."

Bill smiled. His eyes moistened. He continued to say nothing but looked at her with new eyes. Eyes no less filled with the passion of a man for his mate, but sanctified in the permission of heaven. Eyes that imagined his wife walking in a white robe and bathed in Heaven's light.

· · · · ·

"Jill's Pizza and Black Dirt, how'd you like it served up today?" sported Kris into the phone.

"Hi Sis!" replied Luke. "I'll take my dirt with cream, thanks. Place my order and then fill me in on how the new job's going."

"Still sweet as pancakes," she smiled into the receiver. "I really love making Milwaukee smooooooth! So how are things with Rachel, Luke?"

"Actually," he said more as introspection, "she disappoints the hopes of more aspiring young writers than gets them going into big time futures." His voice picked up, "Anyway, she works out of her home reading manuscripts for a Christian publisher. She screens them and recommends the best for further consideration." Another short pause. "She may ride a dirt bike, Kris, but there's more than kicking up trail dust in her. She has a deep Christian faith. In fact, I wish I had her faith."

"First our big brother Bill meets Briggs and ties the knot," observed Kris. "Then I break all odds and fall in love with the guy who fired me..."

Luke broke into her words. "Did you say fall in love?"

"I guess I did," she answered quietly. "Ah, you would have seen it on my face anyway," her voice brightened. "Let's see, today is Sunday. This next weekend we're coming to the Twin Cities. You'll make time to come up and see us, right?"

"Sure!" Luke's voice energized. "What's the occasion?"

"There's a radio broadcasters' convention in St. Paul," she answered. "It's something I'd have shirked this year, until I thought of you. So I talked Rich into going, separate hotel rooms, don't you know. I had planned to call you tonight or tomorrow, but you beat me to it." She paused briefly. "I was saying a while back that it sure seems strange how all of a sudden the Downs' kids are getting matched up. It's as if the Lord were rushing things along for each of us."

"The Lord," repeated Luke. "You sure are sounding religious."

"Rich has a way of doing that to you," Kris said.

"Really!" Luke was genuinely surprised. "He doesn't seem like the religious type."

"Yeah, I know," she admitted. "He's private about his faith, but very committed. Would you believe that I went to church with him today?"

"I'm impressed Kris." Luke was fascinated with this new dimension to his sister's life. She had always been more or less religious. She came by that naturally through their devout parents. Still, he knew something that Kris had concealed from their mom and dad. She hadn't been actively attending church for a couple of years.

"Next Wednesday," continued Kris, "we're going to a neighborhood congregation where I've been attending worship. It's a Lutheran church that does this contemporary service on Wednesday nights. The pastor and people there are very friendly. Would you do this in your church brother? When they heard that I worked for a jazz station, one of the musicians started using a saxophone for some of the songs. I thought that was really sweet!"

"Yeah," said Luke, "that kind of special attention is unusual. I know we couldn't begin to do that in our big parish. Can you imagine trying to add custom features to satisfy over a thousand members?"

"No, I can't," said Kris. "This congregation has almost 850 members, but most worship on Sunday morning at the traditional service. Even so, the pastor announced that if the contemporary service continues to grow at its present rate, the Elders have talked about doing one of the Sunday services as contemporary. That would be a big step for this old, established congregation. In any event, I hope that they don't discontinue the mid-week service. It works really well for my schedule."

"Say Kris, switching gears, did you hear that Bill is back, or at least I think he's returned from Zurich."

"Oh thank heavens!" exclaimed Kris. "I was going to ask you if you'd heard from Bill. Did he say anything about what he saw?"

"I haven't talked with him," he answered. "I got an e-mail from Zurich yesterday. Bill mentioned that he had a flight out of there last night. He didn't go into much, but he did say that the situation there was a nightmare."

"I'm just glad if he's back." Kris had not stopped feeling uneasy about this trip. All kinds of strangely vague news was showing up on the newswire. Stuff filled with disconnect, like "Moscow seems barren of its citizens, but Russian officials believe that the city has withstood the crisis." Kris couldn't see how a city plundered of all human activity had withstood the crisis.

They talked for a while about the news reports coming from Europe and the Middle East. Luke and Kris expressed various opinions about what each thought was taking place behind the scenes. Kris contended that the meat of most stories never broke public media. She often used the Internet to get inside information. What both Kris and Luke did not know, and could not know, was that hell had joined forces with segments of humanity to unleash a deadly plague of terror. As their conversation drew to a close, Luke remembered to ask, "When and where do you want to meet next weekend?"

"If Saturday will work for you, how about an early dinner at 5:00? That fits best with our schedule. That way you'll have plenty of time for driving back to Rochester, too. Pastors need to get lots of sleep for Sunday morning, right?"

"Don't worry about that," Luke interrupted. "Pastor Horton has the message next Sunday. I'll ask him to take the whole service. It's not unusual for one of us to be gone. Every once in awhile the one not preaching travels to another congregation checking out how they do their business. So let's plan on 5:00 and you don't have to worry about your little brother getting his sermon sleep."

"Whatever you say, Luke," smiled Kris. "Let's meet at the restaurant in our hotel. As soon as we're done, I'll send you an e-mail with the hotel's name and address. The meal is on us. Bring Rachel!"

"Hey! That would be great if she could come," he said, pleased that Kris had thought of Rachel. "I'll check with her. I'm not giving in on who's paying for what, though. We gotta talk about that."

"Oh Luke," Kris wanted to catch him before he hung up. "Does Rachel have e-mail?"

"Yes," he said suspiciously, "she uses it mainly to correspond with her publisher. What have you got cooking in that berserk little brain of yours?"

"Give me her e-mail address," she said brightly, "I'll grease the gears."

Luke hung up the phone. It had happened again as he talked with his sister. In fact, lately it was rare when it didn't happen. At the thought of Rachel, the face of the lady in red drifted before his mind taking him captive with intense feelings of longing and lust. "This is messing up my mind!" he hollered out. Luke dove into his bed. Cradling the pillow tightly to his chest, he tried to get this woman out of his head. His heart welcomed her, but his mind fought against all she represented. The emotions were wrong. He pushed and shoved, but the image... the feelings remained

The stranger lived under his skin against his protests. Luke was enamored with Rachel. Why shouldn't he be? She's beautiful, playful, smart and devout. When Luke thought the word 'devout,' the face of the mysterious woman flashed again in his mind, but her face was ripped in pain. Remarkably, at the same time, his longings for her vanished. Again he yelled out, "I'm going insane!"

Gone only for an instant, the craving hunger for the lady in red returned. He wanted to take her, hold her, devour her...

"No! No! No!" cried Luke, squeezing the pillow as if to suffocate it. Tearing his thoughts from the woman, he trained them upon Rachel. He thought of her hair, her eyes, her shapely body. All of it was sweet to his mind, but the satisfaction was fragile. He felt the volcano of his irrational impulses waiting to erupt and destroy the possibility of any future with this woman of spice and faith.

God gave Rachel arresting physical beauty, at least in Luke's eyes. Yet it was her heart that was pure gold—a treasure for any man who would gain her. Lying on his bed, feeling desperate, Luke almost prayed that God would exorcize thoughts of the dark woman from his mind, but he didn't. Luke was unaware of his danger. The mysterious lady in red had come to break apart what Luke was building with Rachel. Lust was to prevail over love, as it often does. Rachel was to be removed from the picture, so that the evil lurking in Luke's future, he would face alone.

• • • • •

Stepping from the curb, Morrell flagged down a taxi outside her apartment. The driver stuffed her luggage into the trunk of his car, but when he offered to take a large hat box, she refused. "I want to hold onto this," she said flatly to the driver. The rope handle of the box had been reinforced with fishing line to manage the extra weight now straining against its bottom. Capturing the driver in the steel of her eyes she said, "Take me to the docks, please." Opening the back door of the cab for his rider, the cabby avoided looking at her face again.

Morrell had chartered the services of a medium-sized yacht owned by a Seattle businessman making his living off the tourist trade. She'd paid an obscene amount of money to have him take her to Vancouver, Canada, no questions asked. The border searches on such vessels were usually very light going into Canada, but sometimes more tricky entering back into the states. Morrell wasn't worried about the trip back. After her "delivery," she wouldn't be carrying anything suspicious.

The cab pulled up to the area of the dock used by most tourists. The charter owner met Morrell at the cab, taking hold of her black suitcase. Offering to take the hat box as well, she insisted upon carrying that herself. He walked her to the boat, then over a small ramp connecting the dock to the charter. Soon they were making their way north by sea. They passed the San Juan Islands. Later, Point Roberts slid by them to their right. Finally, they were pulling into Vancouver. The charter operator had arranged to have a taxi waiting for Morrell when they arrived. Morrell would stay two days in Vancouver. After her short stay, she'd sprinkle the virus from the observation deck of her hotel at a time precisely outlined.

Suddenly a blazing light riveted Morrell's feet to the deck of the yacht. A Canadian customs craft was pulling alongside her charter, checking things out with probing spotlights. The captain raced to meet the commander with an inviting wave. He had nothing to hide. He had no knowledge of what Morrell had brought aboard his ship. Yet, the reason for the woman's secrecy about her trip had troubled him. "Anything on board that I should be aware of, John?" The commander's voice blared from an amplified horn.

"It's tame tonight, Commander. No boozing and partying! Just one passenger with a couple of bags." Morrell fought back racing alarm. She had been assured that customs was loose going into Canada on these "party boats." Straining a smile, she walked forward offering a wave to the customs officer and crew.

"Ma'am, are you carrying anything we should know about? Fruit or any fresh vegetables?"

"No, commander," replied Morrell. Fearing that her voice sounded tight, she took a deep breath, adding, "Just here on a little business, but hoping to enjoy the beauty of Vancouver." She smiled again, broadly.

"You do that, Ma'am," smiled back the commander. Waving his hand, he turned, walking toward the stern of his small ship. The spotlights tore away from the charter, then vanished.

· · · · ·

Rachel was tired. She had enjoyed the picnic that day with Luke. He was charming, but she decided not to rush things with him. It was important first to find out if they were walking the same direction in their Christian faith. "No good to be pulling a relationship in two directions," she thought to herself. It was 10: 52 in the evening when she parked the dish towel, finishing the last of her kitchen duties. Tonight was a good night to hit the sack before twelve. Walking upstairs, she sat down, clicking on the computer. Rachel wanted to check her e-mail before nestling herself within white satin sheets covered with yellow daisy prints.

Two new messages! Neither one was sent by someone she recognized. Click. An offer selling a scanner at, as the ad put it, "a price so low that it almost pays for itself." Click. Delete. The other e-mail was from "JillP&BD@techplace.com." Click. It appeared to be another ad. Rachel almost deleted it, but stopped when, with a quick glance through the text, she caught the phrase "Pastor Luke Downs" near the end of the message. She began to read.

"Dear Ms. Jacobson, This is to confirm your order with Jill's Pizza and Black Dirt. We have you down for two cheese pizzas and four yards of washed gravel. Rochester is out of our delivery area, so we ask that you meet with two of our workers in the Twin Cities around 5:00 p.m. on Saturday. The order has been prepaid. We hope that you find the quality of our products as satisfying as has our long-time patron, Pastor Luke Downs."

Rachel smiled. She was blank concerning the person who had sent the e-mail or what it meant. She was certain that Luke was somehow involved with this peculiar message. It was 11:00. Late, but not so late that she wouldn't give Luke a call. If she woke him up, all the better. She clicked off the Internet, freeing up the phone line. All the lights with the exception of a solo desk lamp were turned off in Rachel's make-shift study converted from the upstairs bedroom of her home. Taking the lamp in hand, she aimed the stream of light toward a sheet of paper taped to the wall near her desk. A long list of frequently used phone numbers was handwritten on a yellow piece of legal pad paper. Spotting Luke's home number, newly scribbled in as a marginal note, she punched it into a lit dial. "Hello, Pastor Downs," came Luke's voice, a bit tired, but nothing there to indicate that he had been asleep.

"Did you order pizza with washed gravel?" asked Rachel.

"Huh?" he quizzed, recognizing but not recognizing the voice.

"Kris is that you?"

"And who's Kris?" she asked.

"Rachel!"

"Yup, Rachel," she smiled, rather enjoying Luke's confusion.

"How do you know about pizza and washed gravel?" He paused only a second. "Usually it's black dirt, anyway." Shaking his head quickly on the other side of the phone, he held the receiver away to avoid bumping his head.

"Well, you see," Rachel continued sporting, "when I was five I learned about pizza, black dirt, and gravel. Prior to that, I'm told that I ate all three."

"Is that right!" laughed Luke. He was beginning to put things together. "You've somehow connected up with my big sister Kris. The only way that you'd put pizza together with black dirt—or gravel, whatever!—is if someone from Jill's Pizza and Black Dirt got to you. Right?"

"Bingo!" laughed Rachel. "I got an e-mail telling me that a prepaid delivery of two cheese pizzas and four yards of washed gravel had been ordered. The message went on to say that my location was outside of their delivery area, but they planned a meeting in the Twin Cities on Saturday at 5:00 in the afternoon. Strangely they did not say where, but they mentioned you as a satisfied customer."

"That's from Kris alright," he chuckled. "She asked for your e-mail address."

"Why?" kidded back Rachel. "So that she could prove that her younger brother dates dimwits? Sure, make me the bumpkin dumb enough to drive two hours for a delivery of pizza and gravel! Is this a Downs' test of some sort?"

"Maybe," Luke continued to enjoy this too, "but for sure I know that she has something cooking that includes both of us for Saturday in the Twin Cities."

"Is that so! Do you mind letting me in on what's going on?" Rachel pretended to be annoyed. In fact, she was a bit put off. Did Luke think that she didn't have a life? Was she to drop any plans that she'd made, just doing whatever with Luke?

"I know this is short notice," Luke answered. "It all came up so quickly. I was going to call you about this tomorrow, but Sis got to you first. Kris and her boyfriend are going to be in St. Paul for a broadcasters' convention next weekend. They wanted to have supper with me on Saturday. They want to meet you, too!" Luke decided to make the proposition more appealing. "Heck, the way I see this, it's a two hour drive to a great meal! It would give us time to talk. And, hey, I'd be eating out with the best looking gal in the restaurant. That's saying something, 'cause Kris is a knockout."

"Give me a break!" cried Rachel. "What have you told them about us? How do two dates add up to a meeting with your sister?"

Luke got the message. The invitation to meet with family looked like he was rushing things with Rachel. He decided to fix this notion quickly. "No, it's nothing like taking you home to meet the parents." Luke forced a laugh. "I mentioned you somehow in our phone conversation. I think it had to do with your mastery of the chicken cuisine. Kris probably thought I'd enjoy some company on the ride up. Besides, you know what they say, three's a crowd. If you say yes, then we're a foursome. It was her idea to invite you, and, well, she took matters into her own hands, sending you off that e-mail."

Rachel knew that Luke had said more to his sister than he was letting on. A girl senses it when a guy is more than casually interested. "What time do you think we'd be back?" she asked. "I've called Pastor Horton," replied Luke, "and he is on for Sunday. I have the day free. You think about it, and I'll see that we are back at the time you set. Okay?"

The wheels of her mind spun as Rachel sought to get a rope around her situation with Luke. After all, it wasn't as if he wanted to see her again tomorrow. The relationship wasn't being rushed. It would be almost another week before their next date. Having no plans to call him during the week, she rather hoped that he wouldn't call her either. It's not the case that she wasn't attracted to Luke, because she was. Still, she had just broken off another relationship largely because her boyfriend wasn't that interested in the Christian walk.

"Well," continued Luke, "what do you think? And don't say no..."

"Sure, Luke, sounds like fun," replied Rachel. Then to herself she thought,

"Heck! It's a week away. I'm keeping my foot on the brake..."

"Great!" Luke's voice beamed genuine pleasure. Inside, the mysterious woman jealously fought against Luke's joy. Luke was soiled. He knew it. He was divided and it hurt deeply. He looked for exits from his dilemma, but his lust had built a windowless, doorless room where the lady in red took aim at his feelings for Rachel.

"One thing concerns me, though." Rachel's voice darkened. "I'm not sure how to get the washed gravel back to Rochester." Rachel's tone caught Luke by surprise.

Forcing away thoughts about the other woman, he was recaptured by Rachel's sense of humor. He bantered back. "Not to worry. I'll have it air shipped from the Metro airport to Rochester! Do you use Visa, Master Card, or American Express?"

"I'll rob a bank," retorted Rachel. A brief pause. "I'll let you go now. I'm heading for the covers real soon. All that fresh air today must have gotten to me."

Luke thought of Rachel lying under the covers of her bed. In his mind, as her face turned toward him, he saw the face of another woman–the lady who had taken captive his mind. He flicked the image away to finish off his conversation with Rachel. "By the way, I really enjoyed today. The food was great and the company even better. You have a good night. Bye!"

"God bless," said Rachel. Hanging up the receiver she headed for her bedroom. Keats, her cat, followed her. Rachel had to avoid stepping on her pet several times as Keats continually ran in front of her, begging attention. Picking up her pet, Rachel folded Keats between her left arm and chest. Keats started to purr. "It's bedtime for both of us, Keats." Keats looked up into Rachel's eyes, looking for a comforting long stroke over her head, then down her back.

Rachel's bedroom walls were papered with both large and small yellow flowers running between and among rows of painted white columns running from the floor to the ceiling. Green vines intertwined with the columns and the yellow blossoms. Two spacious windows, kitty-corner from one another, looked out upon a street and the next door neighbor's large apple tree. Lace curtains were crossed and caught midway with large yellow ribbons.

She had splurged on the purchase of her bed. It was white framed, with a large white and yellow striped canopy above. The dresser and end table were also white, but were compromise pieces made from pressed wood allowing her the luxury of the more expensive bed. At the head of her bed hung a large, but simple, cross, also white. She had attached artificial ivy, making the green ivy on the walls look as if the vine had climbed the cross. At each point where the wounds of Christ would have been inflicted, she had placed one, small, artificial, red rose. Other wall hangings, some religious and others sentimental, hung about the room.

Reading a devotional thought for the day, she then "set the table" for tomorrow by coming before the Lord with prayer and thanksgiving.

Luke walked along a country road. Long, green grass pressed against the gravel. Occasional trees towered skyward from the flat ground as it traced the margins of the road. A huge sun glazed its rays over golden grain held high on long stocks. The field of grain extended in all directions. The sweltering heat had forced the shirt from Luke's torso. It hung to the right, tucked into the belt of his pants.

Luke stopped, taking his shirt to mop perspiration from his face. Tucking the shirt back into his belt, he looked down the road. A green oasis of trees and manicured grass was the only significant break in the sea of golden grain. Straining his eyes toward the oasis, he noticed small patches of carefully tended flowers quilted amid the lush grass. Much of the island of green was hid behind a shelter-belt of trees. Only the front of the lawn was open to the road. The country road Luke walked along seemed to exist for only one purpose. Everything led to that single island of Victorian beauty. Sweat rolled down his forehead, stinging his eyes. Grabbing his shirt again, Luke wiped it quickly over his face.

Continuing down the road, Luke wished for a breeze, even a light gust of wind, to break the uncomfortable heat, but the air hung heavy, suspended in time. Nearing the oasis of green, he passed by the shelter-belt of trees. A house, completely white—sides, shutters, and trim—came into view thirty feet from the road. Sitting on its large, open porch was the mysterious woman.

She was just as Luke remembered her from the brief encounter at the seminary, only her clothes were no longer red. She wore a thin, white gown that fell to her ankles. The gown was pasted to her body by the perspiration drawn out by the breathless heat. She sat on a white swing, suspended from the ceiling of the porch by golden chains. Saying nothing, she seemed to take no notice of Luke. Then, taking hold of him with her eyes, she began to hum softly.

Her voice sounded far away to Luke, but it made his heart race. He desired to move quickly... to get closer to the distant melody. The lady waved to Luke. Perspiration ran down her face and neck. Luke would go to her. This time she was not running away. She was waiting for him. He was sure of that.

"Luke!" Rachel's voice called to him. Turning, he looked back along the gravel road. Rachel was walking with an old man, his dark skin contrasted against the bright day. "Luke! I need you!" Waving her hand high above her head, Rachel wasn't sure if Luke heard her calling.

The woman stood up from the porch swing. "Luke, you don't want her." She spoke softly, her voice filled with incense and sweet promise. "You want me." She leaned over the porch rail. "You can have me..."

Looking back at Rachel and the stranger, Luke's body was being drawn by invisible forces along the path leading to the porch. "Luke!" came the commanding cry of Elijah Jordan. Startled, the young pastor woke from the dream.

Wet with perspiration, Luke craved for the woman on the porch. He convinced himself that they would become lovers. All of his liberal, seminary training had provided him with no protection against his base nature. Pleasure was good. Pleasure between consenting adults was natural and healthy. The bedrock of Luke's social philosophy was not grounded upon theology, the study of God and his revelations, but upon man's wisdom expressed in secular science and psychology.

His body sought to touch her body. The chemistry that drew him to her was simple and natural, not evil—so he persuaded himself. After all, the whole animal kingdom has moved forward, and away from extinction, in the rhythm of the sexual impulse. The longings that he had for the lady in red were part of the primal force that drove all life. Luke felt as if he were having an awakening, an epiphany that primitive Christianity concealed from the uninitiated.

He had no understanding of the forces at work within him because he had no grasp of supernatural things. What he believed to be simple about human nature, had monstrous implications. Luke had become single minded in a universe formed of myriad chords. In the limited vista of what he felt was certain, this woman was there for his taking. Pleasure waited down the path, but one person had to be removed from the journey. He would cool things with Rachel. He didn't want to hurt her. Luke hadn't yet taken the next step in lust's deep descent in which causing pain also brings pleasure.

Moonlight flooded his feelings with velvet night. In this twilight, dark cravings mushroomed that could only mimic and mock true human love.

Chapter 15:
BETRAYED

Looking from her hotel room, Morrell followed the outline of distant lights along the Vancouver shoreline. Other lights moved like ghosts along the surface of the water, the darkness hiding the ships that bore them. Taking a deep drag on a cigarette, she craved the nicotine and tar flooding her lungs. Her glass, now half-empty of her sixth vodka and tonic, tipped sideways in a hand resting on the arm of her chair. Sitting alone on the balcony of her hotel suite, she was unaware of the presence that waited knowingly in the darkness.

Standing up, she walked back into the suite where numerous candles cast flickering shadows against walls and furniture. Removing her clothes, she drew down over her head the robe of her coven. Its large hood extended around her face swallowing up her features within its darkness. She became insignificant as a unique human being. To the entity that watched, she was no longer Dane Morrell, but a nameless-nothing, bred like all other humans as cattle for slaughter.

A four-by-four foot sheet of black plastic was tossed over the carpet to prevent staining. Kneeling on the plastic sheet, she took a surgical knife making slits into the palms of both hands. Thrusting her mutilated hands into the air, Morrell waved them slowly and repeatedly above her head. The blood ran down upon her wrists, dripping over her robe, her hair, and the black plastic. "I conjure you, O great one of darkness, O mighty one of ancient days! Accept my blood as the foretaste to a great feast that I offer up to you this night. The hour of your pleasure has come upon the whole world. Soon all shall die except for your servants. We alone shall live, and you shall be god over all gods. We shall bear your children, children for nurture and children for slaughter."

The Shadow of Death wrapped Morrell in tentacles covering her entire body. She gasped for breath. "Molech, I call upon you by name! Protect me as I seek to fulfill your purpose." Molech, walking unseen by Morrell from the corner of the room, forced the tentacles of Death away from the Satanist's face. She gasped in the air. The Shadow of Death became swollen, as if preparing to engage Molech in battle for the prey. Facing off against the other entity, Molech's eyes glowed brightly, so that they, and they alone, could be seen by Morrell. Something was wrong, and she sensed it. A new emotion, fear, forced its way along her spine until she froze, staring into the bodiless eyes of Molech.

A feast of carnage was being prepared by the followers of Molech. Morrell had her part to play in preparing that feast to come. Molech would not permit her to die until her death would multiply out into millions more. The Shadow of Death did not crave in anticipation for the future, but only in the present. Molech would wait patiently until it could consume the lives of millions. The Shadow of Death thought neither of gain nor loss. It had no mind for more lives or fewer lives; its focus was always upon the present victim that was there for the taking.

Morrell prayed to her god. She continued her adoration of the demon until the radio alarm set earlier began to play loudly. It was soon time. The blood on her body had dried. Morrell laughed out loud. The plastic was unnecessary! No one would be left after tonight. "Goes to show," she thought, "habits are hard to break." The details of her ritual had been enacted many times before. Mechanically she had laid down the plastic, doing all that details as usual when conjuring her dark master.

Standing to her feet, she headed for the bathroom of the luxury hotel suite. The room seemed to move away from Morrell as the Shadow of Death remained stationary, like a helium balloon attached to her by a thousand strings. This entity was always particular to each victim, and yet generalized over all the globe. The Shadow of Death was here, was there, was present wherever human life appeared— its appetite insatiable. It was a universal power let go upon the planet thousands of years ago. Unnatural to man, it had since the time of its release dominated mankind's experience through ominous threats and the harvest of loved ones. Only the blood of the Lamb stood against the tentacles that reached for everything mortal. Those covered by the blood were never harvested, but at the time of their departure, an angel brought them into glory. Their bodies were left behind only for a short time, until their flesh could be restored without its earthly imperfections in a place yet awaited.

The bathroom lit up as Morrell flipped on the switch to her left. Walking to the sink, she washed away the dried blood on her hands and arms. She placed Band-Aids on the bleeding wounds, then brushed her hair. Walking to her suitcase, she took out a swimsuit, stretching it over her body like a surgeon placing on a plastic glove. It was not a suit designed for the modest, but for a dark warrior who used lust as a weapon. She threw a towel over her shoulder. Taking a child's plastic pail filled with sand and sporting a yellow plastic shovel partly buried, she headed for the pool located on the roof of the motel.

She enjoyed the looks that focused upon her as she walked through the hallway. Some were deliberate, inviting some kind of response. Others were discreet, but no less laced with the human appetite to consume another for one's own pleasure. To every open invitation she returned a mechanical smile. Each concealed glance that she captured received a sensual wink. The coven had learned that lust drives much of human experience. Members used this dark appetite to seduce and betray those whom it would add to its own number, or destroy.

"Going to the beach?" asked one of the many men who gave a deliberate look.

Spurning him, she walked by without a word. This was also part of the game. Tonight she wanted no company with her as she executed her part of the plan. She glanced down at her watch. Twenty-eight minutes remained as she hit the elevator button for the roof terrace. Stepping into the elevator, she rode it through several stops. Finally the doors opened exposing the stars in a cloudless night. Children were splashing and laughing in the pool. Looking around at the cluttered pool area, she chose a table on the outside perimeter and sat down.

The outside wall of the hotel continued three feet beyond the terrace floor, forming a barrier enclosing the roof. A white iron railing went up another five feet, allowing a full view of the city and grounds below while protecting hotel patrons from accidental (or intentional) falls. Muttering strange words under her breath, Morrell moved her face slowly toward the artificial light above her. Suddenly the light flashed brilliantly, then died. Morrell sat in the shadows of life cast back from children and adults still enjoying the lit courtyard and pool. Striking a match, she placed it against the cigarette resting between her drawn lips. The perverse pleasure of her intention pumped adrenaline into her veins. At the same time another sensation, an unpleasant tightness, closed in, suffocating her within labored breaths. Throwing her lit cigarette to the floor, it became necessary for her to force each breath into her lungs.

Stupefied, she forced her attention upon the watch bathed in perspiration on her right wrist. Four minutes to go... three minutes to go... two minutes to go. Reaching for the pail of sand she dug her hand in exploring for a small beaker. She pulled it from the sand. Twenty seconds to go... fifteen seconds to go.... ten seconds to go. Standing up feebly, she faced the city and opened the beaker. The time had come. Lifting the beaker's cover she waved the small container sideways and down, emptying its contents into a breeze carrying it for some distance into the city of Vancouver.

At that very moment, coven members on every major continent of the world released their lethal virus. Vortexes opened at each point of contamination. Dark entities spun from their centers running into the shadows to hide from the light. Morrell placed the empty beaker on the ledge of the wall and walked toward the elevator, leaving behind the pail, the sand, the white hotel towel. Returning to her room, she poured another vodka and tonic. Morrell couldn't shake the suffocating presence about her, so she cried to her god. Molech stood watching as the Shadow of Death covered her body completely in a deadly grip. Molech did nothing to help her. She was no further use to it. The other entity was simply tenderizing Morrell for Molech's own satisfaction in her death.

Sweat raced down Morrell's face as she turned on a cable news station. A few days back, during her charter to Vancouver, she had wondered which of the coven members would have initial success. Where would an outbreak first surface? Her whole dark heart wanted Vancouver to start the wave of reports concerning the plague. Pouring herself another vodka, she watched a news report featuring a landlocked whale on the west coast. She laughed. Millions of people were about to die, and national news was following the story of one pitiful animal.

Two more hours passed as she sat alone in the dimness of the hotel room. Her blurring eyes no longer captured the images from the news network. Morrell labored for life. Her swimsuit had become drenched in fluids oozing from her pores. Wiping her hand over her wet forehead, it flamed with fever. Nausea overwhelmed her. She bent forward, vomiting on the rug. The room began to spin and shake, but Morrell knew that it was her languishing body that was quavering. In a flash of horror she realized that she had become infected with the virus. Morrell cried out to Molech. The demon appeared before her.

Frozen across something barely resembling a head was a hideous smile. The monster's eyes burned with lust for human flesh. Waving its hand up once quickly into the air, instantly the Shadow of Death was revealed to Morrell, its countless tentacles wrapped about her. Only her eyes were uncovered so that she might die in terror. The tentacles choking Morrell felt like iron but were translucent as smoke. Sick with the virus and overshadowed by death, she faintly discerned the form of Molech walking towards her, its claws exposed and aimed for her soul. She had been betrayed by the Betrayer. The coven mistress finally saw the face of her god when it "loved" her most. The dark god who served the father of lies had honored its father. Hell was now richer in the poverty of one more lost soul.

• • • • •

Bill finished up his early morning routine that Monday sipping down a cup of coffee before heading out for work. Briggs sat in the study sifting through e-mails. "Hey!" shouted Briggs, her voice rummaging through the apartment. "Guess what? I got an e-mail from Kris. She says that Luke is sweet on some woman in his parish. What about that!"

"He hasn't been there that long." Bill cried back in an older brother tone of voice. "He's moving pretty fast, isn't he?"

Briggs left the computer to sport with her husband. "I suppose so." Arriving in the kitchen Briggs squatted eye level with Bill, delivering a wink. "Of course, you'd be an expert on that. I think you were making moves on me within a few days."

"No. No. No," smiled Bill. "Who was making moves on who?"

Briggs blushed, then stood up to walk over to the kitchen sink. "This new relationship does present us with a problem," she said somberly. "At least if he's getting serious about her."

"I don't need this, Briggs," came Bill's irritated reply. "There's nothing more that I can do. You know that! We did what we could, and that's that."

"We could do a transfusion," noted Briggs.

"I'll think about that if something develops between them," answered Bill briskly.

"You know, honey," Briggs replied, "there may not be much time."

• • • • •

The next morning Rachel was up before the sun to do some baking. With her hair tied back in a bun, she wore a blue apron displaying one large daisy on its front. The stem of the flower started at the bottom of her apron, then with a slight bend it continued toward the top. Passing over the pockets it sprouted dark green leaves. At the top, one gigantic, yellow flower covered the chest. Her hands plastered with flour, she worked a piece of pie dough, making it flat and even. Taking a large knife she slid it under the dough. Carrying the flattened pie dough carefully, she set it over the apple filling in the pie tin. Forming and trimming the edges, she then set the pie with four others waiting to be baked.

Rachel looked through her kitchen window. Everything outside remained cast in shades of grey. Like a cemetery just before resurrection day, the morning was on hold until the sun would rise out of the eastern earth like a great god of light, then life would awaken. Looking up at the kitchen clock she caught sight of Keats walking into the kitchen. The morning news would be starting in a few minutes. Heading for the adjoining living room, she turned on the television, facing it into the kitchen. Keats pestered her mistress for attention, glancing against Rachel's legs as she walked. "Keats," barked Rachel, "one of these days I'm going to step on you!"

Keats was purring madly. Rachel's nine month old hungry kitten wouldn't let up on her pursuit of breakfast. "Okay. Okay!" Smiling, Rachel took Keats up into her arms. Keats pressed her nose against Rachel's chin vibrating against her face in a relentless purr. Scratching behind her pet's ears, Rachel walked over to the pantry, set Keats on the floor, and then popped open a can of cat food. "Let's see," she said, looking at Keats as if expecting some kind of reaction, "for breakfast today we have tuna with chicken. How would you like that served?" Holding the can in front of Keats, she allowed the scent to catch her pet's attention. Keats reached out a paw towards the can. "Oh! You would like it cold, with milk on the side. We aim to please." Rachel served up the morning meal for her cat.

With her cat fed and contented, Rachel looked over the counter to the living room TV. A game show was awarding prizes to contestants. Reaching for the remote control, she searched for the news network, then let the control fall into the left pocket of her apron. Standing over the kitchen counter, she looked sideways occasionally to take in the news. Rinsing and drying her hands at the sink, Rachel reached into a bowl of flour, sprinkling some over a breadboard. Dusting her hands with added flour, she started working out another piece of pie dough.

Suddenly a high pitch squeal blared from her TV. The screen had changed from the cultivated stage of a broadcast studio to the frantic atmosphere of a newsroom where a crew of men and women slaved over switches and monitors. Scrolling repeatedly across the screen were the words, "BREAKING STORY." Wiping flour from her hands with a dish towel, Rachel reached for the remote control. Turning up the volume she began sharing an anxious moment with the world.

The screen changed again focusing in upon the talking head of a female reporter. In the background stood the White House. The reporter struggled to keep her notes visible against a strong wind. "The White House has just confirmed that an outbreak of a deadly disease has been reported in major cities around the world." The collar of her jacket flipped up in the wind so she pushed it back down. Her hair was drawn with the strong breeze and flowed towards the left. "The White House spokesman mentioned London, Paris, Tel Aviv, Morocco, Sydney, Vancouver, and Rio De Janeiro by name. When asked if American cities had been infected, he declined to answer at the present time. He said it was in the national interest not to create panic. The cities suspected to be infected would be evaluated to confirm the actual presence of the outbreak."

Rachel rushed into the living room, taking a chair close to the TV. Her apron brushed against the inside arm of the chair, dusting it with flour. "Just a minute," the reporter pushed the earphone against her head. "We will be switching now to a conference room in the White House. The Attorney General has called a news conference."

Again the screen flashed to a noisy room where the Attorney General worked to get the conference going. "I will answer your questions, if I can, in just a few minutes. Ladies and gentlemen, please sit down." Waiting impatiently, he tapped his fingers against the podium. The room quieted. "As you have heard, there is an outbreak of an unknown pathology reported in large cities around the world. It seems to be the work of terrorists who have deliberately targeted these cities, releasing what appears to be a very deadly virus. The Center for Disease Control and Prevention is tracking any reports of the outbreak within the United States..."

"How deadly is this thing?" interrupted a male reporter.

"I'm sorry," said the Attorney General, "I'm not at liberty to release any details about the virus. We don't know enough about it yet, and we don't want to let speculations generate into unfounded conclusions within the public."

"Is this the same virus that has decimated Moscow?" asked another.

"I cannot answer that...."

"Well, what can you tell us, Mr. Edgewood?" came the loud voice of an irritated reporter.

"Not much right now," the Attorney General, Thomas Edgewood, barked back, glaring at the reporter. He was clearly on edge. The veneer manufactured for the public eyes was torn in shreds by the reporter's question. Edgewood handled subsequent questions poorly.

"Listen," he continued, "we're holding this press conference as a favor to you. Don't push it! I'm doing my job, the Center for Disease Control and Prevention is on top of this, and I suggest you do your job. And your job is not to spread all kinds of unsubstantiated rumors which serve only to whip up public frenzy. Your job is to report the facts. When I have facts to share with you, I will!" Waving off further questions, Edgewood abruptly left the podium.

"Dear Father in heaven," prayed Rachel, "send Your holy ones over the face of this planet to protect Your dear children." Her eyes darted back to the television.

Screen change after screen change popped up as one reporter after another from around the world told about hospitals overrun with the sick and dying. One reporter stopped abruptly to reach for his head. His forehead was wet with perspiration. A look of terror crept over his face. Pulling the monitor out of his ear, he dropped the microphone to the ground. He stumbled away from the camera as the scene switched back to a network command center tracking this story around the world.

Rachel, in the flash of this news report on TV, had seen the disease strike without rehearsal. The terror she saw on the reporter's face engraved upon her mind. Rushing to the phone, Rachel punched in her mother's number, but there was no answer. Panic muddled Rachel's mind. Glancing again to the kitchen clock, she sought to reassure herself that her mother was fine. "Think! Think! Think!" stammered Rachel. "That's right. Mom usually takes her bath about this time in the morning."

Seeking to fight off the gnawing bite of anxiety, she reminded herself of God's love and providential care. Her weakness, however, prevailed. With emotions sliding unchecked into a vortex of despair, Rachel needed to talk with someone. She needed another voice as an anchor to halt her tumbling thoughts. She phoned Beth. No answer. Her friend had left for work. Next she keyed in the number to the church. As Tamor picked up the phone, Rachel interrupted her standard greeting. "Have you been following the news?" Rachel blurted.

"Oh you know me, I always listen to my praise tapes on the way to work," she answered. "Girl! What's wrong with you?"

"It's really bad," Rachel replied. "A deadly virus has been released by terrorists all over the world. Hospitals are overflowing with the sick, and the morgues can't handle the dead bodies... They haven't released the U. S. cities that may be infected. I tried to call my mother in Florida, but I got no answer..."

"Rachel," interrupted Tamor, "I don't think you should be alone. Pastor Luke is in, why don't you come in and talk to him?"

"No," protested Rachel, "I don't need any special attention. If this thing continues to spread, he's going to have lots of our people coming to him. Who won't be concerned about family members who might be living within virus—infected areas?"

"I think you should...," continued Tamor.

"No, really!" broke in Rachel. "I'm coming over later to work on some youth stuff. If he's in then, maybe I'll stop by his office." She paused to reflect. "You know, I started baking pies before I turned on the news. Right now I have five apple pies sitting on the counter ready to bake. Seems pretty trivial now, baking pies. I'll see you later."

"Well, whatever," came a hesitant reply from Tamor. "See you girl. I'll be praying for you."

Placing the pies into the oven, Rachel tackled the job of cleaning up her kitchen. Breaking reports on the television told of death and carnage devouring major population centers around the world. Her mother lived alone. What if something bad was happening to her? Rachel shuddered. Her mother wasn't the invincible woman of her childhood memories. Pam could be hurt. Her body could be assaulted and killed. Rachel couldn't imagine life without the weekly phone visits with her mother. The phone rang, tearing Rachel from her morbid thoughts. Luke was on the line.

"Hi Rachel!" Luke worked to brighten his tone. He found it difficult to set his mind on Rachel. When he thought of her, desires for the lady in red muddled his focus.

"Tamor talked to you, didn't she?" interrogated Rachel. Her voice displayed irritation that Luke had been bothered.

"Now don't get on her case," answered Luke. Focus! He had to focus. "She talked to me because she was concerned for you and concerned for your mother in Florida. I made the decision to give you a call. Would you do me a favor?"

"What's that?"

"Would you meet me for coffee at Griff's?" asked Luke.

"When?"

"Any time," answered Luke. "How about right now?"

"I just put some pies in the oven," she said. "Besides, this situation is becoming a big bother for nothing. Really I'm fine..."

"Can you meet me there in an hour?" Luke continued, ignoring Rachel's last comment. "We can make it brunch if that works for you?"

"Okay," she said quietly, "I'll meet you at Griff's in an hour."
She paused. "Thanks!"

"No problem. See you then!"

• • • • •

Deciding to walk to Griff's, Luke hoped that the open air might help clear his mind. The small family-owned restaurant was a favorite haunt for church members when they finished up choir or board meetings. Leaving the office immediately after talking with Rachel, he hoped to stake a claim to one of the restaurant's booths before the rush. Griff's was too small a business to take reservations, so it was first come, first served.

As he turned the corner, Griff's came into view. The restaurant's small lot already overflowed with cars. Vehicles forced out onto the street, were parked along the curb. "It's busier than I thought it'd be this time of day," thought Luke, "people must want to talk about what they're hearing on the news." Walking through the doorway, he saw that all the booths were filled. Finding Ruthie, a waitress that served him often, he asked how long she thought it would be before a booth opened up. "Maybe ten minutes," she answered. Taking a stool at the counter he waited for a booth, ordering an ice tea to sip.

"Nice day, I'd say," smiled a man sitting next to him at the counter. Luke turned to see the leathered face of an old man with dark brown skin. The man's eyes caught him off guard. They were blue like the sky. "Yeah, a barnburner day," smiled back Luke. He had seen this guy recently, but Luke couldn't place him.

"Sad to hear about that... that virus infectin' all over the place," said the old man. The stranger's smile retreated at the mention of the plague. "Can you imagine anyone doing something like that! ...I mean letting a virus out in big cities so that people will die! That's murder! It's worse than murder, 'cause these evil men don't even see the faces that they kill."

"I really don't know that much about it," replied Luke honestly. "I haven't turned on the news yet today, but I did see the morning paper. Nothing in there. I suppose the news about the virus is just too breaking."

"Yes, a sad thing." The old man shook his head gravely. "All hell is breaking out, and no one seems to know what to do about it." A waitress came with the sandwich ordered by the old gentleman. She asked Luke if he would like anything else. He thanked her, but said that he was waiting for someone and would order later.

"So who do the authorities think are responsible for this?" asked Luke. The old man had more information on the crisis than Luke had gleaned. Knowing something more about the outbreak might help his conversation with Rachel.

"They don't know who dun it," said the man, "but I do!"

"Oh great!" Luke thought, "this guy is a couple quarters short of a dollar. So much for helping me with my visit with Rachel." Masking his skepticism, Luke asked the stranger who he thought was responsible for releasing the virus. It was the polite thing to do, but he wasn't looking for an intelligent answer.

"Well, they ain't all the same, you know," he began. "Some are angry men. Angry because they think that society has done them wrong. So they want to get theirs. And true it is that there are some wealthy and powerful folk who have taken advantage of the world's poor. But there are many more good people who will die in this plague—honest, hard workin' people! Ma and Pa businesses built by the sweat of their many years of toiling and sacrifice." He paused. "Yes, evil men who make no distinctions because they see no faces. You and I aren't important to them." He pointed to a young child sitting in a highchair. "That little girl means nothing. Terrorists will kill her like that," he snapped his fingers, "and think nothin' of it."

Luke was feeling uncomfortable. His liberal education, along with many of its left-leaning professors, agreed with the terrorists' conclusion presented by this old man. The whole economic system of the west was a great mistake. Capitalism was an oppressive system that profited the wealthy, while at the same time exploiting the weak. The man sitting to his side, however, saw it differently. He distinguished between the people who misused the marketplace system and others who worked hard in it making an honest living.

"Yes," protested Luke, "but these Ma and Pa business owners in Western countries have built their little oasis of security on the backs of the world's poor. How does that make them any different from anyone else who profits from global poverty and slave labor?"

"You don't see the faces, either, do you son? All you see is one big face that covers up the faces of good folk, one big face that don't even be real. I don't see the big face of an ugly American, like you." The old man smiled, but his smile had no joy. "I see many faces. I see honest folk who would give the shirt off their back if they came across one of them poor people you seem so concerned about." He paused and looked sideways at Luke. "That looks like a mighty fine shirt you got on. I bet the world's poor wouldn't mind having a shirt like that." Luke was getting the drift of the old man's point so he changed the subject.

"You said that the terrorists are not all alike," continued Luke. "What did you mean?"

"I mean that there are others who act wickedly, not because they want what's theirs or are seekin' some kind of revenge." Again the old man paused. "There are others who hunger for anarchy. They feed upon the collapse of civilizations." He reached for Luke's shoulder. "There are powers not of flesh and blood at work, and they have been busy for a long, long time. Oh—flesh and blood have joined their bloody hands with hell, but this is hell's game that's afoot."

It was time to change the subject again. "You know," said Luke, "I feel like I've met you before—quite recently, actually."

"I get that from a lot of folk," smiled the old man, "but let me finish." He looked deeply into Luke's eyes, forcing the young man to glance down at the counter. "The one thing that drives all of this evil is the lust for pleasure. The pleasure of revenge... the pleasure of the hunt... the lust for power... the sexual pleasures forced or given within a society thrown into chaos."

Luke felt exposed. In a flash, he recognized the old man from his dream. Looking up again Luke examined the stranger's face. "No," Luke thought to himself, "that's impossible. It's just an amazing coincidence."

"Do you believe in providence?" asked the older gentleman.

"Well, yes and no." Luke wondered where this question had come from. "We teach that God is directing things, but I'm not a fatalist."

"I believe in Providence," continued the man. "It leaves little room for coincidence."

Again Luke felt as if his inner thoughts were being displayed for public view. Luke sought to assure himself. "This old man couldn't know!"

"Yup," said the stranger, "things happen accordin' to a plan. Take you for example. There's a plan for you. There's also powers that don't want that plan to happen. They know your innermost thoughts and desires. Bigger than that, they understand ways to work your appetites darkly, so that you become slaves to base impulses, walkin' away from your destiny."

Luke's face turned red. Anger seized him, as if he were a boy tired of listening to a fatherly lecture. And yet, he turned to the stranger as if the old man were his father, seeking answers to questions tearing him apart. "So how does a person keep from becoming a slave to the baser side of his nature?"

"By thinking more about others and their needs, and thinking less about your own desires." The old man spoke firm, but kindly. What he said rang true. If only it were that easy.

"I recall a quote from Shakespeare's The Merchant of Venice," remarked Luke. "It goes something like this: 'If to do were as easy as to know what were good to do, then churches would be cathedrals, and poor men's cottages, prince's palaces.

For I could far better to teach twenty what were good to do, than to be one of the twenty to follow mine own teaching.'"

Just then Luke looked up to see Rachel coming in the door. Quickly surveying the room for a booth, he spotted one near the front windows. Turning back to say goodbye to the stranger, he was surprised to see that the peculiar old man had already left. Leaving the bar stool, he walked over to meet Rachel.

"Who was that old man you were talking to?" she asked. "I could see the two of you through the window."

"I don't know," answered Luke. "I eat here a lot, but I've never seen him at Griff's before. When Ruthie comes to take our order, I'm going to ask her if she knows this guy. Did you see where he went?"

"No," she said, shaking her head. "That's why I asked you about him. I saw you through the window, but when I walked in, he seemed to have vanished. How could he have left without being noticed?"

"This guy was strange," answered Luke. "I've never seen blue eyes like his in a man with such rich, brown skin!"

"Wait a minute!" Rachel served up a puzzled look. "That old man was Oriental—from China or maybe Japan."

"You must have been looking at someone else." Pausing to look around the room, Luke searched for someone who might fit Rachel's description. No one! "Rachel, he had dark skin and eyes blue as heaven's own sky!"

Continuing to talk about what each remembered about the stranger, they walked to the open booth where they parked themselves across from one another. Ruthie came by so they ordered the breakfast special—two pancakes, one egg any way you like it, two strips of bacon, and hash browns. Ruthie had never before seen the man who had been visiting with Luke. Pulling out the odd coin that the stranger had left for a bogus tip, Ruthie expressed her disgust to Luke and Rachel. Dropping the coin on the table, she ranted briefly about the mean joke the old man had played at her expense. "I'd rather he had just left!" exclaimed Ruthie. "What did I do to deserve this? A worthless coin! Funny money!" Looking down at the coin, Luke stared in amazement.

"Let me see that!" Luke's excitement exploded a command. Puckering back her lips, Ruthie pushed the coin across the table. Luke recognized it. It was a Roman coin. It was a coin circulated during the period of the New Testament church. "Ruthie," he said to her as she stood coolly to the side of their table, "I think this is pretty valuable. It's very old. I'd put it someplace safe until you have time to visit a coin dealer to determine its actual value."

"Really!" A beaming smile returned to her round face. "Can you imagine that!" She looked back at Luke. "Thanks Pastor, I will take care of this little item!" Tossing a look at Rachel, Ruthie continued, "When I first saw it on the counter, I thought that it was funny money. You know! A stranger comes in, never plans to come back, so he doesn't bother to leave a tip, only funny money." Slipping the coin into a side pocket, Ruthie bustled away to place their order.

"So what did you talk about with the guy?" Rachel asked, intrigued by the stranger's visit. The old man and the mysterious coin had taken her mind briefly from the morning news.

"The man with the dark skin and blue eyes?" teased Luke.

"Whatever!" Rachel waved Luke off. "What did you guys talk about?"

"It's hard to say, really," answered Luke, gritting his teeth and shaking his head. "The best that I can get out of what he said is that he believes that the people responsible for the virus are either revolutionary terrorists or servants of hell."

Luke gave a quick laugh as if to blow it away. Rachel became quiet. She didn't think that the old man's theory was ridiculous at all.

Ruthie returned with their order. Visiting more with Rachel about the plague, Luke could offer little insight into the discussion about recent events. He hadn't seen or read anything himself. He simply commented off of what Rachel shared. Rachel spoke mostly about her mother, consumed in concern for her safety. "If I don't get her by phone today," she said, "I'm going to get in my car and drive down there!"

"Is there anything else that I can get for you?" intruded Ruthie, passing by on her final visit to their table.

"No, the food and service were great as always," complimented Luke.

Ruthie winked, placing their bill on the table. "In the future," she said, "I'm going to pay a whole lot more attention to strangers when they sit in my serving area. After work I'm making a beeline to Frank's Coin and Gun Shop to find out how much that old coin is worth." Taking it out, she rolled it about in her fingers. "He was a peculiar man—wearing all white clothes and all. How old do you think he was? Twenty?"

"Twenty?" gasped Luke

"White clothes!" exclaimed Rachel.

Chapter 16:
EXPOSED

Riveted to the radio, Tamor watched as Luke entered the office waiting area. "How was brunch?" she asked. Tamor's usual effervescent voice was absent.

Luke shook his head. "Rachel is worried out of her gourd about her mom. I hope the phone lines open up soon. She's sitting on pins and needles until she knows that her mother's okay."

"You can't blame her," replied Tamor. "I've been listening to the news about this virus. Very scary! When I take off for lunch today, I'm planning to call my mother and a few others too."

"Hope you can get through," added Luke. "I'm going to try making a call right now." Walking by Tamor's desk, Luke added, "I want so see how mom and dad are doing." When he reached the door, he looked back at Tamor. "I'm sure they're fine, but like you, Tamor, I'll feel better after hearing their voices. I'm going to insist that they stay out of the metro. They need to avoid the public transit, too. I'd tell that to your mom, too. Everyone should just stay tight." Walking into his office, Luke parked himself at his desk.

It took several attempts before Luke got through to his mother. She and his dad were fine, but very anxious for each of their kids. Loosening things up, Luke shared a little about Rachel and her great chicken recipes. Speaking kindly about his new friend, he avoided any suggestion of romantic interest in her. Betty asked him to get the recipe for the chicken soup. "It was good to talk with you, honey," she said. "I'm going to give Bill and Kris a call right after we hang up."

"It may not be easy to get through," warned Luke. "Rachel has been trying to reach her mother in Florida, but can't get through." He paused. "Say! If Bill has any ideas about this virus," drawing the conversation to a close, "tell him to give me a call or drop an e-mail... Yes, I love you too, Mom. Bye."

Checking things out on his desk radio, Luke discovered that it had become a talking box, with no music playing. Reporters were interviewing various experts or sharing rumors about how the plague was affecting this or that city around the world. Curious about what other radio stations were airing during the crisis, Luke pressed the search button, moving from station to station. No music playing anywhere! He finally returned to his regular radio station. Looking at the call letters on his digital dial, he wondered what Kris was doing right now. And Bill? He must be in the thick of this mess! Whatever virus was out there, it had thrown a black pall over the planet, and, at least for the moment, had sucked the joy from civilization.

Luke started work on a Bible study, but thoughts of the mysterious woman made concentration difficult. After about fifteen minutes of wasted time, the spell was broken by the commanding ring of the phone. Tamor was out to lunch so he answered, "Morningside Community Church, this is Pastor Downs."

"Hi Luke," came a friendly but subdued voice, "this is Briggs."

"Briggs!" Luke lit up. "What a great surprise! How are you?"

"We're doing okay, I guess, under the circumstances."

"I can't believe you called!" Luke continued, registering his astonishment. "I thought about calling you guys, but I was sure that Bill would be lost in his work. And you! Aren't you swamped with patients at Oakland Community?"

"We're getting some patients," she replied, "but they've been people reacting to the news about the virus. Mostly a rash of hypochondria—patients imagining that they have contracted the virus. I think it's only a matter of time before the situation here becomes real. It's not for public record, Luke, but Los Angeles has been hit, and the way this thing spreads, well..."

"I'm just glad you're all right," broke in Luke. "How is Bill doing?"

"It took several tries for me to get through to you," Briggs confirmed the jammed phone lines, her tone sagging. "Bill—he's very busy. I don't think that he's gotten more than a couple hours of sleep since this thing started. Keep him in your prayers, will you Luke?"

Luke was struck by Briggs' request. He had understood that she was a skeptic at best. Luke was unaware of Briggs' life–changing encounter with Elijah Jordan. He simply thought to himself, "I guess it's true that there are no atheists in the trenches."

"I just hung up," continued Briggs, "from talking with Betty..."

"Mom did get through to you?" he intruded. "She said that she was going to try to reach Bill and Kris. Mom got lucky!" Luke smiled faintheartedly over the phone. "She got you instead of Bill."

"Say," said Briggs, moving the conversation in the direction that prompted her call to Luke, "I understand that you're getting pretty serious about a woman named Rachel."

Luke was dumbfounded. "You know Mom," he said, "she tends to stretch things a bit." Another lackluster laugh. He'd been so careful about what he said to his mother over the phone. Maybe she had talked to Kris before reaching Briggs. Well, that cat was out. "I'll say this," continued Luke, "Rachel is an astonishing woman..." Luke heard Briggs take a deep breath on the other end of the phone.

"I'd like to meet her." Briggs was struggling to make sense of what came next. It was going to sound crazy, but she blurted it out anyway, "What about this weekend?"

"Huh?" Bewildered, Luke fumbled for words. How could Briggs get away from her job at a time like this? Why would Briggs want to meet Rachel? And for Rachel's part, well, she'd be reluctant for another episode of "meet the family." On top of all this, Luke was trying to cool things with this woman. If Rachel were asked to meet another family member, that would only stir the coals of their relationship. Still, after his meeting with Elijah Jordan, Luke was feeling a fresh desire not to terminate things with Rachel. Luke's head was spinning as he said, "I was planning to meet up with Kris and Rich in the Twin Cities on Saturday. Rachel was going to be with me..."

"Good!" interrupted Briggs. "I'll fly in and join the four of you."

"Is it safe to travel?" asked Luke.

"Safe for now," answered Briggs.

"Well, okay," replied Luke, thoroughly confused by what was taking place. "I'll e-mail the details to you when I have them from Kris, if I can get an open line, that is. Do you think they'll keep the airlines running?"

"Not to or from any of the cities known to be infected," replied Briggs. "Limited martial law was declared by the president just as I picked up the phone to call you. National Guard troops from uninfected areas along with the military are in the process of sealing off cities known to have the virus. The Twin Cities was not a terrorist target, so until someone infected by the disease starts the plague there, its airport will remain open. The government is desperately trying to contain the epidemic, but at the same time prevent the economy from coming to a complete stop. Every attempt is being made to keep the infrastructure of business and commerce going. Frankly Luke, and I shouldn't say this, but I'm not very hopeful..." She stopped.

"Do you know how many cities in the U.S. have been hit?" asked Luke.

"Officially no," she answered. "Unofficially, Bill says there are four."

"That's not as bad as I thought," replied Luke. He brightened up a bit.

"Oh, it's as bad as you thought," Briggs answered gravely. "OIDC is already getting reports of the plague breaking out all around the infected cities. Bill said that the military is in the process of setting up a secondary buffer by closing off all roads within a hundred mile radius of quarantined cities. All it takes is one infected person to travel out of a city. No longer quarantined, that one person then infects others who travel, and the cycle of contamination spins out."

"Could someone fly out of Los Angeles with the disease," asked Luke, "carrying it to the Twin Cities?"

"No," replied Briggs, "not out of Los Angeles. A person infected with the virus would become deathly sick or would die before reaching the Twin Cities. There have been a number of airlines, busses, and even some trains traveling out of these cities where people have dropped dead because of the virus. Every person on an infected public transport is placed under quarantine immediately. The only good thing about this virus is that it kills quickly, making it easy to track. The problem is that we can't reach everyone who has traveled out of these four cities. No doubt some people have been infected, then died obscurely, but not before passing on the virus. All it takes is... one."

"Have you or Bill ever seen anything like this?" raced Luke.

"We've never seen anything with the deadly characteristics of this virus," came her grim reply. "It doesn't fit within the normal rubrics of pathology. It breaks the rules of physics as we understand them." Briggs was saying more than she should.

"Say, I gotta go. My shift is coming up at the hospital, and I still have a few things to do before I leave. I look forward to meeting Rachel on Saturday."

"I look forward to seeing you," replied Luke, "and once again, welcome to the family."

Hanging up the receiver, he fretted thinking that his family had made Rachel and himself into an item. It was partly his fault. He'd been enamored with Rachel, but he'd worked hard to cover up his feelings for her. Of course, he never mentioned the lady in red to a living soul. In his own head she was a mystery provoking deep introspection. Had he conjured her to take the place of Cassandra? "No," he'd say to himself, "I know this woman." He felt that they were star-crossed lovers–destined to be drawn together. Never managed or tame, his thoughts for the lady in red were wild with mystique and hunger.

On the night when the mysterious woman came to him in a dream, his romantic interest in Rachel faded. Luke became desperately bewitched by the lady in red. The enchantress didn't come alone in that dream, Rachel had been there too. She needed his help. The old man was present, walking beside Rachel. Luke was sure that this was the same old man he'd met at Griff's. How could that be? Luke had never seen him before, or if he had, it wasn't important enough to remember. Still, the old man had read Luke like a familiar book, exposing his innermost thoughts. He'd also placed a key into Luke's hand, though Luke didn't yet realize how it could be used to open the cage of the dark woman's trap. "Think more about others and their needs, and think less about your own."

Luke jumped. It was as if he had heard the old man's voice.

• • • • •

That night white vans and white trucks moved through the streets of a silenced city. Members of the Center for Disease Control and Prevention appeared in their white containment suits like ghosts merging into and out of the buildings lining the streets of New York City. Strapped to the bottoms of their boots were special soles created out of a composite of pressed asbestos and concrete. Crude, hastily manufactured, asbestos mitts covered the usual gloves of the containment suit. Like pads on a cats paws, special coverings were glued onto the tips and at the palm of each glove.

Grim Reapers all, they traveled in pairs to take out bodies, placing them onto the platforms of white, flat-bed trucks. Each dead body was never touched, but manipulated into a black body bag using angled boards to leverage the victim of the plague into the bag. Handles that locked like a vice against the material were attached at each end of the bag.

A shadow ran past a dark window five stories up in a high-rise. A shot burst against the opaque silence, tearing into one of the white suits. A sniper, dying of the virus, decided he would take some of the government cronies with him. As the CDCP team sought shelter, another round of fire broke down upon the street.

A woman of the CDCP team lay dead on the asphalt. She was a mother of three. The murders of these two CDCP personnel were not isolated cases.

All over the city, people dying of the plague had turned against those working on the clean-up operation. Within minutes of the recent shootings, a military truck pulled up in front of the building armed with troops trained for urban warfare. They took aim on the building as the CDCP team emerged from their concealed positions moving towards the military transport. The shadowed figure appeared suddenly in the open window. Instantly shots rang from each trooper's rifle. A man fell from the window, dead before he hit the ground.

The bodies of the slaughtered CDCP team were placed on the same truck as the plague–slain victims in that neighborhood of the city. The truck maneuvered its way down city streets filled with vacant cars, some standing in the middle of the road. The military truck came to a freeway exchange joining onto an interstate where the only vehicles moving were white. Finally, the truck took its place in line with other white trucks, also loaded with lifeless bodies, waiting to enter the Incineration Center of the Municipal Waste Treatment Facilities.

New York City was not the exception. Day after day, incidents of violence and chaos broke out from everyday citizens as the plague made its way through large metropolitan cities.

• • • • •

Rachel sat by the phone. It was Saturday morning. She had tried all day Friday, and several times earlier that morning, to reach her mother. The phone lines throughout the country were so jammed that Rachel couldn't get through to Florida. Unable to ascertain her mother's condition, she felt compelled to drive down to Naples. She would leave that morning—she had already wasted precious time. Her trip with Luke to the Twin Cities would have to be canceled. She felt badly about it, but she wouldn't enjoy herself coming off as a lead balloon for everyone.

Dialing up Luke's home number, there was no answer. Letting it ring until the answering machine clicked on she listened to the recorded message. "Hello, this is Pastor Downs. I'm not able to come to the phone right now, so please leave a message, and if you would like me to get back to you, add a phone number. Thanks. And God bless."

She didn't want to do it this way. "I shouldn't just leave a message," she thought. "This is a pretty big event to be calling off at the last minute." But then again, maybe it was better that she didn't talk with Luke. Had she reached him, Luke might have tried to persuade her not to make the trip to Florida.

"Luke, this is Rachel," she spoke to the recorder. "I'm sorry about this short notice, but I won't be able to go with you to the Cities. As soon as I can get a bag thrown together, I'm heading down to Naples. When I get there, I'll give you a call—if I can get through on the lines. I do feel badly about this, but you wouldn't want your sister to meet me when I'm feeling like this. Frankly, I'm just a wreck until I know that my mother is doing okay."

She thought about how Luke would feel as he listened to her message. "I'll try to make it up to you! Oh—two more things. I'm going to drop a copy of my route in your mailbox as I head out of town. I'm doing this just in case I run into trouble. I hope it's not a bother for you. It helps me to know that if I have problems, that someone would know where to track me down. And finally, would you please feed Keats or ask Tamor to? I'll leave a key under the mat. God bless you too! I'll keep you in my prayers. Please remember me... I," she paused, "do like being with you. Bye."

· · · · ·

Luke returned to his apartment around 10:00 Saturday morning. He had been called to the home of a member who had just received news that her son had died in New Orleans because of the plague. At that member's home Luke struggled to be a comfort to a woman overwhelmed because of death. Once again he discovered that his bag of theology offered him few tools for helping those devastated by death. If he tried to tell the grieving mother that her son was in heaven, he was afraid that his eyes would betray his own skepticism. All he could do was hold her hand and listen. "I hate these kinds of visits," Luke said out loud. Shuffling his feet along the floor to his couch, he flopped into a soft corner, and began to doze.

Soon awaking, he decided to give Rachel a call, finalizing their plans for the day. The face of the lady in red intruded into his mind. Reaching for the phone he was greeted by two beeps. Someone had left a message. He'd call Rachel first and then attend to the message. Punching in her number he reached her answering machine. "This is Luke," he said into the recorder, "I'll call back later. I just wanted to touch base with you about our date for today." Hanging up, he winced. "Damn! Why did I use the word date?"

He called the number that would take him to his messages, then added the security code. He had only one message. He activated the message left by Rachel. Her voice, her words, the reason for her call, stimulated a variety of emotions. He was disappointed that he wouldn't be spending the day with Rachel. She was fun, a pleasure to be around. And yet, Luke continued to be enamored with thoughts about the other woman. Luke was a man divided. Burning passion within him, driven by demonic impulse, reaching for the mysterious lady, while concern knotted his stomach as he thought about Rachel driving to Florida by herself.

Listening to the radio, news reports tumbled with his anxious thoughts. There had been no mention of any outbreaks in Florida. That was good. Naples appeared to be safe for the time. Still, it was a long drive to Naples. Rachel's car could break down. Or, she might drive into a town for gas, or to eat, and become infected. Breaking news stories flooded the airwaves with reports of the plague sending its arteries out from contaminated major cities into small towns around the country. "Damn!" he said again to the empty room.

Luke decided to call Briggs, saving her the trip to Minnesota. The phone lines were thick with traffic. He couldn't get through. It looked like Briggs would be spending time with just the three of them, like it or not. He hoped that his new sister-in-law would not be too unsettled after making the trip and then no Rachel. Trying to call Kris again, Luke continued to run into plugged lines. "There are going to be lots of surprises when 5:00 comes around," he thought to himself. Kris and Rich would be expecting Rachel and there would stand Briggs!

Rushing down to his mailbox, Luke took out the route mapping Rachel's trip to Florida. She had detailed more than just the route. At each major city or planned stop, Rachel had included the times that she expected to be in that area. He noticed that Rachel had scheduled tonight in a motel someplace near St. Louis. In the morning, he noted, plans were made to spend a good part of Sunday with her aunt in Eddyville. It struck him as odd. "Why," he wondered, "would she spend so much time with her aunt if she was in such a hurry to get to Naples?"

· · · · ·

Deciding to leave early for his dinner meeting in the Twin Cities, Luke wanted to be there when Kris and Rich first ran into Briggs. Taking with him the map left by Rachel he arrived at the hotel, parked his car in the ramp, then headed for the restaurant. He ordered a glass of wine at a small stand in the lobby. Sitting down at a table that overlooked the entrance to the hotel restaurant, he waited. Twenty minutes later he saw Kris and Rich walking down the hallway holding hands. They had just come down the elevator from their floor.

Waving, Luke caught the eye of Rich. Rich then pointed Kris to Luke, and they both returned the wave. Setting down his glass, Luke moved quickly to meet them at the entrance of the hotel's restaurant. As always, Kris was the first to vice her brother in a long hug. "It's so good to see you," she said, pressing her head against his shoulder. She gave a second squeeze then whispered into his ear, "I'm so scared with what's happening." Stepping back, she looked over to the table where Luke had been sitting. Next she studied the nearby area. "Where's Rachel?"

"That's a long story," he replied. "She couldn't make it. I'll tell you more over dinner, but right now I want to say hello to this big guy over here." Walking over to his sister's friend Luke was greeted by Rich's outstretched hand. Luke took it with both of his, shaking it heartily. "It's good to see you again Rich."

"It is my pleasure," replied Rich. "I find Kris' entire family to be a delight!"

"She told you to say that, didn't she!" Luke attempted to slosh some humor into the thickening tension felt by all because of the plague.

"No!" smiled back Rich. "I had a lot of fun at your family get-together. I just wish that we were meeting tonight under better times." He paused as Luke let go of his hand. "I'm really sorry that Rachel could not be here. I was looking forward to meeting her."

"Not half as much as I wanted to meet her," added Kris. Rich excused himself briefly to check on their table. Returning with the hostess, they were led to a table overlooking the river. The table was set for four.

"Would you like me to remove one of the settings?" asked the hostess as the three were seated. Luke quickly fielded the question, "No, there's one other coming. Thanks."

Screwing up the left side of her face, Kris took hold of Luke with a stare.

"Guess who's coming to dinner?" he asked, smiling away the chaos outside.

"Don't do this to me Luke," cried Kris, screwing up both sides of her face while shaking her head and finger at Luke.

"Briggs!" he said brightly, still refusing to let the plague infested world into the moment.

"Briggs is going to be here this afternoon?" gasped Kris.

"Yup," said Luke pointing, "and there she is now."

Briggs waved to them from the entry as she walked toward their table. Casting off the usual polite greetings, the first words from her mouth were, "Where's Rachel?"

"That's what we would all like to know," responded Kris.

"What!" gasped Briggs. "She's not here?"

"I'm sorry," said Luke sheepishly, "but something came up..."

"Can I go down with you and meet her in Rochester?" interrupted Briggs. His sister-in-law carried a black canvas bag and a small brown purse.

"No," answered Luke. "Rachel left a message. Said she'd gone by car to see her mother in Florida. She regretted breaking things off, but I guess she felt she had to go."

Briggs crumbled into the empty chair. "Then there's no way for me to reach her," she said softly.

"Not right away," answered Luke.

Rich sat back measuring the situation. "Briggs," he said calmly, "is there something here that we should know, but you aren't telling us?"

Bending forward, Briggs placed her elbows on the table, rubbing her face several times with her hands. "We need to talk," she said. "This isn't going to be easy, especially for you Luke. I really wanted to get to Rachel before I started into any of this."

Luke looked angry, but his expression was masked confusion. He sensed that Briggs was concerned for the safety of Rachel. Something was wrong—terribly wrong. "Why did you want to meet Rachel?" His voice probed into the mystery kept hidden behind Brigg's reticent words. "Frankly Briggs, I've been wondering about this meeting from the moment you suggested it on the phone."

Briggs began to explain about Seda, the first known victim of the plague on the continent. She pointed out that for some unknown reason, instead of dying, Seda lived and her blood manufactured a vaccine against the virus. Seda's blood was vaccine! Its presence was miraculous, completely defying the laws of science. The team at OIDC was working with her blood, analyzing it—seeking to come up with a way to multiply the property that brought about the immunity. They discovered that the immunizing property could not be made synthetically. Seda's blood had to somehow initiate the immunity. It could be multiplied, but it could not be duplicated. Samples of her blood had been sent out to pharmaceuticals, with the same goal of manufacturing a vaccine by multiplying the immunizing property.

"It became clear to those working at OIDC, even before the plague erupted in the U.S., that it was impossible to produce enough vaccine to dent the progress of the virus if it struck within a year," continued Briggs. "This realization—that it would be impossible to mass produce enough vaccine to give any real protection for the world, caused Bill to call a special meeting of the staff directly working with PRN40—the virus." She paused. This was the part that she still struggled to put into words.

"So what was the meeting all about?" prompted Kris.

"They decided that each of them would take enough of a prepared serum of

Seda's blood to immunize their families," answered Briggs directly. She had tears in her eyes. Tears that spoke for all the lives that would not be saved. "The night before the meeting, Bill had asked Seda for a half-pint of her blood. She let him draw it."

Pausing, Briggs looked over the faces at her table. "He worked through the early morning preparing the vaccine. When he met with the OIDC group that evening, even before they had agreed to his plan, Bill had the prepared vaccine with him. He was going to insist upon his plan, even if they were reluctant, but they all agreed. They understood that something of humanity had to survive this plague. It was a stroke of fate that they and their families would be among the remnant to live."

"Wait a minute!" Luke shook his head several times. "Are you saying that we have been vaccinated against the virus?"

"Of course," interjected Rich. "That's why you called the family get-togethers. And the next day we all woke up sick because of a reaction to the vaccination. Am I right?"

"You are exactly right," answered Briggs.

"So we are immune from the virus!" blurted Kris.

"We think so," said Briggs. "Obviously we've not had lots of time to test our research. But by the book, as if Seda's blood chemistry could be explained there, we should all be safe. Everyone at OIDC has been vaccinated. None of us have shown signs of the virus. We no longer bother to wear protective gear unless we're maintaining the ruse, keeping the silence about the vaccine."

"All of us," replied Luke somberly, the reality of Rachel's situation crystallizing in his mind, "except Rachel."

Briggs looked down, away from Luke's eyes. "I came here to help her Luke. I'm sorry..."

"Do you have more vaccine?" he asked intensely. "If I could catch up with Rachel, do you have some vaccine that I could take to her?" This time the mysterious woman made no entrance into Luke's mind. His single-minded focus spotlighted upon Rachel's danger. She needed him. A flood of emotion for her overwhelmed him momentarily. He loved her. He cared for Rachel more than life itself. His concern for another person was the key unlocking the gate that had held him captive to the enchantment of the mistress of dark desires. He didn't realize it at the time—the lady in red was a million miles from his mind—but his love for Rachel had broken the spell of lust.

"It's not that simple," replied Briggs, lifting her eyes to take Luke in. "There's no more available vaccine. Bill took a terrible chance to get what he did. The only way to help Rachel now is by a blood transfusion from someone who has immunity to the virus. Frankly, the blood needed to immunize another is so little that it's not really even a transfusion. The quantity is so small," emphasized Briggs, "that the usual precaution of matching blood types is unnecessary." She looked at the canvas bag. "I brought the equipment in this bag to do the blood exchange..."

"But if it's just a little blood that you need," interrupted Kris, "why is it so difficult to produce large quantities of the vaccine? Just take from those who have been immunized and start making more vaccine!"

"Blood from those immunized by the serum produced from Seda's blood does not act the same way," answered Briggs. "We don't understand why. We don't understand how it is that Seda's body produces blood serum that is an almost free-standing vaccine in and of itself. What we have discovered is that blood from immunized individuals is only effective when transfused immediately. It cannot be put into a sterile bag or beaker and used later like Seda's blood. It can't be produced into a vaccine. There's no scientific answer as to why it works like this..." Briggs looked over the group again. "Seda's blood is for everyone, near or far. But those who benefit from it, must share it immediately, person to person, before the onset of the disease."

"Rachel left her travel route with me." Luke spoke mechanically, his eyes glued on the black canvas bag. Suddenly he looked up, his voice animated. "Briggs, could you go with me, and when we find Rachel, give her a transfusion from my blood?"

Tears formed again in her eyes. "I'm sorry," she said softly, "I'm needed at the hospital. Who knows how many lives will be affected if I'm not there..."

"Damn!" swore Luke. "I'm talking about one life that will die if you don't help me!"

The Guardians standing around the table heard Luke's words. One said, "He is beginning to see faces."

"Yes," said another, "and soon he may learn not to call to his unwanted master."

"Luke," Briggs was finding it difficult to speak, "if you decide that you want to go after Rachel, you don't need me. What you'll need to do is figure out a way to get the transfusion done by someone else. It won't be easy. Clinics aren't used to having people walk in and then ask to share blood." She looked over to the bag that lay on the table. "I'll send this with you. It won't do you much good without someone who knows how to use the equipment, but you can take it..."

"Can you show me how to use it?" asked Luke. It was a rhetorical question. He would insist upon Briggs explaining the procedure.

Briggs shook her head. "I think you should really try to find a doctor or technician to do the transfusion."

"Will you try to teach me?" demanded Luke. His voice was flat, firm—almost loud.

"I'll outline the basics," she said, "but do you understand how crazy it would be for you to do a medical procedure without proper training! It's like trying to make puffed wheat by reading the ingredients off a cereal box."

"Hopefully if I find Rachel in time," Luke answered, his voice was kinder, "we can find someone qualified. But if not, there's very little to lose in my trying the procedure. Right?"

"Right," answered back Briggs. Leaving their table without placing an order they walked back to Kris' room. Taking out the equipment Briggs had brought with her, she explained how each item was used in the procedure. Luke watched without showing any emotion. He had become a machine programmed for saving Rachel at all costs.

Finally Briggs placed everything back into the bag handing it to Luke. Taking it, Luke took to his feet. Knowing that her brother would waste no time in leaving, Kris sprang up from the bed and went to him. She delivered another immense hug to her brother. "You take care, little brother..."

Briggs also walked over to Luke, but Luke took the initiative. Hugging her, he said quietly, "Thanks Briggs. What you did in coming here today was huge. I just don't know what to say..."

Quickly shaking hands with Rich, Luke left the hotel.

Chapter 17:

TRAVELING COMPANIONS

Luke glanced at his watch as he headed out of the Twin Cities back to Rochester. His emotions cried out for an immediate beeline to St. Louis. His head told him to get a few hours of rest. Like a camel storing water, he'd need to soak up sleep for his trip south. Who knew how much rest he would manage in the next few days? Looking at the itinerary again, he noted that Rachel's stop at Eddyville would keep her there until 4:30 in the afternoon. He'd sleep until five Sunday morning and still manage to get to Rachel's aunt's before she left Eddyville. Tired and distressed, Luke pulled up to his apartment.

Fumbling his fingers over the security keypad, he tried several times before landing upon the combination of keys clicking open the door to his apartment complex. Taking the stairs, he noticed a poignant odor impregnated into the air. As he turned into his floor's hallway, he saw smoke passing over the top edge of a partly opened door. Sprinting swiftly to the door, he slammed it to the side, choking against the caustic fumes.

Inside, myriad flames danced above numerous candles cluttering about the room. A woman, unknown to him by name, but recently moved into the complex, lay on a carpet spread over the hardwood floor. Embossed upon the black carpet was a golden pentagram. The woman wore a black robe, its hood completely concealing her head as she lay face down. Her motionless hand held a stick of incense as it burned into the carpet releasing the smoke and foul odor.

"Are you all right?" Luke asked, rushing to the woman. There was no answer. Kneeling beside her, his knee touched against the outside perimeter of the pentagram. Instantly pain impaled his knee as flames shot up at the point of contact. Lunging backwards, Luke knocked against a wooden table, sending candles flying onto the floor. Racing quickly to the overturned candles, he sought to contain the fire. Snuffing out the fallen candles, Luke returned to the woman, standing helplessly above her silent form. All over the room he'd noticed golden coins in random piles, some simply scattered over the wooden floor.

Darting to the kitchen, he filled an unwashed pan with water then returned to the living room. Tossing the water at the smoldering flame, he was thrown back by an explosion as the water passed over the edge of the pentagram. Knocked out for several minutes, Luke came to his senses, fighting the pain of bruised muscles as he got back to his feet. Coughing against the unnatural smoke and smell, he looked for the woman. She was gone. The carpet was gone. All the candles had vanished. Luke felt as if he were waking from a bad dream. But no. He stood in an unfamiliar apartment, his right knee signaling raw pain under pants seared by fire.

Swiftly Luke left the apartment, pulling the door closed. Arriving back at his own apartment, his thoughts stumbled for some stationary point of reason. Should he call the police? What would he tell them? Most importantly, what would they believe? How much of what he remembered had he imagined? Had the stress over Rachel's perilous trip caused his mind to snap?

Hearing footsteps walking down the hall, Luke cracked open the door of his apartment. The newly arrived woman from the apartment was coming his way. Dressed in street clothes, she smiled noticing Luke taking her in through the small crack of the door. It was her! Luke had no doubts that it was the lady in red moving silently down the hallway. Latching the door, Luke dashed madly for the bathroom. Crouched over his toilet, while fighting back the striking pain in his knee, he vomited. The woman he once desired now repulsed him, festering fears and morbid thoughts of death.

Sliding into the soft sheets of his bed, Luke's mind welcomed the idea of a good night's sleep. Suddenly another thought crossed his mind. His torso flew up, throwing his covers to his knees. He had come to grips with the evening's bizarre encounter with the lady in red, but what if he dreamed of her? What if in the unguarded territory of sleep she came to him again? Lying back down he pulled the pillow tightly to his chest. Sleep came, but slowly.

• • • • •

It was late Saturday evening. That morning Tamor had made the decision to travel with Rachel to Florida. It appeared coincidental that she had stopped by at the house just before Rachel was to leave. Yet in the greater hand that belongs to Providence, Tamor was intended to make this trip with her friend. Tamor had called Pastor Horton for a green light to take off a few days from work. After gaining his blessing, she phoned Julie asking her to take over at the office until she returned. Presently Rachel and Tamor were navigating through the St. Louis area on Interstate 55. Rachel had been behind the wheel since they left Rochester. She was showing signs of road-wear. "Say girl," said Tamor, "let's pull off and get a cup of coffee. I'm taking the wheel for a while after that."

"Sounds good," said Rachel. "I'll try another call to mom's."

Leaving the interstate, they drove to an all-night café adjoining a gas station. Brilliant overhead lights beamed down on the concrete creating a bubble of brightness that pushed back the night sky. Rachel looked for a place to fuel her car, finally parking under a broad metal canopy that stood above the pumps. Squinting under the blinding lights above, she left the car to begin filling her gas tank. The black hose from the pump was twisted, forcing her to work it out until she got enough length to reach her car. Stepping from the car, Tamor walked to the café.

She decided to make use of the restroom before recharging herself with black coffee.

After topping off the tank of her car, Rachel walked to the café. Tamor sat at a corner booth shimmering under the light of a neon sign hanging in the window just above her. Rachel didn't join Tamor at the booth, but stood beside the table. Tamor had made her visit to the ladies' room. Looking up at Rachel, she exclaimed, "I needed this stop!"

"Yeah, me too," winked Rachel. "I'm going to check out the restroom and then try to give mom a call. I'll be back in a few minutes. Go ahead and get something for yourself." Rachel started to walk away, but turned, hurrying back to the table. "Say girl, would you mind getting me a cup of coffee at the same time?" She paused. "I'm hungry too!" Rachel picked up a little stand from the table advertising the daily specials. "Would you please order me a bowl of the house chili, too?"

"Sounds good!" replied Tamor. "I'll double that order."

Rachel left, returning before their order had arrived. "I got through on the lines," she said worriedly, "but there was no answer at mom's."

"Did you get her answering machine?" asked Tamor.

"No," Rachel brightened a little, "so maybe the problems are in the phone lines. I'd have gotten mom's voice mail if the lines are up and running."

"She's fine, Rachel!" said Tamor. "But let's have another prayer."

"I'd like that..." Rachel fought back another flood of emotions.

As Rachel slid into the booth, Tamor reached across the table taking her hand. She prayed for Rachel's mom, for her own mom, and for so many who were in danger because of the plague. She asked God to continue to keep Rachel and herself safe as they traveled to Naples. She was praying for God's blessing on the food when the waitress arrived with their order. Glasses and plates rattled around their closed eyes. Stopping, Tamor looked up at Rachel, smiled, and let go of her hand. "Chili looks good!"

"It sure does!" salivated Rachel, her appetite devouring the chili long before it had arrived. She looked across at her friend. "I can't tell you how much it means to have you with me. I still feel, well, humbled that you would do this for me."

"Are you kidding!" smirked Tamor. "This is like a free vacation. You're paying for the gas and all, I'm just enjoying the ride."

"Yes," returned Rachel, "and I'm paying for the meals too." Grabbing the bill she stuffed it into a free pocket.

"Oh no you're not!" protested Tamor. "Now give me that!"

The two quibbled back and forth over who would pay the bill. Rachel, first to nab the bill, prevailed in the end. Tamor, however, said that she would be quicker on the draw next time. She was not going to have Rachel picking up all the expenses! They talked about Morningside, a little more about Rachel and Pastor Luke, concluding with another quick look to Rachel's map.

When Rachel drew out her route Saturday morning, she had planned to stay the night at a motel somewhere around the St. Louis area. She'd need to catch a good night's sleep. Now that Tamor was with her to help with the driving, she could have driven straight through to Naples, with the exception of the one stop she had planned for at Eddyville, Kentucky.

"I'm still going to find us a motel for the night," said Rachel. "I want to visit my aunt in Eddyville. We'd be waking her up in the early morning hours if we drove through. Besides, the itinerary I left with Pastor has me staying at Eddyville until late afternoon on Sunday. I want us to keep fairly close to the plan I left with him." It felt strange to be calling Luke "pastor," but that's still how Tamor related to him.

"I don't get it, Rachel," said Tamor as they walked over to the counter to pay their bill. "If you are in such a hurry to get to your mom's, why are you spending so much time at your aunt's tomorrow?"

"Let's save it for the car," answered Rachel. Leaving the café, they walked through the bubble of light capturing them within the surrealistic environment. Pulling back onto the freeway with Tamor behind the wheel, Rachel kicked off her shoes, then smothered the lower half of her body under a warm lap-blanket. "Okay," she began, "you want to know why I'm taking so much time in Eddyville." She adjusted the blanket around her feet to keep them warm.

"First off, let me explain why I planned an itinerary and left a copy with Pastor Luke." Rachel brushed off some cracker crumbs from her blouse. The chili had come with a plate load of crackers. "When I started my sophomore year at college, I bought a car. Actually, I bought mostly trouble and rust, but it provided me with a way to get to my evening job." Tamor laughed, adding that her first car in America must have been its cousin.

"I also used it to go home for visits with the folks," Rachel continued. "Dad trusted that car about as far as Grandma could spit. He insisted that I detail out a map for the five-and-a-half hour trip. The map included all my planned stops for gas and the like. I also estimated the time that I'd be arriving at each major town along the way. The idea was that dad would know where I was as I drove along the route. Knowing where I was somehow made him feel better." Rachel looked from the windshield over to Tamor. "If something did happen, dad could track me down. It made me feel better too."

"Listen girl," interrupted Tamor, "I hate to tell you this, but you are a long ways past being a schoolgirl who needs to be taken care of by mommy and daddy." Tamor giggled.

"Yeah," replied Rachel, "but you tell that to my mom! When I moved to Rochester, even after dad had died, she still had me send her my itinerary before I traveled to Naples. It made us both feel better about my solo trip. It also became a bit of a game."

"How's that?" asked Tamor.

"Well," answered Rachel, "for example, mom would call Aunt Anne's in Eddyville at the time I estimated to be there. Aunt Anne would let me answer the phone during my stop at her house. When the phone rang, whether it was mom or not, I'd pick up the phone and say something ridiculous, like, "Flat Fly's Swatter Shop."

"You need a cellular phone!" laughed Tamor.

"You bet!" said Rachel. "And I don't have one for the same reason that you don't have one. Just a little short of the green stuff..."

"So why did you leave an itinerary with Pastor Luke?" Tamor was curious about the situation with her friend and the pastor.

Rachel didn't take the bait, not yet, deciding to avoid a discussion about her relationship with Luke. She kept the subject close at hand. "Obviously I didn't have time to send anything to mom. Besides, who knows if all the mail is getting through?" Rachel stretched her head left, right, then back seeking to loosen some stiffness. "Of all the trips I've taken, this wins hands down as the most risky—with the plague and social problems—you know. I wanted someone to know where I was." Looking to her side at Tamor, she concluded, "And that brings me to your question about the time I planned to spend at Aunt Anne's."

"Yeah, what about that?" broke in Tamor. "I can see why you might stop, but you're planning to stay there better than half the day! That's a huge amount of time under the circumstances."

"You're right," agreed Rachel, "it's a lot of time. My stop won't make sense to you unless you understand the family politics. When I was planning the trip to Naples, I had no choice but to schedule a stop at my aunt's. Mother would shoot me if I didn't check in on her sister. But I didn't know how long I should plan for at Eddyville. I wanted to leave definite times with Pastor, and so I had to make a decision about my length of stay." Looking down, Rachel shook her head slowly. "This sounds crazy, but I had this feeling that I should plan for more time, and not less. I couldn't shake that feeling, so when I went back and filled in the times, I planned to leave Aunt Anne's in the afternoon."

"It didn't trouble you," asked Tamor, "about your mom and all? Your stop would delay your trip..."

"Yes it bothered me," Rachel interjected, "but I just had this feeling that I needed to plan some time at my aunt's. I prayed about it too, and the feeling grew stronger. I finally decided that I'd keep the radio on as I drove to Naples—just as we've been doing, and if any reports of the plague indicated an outbreak in Florida, I'd chuck the whole itinerary and head directly for mom's... and as fast as I could get this bucket of bolts to move."

"So you're saying that Pastor Luke knows that we will be leaving your aunt's at," she thought back to the travel plan, "4:30 in the afternoon?"

"Should," Rachel answered, "if we stick to the plan. And I think it's a good idea to keep with the schedule."

"Say, Rachel," Tamor's voice became softer. "If this plague becomes really serious, would you do me a favor?"

"Of course! Just ask."

"I'm not ready to get into it," continued Tamor. "Not just yet. It has to do with my past, and a person who is very special to me." Tamor's voice cracked. "If something should happen to me, or if things get bad in the city where she lives, I may need your help to take care of a few matters. Okay?"

"What are friends for?" smiled Rachel, wondering what was on Tamor's mind.

"I'm sorry to be keeping something back from you." Tamor was crying. "I'll know when the time is right. Are you mad at me?"

"No! I'm not mad at you, Tamor. I've got things in my past too. There are right times and wrong times for getting into stuff. I know that you're just waiting for the right time."

"Thanks," said Tamor, wiping away tears from her face with a tissue.

The two women agreed upon a small motel just off the interstate, its neon sign advertising low rates. There they enjoyed a welcomed sleep that was followed by warm showers and hot coffee in the morning.

• • • • •

Early Sunday morning Luke, red-eyed and packed, was behind the wheel tracing the route that Rachel had left with him. Looking at the dash clock, he took a mental note of the time, 5:23. Luke calculated that if Rachel was following her plan, she was likely still asleep at some bargain hotel. Luke imagined Rachel sleeping safely in a warm bed. He conjured up her face as if it were lit by a faint glow breaking through a crack in the bathroom doorway, its light keeping vigil in the night. If nothing changed from her plan... if there were no breakdowns or unscheduled stops for him along the way... he would catch up with her in the late afternoon at Eddyville.

Continuing to capture the face of Rachel in his mind, he began to pray for her. This prayer was not like the ones he learned at his progressive seminary. He didn't reach out with pre-programmed words to some vague Entity. His concern for Rachel brought him in touch with a Being whom he had lost, but Whom had never been a hairbreadth away from him.

"Father," he prayed, "I feel like I'm a child taking my first steps as I pray to You right now. I lean against Your strength, feeling that I've got nothing to offer. Out of Your love for Rachel, I pray that You will protect her. Keep her safe from the plague. Guard her from accidents, and keep her awake as she travels all alone." Luke was unaware about Tamor making the trip with Rachel.

"I plead with You, please let me reach her before she comes into contact with the virus. I don't ask this for myself." He paused, and then continued, "No, Father, I am asking this for myself. I care a great deal for Rachel. But I also ask it for her. And as I ask for her safety, I do it in the name of... Your Son... Jesus Christ." He felt tears stinging against his eyes as he prayed, once again believing, so personally, in the Savior. And the angels rejoiced in heaven.

• • • • •

Downing a quick continental breakfast served in the motel lobby, Tamor and Rachel were back on the road. It didn't take them long to reach Eddyville late that Sunday morning. Soon they were cruising the familiar territory of her aunt's neighborhood. Driving down the street taking her to Aunt Anne's commodious yellow house delivered a sense of peace and stability to Rachel's unsettled disposition. It always felt good to be there.

Behind the white picket fence boxing in Anne's front yard, her aunt had arranged all kinds of lawn ornaments. Some were plastic moving with the wind, others were molded concrete. An ornate birdbath stood dead center to a flower bed cut kidney-shaped into the green grass. The small flower patch of assorted colors was overrun with perennials of all sizes and shapes. Rachel and Tamor pulled onto the black asphalt driveway of the old yellow house under a cool morning sun. Aunt Anne had lived in this house for as long as Rachel could remember.

· · · · ·

At the same time as Rachel and Tamor pulled into Anne's driveway, back in Oakland Bill was meeting with his pastor before the morning service. Several times he glanced at his watch. He had to catch an afternoon plane for an emergency meeting in Washington with the President. "Do you understand what I'm saying, Pastor?" asked Bill.

"It seems pretty farfetched," Pastor Miller answered, taking a deep breath. "If anyone else were telling me this, I wouldn't believe it..."

"You have to believe me," said Bill, "and I need your blessing. And then, I need help getting things organized."

"So you think that we should begin with the church elders?" asked Pastor Miller.

"I can't give transfusions to the entire congregation at once," answered Bill. "If I get the elders immunized, within a few days they can share their immunity with others. We will work the circle bigger and bigger, until, hopefully, we can get everyone in the parish protected."

"But some could contract the virus before everyone is immunized," added the pastor, concerned for all his flock.

"Yes," said Bill gravely, "but you know, pastor, there's some divine justice in all this. I believe that we are seeing a modern day miracle of God. He is preserving, once again, a remnant. He did the same thing throughout the Old Testament. When God preserves a remnant, He works first with those who are most faithful to Him. In our situation, the same principle is at work. The first to be protected in the parish would be those who worship regularly and give of their time as leaders. Next, we would reach to those who are faithful worshipers. It's the faithful that can be trusted to keep quiet about what we're doing. We'll need to trust that when they share their immunity with family and friends, well, they'll not let the cat out of the bag."

"You know, Bill, they're going to want to protect family and friends. How do keep a lid on this?"

"It's risky," replied Bill, "everything is these days! It might help if Ruby Sorenson, the RN in our parish, were to set up a room where people could come for transfusions." Pausing, Bill concluded, "At some point it will be out of our control. It's messy, but I think we should do it."

"Yes," agreed Pastor Miller, "and there is a divine plan at work here. God's powerful Word calls, gathers and protects those who are faithful. Those who turn from God, well, He leaves them to their own resources, as they prefer. Ironic isn't it? Some want independence from God so that they can live their lives as they please, and in this case, it's more than spiritual death that could meet up with them down the road."

• • • • •

Aunt Anne saw Rachel's car from her sitting room window. Hobbling upon swollen, painful knees, she moved to the side door of her house to meet her niece. A flood of joy rushed through her time-weathered frame, empowering a faster step than was safe for her arthritic condition at the age of 72. "Oh my, oh my!" she repeated over and over as she opened the screen door. Rachel and Tamor were walking up the steps. "I don't believe my eyes!"

"Hi Auntie!" said Rachel, reaching her arms around her aged aunt giving her a gentle hug. Anne had been struck with arthritis in her early forties. The disease aged her, making her feel and move like a person far older than she was.

"What are you doing out on the roads with this virus going around?" scolded Aunt Anne.

"I can't get through to mom on the phones," answered Rachel.

"You too!" broke in Anne. "I've been trying to reach her since Friday afternoon! I keep getting a busy signal or a recorded message about the lines being tied up and telling me to call again later."

"Aunt Anne," said Rachel, stepping to the side, "I'd like you to meet one of my best friends, Tamor Carver."

Tamor placed her hand near her right cheek, grinned, and waved at Anne. Hobbling over to Tamor, Anne gave her a hug. "You two come in, and I'm going to get you some breakfast."

"No, you don't have to do that..." Rachel protested, but Anne just walked into the house her hand waving in the air. Rachel's feeble protest couldn't hide their hunger. They should have done a better job tanking up on the continental breakfast at the motel. Rachel had warned Tamor that Aunt Anne wouldn't be happy unless she could fix a meal for them.

"I won't hear another word!" commanded Anne, stopping to rest at the door. "Rachel, take Tamor to the kitchen and sit down. I'll shuffle along behind you, and we can visit while I get busy over the stove."

"Okay," smiled Rachel, "but make it brunch, because I'm not going to have you fixing us two meals!"

Rachel led Tamor into a large kitchen. Anne's old house was rooted on Thompson's Hill. It was the original farmhouse built by Jed Thompson. The house had been maintained and remodeled but the tattered barn had been torn down years ago. As the city expansion worked out on the east end of Eddyville, new neighborhood houses popped up on what were once fields of grain. Anne's kitchen was a permanent reminder of a day gone by when families were big, ate heartily, and took time together.

White cupboards climbed all the way to the kitchen ceiling encircling a large open area that had plenty of room for sitting thrashing crews during harvest. In this seasoned kitchen, Aunt Anne was thoroughly enjoying herself as she cooked up eggs, fried potatoes, bacon, and even a package of frozen pork sausage. Rachel knew better than to protest all the fuss that her aunt was making. It was this old woman's joy to fill her house with the aroma of her cooking served up for those she loved.

"I'm sure that Pam is just fine," said Anne, moving from the stove to her pantry. At the spur of the moment, Anne decided that she needed to make up a little pancake batter too.

"I know mom's fine Auntie," said Rachel. "But I don't know how bad this is going to get. I want to be with mom if things get," she paused, "well...." Rachel stopped in the middle of her sentence. Changing the subject she asked, "Is Matt keeping an eye on you?"

"He's a wonderful son," answered Anne. "He's been checking in on me several times each day since this plague started. He even came by yesterday morning for a few minutes before he went to work. I'll be fine. It's your mother, down there all alone in Florida, who worries me."

"She has some good friends..." began Rachel.

"Friends aren't family!" interrupted Anne. Rachel looked over at Tamor. Anne gasped. "Tamor dear, I didn't mean..."

"You're right," agreed Tamor, "friends aren't family. There's nothing you need..."

Once again Anne broke into Tamor's words. "Maybe not, but like they say, you can choose your friends and not your family. Sometimes friends are even better than family."

Tamor got up to hug Anne. Anne returned the gesture with a squeeze, then continued with her lecture. "It's good that you're going to see your mother, Rachel." Taking the bottom of her apron into her hands, she used its hem it to remove some flour. "You just stay away from anyplace where they've reported problems with the plague. Do you hear me girl?"

Tamor laughed. "You tell that girl!"

The three of them finished off breakfast. Rachel and Tamor overdosed on Anne's excellent cooking. After the meal, Rachel insisted that she was going to do the dishes. Anne protested but gave little resistance. Her legs were aching from her time at the stove. Tamor took to the dish towel, and soon the kitchen was ready for Anne to fuss over Matt when he stopped by to see her. The rest of the day was spent doing some light housework for Anne. Once again Aunt Anne protested, but Rachel insisted.

Rachel dusted off a picture of her mother with Auntie Anne taken when they were kids. It was an unusual black and white lithograph that had been taken by a photographer on the family farm. It showed the two sisters sitting on a split-rail fence just outside the barn. They were looking off to the distance over a field of ripe wheat. A slight breeze had made their hair look a little blurred because, back then, pictures took time to shoot. Subjects had to sit perfectly still.

Rachel worked around the house doing little things that would spare her arthritic aunt some pain. As she worked, Rachel was troubled by a nagging question simmering in the back burner of her mind. Why had she felt the need to plan so much time with her aunt? Anne seemed fine, and Matt was close at hand. Perhaps she had been foolish. Maybe a quick stop would have been better—just long enough so that she could assure her mother that Anne was fine. "It's too late now," she finally protested, truncating her own doubts. She would continue according to plan and leave at 4:30.

Chapter 18:

SPIRITUAL ENCOUNTERS

"Where is Starkey?" Ahmad's question sounded like a curse. "He was to be back here days ago!"

Giving little heed to Ahmad, Flint's attention was fixed upon an Elishewitz Stryker. Sharpening the razor–wrought edge of his knife he moved a whetstone over its edge again and again. Flint sat at a table, his feet resting over a second metal and canvas chair. The heat had pasted the terrorist's shirt against his torso. Ahmad, also sweat drenched, was pacing the room, his lit cigarette tracing fast patterns in the air as he waved his arms in frantic gestures. Ahmad's dark beard was twisted and snarled, small crumbs from his evening supper still visibly imbedded into tightly knotted curls.

"Are you listening to me!" screamed Ahmad.

Flint smirked. "Starkey doesn't take orders." Flint's voice parroted Morrell's flat, mechanical speech. "Not from me. Not from you. Not from God Almighty..."

"No! But he can die!" screamed Ahmad. "I'll kill him myself if he messes up our operation."

Looking up, Flint's face twisted in disbelief. "Mess up the operation! You tell me, Ahmad, how can anyone screw up a plague so deadly that no one has figured out a way to stop it?" Flint flung his knife suddenly, burying its point into a wooden beam near Ahmad. "You tell me how any of us are going to get out of this alive! Kill Starkey! Hell, we're all as good as dead."

"He is supposed to be back with the antidote," stammered Ahmad. "The Russians gave him the antidote last week..."

"Haven't you figured it out, you idiot," snarled Flint. "There ain't no antidote!"

"Yes there is an antidote!" yelled Ahmad.

"Sure," Flint said, his voice again flat. Getting up from his chair, he took his knife from the beam and walked back to the table. The whetstone once again was traced along the razor edge of the Elishewitz Stryker.

"There is an antidote," said Ahmad, his voice conceding his own lie.

"Just like the one we gave Morrell?" asked Flint. Ahmad said nothing. "Why do you think that Starkey isn't back yet? He's either been ghosted by the Russian

Mafia or by the virus. Either way, I don't think we will be seeing him again."

"Is that so?" A voice sounded from behind Flint. Flint turned to see Starkey standing in the door to the shelter. Ahmad was already walking, almost running, to get at Starkey. He placed his hands on Starkey's shoulders. "Did you get the antidote?" Ahmad smiled broadly, his head nodding quickly up and down.

Starkey breached Ahmad's hold by placing his right hand on Ahmad's left wrist, pulling his arm away, and then walking to the side. Ahmad's right hand fell stiffly to his side. "You have no idea what's going on out there!" came the exhausted reply. Starkey was tired—alive, but worn thin. "You sit in this camp for weeks. You play God by releasing hell all over, and then you just sit here!"

"It seems to me that you had no small part in the plan." Flint spoke without emotion, but his eyes ripped at Starkey.

"And what we did was a mistake," snapped back Starkey, his hands rubbing over his face. "But at least I haven't been sitting here, doing damn little..."

"What about the antidote?" broke in Ahmad, still standing back at the door where he had met up with Starkey. Ahmad was drained, as if cursing the late return of Starkey had spent his energy. He was processing the implications of Starkey's return and the fact that he stood before him, empty handed. Ahmad refused to admit the obvious. He refused to believe that there was no antidote.

"I looked into an isolation ward at the Russian University Hospital." Starkey was present only in his body as he spoke, his mind was back in Moscow. Had he heard Ahmad's question? "It was the research facility where the virus had been secretly produced by two university professors. I looked down through a second story observation window into the containment area of the university. The doors of the unit had been sealed from the outside. Everyone inside was dead. Bodies on the table were dead. Doctors and nurses in white suits with plastic domes over their heads were dead. If anyone had an antidote, they're now dead."

"And if they're dead," added Flint, "then they never developed an antidote."

"But they said they had an antidote!" Ahmad awakened from his stupor.

"And they smiled like damn ghosts as they took our gold," quipped Starkey. Walking over to a metal dresser by his cot, Starkey opened the top drawer, pulling out a picture of his mother. Starkey had a fixation. So long as she was alive... so long as she was well, the whole universe was safe. But if anything ever happened to her... He touched the face on the picture with his fingers. "Have I gotten any e-mail?" he asked.

"Nothing's working," laughed Ahmad. "No phones! No power but what we can generate! Nothing!"

Starkey carried the picture with him to the table, pushed Flint's feet off the chair, and sat down. Placing the picture inside a large pocket on his camouflage fatigues he began raving, "Have either of you..." spewing out a string of profanities, "given any thought to your families?"

Ahmad came to the table, turned a chair around so that the back faced the table, straddled it, then crossed his arms over the back. "All in my family are good Muslims. If we die in battle against the enemies of Islam, then we join the followers of Allah who flow into the streets of heaven for an eternity of pleasures beyond our wildest dreams."

"Is that right?" smirked Flint. "I rather thought that if we died, our bodies would swell up, rot, and leave our lifeless molecules to sit and wait for some damn black hole to swallow our puny planet into oblivion." He threw his knife into the wooden beam.

"Why do you fight for the cause?" asked Ahmad. Once again he opened up the same jaded conversation that never led anywhere.

"Fight!" snapped Flint, his voice showing only the slightest flare of emotion. "... for the cause. You call it a fight. You call it a holy war. I call it hell. We all live in hell. There is no meaning. There is no Allah. There is no place of eternal pleasure. All there is... is hell. I'm not trying to make any difference with my life. You two are the idealists, not me. I'm in this for the pleasure of the hunt and the joy of the kill. I'm not on your side, or their side, or anyone's side. I'm with you right now because doing so serves my own interest as I see things today. Tomorrow? Who knows!"

"You don't have one damn, noble bone in your pathetic body, Porter." Ahmad's head waved disgust into the air.

"And do you think I'm crushed by your opinion of me?" laughed Flint. "I don't give a rip what you think! I don't have any noble ideas, or causes, or concerns for humanity. All we are is yeast multiplying over this planet until there's no more planet to feed off of. If I take someone out, hell, the way I see it, I've given this planet a little more time before we completely run it over."

"You sadistic bastard!" yelled Starkey, leaning to take hold of Flint's shirt. "You get your jollies by killing, don't you? Just like with Lisa!"

Flint smiled, but said nothing, his eyes glued upon the glaring face of his idealistic partner. Molech stood to the side of Flint, its hand resting on his shoulder. Feeling the evil all about Flint, Starkey let go of his shirt, gasping as he did so. He reached up with his hand to rub his throat. Standing up, he walked across the room to a large round container resting on a metal table, a water spigot at its base. Taking a tin cup he filled it, set it down, then briefly let some water fall into the palms of his hands to splash across his face. "You are really messed up, Flint! Do you know that!"

Ahmad lifted his arms into the air throwing his palms toward Flint. "This man is an animal!"

"I'm an animal," returned Flint. "You two are willing to kill millions of people simply because they don't agree with your point of view. That's the bottom line, isn't it? You could be right, you could be wrong, it doesn't matter. All these people are going to be equally dead! The only difference between us animals, is that I have no point of view."

"We at least believe in something beyond ourselves!" snapped Ahmad.

"Not really," said Flint. "You believe in your ideas. They are part of you. They are you! You're no different than me or the tribal African who joins the hunt to genocide another tribe. They have their god's permission, and you have your god's permission. But it's all in your head. Not out there!" Flint pointed to the door of the shelter. "No! It's up in your head." He pointed to his temple. "You kill for your ideas as I kill for mine. There's no difference. You just sanitize what you do with noble nonsense..."

Frosted with anger, Starkey began walking toward Flint, but there remained the sense of raw evil lingering menacingly about Porter. Stepping back, he measured up Flint, then gazed over at Ahmad. "I have no god's permission. I do what I do because I believe in it. I know the evil of Western imperialism!"

"You've unleashed a virus that indiscriminately kills every man, woman, and child that it touches," smiled Flint malevolently, "and you call your cause just? Or are the innocent simply collateral damage?"

"Forget it!" barked Starkey. Walking out the door into the evening air he lit a cigarette.

"I have never known anyone like you," Ahmad said to Flint. "You have no heart! No passion for anything other than death."

"Because I do not sanitize the kill, you call me ruthless," answered Flint. "I can accept that." Getting up he pulled his knife from the beam, sliding it into a harness strapped just above his ankle. Smiling at Ahmad, he cast him a look that spoke of chaos comfortably at home in a human soul. Flint walked out of the door, brushed by Starkey, and headed for the chemical toilet. Starkey felt cold as Flint touched against him, shuddering in the thought of his own death. He looked again to the picture of his mother now gripped in his left hand. Her face shone eerily in the moonlit night. Starkey shuddered one more time.

· · · · ·

Luke was fifty miles from St. Louis when it happened. Making good time, he had been confident of arriving in Eddyville before Rachel left for Naples. Then, like air escaping from his ballooning hopes, steam came pouring out from under the hood of his car. Searching for a place to pull off to the side of the road, he noticed an exit just ahead. He'd take the exit to get off the freeway entirely. As he ramped off the interstate, a red light on the dash indicated that the engine was overheating. "Oh Lord, this can't be happening," he exclaimed. This time it was a prayer, not a slam against the Magistrate of heaven and earth.

Stopping at the side of the country road, Luke exited his car. Opening up the hood he peered through hissing steam to see a cracked, black hose connected to the radiator. Carefully turning the radiator cap; there was no water pressure. The radiator was empty. "Father in heaven, I'll never make it in time to intercept Rachel before she leaves! What should I do?"

A Guardian stood beside Luke on that lonely country road. The wind was blowing fiercely so Luke pulled the collar of his shirt up and around his neck. The Guardian bent his head toward Luke's ear. A thought occurred to Luke. He mouthed to himself, "Yes, I know Father. All things work to the good of those who love You. But if I don't get to Rachel soon, there's a very real likelihood that the virus will."

The radio had been airing reports all morning about isolated cases of the virus popping up to shut down whole communities. There'd been an outbreak in southeast Florida. The graphic depictions of whole families taken out by the disease turned Luke's stomach. He had to get to Rachel, but his car was broken down and mechanics would be reluctant to go out to repair a stranger's vehicle. What was he to do now?

Luke saw a sign for a small town just a little more than a mile from the exchange. Starting down the road in the direction of the town, the wind was to his back and Luke was thankful for that. On the outskirts of the town was a gas station. Passing by an open red door, weathered and old, he discovered no one in the office. Stepping through another doorway he was led into the garage. A muscular young man was working under a car. The mechanic wore a grey work suit with the emblem of the station stitched to the right breast pocket. Over the pocket he saw the name "Mike" in script. "Excuse me," said Luke. "I was wondering if you could help me?"

Rotating on his hip, the mechanic sat up to face Luke. "What can I do for you?"

"My car is broken down," said Luke. "I blew a hose to my radiator. I'm off the interstate just down the road."

Mike shook his head. "We don't inventory parts here," he said. "We're just too small a shop." He thought for a minute. "How bad's the hose?"

"It's not a big tear," answered Luke. "Just enough to be a problem."

"Tell you what," the mechanic said. "I think I may be able to get you going. You'll need to get it fixed someplace soon, but I can patch you up until you get to a station that has the parts you need."

"That would be great," smiled Luke. Mike went to his bench grabbing some silver duct tape. He left the station doors unlocked, with the garage door wide open, merely placing a sign on a hook that let patrons know that he was out for a few minutes. "Aren't you going to lock up?" asked Luke.

"Nope," he said. "I know everyone in town, and they're all honest, Christian folk. Odds are that I'm not going to get any interstate business. I think you're only the second one this year." He pointed to his truck. "Hop in!"

As they drove, Mike turned to Luke, "So where are you from?"

"Rochester, Minnesota." Luke responded.

"You're a long way from home," replied Mike. "By the look of you, I'd be tempted to think that you've lost your best friend."

"I have, so to speak. I'm trying to catch up with her. She's from Rochester too. It's real important that I get to her. That's why this breakdown is such a huge putz! I can't tell you how much your help means to me."

"Glad to do it," smiled Mike. Luke was surprised that the mechanic never asked him why he or his friend were out driving, given what was going on.

"Lots of people wouldn't want to help out a stranger these days," observed Luke. "I'm glad I found one who would." Luke wondered if this man had a family. "Are you married?"

"Nope," replied Mike, "I've been too busy to settle down."

"You're kept that busy at a small town station?"

"I'm not always working there," smiled Mike. "I do other work on the side."

Luke was going to inquire about the other work, but never had the chance.

"Is that your car?" asked Mike. Luke nodded. The small town mechanic pulled up to the car opening up its hood. Wiping the antifreeze off the hose, he dried it thoroughly with a clean rag. He then wrapped the broken area with several layers of duct tape. Reaching back into his truck, he grabbed antifreeze, adding it to the radiator. "That should do it for now," he said. "I wouldn't wait too long before getting a new hose."

"Thanks," said Luke. "How much do I owe you?

"Twenty minutes worth of labor," he answered, "antifreeze and a little tape. How about fifteen dollars?"

"No way!" protested Luke, handing Mike a twenty and a five. "You need to adjust your prices. Thanks again." Reaching out he invited the mechanic's hand.

"My hands are greasy," protested Mike.

Luke continued to hold out his hand until the mechanic took hold and they shook. Grease rubbed onto his hand, but Luke didn't mind. Mike smiled as he left for his truck. "God bless!" the mechanic shouted back. At the time it didn't seem unusual that the stranger should have left with an invocation of God's blessing. Luke watched as Mike drove away.

• • • • •

Mike pulled into the station and parked the truck. Walking behind the garage, Mike saw an older man working over a used transmission for parts. "Nice day!" he said to the older mechanic.

The mechanic, named Hank, continued to slave over the old transmission. Without looking up he said, "Yup! Great day. But it would be a whole lot better if I could get this rusted bolt out."

"Do you mind if I have a try?" asked the young man.

Hank gave the stranger a look. "Do I know you?"

"I'm just traveling through," he answered. Walking over to the transmission, he delivered a wink, placing his hand out for the wrench. Hank reluctantly handed it to the stranger. The young man slid the wrench over the rusted bolt delivering a firm tug. The bolt sprang free.

"Can you beat that!" said the older mechanic, slapping his hand to his side. "Say, young man, I better take over now. It won't do having you get grease all over that fancy white tuxedo of yours." He smiled broadly. "I don't know how you did it. I've been working on that ornery bolt for the last hour. I heated it. I sprayed it with oil." He stopped again. "What's your name, son?"

"Michael," said the young man.

"Thanks, Michael." Twisting his head back and to the left, Hank smiled broadly.

"My pleasure," said Michael, holding out his hand to the vintaged mechanic.

"Ya' don't want to shake these old, dirty hands," Hank backed away, but the young man insisted. Hank finally gave his hand over to the fancy clad stranger.

"God bless!" said the young man as he started to walk away.

"God bless you too, son," said the older gentleman.

Michael walked into the gas station. Removing the sign that he had placed on the door he replaced it with one saying, "I'm working out back." Heading for the counter, the young man touched the cash register; it sprang open. Taking the twenty-five dollars from his pocket, Michael placed the money into the tray. Suddenly he glowed whiter than streaking lightning and vanished. Surprised by the bright flash, Hank got up to see what kind of situation was developing in his garage.

· · · · ·

Luke glanced at the dash clock. It was 2:43. The window of opportunity had shattered. Luke would never make it in time to intercept Rachel at her aunt's. Picking up the pieces of remaining time, he pressed down the accelerator. To the left a gas station came into view. Luke ramped off, driving over to the station. Targeting a public phone, he parked, walked over to the open booth, and checked out the lines. The phone delivered a dial tone. Luke keyed in Anne's number, reading it off the itinerary. The signal was busy. Taking a deep breath Luke hung up the receiver. Should he take time to repair the hose now or keep on with the chase? Walking over to the open door of the garage he spotted a mechanic. He called across the garage, "Good afternoon."

"Hi!" The mechanic placed down his wrench and headed for Luke. "How can I help you?"

"I have a busted radiator hose," answered Luke. "How long would it take to get it fixed?"

"I could do it right away," said the mechanic. "Unless there's something else going on with your engine and all, it would only take ten or fifteen minutes."

"That's not bad," thought Luke. He hated to take the time, but he was already too late to meet up with Rachel at her aunt's. If his car broke down again on the interstate, who knows how much time he would lose? No. Better to fix it now. "Yeah, go ahead and fix it please. And one more thing, do you have anything to get this grease off?" Luke lifted his right hand to show the mechanic the grease, but the smudge was gone. He smiled. "I guess the grease wore off." Luke was surprised. Looking over his hands for a final inspection Luke turned to the mechanic. "I'm going to check out the store and pick up a few things. By the way, I appreciate your getting right to this."

"No problem," said the mechanic. "It's been slow on the interstate since that virus started." He paused. "At least people aren't stopping much. Only if they're desperate for gas." Walking over to Luke's car he sprang open the hood. Luke walked into the station, shuffled through the food racks, and then paid for a stash of junk food and soda. He had no appetite. He hadn't eaten a thing since leaving the Twin Cities. The junk food was there if he should get hungry. Walking back to his car, he waited as the mechanic tightened down the final hose clamp. Luke gassed up, settled the bill, and was back on the road.

· · · · ·

"Yes, Auntie, I'll drive carefully," said Rachel, giving her favorite aunt a final hug.

"And you'll give your mom all my love?" Aunt Anne placed her index finger just inches away from Rachel's nose.

"Yes I will," promised Rachel.

"And I'll be praying for her." Anne wrestled down her skirt in the wind. Taking both of Rachel's shoulders tenderly in her grip, she smiled. "And you know that I love you."

Rachel smiled back, kissed her aunt on the cheek, then headed to the car. Aunt Anne smothered Tamor in a bear hug then released her to follow after Rachel. The two pulled out of the driveway waving to an old lady with moistened cheeks. It was 4:25 in the afternoon.

· · · · ·

Kris and Rich walked down an alley in downtown St. Paul. To the right, about half a block ahead of them, a small storefront protruded from the massive facade of a red brick building. A round, green fixture of tin enclosed a porcelain white interior that lit the store under the stars. Below the light, a glass french door glowed dimly from within. A constant dribble of people entered or exited through the door. Kris and Rich walked inside.

The environment was seeped in age. Black tiles, scuffed and scarred, covered the floors. The walls and tongue-and-groove wooden ceiling were painted white. Gigantic wooden barrels built into the back wall faced forward lying on their sides. The diameter of one barrel was over six feet. A white three–foot counter, with a black linoleum top, stood between them and the barrels in the back. Standing in front of the largest barrel was a man wearing a black suit, black shirt, and black tie. A partly open violin case stood against the wall, exposing the strap of an automatic rifle caught within the case.

Unexpectedly the front of the large barrel separated on a central pivot. Two people walked into its interior. The man in black walked over to Rich. In a deep, Italian voice he asked, "Whatta kanna I do for you?"

"We would like to sample some of your coffee." Rich looked very serious.

"Whatta you think this is!" asked the man forcefully.

"I like Columbian coffee," continued Rich.

The man smiled, "Why dinna you saya so?" He walked over to the large barrel pivoting open its round front. Rich took Kris by the hand pulling her into the opening. Turning to Kris he laughed out loud at the expression slapped over her face.

"What are you doing?" she asked. "Where are we going?"

Suddenly another door opened as they exited from the barrel's belly into the small lobby of a bustling restaurant. "Welcome to 'The Speak Easy'," said the maitre'd.

"Do you have a booth?" asked Rich.

"Yes," he answered. "Do you mind a loft?"

"No problem," smiled Rich brightly. "We would enjoy that!"

They followed the maitre'd down dimly lit aisles, around a number of sudden turns, then up and down several small sets of stairs. A final lengthy run of steps was conquered before the maitre'd led them to a private booth overlooking other booths and tables arranged in the central square below. A small candle burned at the back of the table. Waiting for Kris to be seated, Rich then parked himself across from her in the booth. Within minutes a waiter stood at their table. "May we have two premium cups of coffee?" asked Rich.

"If you gotta the dough," said the young man, "we've gotta the premium coffee!"

The waiter left. Kris looked at Rich, mouth open and eyebrows raised, framing a question. "Where did you find this place?"

"I heard about it from someone at the broadcasters' convention," commented Rich. "It is designed to look and operate like an old 'speak easy' that served patrons whiskey and beer during the prohibition days. It's filled with little nooks built into different levels throughout the restaurant. I am told that the food here is very good."

The waiter returned with a white, round porcelain coffee pot with two white porcelain coffee cups. Each cup sported a thin green band just below the rim. The waiter smiled, serving up a fragrant, red wine from the coffee pot into each of the cups. Setting down the porcelain pot, the waiter handed Rich two menus. "I be backa, soon. Okay!"

Rich nodded, handing Kris a menu. "Holy cow!" gasped Kris. "This place ain't cheap!"

"Today we are not worried about that," smiled Rich. "It is a special day!" He paused, fixing a strand of hair behind Kris' ear. "I need to use the restroom, I'll be back in just a minute. You decide what you want to order." Leaning over the table to within inches of his date, he said softly, "And don't worry about the price. Please! I want you to eat whatever appeals to you. Deal?"

Kris bit her lip, then smiled. "Deal."

Returning a few minutes later, Rich swung into the booth to look intently at Kris. "Well, what did you decide?"

Once again biting her lower lip, she answered, "I'm going to have the prime rib and lobster combo..." Kris blushed. This was one of the most expensive items on the menu. And it was spendy!

"Wonderful!" smiled Rich. "I shall have the same."

The waiter returned to take their orders. Soon after, their salads arrived. Reaching across the table Rich took the hand of his favorite DJ. "Do you mind if I pray?" he asked.

"No," she said softly, "I'd like that."

"Gracious Heavenly Father, You give us all things in due season. Today we thank You for the gift of each other, the food that we are about to share, and for adventures yet to be taken. We ask it all in Jesus' name. Amen."

"Amen," said Kris, opening her eyes to smile across at Rich. "What adventures do you have in mind?"

"Oh!" Rich said, his hand moving quickly to his face and then down again. "Nothing particular. It's just that with a woman like you, I know I had better pray for what's ahead of us. I think that you keep the angels very busy!"

The atmosphere of the restaurant called for the words that Kris now spoke. "These have been the best months of my life!" The enchantress drew the man into her voice as the candle traced dancing shadows over her face. "Rich, I have never met a man like you." She paused. "I just want to say..." her voice broke, the spell vanished, and tears pooled in her eyes, "thank you!"

Returning, the waiter carried a large, round serving tray covered with assorted smaller trays. Each dish was covered with a hood keeping the food hot. The main course delivered to Kris had one other item, a red rose. Looking up at Rich she then fixed her eyes back on the rose. Picking it up she drank in its fragrant petals. "Do they always bring the ladies a red rose with their food?"

"No," answered Rich, his eyes speaking far more than his words. "Only for special ladies on special occasions!"

"Well you make me feel special, I'll say that!" replied Kris, taking Rich's hand with her free hand.

Setting down the rose she lifted the cover from the main course. The plate was empty except for a small black box. Her heart froze—her breath locked tightly within her chest. She bit her lower right lip, but the rest of her body remained paralyzed—her hand motionless like the limb of a statue set above the small box.

"Go ahead," Rich coached, "open it!"

Reaching down, Kris opened the box. A gold ring holding a large, heart-shaped diamond was set into a velvet slot. Rich reached across the table taking the ring from the box.

"My dear Kristin," he said. "There are not many men that can say that they have adored a woman even before they saw her face. I was infatuated with you the day I heard your voice, the manner in which you spoke, the way that you chose to frame your words. Then came the day that I met you..."

"Don't you mean," interrupted Kris, "the day you canned me!" It was a Downs' trait to use humor to control emotions.

"Ouch," winced Rich, "please don't bring that up. It was a terrible experience for me."

"I know," replied Kris. She looked at him as he glanced away. Reaching for his cheek she touched it, softly pushing his face back towards hers. "You were saying?"

"Kristin," he said, taking both her hands in his. He had placed the ring into his side pocket. "I love you. I can no longer imagine the future without you as part of it. I... I called your father last night. I asked him if I might have his daughter as my wife. Now I am asking you..."

Her eyes flooded with tears, but Kris wiped them quickly away with her fingers and sported back, "What did Dad say?"

"Well," replied Rich, somewhat caught by the delayed answer to his question, "it took him a few seconds to speak. When he did, his voice was..."

"I know Dad," broke in Kris, "he was crying! But what did he say?"

"He took control of his emotions by giving a joke," Rich said. "He asked me how much I intended to be paid to take you off his hands."

"No!" gasped Kris. "Dad asked that? Wow! He was sharp under the circumstances! I thought he'd just crumble."

"He loves you, Kris, very much," continued Rich. "I know the feeling. As to his answer, he said, again after a few seconds, that he would be very pleased to have me as a son-in-law."

"Dad has no taste in people," quipped Kris. "He always misjudges them." She paused. "I on the other hand am the best judge of human nature. I know that there's no other man in the world for me... but you."

Kris jumped over the table squeezing herself between it and Rich. Flinging her arms around his neck, she buried her full head of hair against the side of his face. Then she cried.

"I'm sorry," she whispered, "but I've never been happier than at this moment." Pulling back to look at Rich, she again bit her lower lip. "I know I don't sound very happy, but..." Again she brought her head against his as she continued to cry. Finally, reaching down with her hand into Rich's pocket, she pulled the diamond ring out, drinking in the meaning of this moment in time. Rich's hands cupped around hers then took the ring from her hand placing it on her left ring finger. Elmidra stood to the side, his hands placed upon their heads.

Chapter 19:

CROSSING OVER

Patrick Armor, head of the Federal Bureau of Investigation, held a half-burned cigar up to his mouth, then inhaled. He took notes as Nancy Wisely, Director of the Center for Disease Control and Protection, debated hotly with Presidential Advisor Dean Wellington. They had different views about what should be done to contain the deadly outbreak. Bill Downs of the OIDC was also present at the meeting. The President listened intently, his lips pursed together.

"If we don't stop all public transportation," snapped Wisely, "this virus may get out of control! Do you know what that means! It means the death of every man, woman, and child in the United States, if not the world!"

"And if you close down transportation," snapped back Wellington, "we won't need a virus to kill every American. No! Just let the economy collapse and our fellow citizens will be killing their neighbors for food and water."

"Dr. Downs," broke in the President, "or may I call you Bill?"

"Bill's fine," smiled back the doctor.

"Bill," continued the President, "what are we up against with this virus?"

"It's bad, really bad," Bill replied. "It kills within two to three hours of contact. It can be spread person to person or from objects exposed to the virus. It chemically reacts to rubber and polymers enabling it to penetrate our standard containment suits." Bill looked over at Wisely and then around the room. "As you know, the only protection against the virus is the immunization which all of you have received. The problem we face is stopping the spread of the disease until we have the time to figure out a way to effectively immunize the public...."

"Exactly!" interrupted Wisely. "That's why it is essential that we limit the transportation of people and resources. We must stop the spread of the disease until we can develop and implement an effective immunization for the public." Wisely was married with four children; the oldest was a senior at Collingwood Academy. None of her family had received the vaccination. The secret she held from them ripped her apart. If they died, she wanted to die. She consented to the vaccination only after the assurance that she could share her immunity with them after three days. As she met with the President, Wisely was functioning all right, even though she had been deathly sick the day before. Another day, a day feeling more to

Wisely like an eternity, needed to pass before her family would be safely protected by a transfusion of her blood. When that was done, her family would need to be persuaded concerning the absolute necessity of keeping their immunity a secret.

"Mr. President," Wellington stood up, "we are limiting transportation to and from infected areas. In fact, we have stopped it completely! What Nancy is suggesting is the total shut down of the American economy..."

"Dean," said the President, "sit down." He looked over to Patrick Armor. "Pat, what can you tell me?"

"It's hell out there," he answered. "Bill's right about how mean this virus is. The reaction of the public has made matters worse. Sniper attacks on clean-up units have slowed down our efforts dramatically, and as Nancy knows, it has hurt the morale of CDCP personnel deployed within quarantined areas. We've had widespread looting as criminal elements take advantage of the crisis. It's a pathetic joke, because they don't live long enough to enjoy their plunder." He looked over at Nancy. "If we have additional outbreaks in other large metropolitan areas, we won't be able to maintain the quarantine."

"So we must contain the epidemic now!" insisted Wisely.

Getting up, the President walked across the room. He stared out the window into an evening sky. "What's happening in other areas of the globe, Tim?"

Timothy Mandrake, the Secretary of State, was a short, stocky man who usually wore a light brown suit with a maroon tie. "We have it better here than other areas of the world where outbreaks have occurred," he answered. "Most governments don't have the resources to maintain social order. The reports that I'm hearing are straight out of a horror movie. What civilians the virus doesn't kill, either criminals or governments are taking out. We know of several examples where the civil authorities have turned against segments of their own population in an effort to contain the spread of the virus."

"Ahhh," moaned the President, rubbing both hands several times over the sides of his face. "Does anyone know how the virus is getting out of quarantined areas?"

Bill answered that. "We think that the virus has been spread either by mail delivery or the transport of manufactured goods that have been tainted."

"But I thought that we had total quarantine of infected areas." The president, interrupting Bill, looked over at Wellington.

"We do," continued Bill, "but sometimes, before the outbreak is discovered, someone contaminates a letter or goods shipped from a factory. In that case, the tainted goods are carried out of the area before the quarantine is in place. It is this 'onset variable' that concerns Nancy."

"What do you think?" asked the president, looking to the Attorney General.

"My piece of this deals with health issues," answered the Attorney General, Thomas Edgewood, "so I naturally tend to side with Nancy. Dean's point about the social chaos that would result from a total collapse of the economy, however, raises health concerns too. I think, Mr. President, that we are faced with a classic dilemma. If we do everything necessary to contain the virus, the nation would come to a complete standstill. If we don't take these measures, the virus could continue to spread and kill most, if not all, of the non-vaccinated citizens."

Walking back from the window, the president sat down on an overstuffed chair facing into an oval pattern of comfortable furniture. "I think we have to continue to work things just as we are." He glanced over at Nancy. "The economy must keep rolling." Wisely was going to interrupt, but the president waved her off. "Nancy, if the economy stops, we won't have the apparatus or manpower to maintain quarantines anyway. The issue becomes moot." He looked over to his advisor. "Dean, I want us to continue to monitor all systems of transportation and delivery. In any area of the country that has even one certified instance of the plague, I want everything shut down. Mail delivery! Manufacturing transport! Public transportation! I mean everything is bottled! Is that clear?"

"Yes sir," answered Wellington.

"And one more thing," said the president. "I want a plan on how to begin immunization of the American people on my desk in two days."

• • • • •

The staff at Oakland Community Hospital and their immediate families had all been inoculated against PRN40. The initial politics involved with the vaccination of hospital staff was a nightmare. Everyone on staff had a close relative or friend whom they also wanted to protect, but the order from the Center for Disease Control and Prevention mandated that only hospital staff and their immediate families were to receive the vaccine.

Allowing the vaccination of immediate family members was a concession from the Center for Disease Control and Prevention. CDCP had intended to limit vaccination to staff only, allowing them to share their immunity with family members after a three-day waiting period. Briggs argued against this, pointing out that the delay could create a crisis in the morale of hospital staff. "The way this virus is spreading," she told members of CDCP, "some family members could be dying even as we are debating the issue. I need my team sharp and not fretting over their spouses and kids." Briggs prevailed. The staff at OIDC and other key hospitals around the nation were granted a privilege denied to top ranking officials in Washington. Disease control units were on the front lines in the warfare against the plague. Their staff had to keep focused on the job before them.

Staff were permitted, even encouraged, to share their blood with close friends and relatives after their own immunization had stabilized. The process, however, was closely monitored. Family and friends were sworn to secrecy concerning their treatment. The usual germs that can infect needles and plastic tubes during a transfusion needed to be dealt with through proper sterilization. An employee lobby on the opposite end of the public entrance to the hospital had been converted to a transfusion area where employees could meet with family and friends to share their immunity. This lobby had been selected because of its location away from the public view. It also protected those coming for the transfusion from contact with patients who could be carrying the plague.

OIDC staff moved down the hallways of the Oakland Community Hospital as if traveling in a parallel universe. They appeared as living ghosts walking in a world of dying flesh. Wearing white containment suits, they maintained the ruse of staff vulnerability to the plague. The secret of a cure was not shared with the public at large—not yet. Periodically staff members replaced their gloves. Hands-on contact with the virus after a time wore away the integrity of the gloves, prompting their occasional replacement, not to protect the staff from the virus, but from other diseases that were breeding out of control in the cesspool of a plague-weakened society.

Patients in dying misery and staff workers wearing white suits moved slowly, as if caught within a time warp. Unknown to all, a swarming activity was taking place beyond the reach of human senses. Dark entities slithered along the floor, always moving away from the light. The Shadow of Death engulfed room after room, its tentacles sucking sickness and misery into itself. Some patients were smothered in death's grip. Those condemned and dying without faith felt its tentacles tearing into their lost and frightened spirits. The clutch of the Shadow of Death held the faithless victims as this dark entity towered above their sweat-drenched bodies.

The Shadow of Death and the brigade of hell were not the only ones present. Guardians walked the hallways, taking sentry by beds throughout the hospital. A young girl, no more than six years old, was dying of the plague. Two Guardians stood to either side of her bed. The little girl was struggling for air in the last stages of the disease before she would leave this world. The Guardian to her left stood with one hand on her head and the other resting on her hand. "Little Lindsay," the Guardian said, "have no fear. In discomfort you were born from your mother's womb into a world much bigger. In birthing pains you now leave a world of shadows to enter a Kingdom of joy."

"Will it be fun?" came the faint voice of Lindsay, like smoke fighting its way through heavy fog. Her mother, sitting at the foot of Lindsay's bed, flew to her side. The mother's muffled voice struggled through the containment suit to reach her daughter. "Did you call me honey?" Lindsay said nothing. Lindsay no longer heard anything from mortal lips.

"Yes," said the Guardian. "It will be fun! In the twinkling of an eye your body, now very sick, will be restored. It will be beautiful again, and much stronger."

Lindsay opened her eyes. She didn't look at her mother but to the angel to her right. He had also placed a hand upon her shoulder. Pointing toward the right wall of her room, the wall vanished. A brilliant haze, looking like the sun breaking from the horizon through a thick mist, met Lindsay's eyes. There was someone standing there. His arms opened like a father waiting to receive the running leap of his child.

"Jesus," said little Lindsay. A thin smile broke over her pain-torn face. Her mother looked toward the wall, searching for the object captured in her child's gaze. Lindsay stopped breathing. Her mother collapsed upon the body of her child in convulsions of grief, separated from her daughter by the loveless wall of a containment suit. The mother had been told not to touch the body of her daughter, but grief masters all barriers.

· · · · ·

In room 1219, Elijah Jordan sat by an old man midway into the progress of the disease. The Shadow of Death had attached tentacles around the dying man's ankles and chest. Elijah wore no containment suit, which the old man noticed. "Are you dying too?" he asked Elijah.

"No," said Elijah, kindly. Taking a cool cloth he wiped the patient's fevered brow.

"Well, you're gonna die now," the man said weakly. "Why aren't you wearing one of those white suits?"

"I wear the armor of God," smiled Elijah. The old man looked at him, not sure what to make of the stranger's words.

"God won't help you," came the last animated response to surface from the dying patient. "He never helped me." He swallowed down a deep breath. "Just like He's not helping me now."

"You don't know that," said Elijah. "He's closer to you right now than you can imagine." Elijah wiped the old man's forehead with the cool cloth. "Do you think that 'cause you're dying it proves that God don't care?" He waited briefly, continuing as the man remained silent. "Your name is Howard, right?"

The old man nodded. "Well, Howard, if when a person's dyin' it's 'cause God don't care, then He hasn't cared for nobody, except maybe Enoch and the prophet Elijah. Death is a universal judgment against Adam's family 'cause of sin. It's a doorway that, with few exceptions, everyone's gonna walk through." Elijah paused. "But let me tell you a secret," he bent down toward the old man's face, "it doesn't open up the same way for all people."

Howard moaned as death tightened its grip. Elijah's disdain for Death pushed back the muscles of his face until the corners of his mouth traced deeply into his cheeks. Again he dipped the cloth in a basin of cool water wiping the old man's brow. "Even Jesus walked through that door. Yes sir! He did it so He could make another room beyond. A room not allowing for the devil and his evil henchmen. And you know what?" Elijah smiled at Howard. "He did it!" Elijah jumped up as he framed his own face by placing his open hands within inches to each side of his cheeks. "By His blood, brother, you don't have to go to hell. You can be with the angels, Howard! You can be with others known to you in your life and who had faith in the blood."

Tears formed at the corners of the old man's eyes. "Even if He would take me, I've led a terrible life. I wouldn't be worthy..."

"Good heavens!" Elijah slapped his hands in front of his face. "The apostle Paul wasn't worthy! It's not about being worthy. It's about the power of the blood... It's about faith in the Lamb of God and His shed blood and glorious resurrection."

"What's your name?" asked Howard.

"My name is Elijah Jordan," answered the stranger. "And I've come because your name is written in the Book of Life. Will you let me pray for you? Will you let me take that smoldering flame of faith that you've locked away for all these years and help it burst into flame as it lights your way into God's eternal Kingdom?"

Howard nodded, and Elijah began to pray. Suddenly a white light exploded beside the bed where Elijah interceded for the dying man. A sword slashed against the tentacles of death. Howard gasped in air. He continued to lay listening to Elijah as he spoke words to God and spoke words from the Holy Writ that fed the dying man's spirit. A thin smile broke across the agonized face of the old man.

· · · · ·

Turning from the crowded hallway into room 1219, Briggs stopped dead in her tracks. Howard lay dead, with Elijah Jordan still holding his hand. "Are you insane?" she gasped, then closing her eyes she took in a deep breath. "Of course... Of course..." she thought to herself. "Elijah cannot die." She felt certain of that. As Elijah looked up at her from the chair, Briggs soaked in a deep peace. It had been a long time since she had felt at peace—something that had been taken from her when the plague began claiming victim after victim.

"There's a great harvestin' of souls taking place here," said Elijah. "Some are escorted by things ya don't wanna think about." He looked to Howard. "Others, like this old saint, have met up with some..." he fumbled with human language. "He's in pretty good company right now," was the best he could manage.

"Souls," she thought to herself. "What is the soul?" She was still walking with pretty new shoes when it came to her faith. She looked at Elijah. "What happens to the soul? Do bad souls go one place and the souls of good people go to another?"

"First off," said Elijah, "there ain't no good people, only people made good." He smiled. "And souls made fit for heaven are not gonna be with souls destined for hell. The harvesting of souls foreshadows the great division of lambs and goats that'll be fully revealed on the last day." He looked out the window. "Those who aren't made clean in the blood of the Lamb travel from this world with the same powers and principalities that they knew far too well in life. Those marked by the blood of Jesus, well, they meet up with Him and with His friends. They're kept safe till the day when the ground gives forth the fruit of resurrection. Souls ain't just ghosts floating around in some celestial sky. No! Souls are individuals with faces of flesh and blood. Unique they are! Destined for a place made for the redeemed family of Adam." He nodded his head toward the lifeless frame of Howard. "Do you see anythin' strange about this man?"

Briggs walked closer to the head of the bed. Howard looked like so many other victims of the plague filling the hospital. Then she saw it—a thin smile in the lines of the old man's lips.

"Are you saying that all the saints die with a smile, even when it's a hard death?" asked Briggs.

"Not at all!" answered Elijah. "Who cares about the mortal frame that's left behind? The new one that's coming will smile a whole lot, but the body that you wear right now is corrupted." He shook his head looking directly at Briggs. "This smile was a gift from God Almighty for you." Elijah walked over to Briggs, placing his hands on her shoulders. "You have been spendin' entirely too much time thinking about death theses days and forgettin' what's out yonder." He smiled broadly. "Life Briggs! That's the secret the enemy don't want you to know... don't want you to believe. The life is in the blood of Jesus, and you know that now! Think of the life that waits for the Saints! Think of life eternal!"

"And what of those who have no faith?" asked Briggs. "...Those who think we are superstitious to believe in the power of the blood?"

"We can't tell who has faith and who don't," replied Elijah. "We share the good news of God's love to all, letting God judge the heart." Elijah became grave, his arms falling to his side. "And if they die in unbelief," he paused. For the first time Briggs saw deep sadness sweep over his face. "We give 'em over to the justice of God. They're no longer our concern." Elijah shook his head, then left the room.

• • • • •

"Hey you!" cried a man as Elijah walked past his open doorway. Elijah stopped to look into the room. A man in his late forties was doubtlessly dying of the plague. Sitting on a hospital chair he was still in his street clothes. "Do you know when they're going to get back to take care of me?"

Taking a couple of steps into the room Elijah stopped just inside the doorway. He walked as if he were trying to avoid something lying on the floor. "Pardon me," answered Elijah, "I'm not one of those staff people here at the hospital." The man shook his head weakly. "Ain't you the Reverend Herbert Handfelt?" questioned Elijah.

The man looked up at Elijah. "Do I know you?"

"No, but I know you," answered Elijah.

Reverend Handfelt was a leading church figure in Oakland. He wasn't surprised that a perfect stranger would recognize him. Many times his picture had appeared in the area papers because of his work within the community. His religion was constituted in social action. He had long ago given up on prayer, although he would meditate now and then. Elijah saw terror in the Reverend's wide eyes and drawn face. He started to comfort Handfelt saying, "Isn't it great to have comfort in Christ's shed blood..."

Elijah's words fell like acid on Handfelt's ears. The Reverend tossed his right hand at Elijah. "Don't get primitive on me!" He wanted nothing to do with this teaching. "It's bad enough that I'm dying..."

"Yes you are," interrupted Elijah. He looked around the room. It was filling with dark entities that slithered into shadowy places. "And what does that mean for you?"

"It means that I haven't been given enough time to reach my full potential," Handfelt replied. "It means that many of the good things I wanted to do will never get done."

"You're talkin' about what your death means for others," said Elijah, "but what does it mean for you?" Tentacles tightened around the dying man, making it difficult for him to concentrate. He was far too sick for talking abstractly about theology. He continued the discussion, however, because his own dying made theology anything but abstract.

"I have the hope of resurrected life," said the Reverend.

"Because Jesus rose from the dead?" asked Elijah.

Handfelt became irritated again. "I don't have time for this," he answered. "We have no proof for believing that anyone has ever come back from the dead. What I have is the hope that there is life after death."

"It's one thing to hope that we can put a man on the moon," said Elijah. "It's another thing to hope that there are unicorns on the moon. We know that man has set foot on the moon, so there's no good reason to believe that it can't be done over and over again." Elijah walked closer to Handfelt, once again taking his steps with care. "I've got no hope of finding unicorns on the moon..."

"I know what you're driving at," said the Reverend, "and I wish that I had such a simple faith." He looked down. "But I don't."

"But you do have faith, strong faith," replied Elijah. "The problem is that it's in the wrong thing." Handfelt looked up again at Elijah. "You've got faith in the modern world and the things of the modern world. You've got faith in science and believe nearly everythin' that comes from the ivory towers of learning." Elijah looked passionately at the dying man. "All of this changes! All of this passes! But God—and God's Word, they don't change nor do they pass away."

"I've heard all that before," said Handfelt weakly. He was beginning to slip away. "I once preached that too, can you believe it?" He spoke mostly to himself.

"Do you mind if I read to you from the Bible?" asked Elijah.

Smiling, Handfelt moved his head very slowly from side to side. "If it... makes you feel... better..." Handfelt was fading from this world.

Elijah began to read from the third chapter of the Gospel of John. He read the words of comfort about how the Son of God would be lifted up and bring a holy cure to a sin sick planet. The words of comfort, yes, comfort, spoken by Elijah, words calling for hope, but they bounced off Handfelt as if they hit a cement wall. Elijah continued to read in the third chapter, "Whoever believes in him is not condemned, but whoever does not believe stands condemned already because he has not believed in the name of God's one and only Son. This is the verdict: Light has come into the world, but men loved darkness instead of light because their deeds were evil. Everyone who does evil hates the light, and will not come into the light for fear that his deeds will be exposed. But whoever lives by the truth comes into the light, so that it may be seen plainly that what he has done has been done through God."

"I've.... done... good things...." Handfelt wanted to say more, but the room had become so thick to him that his words could no longer penetrate the spiritual darkness.

"Herbert!" cried Elijah through the darkness. "Good works mean nothin' when they come from an evil heart. Hearts without Jesus can't know the truth, so they can never be good! They are filled with the pride of the individual or the vanity of humanity. Herbert, I'm askin' you to have faith in the blood..."

Reverend Herbert Handfelt could no longer hear words spoken by mortal lips. He could hear Elijah's words, but they sounded useless to him, like thunder rumbling within waterless clouds. He was swirling in a vortex, covered by something that was drawing away his life. He could see entities—they looked like grey shadows against a black wall, passing through his body as if he were a ghost. The darkness about him became thicker. He was drowning in mud. He began to hear voices—voices drowning out the beacon voice of Elijah. Yet again, not really voices. Herbert heard the screams and moans of inhuman creatures welcoming him to their misery.

A woman in a cumbersome white suit waddled at a brisk pace toward Handfelt. He lay lifeless in the chair, his chin sunk deeply into his chest. "I'm afraid you must leave this room," she said to Elijah. "Your friend is dead."

"Yes," said Elijah, "but he could've had life..." Elijah started walking toward the door.

The woman turned toward Elijah. "Have you been admitted to the hospital?"

"No," said Elijah.

"I'm going to ask that you follow me down the hall to the front desk," she said. "I'm not sure that we will have a bed for you, but we'll do the best that we can."

Waddling from the room the nurse led the old man to the admittance desk. "You'll need to..." she looked around to explain admittance to the stranger, but he was gone.

Chapter 20:
TERROR IN PASCO COUNTY

Lightning slashed through the ink–black early morning sky with daggers of flashing, ripping brightness. A mixture of yellow, orange and red tumbled around within the racing clouds, butchered by the streaking lightening. "This is not natural," Tamor said, taking in the storm. "It came on so suddenly. I think we'd better be ready to head for cover! This doesn't look good..."

"I'm with you, Tamor," broke in Rachel. "The rain has been getting heavier and heavier." She paused. "Look! Can you see the center line on the..."

"Girl!" Tamor spoke more with her eyes than her words. "We need to get off the road!"

Struck by a great wall of wind, hail followed, pelting the skin of their car. Looking ahead, Rachel spotted a fruit stand closed for the season. A large metal canopy stretched above open ground. "I'm heading for that covering," panicked Rachel, pointing to the tin structure about twenty feet ahead. Hitting the brakes hard, her car hydroplaned fifteen feet past the fruit stand. Rachel turned the vehicle around racing for shelter. Bouncing over the rough, soggy entry, they reached a welcomed sanctuary from the storm.

"I just hope that all the metal on this stand doesn't turn into a lighting rod," stammered Tamor. Rachel turned to her, pain and helplessness painted over her face.

"Not to worry!" Tamor tried to trace a smile on the lines of her lips. "God's still keeping His lambs in view. I'm sure of that!"

Four hours passed within the fury of the storm. Rachel and Tamor said little, each keeping a private vigil of prayer.

$$\bullet \ \bullet \ \bullet \ \bullet \ \bullet$$

A sudden gust of wind blasted against Luke's car making him veer to the left. Huge bullets of water began flattening against the metal of his car. Anxiety raced within Luke. "This is great!" He didn't need another delay. Looking around, he assessed the storm. Suddenly the form of a woman caught his eye. She stood high on a hill, her clothes flapping madly in the wind. Straining to see through the downpour, Luke worked to capture the details of this macabre scene. The woman stood with her palms facing toward the sky. A large, burgundy scarf flagged with the tempest.

"That's no coat she's wearing," gasped Luke. "She's dressed in a robe—a black robe!" Lightening flashed exposing the woman's face. The hood of her robe was torn away by the relentless wind. "Good heavens," exclaimed Luke. "It's the lady in red!" Her lascivious art had not seduced the young pastor, but other crafts could destroy him. An incredible blast of wind slapped against the side of his car. Luke fought for control as the wheels slid across the wet asphalt.

Gaining control, Luke pressed down on the gas. He sped by the storm-locked hill and the mystery woman as she stood captured in chaos. A million questions flooded forward. Flash! Lightning struck a tree to the right, it fell crashing to his side. The falling rain clogged his vision to the road. Up ahead was an overpass. Luke decided to park under its shelter until the storm passed over. Here he prayed for Rachel, her safety, and that she also had found protection from the tempest. He could only hope that the storm had held her up too. He didn't want to get further behind. This was a life—or—death pursuit to vaccinate Rachel before she became a victim of the plague.

As daybreak cut a line across the dark eastern horizon, the violent storm faded eerily into silence. Luke looked at his watch. Precious hours had passed as he waited out the storm. Suddenly a burgundy car bolted by, spraying his car with water. The driver glanced over at him. It was the woman on the hill... the lady in red.

• • • • •

The state capital was animated with fevered early morning meetings seeking to deal with plague-related problems. As the phone rang, Susan Struck was tied up with the same appointment that had brought her to the office at 6:00 a.m. "Susan Struck's office," spoke the secretary to the governor's special assistant. "How may I help you today?"

"I need to talk to Mrs. Struck," demanded Dale Kain. Kain was the sheriff of Pasco County, Florida. He was a no-nonsense redneck born from a southern belle who had married a career officer in the army. At the age of 52, he comported the values of the 1950's like he carried his old Colt revolver. Neither ever left his side. Presently he was traveling 75 miles an hour, lights flashing and siren blaring, barely able to hear the voice on the other side of his cellular phone.

"I'm sorry," said the secretary, "but Ms. Struck is tied up at present..."

"Well, Little Lady," patronized Kain stiffly, "you'd better go work out some of those knots, pronto! I'm Dale Kain, Sheriff of Pasco County. The matter I need to discuss with Mrs. Struck has to do with the plague..."

"I'll ring you through." The secretary hit the intercom key to Struck's office. "Susan, I'm sorry to bother you now," she said, "but I've got Dale Kain on the phone. He's the Sheriff of Pasco County. He said something about the plague..."

"Thanks, Kathy," interrupted Struck, "put him through immediately." The line connected. "This is Susan Struck."

"Susan," Kain's stern voice struggled to penetrate the blaring siren of his speeding car, "I received a call from Art Koehler. He's the town constable in Rockbridge, a small community in Pasco. He tells me that the plague has broken out in Rockbridge. I'm on my way there now and should be pulling in shortly. Art and a few boys from that little town have sealed off the three roads that lead in and out of that pint-sized community. Should I be gettin' some ambulances down there? No doubt there are sick and dying that need to be taken to the hospital in Darby."

"No!" came Struck's emphatic reply. "Let me handle that from my end. According to presidential orders, your job is to keep Rockbridge under quarantine."

"I'll do what I can," replied Kain, "but right now there's only one deputy in the area giving me a hand. If things get rough, it'll just be the two of us, Art, and anyone that he can deputize..."

"Do the best that you can," advised Struck. "I'll warn you in advance. Word is that these situations are getting pretty ugly." She paused. "Ordinary folk are becoming animals when they contract the disease—desperate 'cause they feel there's no hope, I guess."

"You'll be getting some medical help to Rockbridge?" asked Kain again.

"Leave that to me," said Struck evasively. Sheriff Kain had been around bureaucrats long enough to know when double-talk was being served up without forging an outright lie. Kain doubted that there would be any medical help coming quickly to Rockbridge. What Struck was planning to do about the situation in Rockbridge was anybody's guess. Throwing the phone onto the passenger's seat Kain pushed the gas pedal to the floor.

• • • • •

Monday morning Julie Novell arranged the tape dispenser and stapler that sat to the right of the desk at Morningside Community Church. Straightening out a stack of papers, she examined her lipstick in a mirror taken from her purse, and then checked for phone messages. There was only one. Dialing in the security code, she listened to the following message: "This is Pastor Luke, Tamor, I'll be taking a little time off. If all goes well, I won't be gone more than a few days. I'm trying to catch up with Rachel. She's on her way to Florida to see her mother. I've got something that I need to give to her. Oh!—please let Pastor Horton know that this is very serious. I'm sorry for the short notice. Also, please feed Rachel's cat. The key is under the back door mat. Thanks."

Jotting down the message Julie delivered it to Pastor Horton's box. Looking out the office window, she was greeted by a wet, foggy morning. The sloppy, misty weather accompanied her to church, slowing down her morning drive. Thick fog had grabbed onto the windshield of her car, coating it with objects a few feet away, but hiding anything more than twenty feet ahead. Julie looked from the window and back to her desk. Picking up the stack of attendance cards from Sunday's worship services, she turned them sideways, striking them several times against the desktop. Setting the neatly piled cards by the computer, she hit the switch to begin recording information from last Sunday's worship attendance.

At 8:32 a.m. Pastor Horton walked into the office. "Good morning Julie," he said with a wearied smile. "I see that you're already at it. How does it feel to be back in the saddle again?" Horton was masking the same anxiety that gripped the nation.

Julie, who just a few years ago had been the parish secretary before the birth of her first child, smiled back. "It feels like I never walked away from this desk."

"So," asked Horton, "who's taking care of little Molly?" His polite conversation felt strange to him as the nation lay under the pall of death. He pushed the conversation of daily life from his lips but his mind was chewing over the grim news he had watched over morning breakfast.

"Mom just lives down the street," she answered, "and loves to take care of her granddaughter. Molly is her first, so she's pampered to death. Mom has forgotten the 'no' word that she once practiced over and over with me. Tom and I pay a price for what is called 'free' babysitting. Molly comes back to us as Queen of the Universe expecting to have her every wish instantly granted by her slave parents." Her smile faded as she changed the subject. "What do you think about this virus? That's all you hear about on the news."

"It's bad," he said. "I think all of us are taking our family and friends less for granted these days. I find it hard doing any task without thinking of someone that I care about and hoping that they are doing okay." Pastor Horton stopped suddenly realizing something he wanted to ask Julie. "So, Tamor got a hold of you and let you know the important stuff?"

"Yes," answered Julie, "she called me Saturday morning."

"That must have been just after she called me about taking a few days from work," he reflected. "I think that it's great that she wants to help out Rachel, but I'm concerned for both of them. What all did Tamor say to you?"

"She was in a hurry when we talked," said Julie, turning her chair from the computer to face Pastor Horton. "Apparently she'd planned a casual stop at Rachel's on Saturday morning. Pastor Downs had mentioned to her the day before that Rachel was anxious about her mom who lives alone in Naples. When Tamor pulled up at her home, Rachel was already packing for a trip to Florida. Tamor tried to convince her not to go—with the plague and all, but Rachel was determined. Tamor made an on-the-spot decision to make the trip with her. She called you, and after that, she called me. And here I am!"

"Is Pastor Luke in yet?" he asked.

"Oh that's right!" exclaimed Julie. "He won't be coming in either. There was a message on the voice mail from Pastor Luke saying that he was going to try to catch up with Rachel. He said it was serious. I left the message in your box."

Taking the message, Horton shook his head. He read what Julie had taken from the voice mail. "Did he say what was so serious that he had to start tracking her down?" The senior pastor was irritated. He liked Luke, but the Senior Pastor was beginning to fear that his young associate might not be dependable. The pastoral load was increasing as parishioners dealt with the deaths of family members. This was not a good time for Luke to take off.

"No," she answered. "I wrote down pretty much all that he said. And by the way, I'll call Beth about feeding the cat, and if she can't do it, I'll take care of it."

"Please check over his calendar," requested Horton. "See if there is anything I need to cover for him. I hope he's back in a few days! He has the sermon next Sunday. I don't want to start work on one if he's going to be back. If he calls in again, transfer him to my office, okay?"

"Got it!" said Julie, turning back to the computer as she continued to key in information.

· · · · ·

Proceeding on Interstate 75, Rachel and Tamor crossed over into Pasco County, Florida. They'd been looking for a gas station just off the interstate, but nothing was showing up. "I knew that I should've filled up back at Bushnell!" lamented Rachel.

"We're trying to make time," replied Tamor. "I'd have held out for a while longer too. We both thought that a station would be coming up soon. One more fill would've taken us to Naples."

"Best laid plans of mice and men..." interrupted Rachel. She wore an exhausted smile. "I saw a road sign, there's a town called Rockbridge just two miles off the next ramp. I think we'd better take the chance that it has an open gas station."

"I'm with you, girl!" Tamor stared off in the direction of Rockbridge. Distance smeared away the town's detail, but she saw Rockbridge's water tower. Rachel ramped off the interstate taking a right.

· · · · ·

A series of bullets blew out the side windows on Art Koehler's car as it straddled the two lanes of the county road passing through Rockbridge. Squatting down by the side of his car, his pump action shotgun in his hands, he cried out, "I don't know who's shooting out there, but there isn't anyone in Rockbridge that I don't call my friend!" He waited. "Now put your guns down! I've talked to Sheriff Kain. I'm told that he's calling the governor. Help is coming! Folks, we gotta pull together."

Koehler heard the sound of children crying, women screaming, and windows shattering within the handful of downtown stores. Gunfire would break out now and then. Desperate citizens of Rockbridge had been reduced to the lowest denominator of human behavior—predators turning against neighbors they'd known for years. Others defended their property or lives by pulling out hunting guns to fight back malicious attacks. Suddenly a white pickup truck turned the corner, accelerating towards Art's car.

Art stood up waving his right hand above him. A shot pierced the air. A bullet fired from a nearby house ripped into Art's left chest. The town constable slumped dead over the trunk of his car. The charging truck smashed into Art's car throwing the vehicle with his lifeless body to the left. Upon impact, the driver's body lunged forward against the truck's steering wheel. The driver straightened himself, pressing the accelerator to the floor, racing toward the interstate.

· · · · ·

Rachel and Tamor were within a half mile of Rockbridge as a white pickup flew by traveling the opposite direction. "Wow!" exclaimed Tamor. "What's going on with that guy?"

"Well, he'll be having a little visit with the law if he keeps up that speed!" replied Rachel. Looking ahead she saw a car smashed and crumbled to the side of the road. "Looks like there's been an accident. Maybe he's trying to get help."

"Yeah, maybe," Tamor replied. "It could be that the emergency numbers are out. Nine-one-one may be toast—with the phones all messed up and all."

Pulling briefly to the side of the road Rachel looked around to see if anyone needed help. They couldn't see Koehler's body on the other side of the wrecked car. With no reason to stay, Rachel pulled out heading for the business district of the small town. "Tamor!" exclaimed Rachel. "What in heaven's name is happening here?"

The small town was in shambles. Muffled, then piercing, gunfire sounded nearby. Rachel and Tamor hadn't grown up around guns. They were uncertain about the loud cracks that occasionally blasted against the glass of Rachel's car. Just ahead a faded sign advertised the only gas station in town. Accelerating to the station, Rachel pulled up to the self-service pump. "Listen girl," said Tamor, "you let me pump the gas. Just keep looking around and let me know if you see anything funny."

"Okay," replied Rachel, "but just in case this town has something to do with the plague, use lots of paper towels on the pump handle. Will you do that?"

Tamor agreed. Pulling out several blue paper towels from the dispenser, she used them to manage the pump handle. Grabbing another paper towel, she pushed the buttons selecting the cheapest grade fuel. As Tamor filled the tank, Rachel nervously surveyed the buildings near the station. A little girl ran across the street disappearing behind a house. A loud crack pierced the air again. Rachel and Tamor jumped. "Hurry up, Tamor!" cried Rachel.

"I've got this pump at top speed!" shouted back Tamor.

"Stop it at twenty bucks!" Rachel wanted out of this town pronto. "Let's get out of here! I'll go in and pay."

Leaving Tamor at the car, Rachel rushed to the customer door of the gas station. Pushing open the door she entered a small room; convenience items and food were packed on cluttered shelves crowding toward the ceiling. "Hello," she said loudly. "Is anybody here?"

No one answered. Rachel snatched twenty dollars from the interior of her purse. Reaching over the counter, she put the money on the register then rushed out. Tamor was waiting in the car. She'd locked all the doors. As Rachel raced to the driver's side, Tamor hit the button to the electronic lock. The lock sprang open. Rachel quickly slid behind the wheel, closed the door, then hit the switch locking all the doors again. "There wasn't a soul in the station," Rachel gasped. "I just left the money on the register."

"This is spooky!" gasped Tamor. "Let's get out of here..."

Gunning out of the gas station, Rachel was looking for the road that would take them back to the interstate. In front of them stood several men armed with rifles and blocking the road. Rachel slammed on the brakes. "I don't like the looks of this," said Tamor. Her words choked up from a chest gripped in terror.

The car stopped about twenty feet from the men. Rachel looked over at Tamor. "What should I do?" Rachel's unnerved voice pleaded for Tamor to make a decision.

"Girl," replied Tamor, "back out of here and take another street. I don't want anything to do with those dudes."

Shifting into reverse, Rachel hammered the pedal to the floor. The car lurched backward as the men took after them. Intersecting a neighborhood street, she shifted into high gear taking a sharp right. One of the men caught up to the car grabbing the left back door handle and running for about forty feet with the car until he could no longer keep pace. Letting go, he tripped, then tumbled, on the hard asphalt. Rachel sped for a block, took a left turn, then accelerated madly for two more blocks bringing them to the city limits of the small town. Taking another left, then a right, she cruised onto the county road leading back to the interstate.

Traveling over seventy miles an hour, she once again passed the wrecked car of the town constable. In the other lane a sheriff's car whizzed by but didn't stop. "I thought for sure I was going to get a speeding ticket." Rachel inhaled deeply.

"It looks like he's more interested in getting to Rockbridge," observed Tamor. "Say! What's that?"

To their right was the white pickup that they'd met on their way into Rockbridge. It was empty, driver's door wide open. Just behind the pickup was another sheriff's vehicle, its red and blue lights flashing wildly. An officer stood beside the white pickup looking into the ditch.

Tamor screamed! Driving by, they saw a man's body lying in the grass just a few feet in front of the truck. Rachel accelerated to eighty miles an hour. Reaching the exchange, she tried to slow down as she ramped onto the entrance taking them south on Interstate 75. The car's tires squealed against the pavement as she veered onto the ramp. Pulling onto the interstate, they both watched as National Guard trucks coming from the north turned off heading toward Rockbridge.

· · · · ·

Traveling down the interstate, Tamor and Rachel began reflecting on their experience in Rockbridge. "I really need to stop," said Rachel. "I'm shaking!"

Up ahead stood an interstate full-service station with an adjoining restaurant. The outside of the building didn't sport the sharp lines and neon lights that characterize many truck stops. Instead, it was an old house converted many years ago into a business. Inside the restaurant one of the cooks was feeling ill. Living in Rockbridge, the cook had arrived at work an hour earlier. Except for a small fever, she felt fine when she had left for work that morning. She'd heard some shots in town, but just figured that neighbors were using twenty-twos to get rid of squirrels.

"I'm not up for anything with caffeine," said Tamor, "but let's stop at the station up ahead and then eat something light. It'll give us both time to pull together. Besides, do we want to show up at your mom's door on an empty stomach?"

Rachel agreed, ramping off the exit that took them to the restaurant. They pulled into the parking lot near the restaurant. The gas station and restaurant combo sat quaintly on the edge of a small lake. The beach of the lake pressed up against the parking lot. Lovely willow trees grew between the parking lot and the lake, planted at even intervals by past land owners. The willows were planted when the house, now a restaurant, was first built. The mature trees, carried by the occasional gusts that brushed long willow limbs over the water, swept the surface of the lake. Nothing here suggested the chaos engulfing the planet.

Rachel turned off the ignition when her car's wheels bumped up against the curb. The car now sat under the shade of a willow trimmed high enough to allow cars room to maneuver under its branches. In front of them an old man with dark skin and white hair was working an open fire on the beach. "Look at that," pointed Rachel toward the man, "he's cooking fish on the beach!"

Staring in the direction of the old man, Tamor opened the door and got out of the car. She had seen this man before. Someplace in her past his face peered out at her, but the setting was mist and smoke. She couldn't place where she had run into this stranger, but she was certain that he had a part in her history. The old man had one of those faces that planted itself deeply into one's brain cells. Tamor looked over at Rachel. Together they walked toward the restaurant prompting the man to stand up and call after them. "Are you two hungry?" he shouted. A straight line of white teeth broadcasted a glowing smile.

Stopping, they turned back in the direction of the stranger. "Huh?" grunted Tamor.

The old man gestured with his hand toward the frying fish. "I asked if you two were hungry."

Taking tentative steps closer to the man, Tamor took the lead in the situation. "We're on our way to the restaurant for a quick bite."

"They've got good food there, sister" said the man, "that's fo' sure!" He looked down at the fish. "Only thing is, I caught me all these fish, and I sure hate to waste 'em." His eyes twinkled in the mid-day sun. "So when I saw you two pull in, why—I said to myself, 'Elijah, why not see if they'd like to have some fish caught fresh from this here lake.'" Cocking his head to the left he asked, "Well ladies? What's it gonna be?"

Rachel hesitated, then replied, "That's really kind of you, but we don't want to trouble you..."

"No trouble!" interrupted Elijah. "I'm the one that's asking. You'd be doing me a favor. I hate to just throw these fine specimens away." Tamor and Rachel continued to eye Elijah with suspicion. They didn't want to be rude, but they really wanted to visit privately. "I live too far from here to bring 'em back home," he continued, "so I cooked 'em all up. It was a silly thing to do, 'cause I could've just thrown some back into the lake."

"Well..." began Rachel.

"And look," broke in Elijah fearing that she might turn down his invitation, "I got lots of extra sodas and a full bag of potato chips!"

Rachel glanced to the side at Tamor, pleased to see that her friend could still smile. Tamor hadn't smiled much during the whole trip and not once since Rockbridge. "Okay," she said, "I wasn't very hungry, but the smell of that fish that you're frying..."

"...is making us both hungry," Tamor concluded Rachel's comment. Walking quickly over to the fire, they joined Elijah, sitting down on a green wooden bench that he'd commandeered from a small picnic area to the left of the restaurant. "This is kind of fun," Tamor continued, forgetting momentarily what had just happened in Rockbridge. Elijah's presence could make a person forget terrible things.

"I hope you like these," smiled Elijah. "I've used this same recipe since before you two girls were born." Using a fork to lift pieces of fish from the pan, he placed them on paper plates. "Here," he said, handing each of them a serving. Pulling open the top of a new bag of potato chips he then handed the bag to Tamor. "Do you like root beer?" he asked.

"That would be fine," said Tamor. Rachel nodded in agreement. Elijah popped open two cans handing them to the young women. Briefly pausing, they closed their eyes for a silent prayer. Elijah continued to smile.

"Did you see all those army trucks head'n up on the interstate?" he asked as they looked up after their prayer. Then, before they could answer, Elijah waved his right hand in big gestures before his face. "I apologize," he said. "I didn't even introduce myself properly." He reached out his hand, first to Rachel. "My name is Elijah Jordan." Shaking her hand, he reached for Tamor's. "I see by your car plates that y'all are from Minnesota."

"That's right," said Rachel, "Rochester, Minnesota."

"Long way from home, aren't ya?" he asked. "Pretty dangerous being so far from home with this terrible plague showin' up all over the place."

"Brother," cried Tamor, "you got that right!"

Elijah smiled. "So, what brings ya to Florida?"

"I'm concerned for my mom," answered Rachel. "She lives in Naples, and it's been impossible to get through to her by phone." The three continued to talk, but the women never brought up the subject of Rockbridge. Their experience in that chaotic town had molested them, and they felt ashamed to speak about it with others. Several times Rachel tried to draw things to a close and get them back on the road, but each time Elijah did something forcing them to stay a little longer.

Inside the restaurant, the sick cook was handing plates to the waitresses. Her sweat glands wept profusely seeking to cool fevered flesh. Walking over to the owner she said, "I need to use the bathroom." Wiping her forehead with the sleeve of her shirt she added, "I'm not doing very well right now." The owner expressed concern as the cook made her way to the restroom. She vomited violently into the toilet, then returned to the kitchen where she leaned against the counter, supporting her shaking body as she sought to resume her kitchen duties.

"I need to walk." Rachel stood up fixing the waist of her dress. "I've been sitting too long in that bucket of bolts. I'll be back in five."

Tamor's expression said, "Okay girl, but don't leave me here too long." Giving her attention to Elijah, Tamor started telling him about her work at Morningside Community Church. Rachel walked to the restaurant's entrance. She was worried about her mother. It wouldn't be long now and she should be in Naples. Deciding to see if the phones were working she opened the door to the restaurant finding two public phones dead ahead. Each were tagged with a sign telling patrons that the phones were out-of-order. To the far left she spotted restrooms. This would be a good time, she thought, for one final trip to freshen up before reaching her mother's.

Suddenly Elijah's head jerked up from the fire. Springing to his feet, he ran like a man of twenty for the restaurant's front entry. Rachel was walking for the women's restroom, her hand lifted to push against the metal plate on the door. As Rachel's hand drew within inches of contacting the door, Elijah burst into the restaurant shouting, "Rachel!" His voice drew the attention of the staff and patrons. Dropping her hand before touching the door, she turned around. "I need you to come with me immediately."

Rachel blushed, walked away from the restroom, then left the restaurant with Elijah. "What was that all about?" she demanded.

"Let's just say that it's not safe..." Elijah paused, then winked. "Call it an old man's intuition, but I think you need to stay out of that place." He nodded with his head back toward the restaurant. Rachel wasn't in the mood for figuring Elijah out. Returning to Tamor, her friend stood up, confused and anxious over Elijah's sudden dash for the restaurant. Rachel stretched out her hand waving away Tamor's question before it was asked.

Turning to Elijah, Rachel smiled, "Elijah, I really enjoyed that fish."

"Enjoyed!" Tamor repeated loudly, "Honey, that was the best fish we ever ate!"

"Yes it was," agreed Rachel. Reaching out to shake hands with Elijah for the final time she observed, "Not only are you a good cook, but there's something about you that soothes the spirit." And confuses it too, she thought to herself.

Tamor nodded her head in agreement. Elijah just smiled back. "Good to meet the two of you." He squatted down to tend the fire. "Say girls," he added as Tamor and Rachel headed to their car. "I wouldn't take any tours off the interstate. Stay right on the main roads 'til you get into Naples." Waving back and nodding their heads in agreement, they were arrested by Elijah's final observation. "One more thing," he shouted. "I don't think I'd stop off anymore—period!—until you get to your ma's, Rachel. Not even for food! Never know where that plague might show up."

"Thanks!" yelled back Rachel. She and Tamor took to the car.

Pulling out of the parking lot Rachel suddenly braked to a complete stop. "How did the old man know my name?" she asked more to herself then Tamor. "He introduced himself to us, but we never gave him our names. Yet, as we were leaving, he said my name." Turning toward Tamor she asked in amazement, "Remember? He said 'don't stop until you reach your mother's, Rachel.' He also called out my name in the restaurant." They both looked back over their shoulders, but the old man was gone. The fire was gone from the beach and the green bench was sitting back in the picnic area.

"If this day gets any stranger," said Tamor shaking her head, "I'm gonna think that somehow we have both crossed over with Alice through the looking glass." Pausing, she reflected, "You know, the blue eyes... He looked familiar. I've seen him before." Tamor shook her head as she fanned her hand in front of her face. "I studied his eyes!" she added. "He wasn't wearing contact lenses either. Sister, I'd bet my life on it!"

• • • • •

Luke looked up to see Rachel's car merging onto the interstate. "Thank You Lord!" he cried out. Nailing down on the accelerator, he pressed steadily closer to Rachel. "What!" he shouted again. "Is that Tamor with her?"

In less than a minute he had moved directly behind Rachel, just a few car lengths away. Sounding his horn Luke began flashing his headlights on and off. Rachel looked back. "Heavens!" she gasped. "Tamor, Pastor Luke is behind us!"

"Pastor Luke!" echoed Tamor turning to look. "Girl! We have passed through the looking glass!"

Waving back, Tamor let Luke know they'd spotted him. Rachel took the next exit off the interstate, parking along the side of a county road. Flying out of his car Luke met up with Rachel who was already running towards him. Throwing her arms around him, she started sobbing. "I can't believe it's you... I can't believe it's you! Thank you Father God! Thank You!"

Tamor stood awkwardly to the side. When Luke looked over to her, she winked, and with the back of her hand near her cheek, waved to him. Rachel stood there a full minute in Luke's arms releasing a torrent of emotional energy in a waterfall of tears. When she finally pulled away, Luke reached to her cheek wiping away big tears. He looked again at Tamor. This time Tamor came running to give him a hug. After Luke returned the hug, Tamor sheepishly moved back a few feet. She had never hugged a pastor.

"I'm so glad you're alive, Rachel," Luke said energetically. "And Tamor, what a surprise to find you here! Could someone please tell me what's going on?"

Walking together over to long, green grass growing in the ditch, they sat pushing down the blades into soft mats below them. Rachel began explaining how it was that Tamor ended up as her traveling companion. As Rachel talked, Tamor sat quietly. Once in a while Luke looked in her direction. Tamor would smile, raise the back of her hand to her cheek, then wave it again. She realized that this behavior was juvenile, but she hadn't recovered from her sudden display of emotion toward her Pastor.

Rachel stopped when she came to the part about their experience in the small town where they'd stopped for gas. Burying her head within her hands, she whimpered, "It was awful!" Tamor took over telling the events of Rockbridge. Explaining how the community had been in chaos, she paused briefly before describing the terrifying encounter with armed men. Tamor pointed over to the lake on the other side of the exchange. She shared about their meeting with a peculiar old man by the lake. "He had brown skin and the bluest eyes I've ever seen."

"Blue eyes!" interrupted Luke. "Don't tell me that he had hair whiter than winter snow..."

"How'd you know that?" intruded Rachel.

"I don't believe this!" blurted Luke. "And let me guess, his name was Elijah Jordan!"

"How could you know that?" asked Tamor.

It was time for Luke to share all that he knew about Elijah Jordan. When he finished, Rachel asked, "How did Elijah get down here?"

Tamor decided to field that question. "I see it, girl, don't you? This is an angel taken to human form. The Bible has many examples of this. Remember when Jacob wrestled with the angel until dawn?"

"Tamor," Luke had something he wanted to say to both of them. "If you had suggested the presence of angels even a few weeks ago, I'd have smiled politely and written you off. A lot has happened since then." He pointed over at Rachel. "She's helped me to see that life is bigger than my five senses." Luke paused. "I've learned that the supernatural is real. That it has texture. It can be awesome and life saving, or it can be seductive and deadly. Someday I'll tell you both about the lady in red."

"Heaven and hell are all around us, once you have eyes to see," added Tamor.

"Yes," smiled Luke, "once you have eyes to see."

Rachel smiled too. "Luke, I think maybe it's time to do some talking with the Lord, what do you think?"

Luke reached out, taking both their hands. "Father God, we thank You that You have kept us safe through so much danger. We don't know exactly who Elijah is, but we rather suspect that He's here because You want him to be watching out for us. Thank You for Elijah. Please continue to care for us and for those that we love during these terrible times. Protect Pam in Naples. We ask it all in Jesus' name." And the three said, "Amen."

Elijah stood beside them as they sat on the matted grass. Invisible to their senses, he was smiling with his hands facing forward toward the three and his face lifted toward the blue sky. He was not alone. Guardians were ministering to these three as they sat praying. When Luke finished up the prayer, Rachel asked, "So why are you here?"

Luke told about his meeting with Briggs in the Twin Cities and the shocking revelation about his vaccination against the plague. "Do you mean that it can't hurt you!" interrupted Tamor.

"That's right," he answered. "And there's something more. If I give someone just a little bit of my blood, that person also becomes immune to the virus."

Both women struggled to take in the full meaning of what Luke was saying.

"Wait a minute," concluded Tamor. "So not only are you immune to the disease, but you could make us immune too?"

"I know it sounds crazy," he replied, "but I should be able share my immunity. I'm here to give a little of my blood to Rachel and her mother. Now I'm adding my favorite church secretary to the list as well."

Tamor's emotions mixed within her, prodding her to laugh and tugging her to cry. Reaching over to Rachel sitting beside her, Tamor put her arms around her friend's neck, resting her head upon Rachel's cheek. Tears gushed out as all the emotions Tamor had bottled up flowed out like water from a breached dam. Luke placed his hand softly on Tamor's shoulder and waited silently. After a few minutes Tamor was once again master of her emotions. Sitting up she sniffled, "I'm sorry, I didn't expect that to happen."

Reaching over, her eyes also wet, Rachel ruffled her hand into Tamor's long hair. "You've been so strong for me! Thank you..." Taking in a very deep breath she said again, "Thank you, Tamor."

The wind wrestled through the long grass as the three sat in silence. Each of them were thinking over the last few days, often muscling their emotions under control. Rachel wondered about Luke's comment about a lady in red. She'd bring that subject up with Luke when the time was right. Now wasn't that time. They continued to sit quietly until Rachel reached over placing her hand on Luke's hand, asking, "How do you share your immunity again?"

"Well...," Luke's face twisted in confusion, "Briggs explained things to me and I have this kit that she brought with her on the jet. It's in my car." Luke thought for a moment. "Let's not waste anymore time. I'll do the transfusions as soon as we reach your mom's." He glanced over to Rachel, then Tamor. "I've got to admit that I'm a bit nervous about how this all gets done, but we'll do it somehow because we're out of options..."

"We need to scat!" Tamor broke in. Her urgent voice expressed what they all were feeling.

"Have you eaten anything Luke?" asked Rachel.

"No," he replied. "I've been really hungry..."

"Well then let's get you something to eat," interrupted Rachel.

"I've got food in the car," he said, "but..." He was struggling to explain something that he himself didn't understand. "I could devour a horse, my stomach aches, but when I start thinking of actually eating something—I don't know..." Again he stammered for words. "Let's get going! I've got food if I decide to eat. Don't worry about me..."

Chapter 21:
DEATH & DYING

Back at the terrorist base camp, Ahmad lay on a canvas cot, his clothes drenched in perspiration. The large tent that had become his home was now a mortuary filled with dead bodies. Comrades lay on the dirt floor or spread out on contaminated cots. Military issue blankets rested perfectly still over revolutionaries assassinated by their own weapon of terror. Ahmad was laboring for breath, his eyes filled with fear. Flint sat at the table. Molech, invisible to Flint's side, temporarily protected the demon's new pawn from the effects of the plague. Starkey had left for the States to be with his mother. He had to make sure that she was safe.

Ahmad's weakened condition did not prevent him from mustering the strength to scream obscenities at Flint from across the room. "Why you are being spared," he wailed, "I cannot imagine!" He fought for air. "Did you hold back the antidote from us? You..." again a string of soiled speech.

Saying nothing, Flint smiled cruelly at the dying man.

Ahmad soon fell silent, too weak to displace his angst by raging at Flint. The Shadow of Death sucked away the life of this revolutionary, pulling him with each sacrificed second closer to the dark abyss. Fifteen minutes passed. Ahmad spoke again. "Shoot me!" His faint pleading fell without effect upon Flint. "Shoot me! I can't take it any more."

The second plea brought a slitted smile over the face of Flint. Rising, Flint walked over to Ahmad. Taking out his holstered nine millimeter Glock, he fired. Ahmad's pillow exploded, but he was untouched. "It's not that easy, you fool." A voice spoke to the dying man, but it wasn't Porter's. Ahmad's twisted face pleaded for mercy. Flint stood over him, grimacing malevolently, his eyes green and glowing, animated by an unnatural presence. Ahmad froze. The Shadow of Death devoured away the terrorist's soul. Molech shared the feast, putting Flint's hand against Ahmad's chest, savoring his portion of this mortal's fleeting life.

• • • • •

Starkey sat by the bed of his dying mother in Buffalo, New York. The plague had spread to many major cities in the U.S., including some metro areas near New

York City. Infected with the plague while taxiing to his mother, he was swallowed up with grief discovering that she had been infected also. Starkey watched desperately as his mother slipped away from him in terrible discomfort. Dipping a washcloth in cool water, he wiped it gently across her cheeks and forehead. "I'm so sorry, mother," he said.

"It's not your fault," she replied weakly, "there's nothing you can do."

Starkey shook his head. Thank heavens she didn't know his part in her death. "I just wish that there was something that I could do," he whimpered. Tears cascaded down his cheeks.

"I'm in God's hands," she replied. "We're all born to die." Looking up at her son she watched as he also labored for breath. "My concern is for you. I won't live long enough to see you die. I know that you have the plague too." She coughed. "I only wish that I could be as sure of your faith in God as I am of my own." For the first time Starkey saw tears forming in his mother's eyes as they squinted close in grief. "I could gladly leave this world in the arms of Jesus if I knew that I'd see you again."

Reaching over she took her son's hand in hers. Gazing into Starkey's eyes she sought some hint of Christian faith. Starkey looked away, tears continuing to stream down his face. "It's not too late, son," she said. Her words were interrupted by a fit of coughing. "It's never too late. God is always ready to empower your faith and make it grow." Again she coughed. Starkey patted her face with the moist cloth. "I know that you once believed," she said softly, "before you went away to the university. The professors there filled your head with resentment towards God replacing it with an inflated admiration for the things of men."

"Let's not talk about that now," said Starkey. His mother felt his deep affection. The deathly sick terrorist still managed an ember of love that glowed for his mother. The memory of his dad floated in fog. His biological father had walked out on them when Starkey was three. His mother went to work at 5:00 each morning, baking pies for a downtown restaurant. She'd come home exhausted just in time to be there when school was done. Serving him up a sandwich, she'd happily listen to all the details of his day.

"Oh but we must talk," insisted his dying mother. "I know what's at stake. Heaven or hell for my lovely boy... Seeing you or not seeing you again..."

Guardians suddenly appeared in the room behind the veil of what can be seen or heard by mortals. They fought back Entities seeking entrance into Starkey's soul. The Shadow of Death wrapped Starkey in numerous tentacles. Free of death's clench, the terrorist's mother glowed with a radiance witnessed by angels and demons alike. A Guardian stood by, holding a brilliant sword poised above the tentacles entrapping Starkey. The soldier of heaven waited in compliance with the order of things ordained by El Shaddai.

"Mother, you don't know the monster that I've become." He spoke bluntly. "I've joined up with people who are evil. I thought that I was helping to make the world a better place. A world where a single woman raising her son wouldn't have to scratch for a living. Others had tried, and the world was still a mess. This time it was going to be my way. I, and others like me, had a radical solution with short term pain but big time benefits in the long run." He bent his chin to his chest as it heaved deeply under the weight of his words. "What a fool I was. There is no short term fix for this," he checked his language, "...for this screwed up planet."

"This is the beginning of your reawakening," she spoke in hope. Three Guardians now laid hands on the feeble old woman. They would restrain her from entering God's Kingdom until her work was done. The additional time would lengthen the old woman's misery, but each labored second would shine with beauty in the Kingdom of Glory. "Yes there was a short term fix. His work lasted only three years, then they killed Him. But He came back from the grave."

"Mom," interrupted Starkey, "I think..."

"No! Paul," using Starkey's given name, "I'll have my say. The greatest treasure of my life has been knowing Jesus as my personal Lord and Savior." She no longer coughed. "Not by my strength, but by His. Strength given to me each time I went to worship, heard or read the Word, or went to the Lord's Table."

"It seems so long ago," began Starkey, his words interrupted by an avalanching cough.

"I remember how you loved me to sing 'Jesus loves me, this I know' after I had tucked you into bed." Staring at the ceiling she smiled faintly.

"Do you think that He could still love someone like me?" asked Starkey. He caressed his mother's hand within his fevered grip. "Someone who has strayed so far from Him, and for so many years?"

"I know that He loves you," said his mother. She looked back at her son with affirming eyes. "I've never doubted that!" The Guardians withdrew their hands, Starkey's mother collapsed silently into the mattress of her bed, her eyes opened wide in wonder. Starkey could see her mouthing the word 'Jesus' over and over, and then she was silent.

Starkey's torso fell over his mother's dead body. He sobbed deeply until the fast progress of the disease so crippled him that he could no longer remain on his chair. Crawling along the floor he struggled to reach the other side of the bed. Pushing his body up on the open area of the double bed, he lay beside the breathless frame of his mother. Looking across the room, he stared at a large picture of Jesus the Good Shepherd carrying back the lamb who had gone astray. Tucked into the corner of the frame was his picture, taken just after graduation from college. Again he wept. "Jesus," he said softly, "will You carry me back to Your Kingdom?" Instantly the Guardian thrust his sword into the tentacles that encrusted Starkey, slicing the redeemed lamb free forever from the Shadow of Death.

• • • • •

The plague was spreading terror across the globe. A small band of Christians met secretly to worship God and intercede for the planet infested with death. Mohsen Asefi was just finishing up his message. Mohsen was a missionary in Tehran working with local converts to Christianity. That evening his flock had gathered at a convert's home. The curtains were drawn tightly shut. Hymns offered to God were sung in whispered tones. Conversion to Christianity had placed the worshiper's lives into mortal jeopardy. Members within Mohsen's church were game for slaughter if they were discovered. Hunted by family and friends, their execution would be considered an act of patriotism in service to Allah.

"Each of us," continued Mohsen's evening message, "have lost family or friends. They were martyred because of their faith in the Lord Jesus. The loss of our loved ones we feel so deeply. Grief strikes our hearts as it also impales those who have watched loved ones snatched by the plague. We must be clear, however, that our loss is one thing, what has happened to them is another matter. The Savior has gone to prepare a place for all God's people within His Kingdom. The Word of God tells us that there will be a special place in Heaven for those who have given their lives in testimony to their faith..."

In the next room a boy of about fourteen heard the missionary's words while he played with other children. Unlike his parents and sister, he had no intention of converting to Christianity. His family's activities would be reported to officials at his school, but he was in no hurry to betray them to the authorities. Time would lead him to other converts that would be added to his report. Exposing the Christian sect to his teachers would make him a very big man among the boys his age. As he played with friends whom he'd betray and leave parentless, his mind was overcast and drifting from his surroundings. He could see and hear what was happening about him, but his body had been taken over. An entity had invaded and possessed him.

Getting up from the floor, the boy moved mechanically to the doorway. A cloth curtain separated the children from the worshipers on the other side. White foam flowed slowly down toward his chin from the corners of his mouth. Sliding by the curtain he stood silently, back pressed against the wall, the possessed boy fixed his eyes upon Asefi as he preached. Springing across the room without warning, he jumped over his parents as they sat on the floor. The demon shot the mass of the boy's body into the missionary, throwing Mohsen back against the far wall.

The missionary was stunned. Jumping to their feet worshipers rushed to pull the boy from the missionary. Mohsen's face was bleeding from scratch marks clawed by the demonized child. Several men, seeking to subdue the entity, struggled against the unnatural strength of the boy. The child yelled out in his native tongue, but it was a woman's deep voice. "I will kill you!" it screamed. "I will kill you all!"

The men had pinned the youth against the wall but struggled to keep him from continuing his attack against their spiritual leader. Mohsen staggered over to the boy, lifting back his aching shoulders to stand erect before the creature restrained before him. "I know who you are," he said.

"You know nothing!" screamed the demonic.

"I know that you are evil," the missionary continued. "The boy was unprotected by faith, now you have entered into him." Mohsen moved to within inches of the boy's face, studying the young man's eyes. "What are you called?" demanded the preacher of the entity.

The boy broke into a malevolent laugh. "I am not your dirt. You do not walk on me!"

"You're correct," answered Mohsen. "I'm a mouse, and you are the cat."

Again the missionary searched the eyes of the boy. "There is One, however, that commands all creation—things of earth and things in spiritual realms. In the name of Jesus, what are you called?"

The demon-possessed boy screamed, lurching out of the grip of those holding him. Once more knocking Mohsen to the floor, the demonic lunged toward the window shutters. A sudden reach of the missionary tripped up the demonic. Men rushed to the boy holding him to the floor. Women standing to the side of the room were praying silently. Mohsen got up, walked over, towering above the boy. "I command you in the name of Jesus to tell me your name!"

The youth convulsed on the floor. One of the men whispered to Mohsen, "You'd better keep your voice down. We don't want to draw the attention of our neighbors to this meeting."

"You're right," said the missionary. "Thank you." Looking again at the boy wet with perspiration, he watched the child convulse against the constraining hands riveting him to the floor. Mohsen began again, quieter this time, in measured words. "By the name of Him who was crucified, who rose again, who now reigns over all... In the Name of Jesus, by what are you called?"

"My name," yelled the boy, forcing one of the men to place his hand over the child's mouth, muzzling his loud cries. "My name is contempt! I spurn you! I despise your faith. I hate you all!"

"Contempt," said the missionary, pointing to the demonic, "you cannot have this boy!"

"He is mine!" protested the entity. "He will not have you, so he is ours."

"Whether he will be saved or not, God knows," replied Mohsen. "Yet in the name of Jesus I have been given the power to deal with you. If you had possessed a donkey, I could dispel you back into the darkness from which you came." Guardians continued to stand about the missionary, fighting back the legions of hell. One entity bolted through the line of defense digging its claws into Mohsen's neck. The missionary poured blood from where the claws tore into his flesh. A Guardian ripped the demon from Mohsen throwing it back into the throng of evil. Blood continued flowing from the missionary's face and neck.

The boy's face twisted in fear. "I will leave the boy!" The entity forced a scream through the muffling hands of those holding the young man to the floor.

"To return again?" asked the missionary. "No, that won't do. In the name of Jesus I command you to leave the boy and return into the outer darkness."

"Noooo!" shrieked the demonic. Suddenly, beyond the sight of mortals, a dark hole opened. It did not spin or swirl, but snapped apart like a lipless mouth ready to devour its prey. The entities present in the room cried out racing away through the walls out into the street. The hole was black—darker than the deepest, lightless, night. It began to draw a shadow from the boy, like a vacuum sucking up a pile of dust and dirt. Those present witnessed something like a sooty mist coming from the boy. A foul odor permeated the room. With a quick burst, the mist suddenly shot toward a central point in the room just above the head of one woman, then vanished.

The boy lay unconscious on the floor, his body frozen in silence. Rushing over, his mother placed his limp hand into hers. Bending down, the boy's father picked up his son, carrying him to a cot in the corner of the room. "Come with me over to the boy," said the missionary, "so that we might pray for him. Our Lord warned that if one demon were cast out, it is possible for many more to return."

The worshipers followed the missionary over to the cot. Holding hands as they gathered around the boy, some of the women knelt with the mother. "Gracious God, we thank You for the delivery of this young man from the powers of darkness. Yet we know that his greatest danger lies in his lack of faith. We ask that You work greater faith within this young child. We pray that You send Your holy angels to protect him. Help us to defend him from evil. Empower us to lead him through Your Word into faith in the Savior. We ask this in the name of the world's only Savior, Jesus Christ, Your Son, our Lord." The assembly concluded, "Amen."

· · · · ·

"Bill, I appreciate your coming by the White House again this evening," said the President. "I wanted to talk with you and Tim privately." Taking a deep breath the President continued, "Off the record, what exactly are we up against with this virus?"

"Mr. President," began Bill, "if I told you what I think about this monster, you'd want someone else filling my shoes at OIDC." Bill laughed nervously. "I'll tell you this, its ability to penetrate surfaces acts contrary to what we know about all other viruses."

"What do you mean?" interjected the Secretary of State. "What makes this virus so different from the rest?" Mandrake had information about the virus from military research. He was probing to see how the military data squared up against what Downs had to say.

"It doesn't act predictably," answered Bill. "By the laws of science, as we understand them, it does things that can't be explained or duplicated by us in the lab. For example, this virus does something to the integrity of plastic by changing its configuration at the atomic level. It happens very quickly. Once the change has taken place, the virus slips through, well, for lack of a better word, it slips through holes within the atomic bonds of the molecule."

"I'm no scientist," said the President, "but I did take chemistry in college. I can't make any sense of holes being made within atomic bonds..."

"Exactly!" interrupted Bill. He stopped to search for more words.

"Go on, Bill, what is it that you want to say?"

Scratching his head, Bill stood to his feet. Pacing once across the room, he walked back to where the President and Secretary of State were sitting at a large table located in the President's informal office. The table was a mess of strewn papers and computer printouts. Two lamps fought back the darkness, leaving many shadow-soldiers slain throughout the room. One light, a white porcelain lamp with a black shade, remained on guard to the side on the President's desk. In the corner of the room a polished brass lamp stand stood sentry over an olive green reading chair. Animating the lifeless shadows were entities veiled from human perception.

"What do I want to say?" asked Bill rhetorically. "I want to say that these holes created by the virus, and used by the virus to circumvent our protective equipment, are not a physical phenomenon. I want to say that they're not created by anything our science can investigate. The holes cannot be filled by anything our technology can manufacture. I want to say that this virus bridges two worlds, the one of science, the other a world completely foreign to scientific investigation." Bill stared at the President. "I want to tell you that the mechanism used by the virus to penetrate polymers is the same one used by it to quickly move through human tissue, entering the bloodstream, then killing its victims within hours..."

"Damn it, Bill!" shot Mandrake's impatient voice. "What in the hell are you trying to tell us?"

"Yes, what in the hell..." muttered Bill quietly.

"What did you say?" demanded the Secretary of State.

"Mr. President." Intently Bill caught the Commander and Chief with his eyes. "Tim." He glanced away to the man who sat at his side. "I'd bet everything I own and all that my parents possess, that you'll never find a scientific answer to this plague or a scientific answer for the cure..."

"But we do have a cure," intruded the President, "or at least a vaccine that's as good as a cure!"

"Mr. President," Bill replied, "what I said is that it's my opinion that we can't explain our weapons against the virus in scientific terms." Bill ran his fingers through his hair. "The vaccine that now protects each one of us in this room has come from one person, Seda Orhan. Seda became infected with the virus by a contaminated jar sent to her by her mother on Khlos Island before she died of the plague. Seda should have died, but defying any scientific explanation, not only is she alive, but her blood produces something that acts like a vaccine. How her body produces this quality and why it gives resistance to the virus, we haven't the foggiest idea."

"So what's the bottom line?" asked the President.

"Bottom line," repeated Bill, "we need to pray that Seda stays healthy, and we must continue to produce serum from her blood to vaccinate as many people as we can, and as quickly as possible." Loosening his tie, Bill unbuttoned the top of his white shirt. "Three days after vaccination, those protected against the plague can offer their immunity to others by means of a blood exchange. This gives us the means, a rather fast means, of giving protection to the public. Our problem is how to announce and prioritize the procedure without causing a public uproar." Bill hesitated, then continued, "You might say that salvation against the plague comes from one person and then is spread person to person. There's no other way!"

"You sound like a preacher!" Mandrake delivered a disgruntled bark at Bill. His blood pressure had risen. Mandrake's heart strained against two large blockages within arteries feeding blood to his heart. He felt a slight pain in his chest and the fingers of his left hand were tingling.

Ignoring Mandrake's remark, Bill turned to the President. "Our problem is not that we can't fight the plague, but we have so little time to deploy our weapon in an organized manner. We need time to strategize a process for staging the transfusions.

On the other hand, the plague is spreading like a prairie fire fanned by a strong, dry wind. I think that a remnant of the world's population will be preserved, but...." Bill shook his head then glanced towards a window.

The president turned to his Secretary of State. "Tim, what's happening with this thing internationally?"

Mandrake consciously managed the increasing pain in his chest. The Shadow of Death had wrapped the government official in numerous tentacles. Entities were passing in and out of his body, his flesh offering no resistance. "Nancy Wisely directed OIDC to package up some vaccine," he answered, fighting away concern over his agony, while focusing on the President's question. "We have secretly shared this vaccine with selective heads of states as you directed. They, their immediate families, and their personal physicians have received the vaccine. Those immunized are now encouraged to, very privately, share their immunity through blood transfusions as they see fit. The operative word is, privately!"

The Secretary of State was sweating profusely. The plague was claiming a victim without making contact. Stress was killing Mandrake. "Tim, are you all right?" asked the President.

"I'm fine," said Mandrake, "just some indigestion." Taking a tissue he wiped off beads of sweat from his forehead. "What Bill said about the perplexing problems with this virus is confirmed by military researchers." He wiped his head again. Less and less blood was getting through the Secretary of State's restricted arteries. "I think that we're about to see the demise of most of the world's population..."

My God!" gasped the president. "You can't be serious!"

"I'm sorry, Mr. President," Mandrake stood up. "I think..." Suddenly the Secretary of State collapsed on the floor, clutching his chest.

• • • • •

Mohsen Asefi walked home alone after the worship service. His wife had left with the family of the once demonized boy. Mohsen's wife would comfort the mother, also helping her with some household chores. The boy's mother would keep vigil at the bed of her son. At that same time, just about one o'clock in the morning, as Mohsen was continuing down a dark street, a tall Caucasian had taken his own vigil under a streetlight at the far corner. The man just stood there, looking intently toward the orphanage run by a mission society. Mohsen had come to faith in Christ working as a groundskeeper within that mission.

Flint Porter, or what was left of him, stood under the streetlight. Molech, not satisfied feeding off the death and carnage of the young and old infected with the virus, lusted for healthy blood. Flint walked towards a gate of welded iron rods hinged to the backside wall surrounding the mission. Slowly Porter's form strolled from the light into deep shadows. Mohsen watched. When he saw a sudden flash of green light, he ran to the back wall to confront the stranger. "What are you doing here?"

Porter was a few steps into the courtyard of the mission. The lock on the gate was shattered, like china hit by the blast off a shotgun. Turning around, Porter held his hand out, palm forward, in the direction of Asefi. The missionary stopped, as if striking a brick wall. Shaking off the pain, he called out, "I know who you are!"

Molech grinned hideously through the face of Porter. Mechanically Porter's lips began to move. "Do not trifle with me, little missionary!"

"I won't," replied Mohsen, "but Jesus will not allow you to harm anyone in this mission." Mohsen thought about what had happened earlier that evening. His encounter with the demon-possessed child had strengthened spiritual muscles seldom worked by the missionary. "He has prepared me for battling with the fallen ones. I sense in you a mighty presence of evil. I call upon the name of Jesus. Taking the slingshot of David and the stone of God's power, I cast God's presence against you."

Flint's demonized carcass bent over, its arms sprang around its mid-section as if Porter had been hit in the solar plexus. Standing erect again, Molech saw guardians gathering against him. This destroyer, however, could not be dispelled easily. It was present when the disciples of Jesus were sent out on their missionary journeys. It had withstood their exorcisms. "You cannot send me away, missionary," sneered the demonized Porter.

"This may be true," replied Mohsen, "but I can prevent you from harming those whom the mission protects in God's name."

"There is no way that you can do anything to me!" mouthed the lips of Flint, his eyes glowing green.

An invisible guardian spoke into the ear of the missionary. "Yes, there is a way," replied Mohsen.

"There is only one way," Porter smiled malevolently. The life of the missionary would savor almost as deliciously as a young, healthy child. "Are you prepared for that one way?"

Taking a deep breath, Mohsen whispered. "Lord, please take care of my wife, my children, and my community of faith. I give them into your hands as my hands now turn to a task that has awaited me from the day I was conceived in my mother's womb. Father God, into your hands I commit my self, body and soul."

The man of God walked effortlessly in the direction of Porter. When he was within ten feet of the demonized terrorist, Porter lifted his hands again, palms forward. A green light enveloped the missionary. The dark sky encasing the darker moment began exploding with flashes of light. More Guardians were coming by the hundreds, taking their stand surrounding the missionary as he confronted the demon. Each held a golden sword high and tilted slightly to the center of the angelic ring encircling Mohsen as he knelt in prayer.

"Bearers of light," howled Porter, "I defy you! Many times have we faced off! Many times the shadow of the mighty tree has empowered my right to take blood upon this planet of sin and pestilence. You will have Mohsen for eternity, but for the moment, he is my satisfaction!"

"We are here to see that you have no satisfaction in the death of this proclaimer of God!" cried the Guardians in unison. The spiritual realm thundered and quaked because of the volume of their united chord. Suddenly, nearest to Porter, the army of angels stepped back. A light descended from the sky, then grew brighter and brighter. A Cherubim had arrived. It had come to take the martyred saint's soul to the throne room of God. Molech had faced-off with the hosts of heaven many times, knowing that their power was limited under the pall of a cursed garden. The Cherubim, however, was a Creature whom no son of Satan ever sought to see. Molech roared in fear but remained defiant.

In the realm where angels and demons keep watch, the earth and the sky became filled with the Cherubim's words. They thundered in majesty. "YOU WILL FIND NO SATISFACTION IN THE DEATH OF ASEFI MOHSEN!"

"We'll see about that," coward Porter.

Falling level to the ground, still captured in the green light emanating from the demon, Mohsen gasped for breath. His hands remained joined together in prayer, pulled tightly to his chest. The Shadow of Death came quickly in its morbid ritual, then detached the setting from itself. This missionary was not for him. The Cherubim hovered, sending a bright spiritual light down upon the dying martyr. The Guardians continued to encircle Mohsen—comrades in arms with God's warrior of flesh. Over and over they sang in unison, "Blessed are they who die in the Lord, their works do follow them, and they are blessed forever more. Blessed are they who die in the Lord..."

The missionary soon lay motionless on the ground. His soul, now embraced by the cherubim, left suddenly as the heavenly creature blazed skyward. The green light emanating from the palms of Porter snapped off. The demonized man began swaying in an uneven circle. It was sick, gagging as if Porter were about to vomit. The monster of hell was genuinely surprised by what was happening to him. Whatever he had sought to experience in the death of Mohsen had been denied him by the Guardians. In its place Molech was inflicted with pain. The fires of hell were lapping up, inflaming the dark spirit. Porter ran from the mission into a nearby alley. As he ran, streetlight after streetlight in his path exploded into darkness, hiding a mortal face so disfigured that it had to be concealed from sight and light.

• • • • •

Returning to his hotel room, Bill was numb and exhausted. He clicked on the bathroom light, taking in his reflection in the mirror. "You look like a wreck!" Washing his face he sat down on the corner of his bed. Lifting up the phone he was relieved to hear a tone. Dialing in the number to their home, Bill's frame went limp when he heard Briggs' voice. It was a wispy voice, filled with the sleep that had just been interrupted.

"I'm sorry to have woken you up, darling" apologized Bill. "I was hoping that you might still be up."

"I'm a doctor," smiled Briggs, "master of the wake up calls. Right?"

"Yeah, right," he chuckled. "I just needed to hear your voice. It's been a rough day."

"How did your meeting with the president go?"

"How'd it go?" Bill stood up to pace by the bed, leashed by the phone cord to a short routine. "He didn't like what I had to say."

"Was he upset with you?"

"No, it's just that I had no answers for him. The information I shared with the president was pretty grim. You know how the messenger gets soiled by the message."

"I'm sorry Bill. You're just the right guy at the wrong spot."

Bill smiled at Brigg's interpretation, then ran down those details of the meeting that could be shared over an unsecured line. He choked up sharing about the sudden death of the Secretary of State. After that news, Bill really didn't seem to have much more to say. He would let Briggs get back to sleep. "I feel better," he sighed. "By the way, a military plane is bringing me back early tomorrow morning." Bill's tone brightened. "After we land, I'll be taken by helicopter to the Center. I won't see you until supper. Why don't we spend a quiet evening together tomorrow. I'll grill up burgers, then after we eat, let's sit out on the deck counting the stars."

"There are lots of stars..."

"I know," broke in Bill, "but not enough to keep us together as long as I want to be with you."

It was Briggs' turn to sigh. "See you tomorrow. I'm looking forward to numbering the stars. I love you."

"I know." Bill spoke softly. "I love you too. Good night."

"Bye honey."

Bill turned off the table lamp, happily slipping under the covers to the hotel bed. It was a fancy room that had been reserved for his meeting in Washington. The bed was soft with satin sheets. Over him lay a thick, featherweight comforter. It was a room furnished for royalty. Still, nothing felt better to Bill than his bed at home with Briggs to his side. In the darkness of his room, he drank in the welcomed sleep like a lover's kiss. It came quickly—too quickly. Something sinister waited for him in the twilight of his dreams.

Bill walked alone along the beach. There was no sun in the sky, but the day was bright and saturated with heat. He was shirtless. The waistband of his shorts drank in the sweat pouring down from his upper body. Seagulls flew above in the vacant, blue sky. In the distance the form of a woman was walking toward him. He couldn't see her face, but she wore a white two-piece swim suit. A white hat, with a huge red band, encircled the top of her head. She waved, but the features of her face remained cloaked in the distance. Bill's heart was racing. In his dream, he was single again. He was looking forward to meeting the woman coming his way.

When he saw the features of her face, he knew that he had seen her before. She was blonde. She was the woman at the transit in Zurich, but the dream denied him that recollection. She spoke first. "Hello, Bill. I've missed you." Walking to his side she took his hand. Bill turned to walk with her down the beach. As he walked, he left no footprints in the sand. The woman tipped her head back to look up at Bill, the hat's broad rim casting a shadow over her eyes. "Would you like to feed the birds?" Bill said nothing, allowing her to pull him to a large trunk of driftwood that angled up from the sand, supported at its base with a huge limb protruding into the beach. The driftwood was the only object on the ocean shore, besides the two of them and the seagulls flying above. They sat down on the driftwood.

Seagulls began to land to all sides of them. "What will we feed them?" asked Bill. He felt an urgent need to give them food. It was as if the feeding of these birds was the most important business on earth. He looked around but saw nothing to give them. Taking his head into his hands, he grimaced in frustration.

"Bill! Bill!" she laughed. "We will feed the birds. Don't worry." She pulled his hands down from his head. "Don't worry!" Reaching to her hat she pulled two surgical knives out from under the red band. She handed one to Bill. Taking her knife, she cut a piece of her own flesh throwing it to one of the birds. Bill dropped his knife in horror. She looked at him with a ghastly smile. Bill shivered, then glanced back at the seagull having fed upon the woman's flesh. It had been transformed into a hideous demon.

The woman taunted Bill. "Don't you want to feed the birds, Bill?" The muscles of her face knotted together monstrously. "FEED THE BIRDS, BILL!"

"No! God help me, No..." Bill awoke from his dream in screams of terror.

•　•　•　•　•

Later that morning a man stood in front of the check-in line of a transatlantic airline. His clothes were in shambles and his head shot out short hairs in every direction. Dirt covered his face and hands. Airport security was watching him closely. The attendant looked at Porter, then took a step back from the counter. The demonized man's deep, unnatural voice ordered a one-way ticket taking him via transatlantic jet to Oakland. All flights into Oakland's small airport, however, were canceled. The nearest open airport that handled large jets was the Sacramento Airport. Porter booked to Sacramento, reserving a second flight aboard a twin prop plane taking him to Stockton. Arriving at Stockton, he'd work his way by road to Oakland, there putting an end to Seda Orhan.

Chapter 22:
INTRUDER

As Starkey sat watching over his dying mother, Luke, Rachel and Tamor were within ten miles of Naples. Tamor was driving alone in Rachel's car. She had insisted that Rachel ride with Luke, giving them time to talk. "Say girl," she said, "I'm going it alone! Either I'm walkin' or driving—but I'm doing it all by my little lonesome. What will it be? And I don't have all day for you to decide either." Giving in to Tamor, Luke and Rachel took the lead position.

"Luke I have a question, if you're up for it that is." Rachel reached to the dash turning down the radio.

"This sounds serious," replied Luke.

"A while back you mentioned a lady in red." Rachel looked quickly at Luke to read his expression, then glanced back as if to check on Tamor. Rachel avoided eye contact with Luke. "I was just wondering..." she paused.

"She's my devil." Luke trespassed into her silence.

"What?" queried Rachel. Luke's comment startled her. She stared at him.

"The lady in red is everything that I am apart from what I can be for others. She's appetite without labor, desire without principle, and lust replacing love."

Reaching over, Rachel touched Luke's arm. "I'm sorry, I must be witless tonight. Are you saying that she's a symbol for you, or a representation, but not a real person?"

"A few days before I left the seminary I met a woman." He looked over to measure the impact of his words on Rachel. "She wore a red dress. She came on strong. She was a heavyweight flirt. She became stuck in my mind long after that first meeting. The thoughts weren't always fit for a pastor either." Luke now looked straight ahead, fearing that his eyes might betray what he could never share with Rachel. "Every once in a while, I would see her, or thought that I had."

"She was real then?" asked Rachel. "And you liked her?"

"Yes, real as my lust—my craving to have ownership over the property of another's body."

"You're still speaking in riddles, Luke." Rachel gave a light squeeze to Luke's arm. "You don't have to do this. If you'd rather not talk about it, I understand. It's really none of my business."

"Rachel, I want to make everything about me your business! Listen, the lady in red was a real woman who had taken me captive, body and soul." Luke thought about his dreams. "And if she wasn't human... In any event, she had taken away my freedom. The prison, however, was something that I had made out of my own base desires. She had no power except what I gave to her. Nothing ever happened between us. My time with her was mostly in my mind. Our longest meeting took place within a dream. You were there too." He finally looked over again at Rachel. Her eyes looked past him, searching the distance through the window to his left. "Rachel, she's now a memory, like a fading dream, and the only woman who's real to me sits to my right."

A tear slid down Rachel's cheek. She had a difficult time understanding what Luke had just shared. She would never understand what drives the male. Moving closer to Luke, she slid around on the seat, adjusting the seatbelt so that she could rest her back gently against his side. "Thanks."

"Thanks for what?" asked Luke

"Thanks for telling me about the lady in red. It must have been hard for you. Thanks for being honest with me. Thanks for..." becoming quiet, Rachel never finished her last thought. Nothing more was spoken between the two until they drew close to Naples. Reaching the outskirts of her mother's town, Rachel began giving directions. The further they drove into town, the quieter the community became. After they passed Tin City, a downtown shopping center, the people of Naples vanished completely.

"Keep going for another five blocks, then take a right." Rachel pointed down the street. "We're about two miles from mom's." Anxiety was devouring Rachel to the bone. All around them stood homes with boarded up windows and doors. Some homes, apparently abandoned, peered out darkly through broken glass. Luke was traveling forty miles an hour in a twenty-five mile zone. Sweat ran down Tamor's brown skin as she raced behind Luke. Looking from side to side, Tamor was fretful of getting a ticket. At the same time she sought desperately for a police officer patrolling the area. It was eerie. No one was outside walking their dogs or watching children play in neighborhood parks. The only suggestion of life came from inside houses. Occasionally forms darted by windows or turned lights off as they drove by.

Luke turned right. Three houses down the street a man stepped slowly out from a front doorway to stand on an open porch holding a shotgun across his chest. He watched the two cars drive by, his face set in concrete, showing no expression except for a warning that said, "stay away!" A dog darted across the street just in front of them. Luke slammed on his brakes, Tamor veered to the right barely avoiding a rear-end collision. Shaking his head, Luke continued down the street, driving a bit slower. He muscled his emotions under control. The insanity surrounding him must have no foothold.

"I'm sure that your mom's fine," he said nervously. Luke smiled, but Rachel knew that his reassurance, though well intended, was empty. No one could know if her mother had stayed out of harm's way within this embattled neighborhood. Its residents had sought to fight back looters who were taking advantage of the social chaos. Police were unable to keep up with the random violence breaking out all over southern Florida.

"Take a left at the next corner." Rachel pointed. "In four blocks we'll be at mom's house." Continuing to survey the battle worn homes, Rachel knew some of the people who lived in these houses, but saw none of their faces. "Right there!" Rachel's impatience exploded the words from her mouth. "It's the flamingo pink house with white shutters." The shutters on her mother's house had been pulled from the side of the house and nailed over the windows. "Hurry Luke," she coached, her voice barely escaping through the lock on her throat.

Luke pulled onto a concrete driveway. Flying from the passenger door Rachel raced to the front entry. Ringing the bell, she also struck the door with her fist. "Mom!" she yelled, assaulting the door several more times with the palm of her hands. Suddenly the door opened, but only a short distance before the security chain brought it to an abrupt stop. Pam, peering out from the crack in the doorway, smiled faintly. The skin on her forehead knotted together just above the bridge on her nose. "I'm sorry," she said, "I'm not your mother, and I can't take any more people into my home." Pam flashed her eyes several times to the side. Her face pleaded with Rachel to be careful.

"Okay," Rachel said, "I'm sorry to have bothered you." Walking back to the car, she intercepted Luke and Tamor who were heading for the house. Rachel wrinkled up her face, shaking her head very slightly. "I think that someone's with mom," she whispered. Tears began rolling down her cheek. "Someone's holding her captive. Just turn around with me, and we'll drive around the block and figure out what to do."

They took to their cars, driving away from Pam's house. Turning the corner, the three drove until they were out of sight-line, then pulled to the side. Rachel had stopped crying. Instead, she was praying silently. Taking her hand, Luke waited for her eyes to open. Tamor ran over to their car, opened a back door, and jumped in with them. When Rachel's eyes opened, she looked back at Tamor seeking emotional support, glancing next to Luke for some kind of solution. "What are we going to do?"

Luke was expecting that question, but wanted to run from it. He was about to say something—anything—when Tamor pointed to the corner. "I see a phone booth at that gas station. I know it's a shot in the dark, but let me see if I can get through to the police." Before they could stop her, Tamor flew out of the back seat running to Rachel's car. She grabbed the backdoor handle, opened the door, then plucked up her purse. God hid Himself in mystery as Tamor touched the same handle contacted by one of the men during their daring escape from Rockbridge.

"If Tamor doesn't get help," Luke was forced to think things through off the cuff, "I'm going back to your mom's. Give me time to work my way through the backyards, then I'll scope out the situation. I haven't a clue what I'm going to do, but..." He looked anxiously to the side. "If I can, I'm going to slip into the house to see what's going on." He paused. "If your mom is being held captive, and if I can do something, I will."

Rachel felt that she should protest, but didn't know what to say. Turning back toward the gas station, she expected to see Tamor dialing up numbers. Her friend had dropped the receiver. It dangled by the cord. Tamor was walking towards them. "Well," said Luke, "I guess that means Tamor didn't get through, so I'll be taking a hike through the neighborhood backyards." Rachel lunged toward Luke drawing him to herself. "You and Tamor stay here," he spoke softly, Rachel's head resting against his shoulder. "Give me half an hour. If I'm not back," he paused, "then I guess you're on your own."

Pulling from Rachel's embrace, he ran from the car, disappearing behind a turquoise house making his way back to Pam's. Tamor reached Luke's car, opened the back door, then slid into the seat leaving the door open. "What's Pastor Luke up to?"

"He's going back to mom's," Rachel said. "He's going to try and get inside." Rachel's eyes squinted together as tears washed out clinging to her eyelashes. "What can he do alone?"

"Listen girl," said Tamor, her voice masking her own anxiety. "He'll be fine. I'm going to rap on a few doors to see if I can get help. You stay here, just in case Luke comes back. Okay?" Rachel nodded, reaching back to give Tamor a hug. Too late! Before Rachel could hug Tamor, she bolted from the car, running toward a nearby house. She knocked on the door. There was no answer. Running to another house, her knock brought no response. She jogged to another house. Someone moved inside, so she thought, but again there was no answer as she pounded on the door.

Rachel sat in the car watching Tamor work her way down the street. Repeatedly she glanced down at her watch, measuring the time that Luke had been gone. Fifteen minutes passed like hours. "I can't take this," she said to herself. Starting the car, Rachel drove over to Tamor. "I'm going back to mom's. If you get help, great! If not, meet us back at the house. And don't be long at this! It's dangerous around here..." Tamor stepped forward from a white porch to ask Rachel a question, but gunning the gas, her friend sped away.

Speeding to her mother's, Rachel pulled up along the curb, then turned off the engine. She searched for any sign of Luke around the property. "Luke should be here by now," she thought. "Maybe he's in the house." Staring at the boarded-up house, a sanctuary turned prison for her mother, a thought bolted through Rachel's mind. Flinging open the driver's door, she sprang from the car. A diversion could only help Luke if he were trying to do something. Running to the door she pounded on its metal front. Once again her mother opened the door. Pam was clearly unhappy to see her daughter at the door. Pam would gladly face five thugs if it would keep her daughter safe.

"Please," Rachel pleaded desperately. "I need just a little food and water. I have children..."

"I'm sorry, dear" broke in Pam, "but you'll have to try another house."

Rachel continued the charade. Inside, behind the door, a man held a baseball bat menacingly above Pam's head. Luke had slipped in through the back. The intruder had broken the back door lock to gain entrance. Ever so quietly, Luke was moving through the hallway leading to the living room. It stood just off the front entry.

Carefully peeking around the corner, he saw Pam and the thug standing fifteen feet away at the front door. Pam's cat, a white calico, was resting on a deacon's bench. Luke grabbed the cat whispering, "Sorry about this...," then lobbed the cat toward the center of the living room. The cat landed on its feet, racing madly past the front door. The intruder jumped, his eyes following the path of the retreating cat. Luke took three fast steps then lunged at the stranger, driving them both hard against the door, slamming it in the face of Rachel.

The intruder, more powerful than the young pastor, rolled Luke onto his back pinning him to the carpet. The baseball bat lay a foot away from where they wrestled. Luke's adversary held him down with one hand while struggling with the other to reach the weapon. Suddenly Pam stood above them. Casting down her hands, she delivered a large ceramic planter to the stranger's head. He fell to the side unconscious. Pushing himself free, Luke scrambled to his feet. Unfastening the chain, Pam quickly opened the front door. Rachel flew into the arms of her mother as they caved in upon each other's embrace, sobbing.

Slipping by Rachel and Pam, Luke ran quickly to his car. Opening the trunk he took out the bag Briggs had left him. As Luke hurried back into the house, Rachel let go of her mother, embracing Luke. Pam joined them as the three stood locked in each other's arms for several minutes. It was Luke who first pulled back. Looking at Rachel's mother he tried to smile, "I take it you're Pam."

"Yes," she said. "And you must be Pastor Downs..."

"Call me Luke," he interrupted. Luke was in earnest. "Pam, do you have a rope? I want to tie this guy up. After that, I don't want to waste any more time. I'm giving all three of you a transfusion immediately." He looked around. "Where's Tamor?"

Pam left the room to get the rope. She didn't have the foggiest idea what Luke meant about giving them transfusions, but she understood the purpose for tying up the intruder. "Tamor went looking for help," answered Rachel. "It was, as always, her idea. She was working her way up the street knocking on doors to see if she get help. I decided to drive back here to see about you. I told Tamor to come back to mom's soon..."

"I'm going to get you and your mom going on the transfusions," he broke in, "right after I tie this guy up."

Pam returned with duck tape. "Sorry, that's the best I can do."

Luke secured the thug's hands and feet, then went for the bag. Carefully opening the bag, he took out the medical gear. Inventorying each piece in his mind, he laid them out one by one on the dining room table.

"What's all this?" asked Pam. She was looking at the stuff laid out on the table, giving quick glances toward the man lying unconscious on the floor.

"I don't have time to explain." Luke shook his head then laughed nervously. "Frankly, I couldn't explain transfusions if it was the only way to stop a nuclear bomb from going off directly under my feet." Placing his right hand on his chest he looked over at Pam. "Trust me on this," he winked, stealing one of his brother's worn expressions. "Bill, my brother, works with infectious diseases. He came up with a vaccine utilizing the blood of a woman immune to the plague." He motioned for Rachel to sit down. He would get started with her. "I've been immunized. Just a little of my blood transfused directly into the body of another should make that person immune to the plague as well."

He tied a plastic tourniquet around Rachel's upper arm. Taking out another tourniquet, he turned to Rachel's mom, "Pam, would you please tie this on my left arm?"

Luke was as white as a new bed sheet, but he pressed on knowing what was at stake. Swallowing hard, he disinfected both of their arms. Taking out two sterile needles, he attached them to an unused catheter. Finding a vein on Rachel's arm, he took the needle in his hand, but he was shaking so badly that he couldn't get it started.

"Give me that!" Pam winked at Luke with a manufactured smile. "I've put needles into a lot of dogs and cats in my day." Stooping down, she took the needle from Luke, and looked into the eyes of her daughter. "I need you to kneel down and put your arm on the seat of this chair," she said, pointing to an open chair near Luke. "We need gravity to make the blood flow from Luke to you."

Kneeling down, Rachel placed her arm on the chair. "Get ready, honey," she said. "If you bite or scratch, I'm used to that." Pam had worked seventeen years at an animal clinic before her retirement.

Pam eased the needle into Luke's arm. Removing a clamp from the catheter she let the blood flow through the plastic tube dripping from the other end into a paper cup brought from the kitchen. Replacing the clamp, she slowly slipped the other needle into her daughter's arm. Rachel winced slightly. Luke's color had returned, but he wore poorly the responsibility of seeing this medical procedure to completion. "Thank you Father," he prayed silently, "that Pam has the experience to help me out." Luke removed his tourniquet. Pam untied Rachel's. Reaching to the catheter, he released the clamp. His blood flowed into Rachel's arm. Timing it from the first flow, after three seconds he placed the clamp back onto the catheter.

"Pam," he said, "I only have two needles. Briggs set me up for Rachel, with one spare, I didn't know that Tamor would be traveling with your daughter." He shook his head, looked down, then back at Pam. "Would you mind sharing this needle with your daughter?" Gently pulling out the needle from Rachel's arm Luke handed her a cotton swab.

Pam smiled. "It's all in the family, after all." Taking Rachel's spot at the chair she held out her left arm for the tourniquet. Luke tied the tourniquet around Pam's arm, then disinfected an area with alcohol. "I'm afraid one of you will need to put in the needle this time," said Pam.

Looking over at Luke, Rachel stepped forward. Luke could only shrug his shoulders. "Are you sure you can do this?"

"No," whispered Rachel into Luke's ear, "but if mom's willing to help, I'll try."

Luke wiped off the needle using a sterile swab drenched in alcohol. Pam gave Rachel another smile, explaining how to insert the needle into a vein. Rachel's first attempt missed, but Pam refused to show pain. Again Rachel worked to guide the needle into her mother's vein. "Help me dear Father," she prayed to herself. Once again the needle moved to the side of the vein. "I'm sorry, Mom," Rachel said. Tears were rolling down her cheeks.

"Keep going," said Pam. "You almost had it that time."

As Rachel made her third attempt, Pam also prayed silently for God's intervention. The needle slid into Pam's arm hitting its target. "Good!" exclaimed Pam. "Now let's get this thing done."

Luke removed the tourniquets and clamp. Timing the flow of blood for three seconds, he placed the clamp back on the catheter. "I wish that Tamor were here," he said. "I want to get this business over. I want to make sure that Tamor's safe too."

"We've gotta go looking for her," said Rachel. "I'm worried out of my mind about her."

Removing the needles, Luke placed a piece of surgical tape near the end of the catheter marking the needle he had used. He would use it again when they did the transfusion for Tamor. "I agree," he nodded. Turning to Pam, "Would you mind staying here just in case Tamor shows up?"

"Makes sense to me," replied Pam. "I'll take care of this stuff too."

Luke handed her the catheter. "Thanks," he said. "If Tamor comes back, let's get to it right away. Do you have any more disinfectant?"

"Well, this isn't Medical West Hospital," she smiled, "but I think we can make everything pretty harmless. You just see to Tamor. I'll handle things here and disinfect what we've used." Pam looked down at the stranger tied up on the floor. "I've still got one friend left in this neighborhood. I'm going next door. I think Bruce will take this guy for us until he can flag down a patrol car. They do come by, just not often."

"That would be great, Pam." Luke thought it was a good plan. "That mess on the floor is pretty big. Can your friend manage him?"

"Oh yeah," smiled Pam. "And I've got my wheelbarrow. One way or another, if Bruce is willing, this guy's out of here!"

Luke left with Rachel as they headed to his car. He was painfully hungry. He stopped suddenly, bending over with his arms drawn across his stomach. A terrible cramp shot through his empty mid-section. "Are you all right?" asked Rachel.

Luke forced himself to stand. "Yeah, I'll be fine." Rachel was not convinced. She put her arm around his waist until they got in the car. Luke craved food, but the thought of eating anything made him more nauseous. The two drove up and down the street where Tamor had last been seen. Next they took to the intersecting streets. "There she is!" cried Rachel, pointing to a pastel blue house. Tamor was sitting on a bench just outside the front door. The white iron bench was landscaped between two beds of perennial flowers. Luke pulled up to the curb, but before he had stopped, Rachel flew out of the passenger door running for Tamor. Tamor had her back up against the right back corner of the bench. Perspiration poured from her face.

"Don't come close to me!" she shouted to Rachel. "I don't know how, but somehow I've become infected."

Rachel stopped momentarily, but her love for her friend raced her to Tamor's side. "No!" yelled Tamor again. "Stay back!"

"We've been immunized," called back Rachel. Rachel was trying to assure Tamor that they were safe. Tamor didn't understand.

"Wait!" yelled Luke. "I don't know how long it takes for the immunity to kick in." He was recalling the day after his immunization. The process made him sick. Did the body need to go through a reaction to the vaccine before it was protected? Whatever the answer was to that question, it was now too late to protect Rachel if the immunity had not began to kick in. She was already kneeling beside Tamor, stroking Tamor's hair and holding her hand.

"How could this have happened?" Rachel questioned. "We were together all the time. There's no sign that the neighborhood has been contaminated." She looked up at Luke standing beside her. "I just don't get it!" Rachel was in shock.

"I don't know what happened," replied Luke. Turning to Tamor, "We need to get you back to Pam's."

"No," came Tamor's feeble protest, "please don't move me. Not yet..."

Luke signaled for Rachel to come with him to the car. Rachel was reluctant to leave Tamor, but Luke's look insisted upon it. When they were out of earshot, Luke said softly, "I don't know if your immunity is built up yet. We're taking a terrible risk..."

"This is Tamor," said Rachel stiffly. "She risked her life for all of us. I'm not going to do any less for her. If she doesn't want to travel, let's get the medical gear and give her the transfusion right here."

Luke stopped, looked down, and said slowly, "I'm sorry Rachel, I thought that I had explained that to you. A blood transfusion will only work before a person has been infected." There was nothing that he could do for Tamor. It was too late to give her a transfusion. All they could manage now was to make her comfortable.

"Since Tamor doesn't want to travel," said Rachel, softly now, "would you please go back to mom's and get a blanket—maybe a pillow, too?" She felt badly about her harsh words. "I'll stay here with Tamor. If the immunity isn't working for me, it's already too late."

Luke closed his eyes tightly. Tears protested against even the possibility of Rachel's infection. "Okay," he said, "but if something happens to you...." he swallowed. "I don't want to live without you Rachel." Rachel smiled, kissed him on the cheek, then ran back to Tamor. Luke drove his car back to Pam's.

"Tamor, I'm so sorry!" Rachel knelt again beside her friend. "You'd never have been infected if it wasn't for me."

"You don't know that, girl," said Tamor. "How do you know what lies ahead for me or for you? Only God knows what's in our future. I could've gotten sick back in Minnesota." Tamor smiled faintly, taking Rachel's hand. "I hope that vaccine is working on you, Rachel." Then she prayed, "Lord Jesus, take care of Luke and Rachel. Allow the immunization to rush through Rachel's body building a wall that cannot be broken, even by this virus. We ask it in Jesus' name. Amen."

"Tamor, you're like Jesus," sobbed Rachel. "Here you are dying, and like Jesus from the cross, you are ministering to other people."

"No," replied Tamor, "no one is like the Savior. The only thing I know for certain is that my time is in His hands. I'm not going to leave this world until the Shepherd calls His lamb. If Jesus calls and says, 'Tamor, today it's time to head for glory,' then I'm ready to follow where He leads."

Crying, Rachel laid her head down in Tamor's lap. "I know... I know..."

"Will you do me a favor?" asked Tamor.

"Anything!" replied Rachel, lifting her head to meet her dying friend's eyes. "Anything! Just name it..."

"Do you remember the secret that I told you about?" began Tamor. "I've never shared it with anyone." Tamor coughed. "Just after I got to America, I met a young man. I thought I was in love with him. I had made a decision not to have sex until I was married, but..." Tamor touched Rachel's face then looked away, "I did not live up to my decision."

Tamor coughed again. "I not only had relations with that boy, but I ended up becoming pregnant. I refused to have an abortion, so the father left me. I never heard from him again. He left me more than pregnant. He left me empty, filled only with guilt and shame. Guilt for what I had done knowing it to be wrong. Shame for dishonoring my faith. When my baby girl was born, I gave her up for adoption, but the guilt remained. I was trapped in my sin and, it seemed to me, beyond the reach of God.

Then one day a man..." she stopped abruptly to remember back. "It was Elijah Jordan!" she stammered. "I'm sure of it! And he was giving out religious tracts on the street. He handed me one showing Jesus carrying a lamb that had gone astray. It had the words of the spiritual on it—you know, 'I am Jesus' little lamb.' Suddenly," Tamor coughed, "I knew that the Lord still loved me, and that He was carrying me. I'd always be His little lamb."

Rachel sobbed on Tamor's lap. "Will you do me that favor?" asked Tamor again.

"What do you want me to do?" answered Rachel. She had to force her words through a minefield of emotions.

"The family that adopted my little girl is very close with the Lord. We had an open arrangement. I visited Shanai—that's what they named her—I visited her every so often." Tamor was struggling for breath. The disease was moving quickly. "There's a small chest that I keep in my apartment. You'll find it in my bedroom. A cedar chest engraved with a cross on the front. It has some things I saved to share with Shanai on her wedding day. Would you please see that she gets it?"

Rachel erupted in grief. Tamor would never share in Shanai's wedding day. Tamor became quiet. She was dying. "It's happening quickly," Rachel thought to herself, "God willing, Tamor won't suffer long."

Standing up, Rachel lifted Tamor away from the edge of the bench, and sat down with her. Holding Tamor in her arms she prayed tenderly into her friend's ear. Her prayer spoke of God's love and mercy and presence. Luke came, his voice breaking into her prayer. "I brought you a blanket," he said to Tamor, placing it gently around her body. Tamor didn't respond. Luke looked over to Rachel. "I took the blanket from a closet. I didn't see your mother. She must have been with Bruce taking care of that guy who broke in on her."

The minefield of emotions exploded within Rachel. Her eyes were tightly closed, but tears broke through the barricade washing down her cheeks. Rachel took a deep breath. Softly she began to sing. "I am Jesus' little lamb, ever glad at heart I am; for my Shepherd gently guides me, knows my need and well provides me; loves me every day the same, even calls me by my name."

As Rachel sang the second verse to the children's hymn, Tamor stopped breathing. The Guardians of heaven had encircled the three as the soul and spirit of Tamor left its earthly tent to await a new body. At the center of the ring of angels, Tamor danced within a soft, white mist. She wore a beautiful white robe running down the length of her body all the way to her feet. The white robe swayed about her as she danced in perfect rhythm to Rachel's song. Round and round she danced in light, her face radiant with joy. She couldn't hear Rachel singing as mortals think of hearing. Yet her body moved in perfect unison with her friend's earthly song.

Rachel came to the last verse of the song, "Who so happy as I am..." Tamor began to sing with Rachel, continuing her dance, hearing, but not hearing—joined, but not joined, with saints on earth. Tamor's white robe flowed this way and then that way, without one crease or wrinkle forming in its radiant fabric. "...Even now the Shepherd's lamb? And when my short life is ended, by His angel host attended, He shall fold me to His breast, there within His arms to rest."

In the white mist where Guardians stood sentry, Elijah Jordan watched with his blue eyes, wearing a grin so wide that even the Guardians turned to see.

Chapter 23:

THE ENCOUNTER & THE QUEST

The sun had toiled out its work for the day then sunk exhausted in the west. Shadows grew longer until they tangled together. Rachel continued to hold Tamor. Luke sat with her on an island of green grass held captive by a sea of surrounding white flowers. Resting his back against the front leg of the white garden bench, he hardly noticed as Rachel lightly stroked her hand over his hair. Pam, concerned that they had been gone so long, was walking down the street looking for them. She carried her kitchen broom, a womanly weapon should she run into another stranger. Spotting Rachel on Martha Draegor's garden bench, Pam picked up her pace in their direction.

Pam was about to yell over to them when she saw Tamor lying still within her daughter's arms. Saying nothing, she walked over to Rachel, bent down, wrapping her daughter in her arms. Kissing the top of Rachel's head, she said softly, "I'm so sorry, honey. I'm so sorry. Her troubles are over," she sighed, "but ours still roll on. What happened?"

"It's the plague. I don't know how she got it and I didn't, but..."

Pam sought for words of comfort. Her Christian journey had taught her that tossing out religious truisms can do more harm than good at a time like this. The power of heaven was there at that moment, but her words were earthen and unable to capture the glory that now embraced Tamor. "When your father died," Pam sought to find the words remembering her own pain, "I told myself not to push God away. The storm had struck, but God is not the storm. God is the anchor. God is the one who claims us, refusing to let our broken world take us from Him in the shades of death."

Smiling bravely, Rachel bent her head back to look up at her mother. "She is Jesus' little lamb..." she started repeating the words of the song, but tears again flooded down her cheeks carrying away her words. Pam cried with her. Luke's tears fell on the inside. To the world he appeared tired and numb. His soul, hidden to the eye, was an active volcano erupting in grief.

Anger boiled within him, a molten lava with a mind of its own—driven to pour down upon a world that had crushed Tamor's beautiful life and paying no penalty for the wrong. Grabbing the stem of a white daisy growing to his side, he ripped it from its base. Holding the blossom in the palm of his hand, he was about to crush it when Pam reached down taking the flower from him. "The grass withers, the flower fades," she quoted the prophet Isaiah, gently placing the white flower into Tamor's coal black hair, "but the word of God stands forever."

Glaring forward, Luke refused to meet Pam's face. "The flower's beautiful," remarked Pam. "Sad that its beauty is only for a little while." Leaving Rachel to squat down beside Luke, Pam used her broom as a brace. It was a painful maneuver for her vintaged frame. Positioning herself directly in front of Luke she became the target for his glaring rage. Brushing the sleeve of her shirt over her cheeks, she wiped away spent tears. "I didn't know Tamor, except for a few things that Rachel had mentioned to me as we visited over the phone."

Smiling up at Rachel she continued, "I'm sad right now because I see my daughter's pain." She reached over with her free hand placing it on Luke's shoulder. "But I'm not real sad, because Rachel and I are going to have many long visits with Tamor in God's kingdom. Many long visits..."

"You and Rachel trust God." Luke tore into her sentence. "I say to myself that I am finally beginning to experience what you have with God all the time. I even dare to think that I'm growing in the Lord, that my faith is beginning to happen. Then the world turns upside down, like now, and what I thought was faith falls apart like a grand house of cards. There's no justice, Pam! There's no justice!"

"You're right, you know," replied Pam. "This broken world has no justice to offer us. Instead it serves up misfortune and untimely ends. Yet God didn't run from our misery and pain. He took all the suffering that this world could dish up and more, just like you plucked up the flower I've placed in Tamor's hair. God wove together all the sadness and suffering of this miserable planet throughout all its horrid history and made a cross out of it all. There He let the injustice of this world impale His Son upon rough and blood-soaked wood."

Pam looked up into the sky. "The innocent Lamb of God became a sacrifice offered over for torture and death. That wasn't fair. This broken world isn't fair. But justice broke out of that cross through an open tomb. That justice says Tamor is still alive, and all the darkness of this world has lost the game." Looking directly into Luke's red-washed eyes, she concluded confidently, "Luke, I believe to the bottom of my heart that Tamor is alive because God is just, and loving, and keeps His promises."

Pam's voice broke through the prison of Luke's years of dark struggle with God. Tortured tears washed out from his soul spilling down over his face. His head slowly lowered until his chin rested on his chest heaving in rhythm to deep soul sobs and sighs. He wept, not because he was sad, but because he was overpowered by joy. The shroud of death that had covered his life for so long had slipped away at Pam's words. Peace, surpassing all understanding, flooded into his soul, replacing the spent tears. Quaking epiphany had thrust him from a bastille of darkness to stand in the kingdom of light.

Deep within Luke, buried under all the doubts, a seed had been planted long ago by the work of God. This seed was life, and life everlasting. It cried in protest against a world where everything appears to move in a mechanical march ending in death and decay. As a child, he didn't fear death. It just felt unnatural to him, unnatural to all of humanity.

Standing up, Pam spoke matter-of-factly. "It's getting dark. It's not safe to be out any longer. The looters are already making their way to the streets." She took a deep breath. There was an uncomfortable subject that had to be brought up. "Ordinarily we are to place the victims of the plague into the garage, or lacking a garage, into a room that can be locked until a decontamination unit can be notified. They then pick up the bodies..."

"No!" broke in Rachel. "I won't have Tamor taken to some mass grave or her body burned like trash."

"I said ordinarily," continued Pam. She thought for a moment. "When your father died, I purchased grave plots at Sun Valley Cemetery. I bought three that were side by side." Pam sighed. "I never knew why, either. I guess it didn't feel right for Roy and I to be buried only with strangers keeping us company. I had no idea that my daughter's best friend would be lying beside us."

"Will they do burials?" asked Luke.

"Not exactly," replied Pam. "I've got a garden shovel. Early in the morning we'll do our own committal for Tamor."

Rachel was shocked. Tamor deserved better than this. Besides, you can't just go and start digging a hole in the cemetery. Shooting a puzzled look over to her mother, words stuttered to her lips. "Will... they... let us?"

"My guess," replied Pam, "is that the authorities are dealing with things far more pressing than watching over cemeteries." Walking stiffly over to Rachel, she took her daughter's hand. "Yes, we'll be taking a risk, but we need to try!"

Tenderly placing Tamor's body into the back seat of Luke's car, Rachel closed the door. Grabbing the garden bench, Luke wedged it into the trunk, a token attempt to protect the neighborhood from contamination. Driving back to Pam's, Luke waited as Rachel backed her mother's car out of the home's double garage. Pam shifted a few boxes, moving several pieces of patio furniture to free up two stalls. Luke's car would transport Tamor's body to the cemetery. After her burial, Luke and Rachel would leave their cars in Pam's garage until she could notify a decontamination unit.

· · · · ·

The small part of Porter that was still left to him was frustrated at the delay intruding into his trip to Stockton, California. He was driven. He suffered an intense compulsion pushing him madly to Oakland—demanding that he must at all costs put an end to the life known as Seda Orhan. His airplane had been diverted to a military landing strip. The passengers were not told the location of the field that now held their plane in limbo until some undisclosed issue was resolved. The authorities assured the passengers that the flight would be continuing on to Stockton, but refused to give a definite time for the departure.

One frustrated woman sought out an attendant, protesting the delay. "I need to get to my mother and father," she spoke angrily. "They're old, and I need to help them. They'll be terribly anxious for my safety. I have to get to them because of the plague."

"I'm sorry," said a flight attendant coolly. Margaret Saunders was tired of working flights during the outbreak. Passengers were irritable, and delays were routine. Flight attendants had become the convenient targets for patron frustration. "It will be at least twenty-four hours before we will be able to leave."

"Where are we going to stay?" asked another passenger overhearing the conversation.

"We're all staying on board," replied Margaret. "We will be handing out pillows and blankets to make you as comfortable as possible. Some boxed lunches will be delivered shortly."

"Do you mean that we can't leave the plane?" protested another passenger.

"Martial law allows you to stretch your legs outside the jet," she replied, "but you must stay within thirty feet of the aircraft." Margaret had tied her red hair up into a bun, cooling down the back of her neck. She no longer cared how she looked to the patrons. The way things were going, she was seriously considering quitting the airlines after this trip to spend more time with her family.

Walking away from the passengers gathered around her, Margaret passed by the aisle seat where Flint Porter was sitting. Coming alongside his seat she felt suddenly chilled. Molech stood invisible to the mortal eye in the aisle beside Porter. Each person passing through the demon felt a sudden drop in temperature. Molech was keeping Porter alive until he finished his business with Seda. The monster was also there confining the virus so that Flint did not communicate it to others. If Flint were allowed to spread the virus, everyone on the aircraft would be dead within hours. The plane would then be quarantined, and Porter would never make it to Oakland to dispose of Seda Orhan.

· · · · ·

Feeling his way down a dim hallway, Luke stepped over one corpse after another, often stumbling over the carnage. He was alone. Something sinister waited for him up ahead. He wanted to run, but his legs kept moving him forward, driven by a mind of their own. Coming to an intersecting hallway, his legs turned him to the right. Reaching out from the darkness below, a hand grabbed his leg. Luke jumped. The face he saw beneath him pleaded for help. No use. Luke's legs kept moving him to some unknown destination darkly awaiting his arrival.

A mordant mist suddenly poured into the hallway from all directions. Luke took five, maybe six steps. After that he could see no more than the width of his hand before his face. He tripped over another body, but no, it was an old gnarled root of an ancient tree. Moving his hands over the rough bark, Luke pushed against it, bringing himself to his feet. The mist had settled, floating waist high in all directions. Above him an old tree towered amid wisps of vapor drifting in a vacant sky set aglow within green iridescence. Mechanically his legs carried him toward the trunk of the tree. At the base of the tree a green haze clung about a hideous monster poised before the mammoth trunk. "You cannot defeat me," said a voice low and resonant. "Better men than you have tried, but they are all dead."

"I don't know who you are," cried Luke. He had to force the air up to make the words explode from his mouth.

"I am the great destroyer of innocence and life." The monster's green eyes glowed brighter and brighter. "I am your destroyer!"

"Dear Father in Heaven," came Luke's silent prayer. "I have no strength to fight this creature. Help me, I pray. Tell me why I'm here and what's happening to me. Defend me, God Almighty, for Jesus' sake. Amen."

Suddenly Mike, the mechanic who had helped Luke out along the interstate, appeared at Luke's side. His hand carried the simple wrench of a mechanic. Molech cried out, "You have no business here, Guardian! Be gone!"

Mike smiled, extending his hand toward Molech. The tool he gripped began to elongate until it was transformed into a sword, a golden sword. His mechanic's uniform dissolved into a white robe, showing a muscular creature powerful enough to engage the monster. "You have no place in this man's soul," replied the Guardian. "Leave or face the sword of righteousness."

Molech howled. "I will leave, but not even the Guardians of heaven can equip this puny mortal to do battle with me. Look at his heart! His faith is young and will waver." Again Molech screamed, then dissolving in the mist, it vanished.

Turning toward the Guardian, Luke's face asked the question before the words were formed at his lips, "What's happening to me?"

"The Destroyer intends to take the life of Seda Orhan," replied the Guardian. "You will prevent that from happening."

Luke fell shaking to his knees. "You can't be serious. Who is Seda Orhan? What can I do? That monster will kill me. There's nothing that I can do..."

"You're right, there is nothing that you can do." The Guardian lowered the sword to his side. "Nonetheless, you are to leave tomorrow for Stockton, California. From there you will travel to the Oakland Infectious Disease Center where your brother works. There you will find a patient named Seda Orhan. You will protect her from the powers of hell. You will stand in the power of the blood against the evil that seeks her death. You will protect Seda Orhan with your life if that becomes necessary."

"No... No... No..." shouted Luke. Hearing Luke cry out, Rachel rushed to the couch where he slept.

"Luke," she said quietly but firmly, "Luke wake up, you're having a nightmare."

Opening his eyes, Luke sat up grabbing the front of his shirt. It was wet with perspiration. The image of the Guardian, the grave implications of his words, were etched in his mind. Whatever he faced, no matter what his fears, Luke knew that he must leave for California. The destination awaiting him mastered his mind, overwhelming Luke with thoughts of danger and death laying just ahead. Luke craved to plant his feet like roots into Naples' soil. He'd rather do anything but travel to Oakland!

Yet with the divine command had come a yearning to do the deed appointed; a yearning superceding all his fears. There was no time for idle intent.

After Tamor's body had been laid to rest, he would leave immediately for Stockton. "I've never been big on dreams and visions," Luke confessed to Rachel, "yet something real happened in my dream. I've been visited! Joseph in the Bible was visited so that he'd accept Mary's pregnancy. Later an angel told him to protect his family in Egypt." Luke paused. "But, Rachel, there was something else present in my dream. Something..." Luke shivered. "Rachel, I need you to help me... help me find faith and courage."

Rachel gasped. "What does God want from you? What did the angel say?"

Relating most parts of the dream as best as he could remember, Luke included his vivid encounter with Molech. Rachel, sitting beside Luke on the couch, leaned back into his arms to pray. Her will became united with his duty. Together they would fly to California. After the committal service at the cemetery, they would scramble to catch the next flight to Stockton. Right then, however, Luke was content to hold Rachel in his arms. Dark thoughts sought to invade the silence between them. He fought away the mental tormentors assaulting him with the knowledge that he may die, never again to cradle his love within his arms.

Finishing her prayer, Rachel turned to face Luke. Kissing him gently on the lips, she left the room to wake up her mother. Pam offered to make them a quick breakfast of scrambled eggs and toast, but they politely declined. Rachel took time for a bowl of cold cereal but left most of it unfinished. Luke ate nothing. His empty stomach rumbled, calling out for attention. Pam coaxed him to eat something. "Thanks," he said to her, "but I feel..." he searched for the words, "I feel like I just can't eat right now."

• • • • •

It was early in the morning as they drove to the cemetery. Dew rested as a heavy blanket over green grass patched with dripping spider webs. The unkempt cemetery was no longer manicured by grounds keepers. An eerie silence rested over the graves. Freshly dug holes revealed that, under the cover of darkness, grave robbers had been shoveling away dirt to plunder graves. Pam led the way to the family plots where Luke began digging a grave. Pam had placed one of her handmade plaques into the hands of Tamor before sewing her body into a quilt.

The quilt had been made by Pam for Rachel's wedding day. The plaque read, "I am leaving you with a gift—peace of mind and heart! And the peace I give isn't fragile like the peace the world gives. So don't be troubled or afraid." The bottom of the framed picture displayed a water-colored picture of a shepherd leading his flock to a distant oasis.

"Hey, what are you doing over there?" yelled an old man kneeling by a grave. His body had been hidden by his wife's gravestone. "Leave the graves alone! Have you no shame?"

"It's a fresh grave that we're digging," cried back Pam.

"Oh," he said, "I'm sorry." Standing up the old man struggled against the pain in his arthritic joints. "You decided not to give the body over to the decontamination teams, huh? I don't blame you. If it were my wife," he pointed to her grave, "I could never have given her body over to be treated like infected garbage." Wiping a spent tear from the corner of his eye, the stranger slowly walked away.

Luke, Rachel and Pam took hold of the quilt lowering it tenderly into the shallow grave. Luke offered a prayer, then recited from memory, "We now commit her body to the ground; earth to earth, ashes to ashes, dust to dust, in the sure and certain hope of the resurrection to eternal life through our Lord Jesus Christ, who will change our lowly bodies so that they will be like His glorious body, by the power that enables Him to subdue all things to himself."

There was more to the liturgy, but Luke couldn't remember all the words. He continued as best he could. "Almighty God, by the death of Your Son You destroyed death, and by His rest in the tomb You made the graves of the saints a place that is safe and a doorway to light. We thank You for this victory that came by way of the suffering death and glorious resurrection of Jesus. Strengthen our faith, we pray, so that we might join Tamor and our Lord Jesus Christ in the kingdom that He has prepared for us. We ask this in His powerful name. Amen."

Covering the body with earth, the three concluded with the Lord's Prayer. Rachel and Pam then joined hands, closed their eyes, and sang 'I am Jesus' Little Lamb.' This time there were no tears. The faces of Rachel and Pam glowed with joy and confidence. The body was laid to rest, for a time, but all that made Tamor uniquely special lived on in God. Rachel thought of her smile, her crisp British accent and humorous slang, her love for God and others. Tamor, who had given a powerful witness of her faith, was very much alive, and they knew it without reservation.

Making a trip back to her car, Pam took a yellow tablet used to make out a grocery list weeks ago. Tearing off the dated list, she crumbled it, shoving the scrap into her pocket. Writing a message on a fresh sheet, she tucked it into a clear plastic bag that had blown against a grave marker. Pam arranged the note on the freshly dug earth, placing stones on the corners to hold it down. The note read, "The saint here wears no riches but the blessings of Christ. Please do not disturb this grave."

· · · · ·

Driving back to Pam's house, Luke parked the infected car in the double garage then closed the door. Rachel showered quickly, then Luke. It worked out well that Rachel's bedroom furniture still had its place in Pam's house. Rachel's closet and dresser stored clothing left behind when she went off to college. Rummaging through her old clothes, Rachel pieced together a dated patchwork outfit for their trip to California.

Pam found Luke a shirt and pair of pants still in the bottom drawer of a dresser once used by her husband. They were too big for Luke, but looked and smelled a whole lot better than what he had been wearing. Everything that had been in the infected cars was left behind with the vehicles. Even the clothes they wore to Florida were ditched. Clothing may have become contaminated. Washing them gave no guarantee that the virus would be destroyed.

• • • • •

With hugs and kisses Pam left them at the Ft. Myers' airport. A declining number of passengers walked the terminals in silence. Tickets were still available on a flight that stopped over in St. Louis, continuing then to Stockton. Luke and Rachel had forty minutes to kill until their flight boarded, so they stopped at a small airport café. Choosing a table overlooking several runways, they waited for the waitress to take their order. "I'm sorry," said the waitress when she arrived, "we're out of many menu items."

"All we want is something to drink," replied Rachel. "What do you have left in that department?"

"Some flavors of soda," she answered, "and ice tea."

Rachel and Luke agreed on the ice tea and it was delivered to their table within minutes. "You know," said Rachel, "Tamor never told me the address of her biological daughter. She wanted me to bring her daughter a chest that she'd been keeping for her wedding day."

"Tamor has a daughter?" Luke was startled by the disclosure.

"Yes, she does," answered Rachel. She told Luke about the details of Tamor's daughter. Feeling the clutch of death, Tamor had labored her words one by one as she spoke with Rachel.

"When we get back to Minnesota, we'll go to her apartment," said Luke. "I'm sure that there must be an address book somewhere that'll give us what we need. Do you remember what the girl's name is?"

"Yes," said Rachel, "at least her first name. It's Shanai."

"What did she tell you about Shanai?"

The answer to Luke's question would wait. "Luke Downs!" called out a voice, "now don't that beat all!"

Looking behind him, Luke saw a man smiling brightly—too happy, it seemed, for what was going on in the world. "Elijah Jordan!" stammered Luke. "What are you doing here?"

"Do you mind," questioned Elijah rhetorically, "if I pull a chair over and join ya?" Whatever their response, the messenger had no intention of leaving.

"We don't mind." Rachel was the first to speak. Her electrified spine drawing her straight up in her seat. Before her, if she were right, was a holy one of God. She looked over at Luke.

"Of course! Sit down Elijah." Luke pulled over a chair from a neighboring table. As he did so, he shot Rachel a discreet look of frustration.

Broadening his smile in appreciation, Elijah sat down slowly, appearing like an old man easing his arthritic frame onto a chair. Before he could speak again Rachel rifled a question at Elijah, "Who are you, Elijah Jordan? Who are you really?"

Elijah tottered his head back and forth above his neck, continuing as if the question had never been asked. "Nice clothes you're wearin', son. The ample vintaged look I see!" Luke smacked his lips, shaking his head several times. "So, Luke," continued Elijah, "you're headin' for the place where your brother hangs his hat. Now why would you be a goin' to a city infected by the plague?"

"I think you know," answered Luke.

"I guess you're right about that!" Elijah's smile vanished. "You'll be standing against a mighty warrior of hell, son. Are you prepared for that?"

"No, I'm not," said Luke flatly. "I'm not ready for any of this. Yet here I am, throwing away common sense like a moth flying toward an open flame."

"There's no brightness in the Destroyer," came Elijah's knee-jerk response. "It's dark and mighty. The disciples of the Lord couldn't defeat it."

"Then how on earth can I go against it?" Luke was astonished. "If the holy apostles couldn't take this monster on, then what in heaven's name am I doing here?"

"Yeah, in heaven's name," parroted Elijah. "You must engage it in heaven's name." Elijah paused. "You mustn't seek to banish the beast of hell by what lies within you. You must stand in the blood of the Lamb. You must remember the pain that came upon the Savior when nails were driv'n into His hands and feet." Elijah looked down. The words he had spoken were precious to him.

Taking hold of Luke again with his eyes, Elijah's words followed. "And you must fast. Eat nothing from this time forward 'til you have confronted the evil one. Each time you feel pains of hunger, think upon the pains of Jesus on the cross as He faced your mortal enemies in a great spiritual battle. Pray, and pray again. Let the Holy Spirit move with'n ya as God molds your frame within His everlastin' hands. Then, and then only, can you face the Destroyer."

"The Destroyer came to me in a dream, you know." Luke shivered. His empty stomach ached.

"I know, son," replied Elijah, "I know. But you weren't alone were you?"

"No," answered Luke, "an angel was present with me. This angel had helped me before as a mechanic when my car broke down on the interstate." Luke looked over at Elijah. Elijah knew all about angels taking on human form. Elijah knew it all! "Suddenly," continued Luke, "in the thick of that gruesome nightmare, the Messenger appeared at my side."

"Then what happened?" The old man asked the question, but he knew the answer. He knew...

"He changed," replied Luke. "And in his hands..."

"In his hands," interrupted Elijah, "was the sword of righteousness—golden and bright!"

"I guess so," said Luke.

"No, there's no guessin' about it!" came Elijah's emphatic voice. "Your journey of faith must dispel the doubts and grasp tightly the promises of God. It's in righteousness that you find strength!"

"Then we are in deep trouble, because I don't feel very righteous..."

"No, Luke," broke in Rachel, "you know better than that. God has placed on you the righteous robe of His Son. You are declared forgiven and pure! You are righteous!"

Elijah smiled. "Take your eyes off yourself, boy, and put them on the cross." Elijah's eyes drilled into Luke, as if trying to pour his understanding into the young man before him. "Yes, you are righteous! Yes, you're pure! You wear the righteousness of the Son of God. Call upon that righteousness to protect you against the demon, and then the agent of darkness cannot prevail."

"But what am I to do when I meet up with it?" asked Luke. "I don't get any of this! I don't know how to find the demon or what to do if I do find it."

"Continue your quest, son. Resist the reason bringin' the monster to Oakland and it will find you." Elijah leaned over the table. "As to what ya do when you face this evil, I can't tell you much. It can't be destroyed, but it can be sent back, at least for a season, to the belly of hell. That's what you must do. Send it back to hell!"

"But how do I do that?" asked Luke. Elijah never answered Luke's question. Standing up, Elijah started walking away. "Wait!" cried Luke, but with each step Elijah's body grew fainter until it vanished into thin air.

Luke turned to Rachel. "What do you make of that?"

"That is an angel of the Lord," replied Rachel. "I'm tingling all over. I've never had anything like this happen to me, although I've heard reports..." Rachel gaped at Luke. "He has come to give you a message from God."

"Yeah, sure," said Luke impatiently, "and what good is his message? Rachel, I'm terrified! If you saw what came to me in my dream, you'd understand. I can't imagine facing this thing in the flesh."

"I think what's happening here is beyond anyone's imagination," observed Rachel. "And Elijah did have a message for you. The messenger told you to fast. Remember Luke, the Lord told His disciples that some demons can't be exercised without fasting. I don't understand why, but that's what the Lord told them." Rachel continued to glean insight out of the special visit. "Elijah also said that you're to fight the demon in the righteousness that comes from God."

"I'd rather Elijah would give me a magical sword or something," Luke replied. "I still have no idea what I'm going to use against the demon when we face off..."

"I understand your fear." Rachel moved her chair closer to Luke. Putting her arms around his neck, she pushed away all other faces that busied the small café. "Those things that could not wait—that had to begin immediately, have been told to you. I believe that God will let you know everything you need to know, but it will be by His timetable." Smiling, Rachel kissed Luke's forehead. "If we meet up with this demon today, our fast will have been a short one, and yet, you haven't wanted to eat since our meeting on the interstate. God Himself began your fast before He sent Elijah...."

"This is too much for me, Rachel," moaned Luke. "My head is spinning!"

"I know," assured Rachel, pulling closer to Luke, "We'll take this one step at a time. Today, when we feel hungry, we'll remember the suffering of Jesus. "

Luke nodded his head. Reaching his hands over to Rachel, he held her face in the palms of his hand. "I think that the Lord brought us together because without you, I'd never gone through this. You fill up the holes in my life, giving me strength and hope. I love you, you know that, don't you?"   Rachel smiled back, "I know."

Well?" said Luke, inviting something more from Rachel.

"Well, what?" Rachel was coy.

Luke was flustered. "Well—how do you feel about me?"

"Oh, that," said Rachel. "I loved you before you were certain of your feelings for me."

Luke relaxed. Her words felt better than spring. "No, that's not so," he protested. "You caught my eye long before I had your attention."

"Yes," smiled Rachel, "I knew that you had noticed me—that you had feelings for me. But feelings are not the same thing as loving. Lots of people have feelings, but they never know true love. I started to love you before I was sure that I would want to spend my life with you. I liked being with you. I imagined myself doing so many things with you, even kicking up dust together on dirt bikes." She paused. "But I'd never think about marriage until I was sure that the man I loved was godly."

"I'm a pastor!" blurted out Luke. "Wasn't that enough proof of my faith?"

Rachel smiled. Luke understood how foolish that argument now sounded, even to him. "I have grown a lot," said Luke, "but I have a long way to go."

"We all do," said Rachel. "The important thing is that you're now walking along the path. God has done a big thing in your life."

"Would you... ever consider walking that path with me," said Luke softly, "for the rest of my life?"

"I think that after we're married," replied Rachel, placing her head against Luke's shoulder, "we should have children. If the child is a boy, I'd like to call him Elijah. And if we have a girl, we should name her Tamor."

Chapter 24:
THE SACRIFICE

Arriving at Stockton, Luke and Rachel immediately grabbed a taxi to a small car rental near the airport. Giving them a list of cities declared under quarantine by the government, the attendant added, "This list changes hourly, so don't be surprised if you find military trucks blocking another city." Looking the list over, Luke shook his head when he saw that Oakland was under government quarantine. All of the major roads into the city would be blocked.

Leaving the rental center office, the attendant took them through the car lot. Luke leaned over. "Rachel," he whispered, holding the list in front of her, "how are we going to get to the Center? Military blockades will have a stranglehold on Oakland."

Rachel shrugged her shoulders. "I'm not sure," she said quietly. "We just go for it! If God intends for you to get there, and He does, then He will make a way for us."

Handing Luke a set of keys, the attendant glanced over to Rachel. "I don't know why you folks are out traveling." Pausing to look the couple over for a final time, he added, "Don't get me wrong! I'm glad the boss is getting some business or I'd be out of a job."

Rachel offered half a smile. Luke's mind drifted beyond the casual conversation. They would be taking to the road in a red, mid-sized car. Climbing in, Luke headed out of the lot navigating their rented vehicle onto a frontage road. Flint Porter, who had rented a car at a nearby competitor, shot by Luke traveling seventy miles an hour. Catching Porter's look in their direction, Rachel shivered. "That guy's crazy," she said.

"He's ticket bait," laughed Luke. "Wherever he's heading, if he keeps up that speed, he'll be having a little visit with a badge along the way."

Hitting a button on the radio, Rachel searched for a local station. "Reports from around the globe," said the newscaster, "are telling of churches filled to capacity. If nothing else, this plague has brought the people of the world to their knees..."

As the announcer continued reporting about religious revival blazing over continents, Rachel turned to Luke. "What do you think?" queried Rachel, "has

God allowed this plague to bring the world back to Himself?"

"It's the way God worked throughout the Old Testament," replied Luke. "When His people rebelled, He let forces within nature, or the power of conquering armies, crush their rebellion, bringing them to repentance." He glanced sideways at Rachel. "Whatever else, this terrible plague seems to be bringing the world to repentance. I wonder if church leaders are seeing things as clearly as everyday Christian folk? Much of the world's problems can be traced back to a Church whose leaders floundered on God's Word, leading their flocks to the wolves. I should know," Luke took a deep breath, "I invited the wolves to prowl among my sheep."

Rachel turned off the radio. The two continued their drive in silence. Luke looked repeatedly over to Rachel. Each time her eyes were closed, her lips moving in silent prayer. He prayed too. Luke prayed that God would provide a way to avoid the blockade. Above all, Luke prayed for courage to face an entity that had withstood the power of the ancient apostles of Christ.

· · · · ·

"No!" snarled Molech through the drooling mouth of Porter. Secretly a Guardian had come, but the demon could sense his presence. Abruptly the engine stalled as invisible hands pulled spark plug cables loose from the engine. Molech was enraged. Swelling out from the body of Porter, the arch-demon filled and possessed the entire car. The Guardian, having finished his task, was now visible to the evil lord. Heaven's warrior stood briefly in the center of the road, then vanished. The demonized car rested invisibly to the side of the road as cars and trucks passed by. Molech began moving cables with its mind, attaching them one by one back onto the spark plugs. The monster had been only briefly delayed.

· · · · ·

Cruising along the highway heading toward Oakland, Luke and Rachel passed the cloaked vehicle. "At some point as we get closer to the city," noted Rachel, "we'll be forced to find the back roads."

"Agreed," said Luke. "I keep looking for..." Without warning, a military truck heading towards them in the other lane pulled across into their lane and parked, blocking their way. A uniformed man got out of the military transport signaling them to stop.

Luke hit the brake. The rental car slowed down quickly, pulling he and Rachel toward the dash. Luke rolled down his window. The soldier placed his left hand on the fender of the rental car. Wearing a white mask over his mouth and nose, the soldier bent his head down to size up the occupants and the contents of their car. "What brings you folks out today?" he asked. The top strap of his holstered gun was unfastened.

"Hello," strained Luke, his voice in a vice. "To be honest, we're curious about what's happening outside of our small town."

The officer did not look pleased. "This is no time to be sightseeing," barked the officer. "I think you folks should head back to that small town of yours. And by the way, what town are you from..." Suddenly Porter flew by on the shoulder of the road, his gas pedal shoved to the floor. The man in uniform ran to his truck, taking the wheel and gunning down the highway after Porter. Radioing ahead to another sentry, the soldier reported that a speeding vehicle was heading toward Oakland.

Quickly shifting his car into gear, Luke hit the accelerator. Perspiration beaded over his forehead stinging into his eyes. Wiping his hand over his face, Luke said to Rachel, "I told you that guy was road bait." Looking to his side, Luke watched Rachel take in a deep breath as she lifted her hair from the back of her neck. "I think it's time to start looking for the back roads," he continued. "I don't want any more run-ins with the law."

"Agreed," said Rachel. Folding open a road map she checked for roads less likely traveled. "Just a little ways ahead there's a country road. Hopefully it'll take us behind the roadblock to this major highway heading west." She pointed to a road on the map. "If we can get that far, the map shows that this highway will take us into the city near the OIDC." Looking up from the map Rachel scouted down the highway. "That's the road!" Rachel's hand flew from the map pointing to a road sign. "Take it north."

Up ahead, a few blocks before the next turnoff, they saw a military truck. Flint Porter's rental car was pulled over to the side of the road. "Well, I guess he's having that little visit with the military instead of the State Patrol," quipped Luke. Neither he nor Rachel saw the dead soldiers lying near the road, victims of an assassin's cunning and skill. After the killings, Porter commandeered a military truck. One of the men taken out by Porter had his same build. Porter intentionally shot this man in the head. Carefully taking the shirt off the slain soldier, he placed it on himself. The hat was bloodied, so he grabbed a hat off a soldier he had taken out by a hit to the chest. Against military regulations, Porter wore the military hat recklessly to the side of his head.

Luke continued north on the country road. "Look, Rachel, do you see the dog over there caring for her pups?" A thin female, lying out on reddish clay, nursed five or six new pups. "So much life out there! So much beauty!" The sun polished a cloudless sky resting above a peach of a California day. "But you know, Rachel, I can't take the beauty in because I'm scared—it's gnawing me away inside."

"What we're up against is hard to know, Luke. It's real hard." Rachel again lifted her hair to cool the back of her neck. "You're close to experiencing what Christ must have felt, alone in that garden. But He knew what He was going to face—death by crucifixion." She turned sideways resting her back against the door. Luke was white as a streak of lightning. "Our problem is that we're clueless about what we're up against..."

"That's right," interrupted Luke. "What weapons do I use against... whatever it is that I'm to stop? My mind spins, Rachel, it just spins!"

"Luke, God's going to get us through this. I don't think He's going to have you face this... demon empty handed. Why the dreams? Why the visit by Elijah? Why this chase if none of it will matter?" Letting go of her hair, she waved it back and forth in the air. "We just have to keep going... keep the foot on the gas. God will provide what we need to stop this creature. Nothing's happening to you that is strange to Christ. He's got the final scene of this chapter in your life all figured out."

"Yeah," sighed Luke, "I just don't want this to be my last chapter." His words tore into Rachel. She too was afraid, but she had to put up a strong front for Luke.

Coming into view was the intersecting highway that would lead them into Oakland. Luke turned west. After driving for better than twenty minutes, they came upon a shopping mall nestled into a hill just outside city limits. It was empty. "This place is eerie," remarked Rachel, "a modern ghost town." On the west corner Rachel spotted a store advertising, among other things, trail bikes for sale. "Turn into the mall," she said abruptly, "I have an idea."

"What idea?"

"I've got a plan for getting us into the city." Rachel pointed out a store in the mall. "Head over to Parkway Bikes."

Pulling into a parking stall in front of the store, Luke turned off the ignition and asked, "You're not seriously thinking..."

"Come on," interrupted Rachel, "let's see what they've got."

The store was closed, the doors locked. Peering through the glass they could see a variety of bikes partly hidden in shadows and darkness. "Do you have your credit card?" asked Rachel.

"Yes," replied Luke, "but I don't think that the store's open for business."

"Today's the grand opening!" Looking around for something hard, Rachel spotted a row of rocks bordering a small bed of sand and cactus plants. Grabbing an egg-shaped grey stone she slammed it into the glass. It cracked. Again she struck the glass door. The glass exploded, shattering fragments onto the showroom floor. "Today you are buying two bikes and a glass door."

"I'm seeing a whole new side of you," said Luke.

"A coin of value has two sides, right?" Smiling, Rachel bent down, sliding under the metal crossbar. Luke followed, carefully avoiding the jagged glass sticking out from the metal frame. Rachel jogged over to two bikes standing in the center of the showroom. Knowing dirt bikes, she looked for features that would help them with the trip ahead. Pointing out that there were no keys in the ignitions, Luke asked Rachel, "What do we do now?"

"I've been in lots of dealers like this," she said. "They all keep their keys somewhere behind the desk." Leaving the bikes she climbed over the counter, not bothering to walk around to the back entry. Rummaging through doors and drawers she looked for a stash of keys. "Bingo!" she said at last. She had discovered a cupboard holding a dozen keys or more, each hanging from a separate hook. Grabbing seven of the keys, she hustled back to the bikes. "Two of these will fit the bikes we're after," Rachel said, trying them one by one in the ignition of a bike. A silver key slid in and turned. Throwing the other six keys to Luke, she pointed to a similar bike saying, "Give the silver keys a try on that one."

The last silver key did the trick, firing up the bike under Luke. "I haven't done a lot of this," he shouted to Rachel over the blaring engine noise of their bikes.

Tossing Luke a quick smile she quipped, "Dogs are experts after the first bark!" Walking to the counter she found a pad of paper. "I think we'd better leave our phone numbers, and not any credit card information. Who knows who might find the note!" Quickly she scribbled Luke's home phone number and her own. The note said, "Please call us and we'll settle up for the door, the two bikes, and the helmets. Thanks." Taping the note to the cash register Rachel grabbed two helmets tossing one to Luke. Saddled on her bike she shouted, "Let's ride!" Gunning her bike for the button used to activated the electric door opener, she gave it a hit. Nothing! The electricity was down.

Leaving his bike, Luke muscled open the metal door. Rachel waited as he mounted his bike and adjusted to its feel. Luke lacked Rachel's rhythm for biking. Pressing the throttle, his bike pealed forward, the quick jump nearly pulling Luke off the back of his bike. Rachel sped out of the showroom, tracing the dust after her novice partner. Side by side, the wind fingering Rachel's hair as it left her helmet, they continued west on a road that would take them within miles of the OIDC. Rachel searched the horizon for roadblocks. The hilly terrain and many orchards made it difficult to see into the distance. "How does it feel, Luke, to be a criminal?" she shouted.

"What's that?" he yelled back. It was almost impossible to hear over the roaring engines and racing wind.

"I said, 'Hi Clyde! I'm your Bonnie!'"

"Yeah, I get it!" shouted Luke. "...Parish pastor to prison inmate!"

Rachel smiled, her eyes ferreting the land for military patrols or roadblocks. Seeing something, Rachel throttled back, quickly raising her hand to catch Luke's attention. Luke slowed down stopping beside her. Pointing to a military blockade dead ahead she said the obvious. "There it is. That's what we have to get around."

"What's your plan?" asked Luke.

"We need to backtrack for a few miles. When we get out of sight we'll leave the road and make our way across the open field." Luke agreed. "After all," smiled Rachel, "that's why these are called dirt bikes." Luke attempted a weak smile, but the danger he faced erased all sincere joy from his eyes, mouth, and cheeks.

Heading south, they soon veered off the road as Rachel led the way west. The two bikers bounced along the rough terrain, avoiding random rocks and ditches. Rachel navigated them slightly north, seeking to stay a good distance away from the sentries at the blockade. Making it past the blockades and into Oakland meant that they had to keep their growling engines out of earshot. Finally, after about forty minutes of biking over the field, the outskirts of Oakland's suburbs came into view.

• • • • •

Looking ahead, Porter saw a military blockade standing between him and his destination. Random military vehicles patrolling the area had threatened him before. It would be more difficult to get past this military post on his way to OIDC and Seda Orhan. Pulling up to the blockade, Porter watched as two guards stepped forward holding automatic rifles with their safeties off. One stopped directly in front of the truck as the other continued to the driver's window. The soldier smiled until he noticed Porter's hat tilted to the side. Instantly frowning, the soldier at the window stepped back raising his rifle. Porter pulled out and fired his pistol, shooting the man through the forehead. The other guard began firing a spray of bullets at the truck.

Porter sprang from the truck, somersaulting over the hard asphalt, landing on his knees. A trail of mismanaged bullets followed after him. Sighting the soldier, Porter fired several shots. The man fell dead to the ground. Another soldier ran from a military car sitting off to the side. The sound of gunfire had torn him from an afternoon nap where he'd dreamt of fishing with his son on a deeply forested stream. Waking to the gunfire, his view was blocked by another military truck. Running toward the action, he held his rifle locked to his shoulder, ready to fire. Porter shot first as the guard turned the corner, moving into the terrorist's sightline from behind the truck. The soldier was mortally wounded. Dashing for the vacated car, Porter left the soldier to die in a bath of blood. The keys were in the ignition. Jumping into the car, Porter fired the ignition and continued his pursuit of the kill.

· · · · ·

Rachel and Luke arrived at the eastern edge of Oakland's suburbs. A wide variety of fences butted up against one another forming a fortress of protection for the neighborhood. Rachel drove along the patchwork of fences until she spotted an unlatched gate. Racing through the opening, she knocked into the gate with her bike. Luke followed. Traveling through an unkempt backyard they spotted a two-story house. A small pool to their right spoke of inactivity, its gaping mouth filled with leaves and debris. Luke caught motion inside on the second level. Suddenly gunfire ripped pellets of steel at Luke and Rachel. "Move it!" yelled Rachel over the roaring engines of the bikes.

Dashing by the house, the bikes headed for a front gate hanging broken on a single hinge. Hitting the side of the gate forcefully, Rachel broke the remaining hinge free, burying its bottom front corner into the sod. Luke was a few feet behind her as their bikes burst out onto a suburban street. Rachel tore away as the sniper ran through the house seeking to pick them up on the other side. Tat... Tat... Tat... Bullets flew by, breaking a picture window in a house across the street. "Go!" screamed Luke.

Safely away from the sights of the sniper, Rachel stopped. Luke circled back to join her. "Do you know where we're going?" she asked.

"Not yet," said Luke. "We need to find a major street, then I think I can figure a way to get to the Center." As Luke took the lead, they drove around for nearly three quarters of an hour before Luke recognized a street. He was sure that this road would take them to within a few blocks of OIDC, but they were traveling the wrong direction. "This is it!" he yelled over to Rachel. "But we need to turn around and head back the other way." Luke nodded his head several times. "I know where we are now!"

· · · · ·

Parking his car in the middle of the street, Porter walked away with its engine running. Having survived the military gauntlet, he was now one block away from OIDC. Like most of the city, this area had become a ghost town. No one was out. Porter, more animal than human, instinctively sought to conceal his movements. Arriving at the Center where a private was guarding the main entrance, Porter worked his way to the side of the Center, sliding his back against its outside wall. Turning the corner with a single motion he quickly threw his knife into the neck of the soldier. The victim fell without a sound.

Cautiously Porter looked through the glass door sizing up the operation inside. Walking the hallways without protective suiting, the personnel at OIDC had all been immunized against the virus. A white lab coat with large pockets sewn on the front at waist level was the standard uniform for the staff. "The lab coats may prove useful later," Porter thought to himself. Porter waited and watched. Finally, with one exception, the area was empty. A nurse sat alone at the front desk, consumed in paperwork.

Bending low, Porter opened the entry door, crawling over to the four foot wall separating the front desk from the lobby. The nurse saw nothing, continuing on with her work. Moving along the edge of the partial wall, Porter reached a door and quietly shoved it open. A plate on the door stated, "Staff Only." Crawling through the doorway, he stood up, surprising a man standing across the room. Like a lion pouncing upon its prey, Porter sprang across the room slamming the butt of his pistol into the man's head. Stan, Bill's friend, fell to the floor unconscious.

Working against the unconscious dead-weight of Stan's body, the assassin removed his lab coat, putting it on himself. Removing Stan's identification card as well, he repositioned it on the lab coat so that the picture and personal information was hidden under a flap. Dragging Stan through a door leading into the men's locker room, he placed him into a shower stall, pulling the curtain shut.

Porter would have had a difficult time getting through the Center's defense if Seda were still in the maximum security area of Black Knight. Instead, OIDC had converted a second level area into a small apartment for her use. Using the roof over the single level of the front entry area, the Center had designed a small outdoor patio. Seda used the patio to escape the white walls of the institution—or at least, feel like she had.

It dawned on Porter how difficult it would be to avoid the scrutiny of the regular staff. They were no doubt a close-knit group whose intense work at OIDC forced them to know one another well. The white coat might fool the soldiers guarding the Center, but it wouldn't take away suspicion from the staff. Looking again at the white coat that he wore, Porter grabbed his head, grimacing in frustration. The coat was useless! Opening up a crack in the doorway, he sized up soldiers as they walked by the staff lounge. Several passed, but none were the right build. Finally a soldier entered the hallway with a similar constitution. Walking through the doorway, Porter intercepted the soldier. "Would you mind giving me a hand?" he asked. "I need to move a piece of equipment from the staff lounge, and

I could sure use a strong back." Working hard, Porter tried to make his lifeless voice sound congenial.

"No problem," said the guard, following Porter into the lounge. "You must be new here."

"Just arrived today," Porter answered. "I suppose that's why I'm the grunt moving around furniture." He faked a laugh. "The item's in the men's locker room," smiled Porter stiffly, pointing ahead. The soldier walked into the locker room, then turned to face Porter. As he turned, Porter's gun clubbed across the side of the soldier's head. The blacked out soldier was dragged by the terrorist into the shower room. Exchanging clothes with the soldier, the demonized Porter placed his victim into another vacant shower stall, closing the curtain to conceal a second victim. Porter would need to avoid the guards, but they were far fewer in number than the OIDC staff. Disguised as just another military uniform, the staff would consider him to be newly stationed at the Center. They would ask no questions unless he gave them reason.

• • • • •

Waiting for Rachel to meet up with his bike, Luke pointed west. "The Center is just a few blocks away. Let's ditch our bikes and walk the rest of the way." Taking off his helmet, he gave it a toss. "Remember, to the military we're criminals breaking the rules under martial law," he shouted to Rachel. The roaring engines made it difficult to speak. "The bikes are too noisy and this place is like a cemetery! Riding these roads, we stick out like a warship cruising down Lake Minnetonka."

"Yeah, we don't want to wake the living," joked Rachel. Luke didn't bother to fake a smile.

Jumping her bike over a curb she parked it on a grassy knoll by a large brick house. Luke, not as handy with his bike, traveled a nearby driveway to reach Rachel. Leaving their bikes, Luke led their way on foot to OIDC. Reaching the Center, Rachel and Luke spotted the guard laying in a pool of blood. Jogging quickly over to where the guard lay, Luke motioned for Rachel to come over. As they pulled the door open, the nurse at the desk looked up from her paperwork, immediately hitting a button signaling for security. Two uniformed men hastened into the lobby, their rifles in hand. "What can we do for you?" demanded one soldier.

"I hope you have business here," said the other. "If not, we're mandated to place you under arrest."

"My brother is Dr. William Downs," Luke gushed, next sucking down deep breaths to control his anxiety. "I need to see him!"

The soldiers knew Bill. He was familiar to all at OIDC. "I'll check this out," said one soldier as he walked over to a phone. The nurse looked on, skeptical of the stranger's story. "Why have these two shown up at the Center during the quarantine?" she thought to herself. The soldier returned. "The doctor will be right down," he said. "Please wait here." Walking to the side of the room, the uniformed men kept their eyes pasted on Luke and Rachel, their guns in hand and ready to take action.

Flying into two swinging doors banging them open, Bill rushed into the lobby. "What on earth are you doing here, Luke?" he barked, his voice saturated with surprise and irritation.

Luke rushed to his brother. "Bill, I don't have time to explain. You must take me to Seda! You must take me now!"

Quickly the guards moved to block the door leading to the stairs and Seda's apartment. No one was going to see the Center's premier patient unless there was a clear green light. "What's going on?" Bill demanded. "What do you know about Seda?"

"She's in terrible danger," Luke exclaimed, still breathing hard. "A man has been sent to assassinate her." Looking over to the main entrance, Luke continued, "There's a dead soldier out there. My guess is that the killer is already in the building." Racing to the door, one of the soldiers found the dead body of his friend. Feeling the slain soldier's neck, there was no pulse, but the flesh was still warm. The killer must be close at hand. Looking toward the doorway still under guard, Luke shouted, "There's no time to explain! Take me to Seda!"

• • • • •

Molech divined the location of Seda, moving Porter like a game piece up the stairs, and then down the second story corridor leading to her apartment. Seda sat outside in the small patio area as Porter tried her door. It was locked. Seda had been instructed to keep her door locked at all times. The staff would knock, she was told, then she was to look through the small window making sure that she recognized whoever was there to see her. Taking out his knife, Porter quietly sprang back the bolt on the lock. Slowly opening the door, he slid through the doorway, closing the door behind him.

• • • • •

A quick jerk of Bill's head motioned to the soldier to lead the way. Running up the stairs with the safety of his automatic rifle turned off, the soldier led as Bill, Luke, and Rachel followed. Racing down the hall to Seda's apartment, the four reached the door just minutes after Porter had broken the lock. Seeing that the door had been forced, the soldier struck it hard with the bottom of his boot. Looking down, the four saw Seda laid out on the floor.

Porter had gagged his victim, binding her with curtain cords. Her arms stretching above her head were tied to the foot of a couch. Her legs were fastened to the leg of a heavy, oak table. Porter, preparing Seda for ritual sacrifice, had already cut marks on her arms with his knife. Blood seeped from Satanic wounds etched on her skin by a razor sharp instrument.

Looking up, Porter's demonized eyes glowed green with Molech's hatred. Opening wide his mouth, he roared like a wild beast. The four who had surprised this pawn of Molech were lifted into the air by an invisible force, then flung against the wall. "Get out of here, Rachel!" shouted Luke. "All of you, get out of here!"

The soldier, Bill, and Rachel were riveted against the wall. Evil powers held them captive. The stench of Molech hung so thickly in the air that they gasped, fighting impulsively against each breath that brought his contagion into their lungs. Slowly Luke's body alone descended to the floor until his feet hit the carpet. Invisible Guardians had overpowered Molech's grip, landing Luke to his feet.

Springing up from where he had knelt beside Seda's quaking form, Porter faced off with Luke. "So, you would fight me," mouthed Porter, but another voice spoke. It was deep and unnatural.

"No," replied Luke, "I'm not going to fight you." Luke was terrified. His nerve would have drained away if not diked by the supernatural presence of the heavenly warriors. Continuing to breathe deeply and quickly, he shoved out, "God is sending you a message. I'm the delivery boy here to send you back to hell."

Opening its ghastly mouth wide, Porter roared. "Send me back to hell, boy? I don't think so!" The demonized terrorist shot his left hand forward with its palm facing forward. A green light swallowed Luke up in the monster's hunger for revenge. Luke, the object of Molech's rage, fell to his knees in terrible agony. His right knee, injured when he tried to help the woman at his apartment complex, throbbed with insufferable pain.

"I see you met up with my friend," hissed Molech through Porter's lips. "You shouldn't always be trying to save people." Porter smiled. "Leave now, and you can live."

"I can't do that," shot back Luke.

Reaching out his right hand, Porter pointed his weapon toward Luke, its edge traced with Seda's blood. Again Luke's knee exploded in agonizing pain. Searching through his anguish, Luke sought to find a storm-torn hill impaled with a bloodied cross. Luke tied his pain with the torment of Christ on the cross. As he had practiced with each supernaturally augmented pang of hunger, so now he joined his suffering with the torture of the Savior at Calvary's cross.

The green light faded as Porter's hands dropped to its side. The knife in the monster's right hand fell to the floor. Molech's sorcery was transforming Luke's environment. Like sails on a boat hit by hard gusts of an undulating wind, the walls of the room began to waver. Their solid surface became translucent, then vanished. Standing alone, Luke now faced off with Molech within a storm raging in purple light. A huge, ancient tree towered from the jagged facade of black rock. A green mist hovered a few feet above the rough, rocky surface. Dragged into his nightmare, Luke stood in terror.

Molech, unsheathed from the body of the terrorist, stood near a mound of rock at the base of the great tree rising above the mordant mist. Porter's body was tied over the mound, like an animal prepared for cultic sacrifice. Luke didn't know if Porter was alive or dead. Unlike his dream, there were no Guardians in this place.

Whatever Luke faced, he faced it alone. "Send me to hell, boy?" cried the entity again, mocking Luke's own words. Gazing at his unnatural enemy, Luke's stomach turned. The beast was hideous! "I think you have things confused," continued Molech. "I take souls for hell. On the day of the awakening, many will come with me to my father's house."

Luke knew that Molech spoke of the day of the resurrection of all flesh. The demon's father was Satan. Closing his eyes, Luke prayed to his Father. "Dear God," his words were a sigh, "I trusted that You would tell me what to do when the time came for confronting this demon." He swallowed deeply. "I don't know what to do..."

Luke stood about twenty-five feet to the one side of the tree. Fifteen feet to the back of the tree the mist fell over a ledge. Luke could see nothing beyond the ledge but darkness extending in every direction. Surveying the area, Luke searched for anything that could be used as a weapon. Protruding above the mist just a few feet to his right stood a solitary boulder, about four feet high and two feet across. The black, rough rock slanted out of the water. Sharp spikes jetted out of it in all directions.

Suddenly a bolt of white lightning struck down from above them, hitting the jagged rock. Molech howled in rage. "No Guardians here! He must face me alone!" In a ledge formed at the base of two spikes, lay three round stones. Glowing with a silver light, they appeared like rays of sunshine breaking through a storm tossed sky. The presence of the stones brought a sense of hope to Luke's dark circumstances. Drawing in a deep breath, Luke faced off again with the beast of hell.

Lifting its hand to draw darkness out of the purple light, Molech flung the unnatural vapor at Luke. Luke was tossed backwards, falling under the green mist. The suffocating mist would have drawn into his lungs like putrefied Jell-O, but his first breath stuck in his mouth. Luke couldn't breathe.

Springing up, Luke spit and gasped when his head rose above the hellish mist. Flinging a bolt of darkness toward the tree Molech shattered loose a branch, sending it like an arrow straight for Luke. God's warrior sprang to the side, but a fractured piece of wood tore across his left shoulder drawing out blood. "See mortal!" scorned Molech, "you bleed. You die!"

"My strength is in the blood of the Lamb," cried Luke. "My strength is in the blood of the Lamb... My strength is in the blood of the Lamb..."

"There are no Guardians here, mortal," sneered the beast of hell. "You are injured. You are helpless. You are alone." Taking a few steps closer to its prey, Molech drew more darkness from the purple storm, casting it at Luke. "You are mine!"

This time the darkness didn't shoot out at Luke, but moved slowly in his direction. Making contact with Luke, it contoured around his body, swallowing him whole. It carried Luke, inch by inch, toward the protruding spikes of the boulder. The dark force began to press Luke against the spiny rock, the spikes beginning to pierce into his body. Luke thought of the nails entering the hands of Christ. Not clear why, Luke searched his hand along the boulder for one of the silver stones. Taking hold of a rock, the dark wall pressing against his body vanished.

Like a rocket fueled by the adrenaline racing within his veins, Luke threw the glowing stone at Molech. It was a bad shot, but as it struck the surface of the mist it exploded into light. Molech stammered backwards toward the abyss. Looking at the darkness behind it, the monster turned menacingly back toward Luke. But there was something else. Molech was terrified. It feared whatever was beyond the rock ledge where the green mist poured over into the oblivion.

Grabbing another stone, Luke hurled it quickly at Molech. Again his weapon missed the mark, but the mist and ground four feet in front of the beast erupted into light. Molech fell back, disappearing under the green haze. Immediately springing to its feet, the monster lifted its hand into the air, again summoning forces of darkness to hurl against the young pastor. Luke grabbed the final rock. "I stand in the blood of the Lamb!" he shouted. His words shot at Molech as he fired the stone with another rush of adrenaline. Striking the right arm of Molech, the stone detonated into light. Molech howled!

The injury surprised the beast and inflamed its hatred. "You have no more stones to throw, boy!" The monster's voice screamed with rage and intimidation.

The demon was right. There were no more stones. But the injury to Molech's arm prevented it from conjuring its dark weapons to use against Luke. Man and the monster had been reduced to battling hand to hand. Luke knew that he couldn't defeat Molech in a battle of might. He thought again about Molech's terrified look when it had fallen toward the abyss. There was perhaps one way to send this monster home, but it would mean his death as well. Or worse, the plan risked his facing realities more odious than death waiting in the darkness at the far side of the ancient tree.

Luke thought of Rachel, his eyes squinting against stinging tears. "I've got one thing to say to you!" yelled Luke. "I'm not your boy! Not anymore!" Taking a deep breath he ran with all his might in the direction of Molech, yelling as if to shake the deep with the cry of a great, mortal warrior. Striking the hard body of Molech, they fell backwards, but not far enough.

Luke's injured arm shrieked pain throughout his nervous system. He thought of Christ suffering the spiked, lashing whip as it tore into his back, legs and arms. Luke drew strength for his legs from the might of his heart. Making fast, repeated steps against the rocky floor, he shoved against the beast, but moved it very little. Most of his steps simply slid uselessly over the black, slippery stone.

Molech turned to see how close it was to the ledge. Its fear provided its fatal mistake. Grabbing Molech's injured arm, Luke turned with the monster in the same direction of its horrified gaze. Luke then simply stopped pushing against the demon. The monster's own resistance against Luke's efforts suddenly sent it flying with the Lord's warrior toward the darkness. Molech bellowed as they fell over the ledge and into the abyss. "Father, into Your hands..." cried Luke as he fell linked with Molech through the darkness.

As the two fell down, and down further, above them the darkness over the ancient tree became filled with millions of tiny points of light. At the same time, all across the planet a mist rose from the victims of the plague, both the dead and the living. Objects contaminated by the plague also produced a residue that vaporized into a mist. The mists were sucked towards the earth, drawn irresistibly into the tiny points of light.

Each unnatural substance, caught within one of the points of light, turned black, then fell like rotten fruit around the base of the ancient tree. The head of the snake had been smitten. With Molech banished, there was no more life in the evil it had let loose on the planet.

Luke continued to fall, attached to the monster by its panicked grip. Pain and fear flooded into Luke's consciousness. Unable to endure what was happening, he blacked out. Suddenly streams of light, appearing like lasers, shot down from above. Four lights, one to each side of Luke, formed six-foot high beams that fell with Luke through the darkness. Transformed within seconds, the beams revealed Warriors of Heaven. Molech grimaced, then pleaded for mercy. Taking hold of Luke, the Guardians broke him free from the grip of the demon. "Don't send me away!" cried the monster.

Saying nothing, the Guardians ascended away from the smitten denizen of hell. Crossing over, they broke out into a city of gold and precious stones, brilliantly lit by an unseen source. Reaching to the limb of a tree, a Guardian plucked a large fruit from its branches. Instantly it was replaced by another. Breaking open the flesh of the fruit, the Guardian rubbed its fragrant nectar over the terrible claw-marks gouged into Luke's body. The wounds disappeared. Once Luke's body was fully restored to health, the angels joined hands in a circle about this man of God. Brighter and brighter the circle glowed until it exploded with light.

Awaking on the floor in Seda's apartment, Luke found everyone in the room unconscious and lying on the floor. Luke turned his head to see how Seda was doing. There sat Elijah on the floor with his back against the couch. Seda was untied. Elijah had placed her head on his lap. Stroking her hair with his wrinkled hand, he asked Luke, "Is it over?" Luke nodded.

Tenderly placing Seda's head on a pillow taken from the couch, Elijah walked to the door and turned. A great smile broke across his face as he bent down, tucking his arms against his chest, sending his hands flying freely in the air about his neck. Spinning around and around, he finally stopped to face Luke once. "So it ends well," the Guardian Elijah said. "You were willing to give yourself—give yourself to death and worse! Hell is never prepared for that, you know." A look swept across the face of Elijah that spoke more deeply than words. His blue eyes locked with Luke's.

"Three stones," continued Elijah. "Three wounds of Christ on the cross. Light breaking upon the darkness. Wounded He was, that all mortals—that you—might have life. The fourth wound carved by the Roman spear, a wound of blood and water, fell with you into the darkness." Suddenly standing erect, Elijah was transformed into a creature so bright that Luke was blinded by the light. Lifting his hands above his head, the Guardian turned around three or four more times clapping his hands, then vanished.

Weak and numb, Luke crawled over to Rachel. Sitting up against the couch, Luke stretched his legs out on the floor, drawing Rachel's unconscious body into his arms. He stroked her hair until, opening her eyes, she turned her head and smiled. Suddenly bolting up, Rachel looked around the room. She saw Seda lying with her head on the pillow; the others were still unconscious on the floor. Looking at Luke she exclaimed, "Where's the assassin?"

"He's gone," answered Luke calmly.

Rachel searched her memory. She was confused about what was happening. Then, remembering the evil that they'd faced, a second question jolted at Luke. "And what about the demon?"

"I think it's gone too." Luke was exhausted.

With a sudden realization of what Luke must have gone through, Rachel threw her arms around him. "Are you all right?"

"I've never felt better in my life," smiled back Luke.

"Did you see it?" she asked. "Did you meet up with the demon?"

Luke determined then and there that his experience in the battle with Molech would remain with him, and him alone. Words would fail miserably in capturing what had taken place in Molech's domain. "I've done what I was sent to do," he replied simply, then paused. "There's at least two good things that have come out of this. I'm holding you in my arms, and that may never have happened without the plague."

Rachel smiled. "And what's the other good thing?"

"People have started to think about God again, and of things more important than what kind of car they're driving, or the square footage of their homes."

"For how long?" sighed Rachel.

"I don't know." Looking out a window, Luke drew Rachel again tightly against his chest. "I just hope that it will be long enough for our children to grow up in a world that smiles towards heaven." He lifted her face away from his shoulder. "You're still willing, aren't you?"

Rachel smiled.

· · · · ·

The plague, delivered from hell by mortal hands, was vanquished with human hands empowered by the sacrificed Lamb of God. Luke and Rachel were married seven months later. The family had gathered at the Downs' cabin for a double wedding as Kris stood beside her brother to join her life with Rich. Rich and Luke were each other's best man, and so too, Rachel and Kris served as each other's maid of honor. Their wedding service proclaimed the presence of Christ as the honored guest. The lessons were read by Bill and Briggs. Mother Downs wept throughout the service. When the couples had planned the part of the service where the unity candles would be lit, Luke was the first to insist that the individual candles be extinguished.

Fourteen months after the wedding, Rachel gave birth to twins, Elijah Jordan and Tamor Pamela. Tamor had a smile warmer than the sun in mid-July. Elijah had the bluest eyes; eyes bright as a cloudless day under a summer's sun.

About the Author

Serving as a parish pastor in southern Minnesota, David Paul walks with his people the hills and valleys of everyday life. Over twenty-five years earlier David Paul studied philosophy and English, followed by the rigors of seminary training. It was just before starting at the seminary that he was united to Nancy his wife and companion. After receiving his Masters of Divinity Degree, David Paul and Nancy together have served parishes throughout Minnesota and North Dakota.

Stimulated by a deep-rooted desire to reach with the Gospel beyond the walls of his congregations, David Paul has written manuscripts in the genres of theology and fiction. He has also authored or co-authored a number of Bible studies and books for Concordia Publishing House, including *Pathlight; Faith Alive; My Christian Faith; Free in Christ Free to Serve; Managing Finances;* and *Communication: A Scriptural Foundation for Marriage.* He has served as editor to a District monthly magazine for almost fifteen years.

Recently David Paul has joined hands with River City Press. Great Evil...Good God presents a concise and cogent answer for the dilemma that has faced off with Christianity from the beginning: If God is completely good and limitless in power, why does He permit the terrible evil that we see within the world? Plague of Terror is a Christian thriller weaving together spiritual powers and human intrigue as a plague released by terrorists and Satanists begins wiping out cities around the world. It is a novel of action and romance.

David Paul and Nancy live in Fairmont, Minnesota. They have five children, a dog and a cat. They are deeply appreciative of the parish family and the staff of Immanuel in which David Paul serves the Lord Christ as Senior Pastor.